UNDERTAKER'S WIND

A SEA OFFICER WILLIAM BENTLEY NOVEL

JAN NEEDLE

Broadsides Press

Printed in the United States of America

ISBN 0-9726303-5-X

In memory of my dear friend
Carole Docherty, of Glasgow and Toronto

Chapter One

The light was mild when they came across the body. The light was mild, the breeze was non-existent, the smell off the unseen shore was exotic, sweet, and rather wonderful. Sensations came to Lieutenant Bentley slowly, almost peacefully, as London Jack shook him to consciousness. He made out the large face, bland and smiling, then the dark blue of the sky, with daylight spreading through it like pale fire. He sighed, but inwardly. He had had a dream of Deborah.

"There's a boat," said London Jack. "We've paddled up to it. It's got a dead-'un on the bottom boards. A dead old black 'un."

"God," said Will. He shook his head, emerging out of sleep. "Where's it come from? How far are we off of land? Smells strong enough."

"No distance. Half a mile, maybe. A mile. We'll see it when the light comes up. He's had a sail up, but it's halfway down. The mast has snapped, by look of it. It's the dandy skiff."

Will Bentley was awake now, fully. What dandy skiff, though? He did not know a dandy skiff. Except — He jerked himself upright and seized the gunwale of the jolly-boat. He caught a glance from Ashdown, who was balanced in the bow. He seemed to read the young lieutenant's mind.

"Aye, sir," he said. "The one the Scotchmen stole off of the *Santa*. Here she is again, not much the worse, all things considered."

"Good God!" said Will. "The treasure?"

Both Jack Gunning and Jack Ashdown laughed.

"No treasure," said Jack Gunning. "Just a stinking corpse."

Bentley, who was, all said and done, commander of this leaky little craft, this unarmed and unprovisioned cruiser of his Britannic Majesty in England, scrambled to his feet. A pang of hunger gripped his stomach, and his mouth, indeed, was foul, tight and dry. He knew it was his duty to perform. He knew it, but he did not know quite what. He saw the body lying there, and he had another pang. It was old, and skeletal, and almost moving in its utter pathos. Pathetic true; but somehow peaceful. The mouth was open, the gums exposed and with not a single tooth. The black face, eyes closed but not hard-compressed, was fringed with curly hair and whiskers of a startling whiteness.

"Good God," he said again. "He *is* old. What did he die of? Have they butchered him?"

All three somehow expected that. The Scots, the wild Lamont brothers, had proved themselves as bestial. As bestial as they were brilliant, shining brightly with intelligence that was without fear or pity. But the old black corpse, as far as they could see across six feet or so of sweet green Caribbean water, was unmarked, unmutilated.

And then the corpse, in tattered shirt and ragged britches, moved slightly. Ashdown, although a seaman born, damn near fell overboard, and let out a stifled cry. The corpse than jerked and wriggled, opened its eyes, and stiffly, with a lot of effort, sat up and looked at them.

"Are you English lads, by any chance?" it said. And took their looks and silence for affirmative, and added: "Why, I thank the holy Lord for that! And do you have a bit of bread or drink on board you? I'm English too, and mortal bloody hungry."

Will wondered, when they had got the old castaway on board and sat him down, and shared a morsel of their own tiny stock of biscuit and water they had rescued off the *Biter*, what was the protocol in such a circumstance as this. Dick Kaye, for certainty, would have assumed the old man guilty of some offense or other, and would have questioned him accordingly. Perhaps he was in league with the Lamonts (he had survived them, which was in itself suspicious), or perhaps had found the skiff abandoned and stolen it, the property of the British Navy if only by conquest. The withholding of his portion of their morning ration would have freed his tongue, if nothing else. But neither Bentley nor his two companions were made of such stuff. They watched the old man eat — with care and slowly, which argued he had been in likewise circumstances in his life before — and they merely wondered what he would tell them when he was ready. His eyes, though pale and washed, shone very frank, and as the food went down, he was prepared to smile.

Indeed, he looked extremely comfortable, and stretched his long, thin shanks out across the bottom of the jollyboat, and tutted at the water slopping there.

"Not very shipshape, mates," he said. "Ain't there no officer among the three of you? Give me the order and a bailer and we'll have her dry fer you in half a minute." Although Jack Ashdown was most clearly attired as a common man, he turned to him. "You, sir," he said. "Ain't you prepared to say the word?"

This was a dangerous tactic, as Bentley wore a blue coat and Gunning also had some marks of gentleman about him. But the castaway, apparently, was an expert judge and had no fears that they would throw their weight at him. And indeed, both smiled.

"There's a breeze springing up" said London Jack. "When she's heeling over she'll dip out easier. Why ain't you on the shore? We was going to put in there to find some meat and water. Waste of time would that be?"

The smile broadened. The man exposed his gums, and stuck a tip of tongue out, fresh and pink, not furred at all like theirs, to lick his lips.

"Can't get back in, can I? I drifted off but can't set sail enough even if the wind would blow on shore, which it ain't inclined to do. They broke the mast, d'you see? And smashed the oars. Likewise the rudder. Might have stove the bottom in, 'cept they was being watched and thought they'd better use their time in disappearing, maybe. It's a tantaliser, ain't it, lads? Sitting a mile away from home and watching Goodman Death creep up on you? I'd have swum it, 'cept I can't. Too old to learn now, though, ain't I?"

Gunning laughed.

"Ain't you a seaman, then? Why'd you put off from the shore if you knew you'd not get back? Or are you so old you'd learnt it but forgot?"

A light, sweet puff put new ripples on the water. The slack sail of the jollyboat half filled, then flopped once more. But the breeze was coming.

"Gather yer rosebuds while ye can," the old man answered. "That's what's the purser on my last ship said. The breeze was blowing off the beach, them murderers were on it, and them blacks were in the trees. The devil and the deep blue sea."

Gunning grunted, once more amused.

"Fear black men do you? Find 'em dangerous?" he said, laconically. "Well, if we're out on the water, that makes them the devil, eh?"

"Them black men savages," he replied, simply. "And them white men worse. Wind blow offshore, I borry them boat. Either steal or die. I steal."

His face cracked in a grin. Hard, bright gums. His pale eyes twinkled.

Ashdown said: "These white men. Were they Scotch?"

Will said gently: "You won't know Scotland, I suppose? Are you from Africa?"

A cloud passed across the eyes. They narrowed, as frankness was replaced by guile.

"Not from Africa," the old man said. "I come from England. Lunnontown. You know Lunnontown?"

The three *Biter* men exchanged glances. A very simple guile, it would appear. The man's accent was most peculiar, they could not place it by location — but English it was not; there was nothing of England in it in any way.

Gunning said: "I know Lunnontown. I was born there. Scotland is across the river. You can see the mountains. Volcanoes. Maybe you've never been across?"

"Aye, oh aye indeed," said the black man. "High smoky hills, yes, fire-tops. But I never crossed 'im river."

But he knew he'd lost them, and suddenly he laughed. It was open, pleasant, genuinely amused.

"Born in Virginia," he said. "Mama a slave. I run a long, long time ago, become sailor man. And a buccaneer. And a pirate. And in the English Navy, and a merchantman. I sailed with Henry Morgan. You heard of him?"

"Henry Morgan?" said William. "But that means you must be..."

"Hundred," said the man. "Thereabouts. Long long time ago. Soon be dead though, eh? Even sooner if them Maroons get hold of me! Or them white devils. Or them French. I run away from Frenchmen first of all."

The breeze was blowing steady by this time. Ashdown secured the skiff astern of them on a painter, and hardened in the mainsheet of the jollyboat. The rising wavelets began to slap against her clinker planks.

"Frenchmen," Ashdown said. "And the Scotchmen and some savages, by the sound of it. Well, sir. What you want that I should do? Twenty minutes in this blow will see us on that shore. It's a rocky one, however. In more ways than half a dozen."

"We've got no weapons, Mr Bentley," put in Gunning. "Save three cutlasses and a brace of pistols. Powder damp, for certainly. If the Lamonts are there and armed, God help us, let alone our friend here's wild black savages. Hey, Mr Worm," he added. "Can you fight?"

The gums again. Mr Worm — long and skinny; it seemed a proper name — did not give a voiced reply. But seemed contented at the prospect, if it became material. Will, though, was puzzling.

"Frenchmen, you say? Why Frenchmen, where? On the shore there? With the Scotsmen and Maroons? Is this a story?" Like you're a Londoner, he thought. But it was all peculiar. Here, for instance, was the dandy skiff. And there, not far away, the three Lamonts, presumably. And then the stolen treasure, from the Spanish ship, the *Santa*. Was that here, too? Good God alive — when Slack Dickie Kaye should hear *that* news!

"Not story, sir," said their castaway. "I run from off of French ship. I been on her age-long, I don't know, but I don't like their language, can't 'compreehenny' ten words out of six. We come ashore after them storms, I showed 'em the place. She lost a mast, some spars. They careen her on a little beach, inside the cliffs so they can set new mast up. They can't climb off of beach because the cliffs too steep and rocky. I can, though, I knowed the way. And when I run, I found the little boat along the shore a way. Good boat, eh? Give me an oar to make a new mast, and a board to make a paddle, and I go off again. I can live on the shore, not difficult, I know this bit of coast years on an' off. The Frenchmen starve, they know no better, but I can eat. Only them black man give me fear."

The sun was rising fast, the temperature was set to soar. The sky was cloudless, the land green, luscious and close. But their task was to sail to Kingston or Port Royal, as fast as maybe, and bring succour to the stranded *Biter* men. Their duty was to race around the coast, guided by Ashdown, who had some knowledge of the waters, and tell Captain Shearing at the Navy Offices that their brig had come to grief and that they would have to mount a rescue. But Ashdown, unbidden, had set a course towards the shore. The skiff, a docile pony on a lead, was jogging on astern of them, her bow-wave growing in the playful wind. It was left to Gunning to put the common thought to word.

"A French ship," he said musingly. "Two masts at least, as Mr Worm says one of them is gone. Which means food and drink and guns and ammunition. But most of all a ship. Now that would be a pretty prize, indeed. These men?" he asked of Worm. "These Frenchmen? Are they King's men or of the common herd? Does this ship have guns and soldiers?"

"She can't be Navy," said Will. "Captain Shearing would have warned us when we went out to find the *Santa* if there'd been cruisers. He said the waters swarmed with Spanish, not with French."

"Aye," said Gunning. "But what would he know? One arm, one leg, one idle shoreside berth. And why's the Squadron standing off? To watch for Johnny Crapaud, in case he comes invading! This could be a scout, a spy maybe. Sent in advance. Come on, Worm — how many guns? Is she a trade ship or a rover?"

"No piracy," the black man answered, smiling. "Not Navy neither, I don't think. But she got guns, 'bout eight or somesuch, I dunno. Captain wear a hat. In Carolina, where they pick me up, they did trade with cotton men. And they sold two slaves as well, I think. Some nutmeg maybe. Them smugglers."

"What, Afric slaves?" asked Bentley. "Did you not speak to them?"

Old eyes regarded him. They were gleaming with amusement.

"Speak with Africans? What language should I speak with, then? I told you, sir — I am an English man. Not Lunnontown, maybe — but I am Carolina born and bred, and loyal subject of our King."

Ashdown, at the tiller, laughed.

"God Jasus," he said, sounding for once, despite his normal London accent, like the Irishman he was. "Born in Carolina, is it? Or Virginny, like you said just now? You are truly talking like an Englishman, God help you!"

"Steer a course," said Bentley, snappily. "I am seeking useful information here."

"Aye aye," said Ashdown, equably. "Talking of which, sir, beg your pardon, which part of that faceless shore do you want to set upon? For myself, sir, I can see nowhere to put foot to land at all, except for mountain goats. And they can swim, sir — which I indeed cannot."

The three white men fell silent, contemplating. They were setting in towards the island certainly: but the line of whiteness had emerged in daylight not as sandy beach but as sheer cliffs. Their tops were fringed with luscious green, which made Will lick his lips. Lush green meant water, which they had little of. The lack was growing stronger by the hour.

"Where is this French ship?" he asked, decisively. "Mr Worm, how long ago were you blown off of the island? Do you know counting? Do you know how to get back to where she is? Do you know anything at all?"

"I doubt he knows his name as Mr Worm," said Jack Ashdown. He said it quietly, almost to himself, but Bentley heard it, as had probably been intended. He needed food and drink. He had to keep his head. He gestured; half apology.

"Your name is not Worm, and am sorry for my lapse," he said. "I mean no insult, sir. I take it you are a free man now, and should be held accordingly. What is your name, pray? In reality?"

"Sir," said the black man, "if I ever had a proper one I can't remember it, nor do I miss it neither. As to being free, I suppose you will sell me so it does not matter, does it? The French had hopes to sell me but I am very old, and I can play very touched and stupid if need be. I am not worth a lot, but you can keep me if you will. I do not eat and drink much, sir."

Gunning let out a burst of laughter, and indeed it was hard to believe the man was not mocking them. Bentley found he did not really care. But he would call him Worm then, from now on, and to hell with it.

"Worm," he said. "I am weary and not in a mood for jesting. Know you where we are, at all, or are you merely useless? I presume your ship is in the way we're going, as we have not passed a cove. Unless in dead of night, of course. I guess we could have missed it."

"You could have done," said Worm. "You would have done, daylight or no. But nay, it is ahead, and still some leagues. I set off and drifted full two nights ago. I had little wind at all, thank God, but it is still a tidy way. We need the wind to keep up pretty strong, and in these parts..."

They looked at him. They wondered if he really knew or would just blow hard, like sailors do. The black man sighed.

"Spread all sail is what I would do," he told them. "We have another windy hour at the outside. Then we'll be hot and flopping. How much water is there left to sup?"

No point in arguing, so they took him at his word. Ashdown kept the tiller, Will tended to the canvas, and London Jack helped Worm bail out the bilges, to get the very best of speed. They contemplated abandoning their tow, but they decided they might need her if and when they found the hidden Frenchman and they had to fight and run.

After two hours, they were confident the black man had been blowing harder than the wind, and London Jack, indeed, had opened up his mouth to say so. Good luck he did not, though, for it dropped at the very instant, and went to nothing, without even so much as a warning puff, or fluke. One second they were heeling merrily, creaming through a short steep onshore sea, the next the sails hung like nightgowns, the boat lurched sharply back to windward, staggered into the trough again – and then they wallowed. The lightweight skiff astern slipped through the sea to butt them on the transom.

"God's cods!" said Gunning, coarsely. "The bastard! It's like as if it's never bloody blown!"

Their forward motion was at zero. The heat, masked by the breeze before, hit them like an exhalation from a baker's oven, and almost as sweet. The shore, a mile off, sat and shimmered, the blue sky above the green tree-line began to shake and waver like a belly dancer's skin. Sweat broke out suddenly on all their faces; except, Will noticed, their ancient black companion's. Who glanced from one to other to see if he must take the blame. Reassured, he murmured: "It sometimes comes back in the afternoon. But then, it might be blowing out to sea."

The motion, as they sat there, was pretty much unbearable. Without a sail to hold her down and steady, the boat rolled and battered like a cockleshell. The sun above seemed cruelly close, deeply malevolent. Mouths that had been merely dry before were parched, almost instantly. The sweat in Bentley's oxters became a drip, thin trickles down his side, and then a sort of torrent. It was not the most unpleasant of his problems, though. He had been keeping a transit on the shore. Two trees. A rocky outcrop.

"We are drifting west," he said. "We are going back the way we came. It's either row ashore and look for water, or it's row ahead until the wind comes up again." He licked his lips. "Or does not. If so, my friends, it's merely row."

"I can pull an oar," said Worm. "I stronger than I look. I had plenty practice, sir. Believe me!"

Plenty experience, as well. They could all see the new-raised surf beating on the rocky shore to what had been their leeward, and they could all see how high and hard the Caribbean rollers were throwing it. But the Worm knew also, so he said, that there would be no drinking water there even if they could get on the beach alive. He knew it, so he said, and they were disinclined to disbelieve him. Doubtless but he was thirsty too, and hungry. And he was already freeing an oar and plucking out the poppet from a rowlock.

"Christ," said London Jack. "How far then, old-timer? How long?"

"We could use the exercise," said Ashdown, eyes glinting with amusement. "Make sure we're fresh and full of vigour when we have to kill the French!"

"Stick to the tiller," said Gunning. "We'll take it in turns to have a rest. It might be a long job."

"No," said Will. "Lash it amidships please, or unship the rudder. We'll all row, but take it easier. Two men in a tub like this will be a killer. This way we'll keep it up for hours. And we've got to cover land."

No one disagreed, and they ranged themselves to pull. Ashdown took stroke oar, Gunning took the thwart ahead of him, then the Worm, and William — commanding officer maybe, but short and very light — a natural bow man. In some boats' crews this position would have been impossible; taken for humiliation. In this boat, happily, not one man had the thought. At a word from Ashdown they laid their backs to it, and the jollyboat recovered her sea-kindly equilibrium. She rolled, yes, but it was a roll that all could handle, and every blade was poised and angled right to cut the water whether high or low beside them. The skiff moved easily astern of them, and the breeze they created as they slowly plugged along made the heat seem less, the sweat more bearable. There was even conversation for a while. But desultory; and it did not last for long.

It was not an endless pull, and the breeze did rise again to help them eastward along Jamaica's southern shore. They pulled for three hours the first time, then they lay and rested in the bottom, seeking shade, when the sails had filled once more. They shared a little water — Bentley would not increase their ration, just in case: there were four of them to drink it now — and the Worm insisted they could soften their tack in water dipped from overside, and did so, eating it with relish. The white men, though, having heard the tales of madness, were not inclined to try. Apart from anything, it smacked of desperation which they hoped was premature. Short-lived hope, perhaps. Within ten minutes of their rations going down, the wind went down as well, and they rolled, and flopped, and suffered once again. They unshipped the rudder, shipped their oars, and set off doggedly along the coast.

But clouds were rising in the south, and gradually increased throughout the afternoon, although they brought no wind for several hours. Then, as the masked sun was dipping down, a zephyr blew, then a light breeze, then a stiffer one. They made sail, then took a reef down, and they fairly flew along. Best of all was when the Worm announced that the headland up ahead — he was almost certain of it — hid their secret cove.

Oh Christ, thought Bentley. And now what do we do? In half an hour they would round the point and find a Frenchman lying there, armed and manned. He had asked how many men, roughly or precisely, and Worm had said "a lot." Pressed for a figure, his fingers had indicated twenty maybe, or maybe more. And they had guns and cutlasses and daggers in their belts. He smiled a happy smile. Good sailor men, he told them, good fighters, too. Just around that little headland. Yes.

"Shit and muffins," Gunning said to Ashdown. "I hope our laddo's got a plan."

Will heard him, naturally. He was meant to. His tight smile said it, though. No plan. No plan at all.

He would have to form one. Fast.

Chapter Two

At the self-same moment, but in a different zone of time, a different longitude, Post Captain Daniel Swift drank port to help his dinner down in Hertfordshire, England, and spoke of his nephew Will Bentley as if their lives were still contiguous. It was years, in fact, since they had spent much time together, but Swift was a man of strange imagination, and very large ideas. He envisaged Bentley as an open slate that he could write the future on. And make a fortune.

"It is a well set up young man," he said, "although slight of build and low in height, my lord. But best of all, it is obedient. I shall instruct him, he shall obey. With your son out there also — and firm friends indeed already — I can see no impediment. They shall rise, and so shall we. Great riches shall accrue."

It was pitch black in England, and the Kaye family estate, near Ware, was far into the country. Lighted as they were by flickering logs and the yellow glow of one coal-oil lamp, the two men had not a clear view of each other's countenances, or expressions. It is doubtful, in any case, if the Duke had any idea of just how startling was Swift's claim that his nephew was obedient. Swift's views were strong, and fixed, not modified by many normal doubts.

The Duke, moreover, had met Will, and had been most impressed. In correspondence he had revealed to Swift some of his own son Richard's failings — perceived or real — but declared that the young lieutenant, and his constant friend Sam Holt, just the very ticket to put some muscle into him. He was a pragmatist. His son was a disappointment in himself, but he had potential, with the right direction. He had also brought off a recent coup which had heartened the doubting father considerably. So much so, he was prepared to boast about his offspring; something he had never felt the confidence to do before.

"Aye," he said. "Well Dickie's on the up and up himself, and not, for once, through others' influence. That master, Jack Gunning, ran — you did not know this, Captain Swift, I would have feared to tell you. They were left by his abandonment to sail the *Biter* to the Carib by themselves: no master, your nephew and his lowly friend as officers, and Dick First-timer in command. She would not have got beyond the Nore is my belief."

Swift stared at him, through the dimness. Without Gunning, they would not have got so far.

"Good God," he said. "He ran? So what was your son's coup?"

"He had him kidnapped," smiled his lordship. He reached for the decanter, held it aloft. "He went ashore, and found him out, and got him drunk. His stalwarts knocked him on the head to keep him quiet down the river, then they chained him down below. Got a pilot to take *Biter* to the open sea, then hit Gunning with the fate accomplished. It was the stoutest action Richard's ever did, and off his own bat also. More port, sir? It is excellent, though I should not say so, who has it shipped."

Swift nodded, savouring the delightful story. He savoured the port wine, ditto, drinking both the pleasures in.

"Good man," he said. "No, *two* good men. No, three and four with Holt and Gunning. Gad, sir, it is a winning team! Gad, sir, I am certain now that we can bring it off! And what is more, it meets my first criterion — it is for the country's good!"

The duke made no comment on this, because he knew that anything he was involved in was for England's good, it was his watchword. He perceived the nation's power in terms of wealth acquired — by whatever means — and to win wealth as, therefore, his patriotic duty. Swift sought to rise for Swift alone, was his suspicion, whether from need or greed he had no real idea, and however hard he evoked the common wealth. It suited him, however. Their ends were similar. And that was admirable.

"Four good men," he said. He opened up a snuff-box and pinched substantially, and sniffed, and blew, and offered it across the fireplace to Swift, who joined him with alacrity. "Aye, four," he said, when they had both recovered. "But what would please me, Captain, what I think we *really* need... is you. What think you of this Cuban snuff? Is it not a marvel, newly down from God on high? What say you to that proposition?"

Swift, it seemed, nearly licked his lips. It could have been the fiery Cuban dust, but it was not.

"The proposition that this snuff is God's gift borders on the blasphemous, my lord," he said, smiling. "But the other one sounds positively devilish. Your son, my nephew, the keen and eager poor-boy Samuel Holt, and that rogue Jack Gunning. 'Tis pity he's a drunkard, but there are few men primer in my experience. In any way, I will handle him. Men dare not cross me when I take command."

He sat back in his deep chair, small, square-shouldered, and ineffably pugnacious. His eyes — peculiar and bright – gleamed intensely for a long moment, then he suddenly relaxed. The smile that lit his face had dazzled many men who ought, perhaps, to have had second thoughts. The fat man across the fireplace was only dazzled.

"Take command," he repeated. "So that means you can go to the Carib, Captain Swift? By George, but that is excellent! How?"

Swift rose to his feet, as if on springs, too full of energy to remain in one place for long. His height was not impressive but his demeanour was. He almost strutted, his blue coat setting off the piled white ruffles at his neck. He began a gesture with his right hand, then seemed to remember, and obscured it, to end the waving with his left. The duke had noticed, when they had shaken hands, that Swift was short two fingers, and a half. A recent injury, the scarring still bright, and not a welcome badge of honour to so vain a man, it seemed. Swift saw his glance, and laughed, and nodded.

"Aye, you see my damaged flipper, sir. Well, that is how, amongst other things. I lost it in the Straits in a bloody little skirmish with the Moor and it helped convince their lordships I was a hero! So that is useful, when they want men for a certain mission; and more useful, I can call the shots!"

The men had been correspondents for some months, since, indeed their families had been interlinked, however tentatively. His lordship was a money man — had wealth in land but a constant urge to fatten up his store — and he recognised a tide in nature that should not be left to run away. His eyes, at this certain moment, were growing positively dreamy.

"Gad," he said. "Those golden, golden isles! My son has money — mine, to lose or grow — and not a jot or whit of hard good sense. Your nephew has wit but not the shekels. Between them they will find something for us, and my boy will get it wrong in probability, and yours will put him right. Then — just at the proper moment, when the die is to be cast for good or ill — you turn up and make certain that between them they are right. Oh, excellent, most excellent! When do you sail? Is it in a squadron, or just yourself?"

Swift was by the fire, kicking at the logs. He stood upright, distaste flashing across his features.

"Pah! Squadron!" he said. "Sir, I would rather die than undertake patrol, and their lordships, thank God, well know it. I was private in the Straits, and I done them excellent! I go private once again to the Western Indies."

"What?" asked his lordship. "Letters of Marque, is it?"

Swift gave a log one last kick and threw back into his chair.

"Nay, private, not a privateer. It is a Navy thing. I sail alone, no flag man or admiral to send me here and yon. The Jamaica planters have expressed a need, they've set up a caterwauling that won't be gainsaid, and the Office seem to think there is advantage in it. They get me off their hands once more, they know I'll turn in some prizes for them willy-nilly, and I'll harass Johnny Crapaud far and wide. My orders are, unless I'm much mistaken, to link up with the *Biter* and her goodly Captain Kaye. I've not seen them yet of course, on parchment with the ink blotted dry, but I'll put a wager on it, any day. It suits us perfectly, my lord."

The duke was nodding, his jowls all ashake. He had the decanter-neck in hand but was distracted. There was treasure in the air.

"A two-man squadron, then. Your very own. With orders to... to what, sir?"

Daniel Swift raised his hawk nose to the ceiling and barked with satisfaction.

"To search out and destroy the Frenchmen. Warships if I have to, within scope of size and weight of metal, naturally, but their sugar men for preference, and any other commerce I can find and harry. The French grow and market their produce too damn well for English comfort is the backside of the tale, I'm told — one good reason why we are at war with them. And then there's slavers to knock down, and smugglers, and even privateers. Disruption is my watchword. Find out a Frenchman, in whatever guise, and give him a taste of good old English boot. Or steel."

"There will be prizes in it then?"

"It is possible. More than possible. But that is not an easy line, in the circumstances. First one has to get the ships, then one has to find prize crews and a near destination. A destination not stuffed with Johnny Foreigner, which is not a simple prospect in the Caribbean. The islands are French, Dutch, Danish, let alone the bloody Spaniards, who are meant to be our allies, so they tell me, but what man except a fool would put his trust in that? Their Guarda-Costa ships are privateers to a man and they will prey on anyone. The best way to deal with evidence, in piracy, is what it's always been – remove it. The sword, knock out the bottom, no one to tell the tale. If I got a ship to friendly shore there might be pelf, I grant you. But my job will be disrupting trade, not setting up a trading house. For me and Captain Richard, the Jamaica plan is where the cash will lie. Your son will help me kill the enemy, my lord. Then we'll milk our new acquaintances..."

If Swift had a conception that such cynicism was best unsaid to a man he hardly knew, he showed no sign of it. In fact, he gave another bursting laugh.

"In any way," he said, "my men are men of war, not men of business. Give them half a chance and they'll sink, not save, and they know damn well the Squadron is patrolling, which means the French fleet might heave up at any time and take their prizes back as sure as sneeze. Further, they got the taste of blood from off the Moormen. Some of them use scimitars instead of cutlasses and to such breaches of King's regulations I turn the blindest of blind eyes. It is a fearsome weapon."

Absent-mindedly, as it were, he waved his right hand through the air.

"I lost twelve men and half my fingers in the bloodiest of the fights," he said. "We lost twelve and they lost some eighty three as near as we could judge. They keep their blades as sharp as razors, but chain shot is still best, when all is said and done."

"Twelve Christians dead is still a dreadful loss," said the duke pontifically. And Dan Swift laughed.

"Fourteen," he said. "Two of the Moors were English renegades. The captain and the mate in fact, the turncoat bastards. One of them was a Portsmouth man, who said he had been a galley slave until he agreed to be a commander of some sultan's ship. He could navigate, you see, as could his fellow, who had also been taken from a British hull. It was either join the rovers or row themselves to death or hang."

The duke was suitably impressed.

"Still, they should not have done so," he postulated. "An Englishman's duty is not so lightly betrayed."

"As I told them before my men beheaded them," said Swift. "We used scimitars, it struck us as appropriate. Sadly, this sort of thing is not uncommon, most of their galleys are officered by turncoats of our race. And of French and Spanish, but that is natural I suppose. They sell their souls merely to save their lives, and then they prey on English ships and English wealth. And women too. The sultans use them in their harems. Fate worse than death in so many words, although there *are* women of my acquaint would surely benefit from such a treatment. I'm sure you take my meaning, sir."

The logs were low, and his lordship rang a bell to have then stacked again, and more port procured. As the decanter was not nearly finished, it seemed the night might be a long one, although Swift would not drink much of it, in his normal way. While servant ears were flapping they talked of neutral things, like cash and hopes of it, beyond the Western Ocean. Dick Kaye had sent back letters — the post was excellent, despite the wars — and seemed to be confirming that estates were coming vacant all the while, that the sugar planters — no guts to fight, no brains to think — were in a state of daily funk and ripe as medlars to be culled or gulled.

"He claims, indeed," his father continued, "that he could have one signed for any week. I've urged him caution — nay, to keep his fingers out of my credit letters until he gets the nod. That will come from you, sir, naturally. You must be my main assessor, my brains and mentor in all this. Do you believe, sir, that I have never been abroad, not from these shores so far as the Isle of Wight, even? Can you believe that, sir? Ships hate me, sir, and I hate ships. Did you ever meet in all your life with such a milk sop?"

They shared a hearty laugh, and Swift demurred that he had travelled enough for twenty men, and that between the pair of them they formed the ideal team. They would rise together — he to undreamed of heights, his lordship to yet giddier even than he had achieved so far. When the footman finished his small tasks and left, neither of them bothered to wonder what he might have made of it. He was a servant — a necessary nuisance — and he was gone. When they were alone though, Captain Swift let out a sigh.

"I don't hate ships," he said, "but I must say this current one leaves much to be desired. She is called the *Beauty* and it is a downright lie. She was old before I got her, and she has had hard waters and hard knocks. The Straits was constant battering, both inside the Middle

Sea and out in the Atlantic. That corner of Africa brings you everything, sometimes in one day. Seas blown from the Americas rolling like mountains, snap gales and hurricanes of wind, and days of calm when the water damn near boils. And the Moorish galleys go like lightning and fight like bloody demons, which is what they are, of course. Black devils led by blacker Englishmen! I'd hang the lot of 'em!"

He reached across and took some proffered snuff. They sucked, and blinked, and blew like trumpeters. Then they cleared their throats with port. Swift sighed.

"The ship is dead, and that's the truth of it. How she will get to Jamaica is a matter of philosophy. First thing their lordships require that I do is take a better one, and let my old tub rot. Wars are costly, is what they say, which begs the question — why conduct them, then? Answer: to win more wealth and power in this world. Wealth, note. I am not political, my lord, but I do not understand this as a proposition. It seems they will not lay out cash to earn themselves some more or save themselves from loss. Even the risk of losing ships and sailors does not appear to move them. It is said we are small-minded when it comes to spending cash, we English. Maybe it is true. Certainly if I envy the Frog across the ditch anything it is his flair. They spend money on their ships like water, even if they fight them like old women."

"Aye, seed corn," grunted the duke. "That is what we farmers call it, Swift, seed corn. But you have another ship already, do you not? Will the admirals not commission her?"

The Captain laughed.

"Too small. I built her to a purpose, and the purpose passed. In anyway, the Office will not pay enough for her. No matter. There is no hurry, wars cannot last forever, and all the time she is unfinished in the yard there need be no final payment. When I need her, there she is. Seed corn!"

"But when the war is over, what is she good for? It is not a merchant man, I ween?"

"Any hull can carry what it has to, my lord. If worst should come to worse there is always slaves. She will be fast, indeed. Now there's a plan! Express slaves, to fill an individual need!" He sipped. "Nay, if they should put me on half pay I'll set up as a privateer somewhere. There is always a war on if you care to look for it. Or failing that, a smuggler."

They shared a look, but did not go into words. As a joke it was possibly too near the mark. A log fell, and showered sparks. Swift sighed.

"The truth is, I need the men I've got already, they are trained and hardened to my ways. They would not be fitted in such a little ship, and they're close to mutiny in any case. I've had to moor downriver at the Nore, which after a long voyage did not enrapture them, precisely, nostrils full of quim-scent as they are."

" Close to mutiny? How close?"

"This close: if they could they would. But I have had experience of mutiny, my lord, and well they know it. When I tell them we are sailing off once more, and for the Indies, it will go very hard. And I will handle it, I promise you."

The two men lapsed to silence. There was another matter they had broached in letters, but face-to-face even Swift considered it as delicate. He did not hum and hah for long, though. His way was bull-headed, at a gate.

"My lord," he said. "You said that when we met at last, there was something that you... that you and I should... the mutual advantage of our venture."

Hard to embarrass; it was another of Swift's claims to fame. The duke shouted with laughter; he was very pleased.

" Hah!" he said. "Felicity! She is the woman made for you, my friend! It is a match that's made in heaven!"

But his satire had gone too far to be believable. Swift smiled very tightly, but was being teased, and knew it.

"I am married already, as you clearly don't recall, my lord," he said. His bright, clear eyes spoke things much better left unsaid, but it was far across the fireplace. "A pity, sir, but there it is. Your young lady, alas, is not for me."

"Aye, damn inconvenient is it not? For you, and her indeed, to boot. She needs a mate, the matter's urgency itself, for otherwise I fear she might go wild. Gels do, these days, the old certainties are becoming hard to keep a grip on. My lady wife says the horsewhip will no longer serve the turn, although it was damned efficient in my young days. She might go wild, and like it or not that would cost me. I have money riding on her, Swift, that is the way it is with family. Inconvenient? She is a brassbound bloody nuisance, doubled."

"Ah indeed," said Swift, carefully. To an extent he knew this was a game, or he suspected it. After all, the ground had been prepared in correspondence. "Indeed, my lord, if we could treat them like we'd wish, how easy life would be. A wayward daughter is not the ideal choice."

"Choice! Pah! You talk of choice, sir! Oh God, that we could choose our family like our mistresses or friends! I have a wayward girl, and money to be lost, and that's a worry. But you sir, have a nephew, do you not? A nephew of whom one hears naught but the opposite. And there, sir, surely there, is where advantage might be won... For both of us."

"You mean?" said Dan Swift, rather delicately.

"Of course I mean! Indeed I mean! My God, sir, let them marry and put an end to it! Your nephew, my daughter, and a store of gold in sugar and in slaves! What say you, man? There cannot be an objection, surely?"

Swift was enjoying this. He had a sense of mastership, he felt that whatever, he could but win. But to show consideration (if only for the joke that they were sharing) he said this: "But I have heard, my lord... I scarce know how to say this, that she is somewhat..."

He did not say the word, but it caused a great explosion.

" Yes, yes, she is!" his lordship roared. "Ugly? She is somewhat like a horse. But then — so what! He can fuck her with his eyes closed if he has to, he only needs to get an heir, and once might do for that! She'll bring up children — badly, like she was herself, no doubt — and she'll beat his servants for him, what else does any man deserve or need? My younger girl, my little Arabella, would tend his horses, also, but I fear that she will grow up beautiful, a thing far worse than ugliness in a gel, for adventurers will come to strip me of my fortune. So what say you, then? Will he be willing, do you fancy? For, say, twenty thousand pound?"

Swift, who, if truth were told, was not entirely a stranger to debt in any way, went dry about the mouth, but hid it rather well. He nodded, as if sagely.

"Aye," he said. "I would wager he'll be willing, sir, I would wager anything on that. Indeed, as I thought I had hinted, in the very least, I've told him of the possibility, in my own mails to Jamaica. He has not yet responded, but I have no doubt what he'll reply. But, my lord... the young lady herself...? Has she made indication? Would she be willing for her own part of the bargain?"

"And what's it got to do with her?" asked her father hotly. "Yes, sir, indeed she would be willing — or she can starve, for all I care.

She could not keep herself with whoring, that I guarantee! But judge for yourself, sir. I shall bring her in."

The bell was jangled, the word was passed, and very shortly Lady Felicity stood before them. She gazed into their faces completely unabashed, and Swift — standing as a gentleman must be in the circumstances — was made conscious by something in her eyes that she was looking down on him from her height superior, and somehow mocking him. Introduced, she announced in clear tones that she was honoured, and made him feel the very opposite. Dan Swift was forced to tell himself that she was very ugly. And also very rich. Superior, inferior. He was utterly confused.

And when her father mentioned Bentley's name, she asked with put-on openness "Which one was he?" Then she remembered. "Aye, the little one," she said. "Indeed, he seemed quite pleasant, for a youth. He had a very handsome friend, as I recall."

Swift felt rage begin to rise inside him, not sufficiently countered by her plain face and scrappy ringlets, by her ill-chosen clothing, by her big bony feet and hands. Her father ditto, it would appear. The colour rose sharply in his face, and his voice became instantly congested.

"You may go, Miss," he ground out. "You had better go. Indeed you have displeased me, child. Oh no, don't ask me how!"

From her expression, Lady Felicity had had no such intention in the slightest. She bowed — and only very slightly — then she turned and left the room. Swift was genuinely shaken. Women were a mystery to him, and always had been. He had wild thoughts of a whipping, though, a whipping that would bring her weeping down.

When they were seated once again, with more port in glass and puffing at cigars from Spanish Cuba, they regained their equilibrium. The slighted father gave a laugh, though gruff and short.

"A terror, eh, sir? A temper like a lioness, and ugly as an ape. Perhaps your Will won't be so keen as you might think him. Felicity, however, will agree. You have my pledge on that. And twenty thousand pound, remember. Twenty thousand pounds. That buys a lot of married happiness, my friend. It is satisfaction guaranteed..."

They shook hands on it, wreathed in smoke and bonhomie. They shook hands on it and drank.

The future. Aye. The future.

Chapter Three

Will Bentley's plan — when it came to it — was more a testing of the water, he explained to Gunning and Ashdown, to gauge what their chances were, or if they had a chance at all. By the time they reached the headland the night was black as pitch and the wind was blowing hard enough for them to run to blazes and beyond if need be, but from their distance off they could make out waves bursting into a cove mouth that looked exceeding narrow. The Worm, though, tapped his nose. The entrance held a useful secret, was his hint.

As they rounded, they could see what he had not explained. There was a long nose of rock that obscured the entrance to the cove, but sheltered it as well. From offshore there appeared to be a maelstrom, but there was a passageway, narrow but almost calm. Inside, and on the right tack, one could take the breeze and scuttle out again at speed. It was the perfect pirate anchorage. On shore there was a fire burning high and bright, which was also invisible from the outside world. It threw the tall cliffs behind it into a stark relief, and also backlit the brig pulled in almost to the beach. At that moment, rain fell down, a hard and sudden burst. They raised their open mouths in gratitude, and their hearts rose also. Visibility, to their enemies, was almost nil.

"Luff up," said Will to Gunning, who was at the tiller. "Worm, hold off the skiff, don't let her crash and make a row." His voice was low, as were the others' when they spoke. As Gunning brought her head to wind, Ashdown and Bentley muffled the flapping sails, while Worm pulled the skiff short on its painter.

"Right," said Will, decisively. "We'll anchor off the jollyboat and go in in the skiff. Jack — get down the mainsail, handsomely. I'll douse the fore and get the killick ready."

The plan was formed, and each man grasped it instantly. They were four hundred yards from their prey and with care would not be seen. The hook was dropped, the jollyboat was eased astern to lie behind a rocky outcrop, her sails were stowed, and two oars — too long but never mind — transferred to the dandy skiff. Within five minutes they were rowing almost silently towards the darkened brig. With luck, Will hoped, she would not even have watchmen on board. With luck there would be liquor round the fire on the beach. With luck they would step over the bulwarks, find swords and firearms, and be masters of a floating fortress, just like that.

Just like that, though, the breeze dropped once again completely, and the rain stopped, a celestial tap turned off. On the instant, through a rending of the bundled clouds, the moon burst through as bright as sunshine, but white and far, far starker.

Stark naked in the quiet waters stood the dandy skiff, not thirty feet from the French brig. And on her poop deck was a watchman, smiling quietly at the scene on shore. As the skiff came to a standstill, two men resting at their oars, Will Bentley at the tiller like a statue, the black man black and silent in the bow, this watchman turned and looked at them. Will felt his stomach turn to water. He was staring into the Frenchman's face. And the Frenchman showed no reaction, he stared straight through him.

It dawned on Bentley slowly, that they were in some strange way invisible. Perhaps the lights on shore, perhaps the moon, perhaps the fact that they should not, could not, be there so close. The watchman's eyes were full upon him, but they held no recognition of the fact. The four men and the dandy skiff did not exist.

Will, in fascination, recalled that he had seen the like before, in Portsmouth harbour, on another ship. It had been a friendly wager, between two captains for a puncheon of Madeira wine, and ale unlimited for their successful people. After rowing races in the day, and milling matches as the sun went down, a prize had been secreted on a neutral ship, with two boat's crews from the rivals sent to try and snatch it. The target ship had not been warned, but they kept the normal wartime lookout, naturally. The first boat's crew, under a cloudless sky, with half a moon, had paddled up to the target, right beneath her bowsprit, and three of her men had gone on board. They had been seen on leaving, true enough. But the deed was done. They brought back the puncheon, their shipmates had ale all round, and the neutral lookouts — as was the Royal Navy way — were flogged next morning at the gratings; but only lightly. Looking at the Frenchman's cheery face, cheery perhaps because the rain had gone, Bentley could not believe it, still.

Then the Frenchman turned away. The noises on the beach were louder, there was a ragged cheering, and the sound of crashing logs feeding the fire. Showers of sparks flew up, and it was like a carnival. Bentley was not inclined to cheer, nor were his fellows. They exchanged glances, relief and disbelief combined maybe, and old

Worm, up on the stem, could be seen shaking his black and silver head.

"Look," hissed Gunning. "Bloody fire and damnation! There's another one!"

As their watchman moved slowly forward, they could see a second coming down along the deck in his direction, and in theirs. Not one of them believed in double-providence, but Bentley, without conscious thought, knew what to do.

"Worm," he whispered, urgently. "Take her in! Gunning, Ashdown! Under the sail! Quietly now, quietly! Leave room for me! Oh, *move*!"

They took the thought immediately, with not a word of doubt. Ashdown spun his oar forward to the black man, who turned it deftly for a paddle, his legs straddling the bow, while the Irishman slid beneath the skiff's torn sail. Gunning unshipped his oar without a bang or rattle, bringing it below the canvas cover beside his body. Bentley left the tiller swinging and went down too. It had taken seconds. They lay in a bundle, not daring to pant. They had put their trust in a mad old castaway they did not even know. They heard him dip his makeshift paddle, and they felt their little vessel give a forward surge.

It was unbearable. Will clutched the handle of his cutlass and he damn near groaned with tension. If Worm should indicate their presence they would be shot or speared like fish beneath the canvas. His ears ached to hear the Frenchman's shout of warning.

But it was the Worm who spoke at last, and he spoke extremely cheerfully in what, perhaps, he hoped was French.

"Hey! Ho! Mushoor, Mushoor! C'est moy, your servong! I come back!"

First one, then two men answered, and their French was shocked, and voluble, and — beneath the bundled sail — completely incomprehensible. "No, no, friend, amee!" they heard Worm call, then the bow bumped into the brig, and the skiff jerked and rocked as she was hauled and pulled alongside. Then she lurched as the Worm, presumably, clambered out, then knocked against the side again, but light and loose. Nobody else had jumped aboard.

"Ola! Black man! Where you go, eh? D'òu 'ave you get la chaloupe? You bad man! Where you been gone away?"

"*Donne-moi la ligne*," came another voice. "*Oui, ça, ça! Bon. Voilà.*"

The skiff bumped once more, then floated free. The voices receded quickly, and beneath the canvas Bentley and his companions lay still.

"By Christ," said London Jack. "By holy bloody Mary."

"We've got to move!" hissed Will. "He'll tell! They'll search in any way. Unless they're lunatick!"

"Gently, gently" Ashdown said. "Your foot is up my arse."

"Be ready with your blades," said Bentley. "Ah, Christ, I'm jammed. Ow! Shit!"

The boat was rocking and the noise was terrifying. They scrambled out from under fearfully, expecting to be greeted with bullets or cold steel. The moon was bright, but Will noted with relief a ragged edge of cloud heading towards it. He felt a spot of blessed rain.

"Where are they, sir?" It was Ashdown, crouched beside him. He had a cutlass with a ragged blade. "God, listen to that row up on the beach. Have they took old Mr Worm ashore already?"

Alongside now, they could see the brig was almost at the shore, held by lines up to the trunks of slender palms and two anchors off the stern. Aloft, the new foremast was half-complete, with shrouds fitted and some running gear, although no yards as yet. No topmast neither, but no matter. There was a forestay rigged so they could raise a jury headsail or so, and the main course and topsail were lashed on their existing yards and could be loosed in double time.

"Christ Mr Bentley, look at that!" breathed London Jack. "They've got no boats ashore! They wades out and clambers up the bobstays or a ladder. Where are their watchmen? Surely not them two only? And where've *they* gone, and our lovely Worm?"

The rain began to fall, soft but insistent, very warm. Will caught a movement at the bow. The Frenchmen were emerging from a hatchway, but the Worm was not. After a moment's conference, they began to amble towards the foredeck.

"They're going ashore with the news," Ashdown, excitedly. "Shall I nab them, sir?"

"But if they're ashore," said Gunning. "And we're on board... Eh, Will?"

"Fine well," Bentley replied. "But if the men on shore don't know there's aught amiss, think of the time and leisure we'll gain. Ashdown, you go to larboard, I'll go to starboard. Silent as the grave."

"The Frenchmen's grave," said London Jack. He had a mordant wit. "Or ours," he added, "if there's other men on board this tub that we ain't paid mind to yet." He headed for a companionway. "I'll go and take a look."

As the clouds slid across the moon the light grew dimmer, and was then cut off. The guards, not hurrying, had only reached the bowsprit heel when Ashdown and Bentley had made it to their flanks. Ashdown held the cutlass still, but saw that the lieutenant had seized a belaying pin of iron, and made the swap himself, on Bentley's cue. How good to have command of thinking men, thought Will. If they killed the sailors they would have no hands to help them the sail brig away. And sail the brig away they must — or most likely die themselves.

They moved in like a pair of cats, black cats, black night, and struck blows simultaneously. Both men had seen such stunning-clubs in use before — Ashdown may well have used one — so struck neither too hard nor soft. Both Frenchmen dropped without a cry, and lay there breathing almost gently, and not a drop of blood at all.

"Well done," said Will. "Now stuff a kerchief in their mouths and bind 'em. I'll go back and help Mr Gunning, who I think has disappeared. God hope he don't find no sleeping Froggoes down below and wake the bastards up."

"Aye," Ashdown. "God help he don't find no drinkables, an'all..."

Will glanced ashore before he left and saw the ship's crew still gathered round the fire, which was burning bright. There were awnings rigged, but most seemed not to mind the rain, and lounged about and drank from bottles, which were plentiful. There was a heady smell of roasting from one end of the blaze, and a hunger-clench near turned him inside out. Going down a ladder cautiously, he met Worm coming up, who gave a great gummy grin as Bentley jumped nervously. He had two pistols in his hand and a short sword hanging from his waist. Behind him Gunning came. Both his arms were loaded up with guns.

"Pennies off a blind man," he said cheerfully. "There's food and drink in plenty. Me and Wormie have already stuffed our mugs. Bleeding wonderful. Like a coaching inn without the horse shit."

"No other men, though? No more guards, no watchmen, sleepers? Did you look everywhere?"

Gunning nodded.

"She's not a big'un. Armed trader, quite a handy little craft when we've got her rigged again. I checked the usual lurky-holes. Why would men hide? They didn't know we'd come avisiting..."

Will eyed him curiously. He had not mentioned the one commodity most men would have taken as priority. Dick Kaye, thought Will, would have grabbed and hidden it, and then kept quiet. But this big, bland Londoner had no such venal interests. He made money easily, but seemed to have no lust for wealth at all.

"No treasure, then?" asked William. "The hold ain't stuffed with gold?"

Gunning laughed.

"There's treasure in plenty, Mister. There's treasure beyond price. But it's the liquid kind, that well brought up country boys like you quite disapprove of. Wine and brandy enough to satisfy a bloody pirate. Christ, I can't hardly keep me tongs off it."

Tension crept into Will's gut. He needed Gunning, the need was desperate. He said lightly: "But you did not open up a bottle, just to taste it? Very good. Ah — but you do not take liquor, do you? These days you never touch a drop."

When bantering about hard liquor, one could never tell with London Jack. But his smile expanded.

"I have been known to," he conceded. "Now *there's* a rare admission! But we've got work to do. Four men, one mast, four cables on the head and stern, two hundred Frenchies on the beach with guns and swords and bottles. Shit and buns, Mister, do you take me for a Bedlam?"

"Two hundred! Christ, man, are you serious —"

Jack was not, and William felt relieved and foolish. But the great relief was to hear Jack's credo. If he opened a bottle, if he even took the cork out so the genie could escape, then London Jack was lost. He was a seaman, though, and he did not want to lose his life. It occurred to William in the instant, that Gunning only ever was incapable when he was surrounded by good men. This time, he needed every ounce of strength and wit to get out with his skin. Then, maybe, the rumpus could explode...

A low hiss came down the companion ladder. It was Ashdown, straining eyes into the gloom.

"What goes on below there? We haven't got all bloody night, I doubt. Begging your pardon, sir, for my bloody cheek."

"Quite right," Will said. "I stand rebuked. Are they bound? Any sign on shore that we've been rumbled?"

Pointless questions, no answers needed. The three men below returned to the deck and looked about them with their seamen's eyes. One headsail bent on ready to hoist, enough sails on the yards to drop and brace, a brailled-up lateen at the stern. Still black and spattering, thank Christ, the carousing on the beach quite unabated. Gunning slipped into sailing master guise.

"With your permission, sir?" he asked Will, sardonically. "We need axes to cut off the warps that go to shore, we need to let go the anchor off the starboard quarter so the wind'll swing her along the beach with a jib or two up, then we can drop the mains'l and cut the port quarter anchor free. We need men aloft though. The Worm's too bloody old, the bloody skeleton. He can use an axe. I'm going to take the tiller. Which leaves you and Mr Irishman to do the scuttling about. I take it your namby hands ain't too soft to go aloft, sir?"

"Navy discipline, Jack," said Will, equably. "You'll never get the hang of it, will you? What about our Frenchmen, though? They've got muscles, haven't they?"

"They're French," said the black man. "You cannot trust them, sir."

"They've got headaches," said Ashdown. "As much use as a putty prick."

"I don't need no bloody Frogs," said Gunning. "I'll get this tub out single-handed if I have to. Big gun would be useful, though. Just in case."

"There's a swivel in the waist," said Ashdown. "Larboard side. Two pounder I would judge. Be nasty if we had some grape."

The Worm showed his gummy grin.

"I know where the powder's kept. And the shot. You want me to break it open?"

"Surely no need," said Will. "Even a Frenchman would leave his pieces up and ready in a trap like this place. What if an English ship chanced in? A rout."

This seemed most likely, and Ashdown confirmed it by a check. The black man went to the galley to ignite a slow-match "just in case". Then they gathered, amidships. The tension was on the rise. Bentley looked from man to man.

"Right," he said. "Mr Worm, nip down below again and bring some vittles up in case we get stuck on deck here a long age. Everybody seize a pistol and check it's charged and primed. There's axes there and there, and when we're set we'll use them to cut our bow ropes off. Now, Mr Gunning. I put the sailing in your hands."

"Good," said London Jack. "Mr Ashdown, if you please. Get up aloft and prepare the course to loose, Mr Bentley, single up down here so you can brace her round to starboard, and lay on tacks and sheets. Worm — go forward now and check that headsail's ready to rouse up."

"And everybody," Bentley added. "Keep your heads down and your movements gentle. If they spot us there'll be bullets flying, at the very least. They might have got a gun ashore as well. We'll know it when they open fire."

"Right; scoot!" said Gunning. "Ashdown, on that main yard. Don't holler when you're through, I'll keep a look out for it when you wave."

"Aye aye," said Ashdown. And, like a feline in the dripping darkness, was gone.

The operation — four men to unmoor a good-sized brig and get her rigged sufficiently to sail, and all un-spotted by thirty sailors not ten fathoms distant — struck William as probably impossible, and an awful lot of fun. While Gunning hacked through the lightish warp by which the starboard quarter was anchored, he sorted out essential lines for when the mainsail should be free to drop. Even aware that Ashdown was on the yard, he could hardly see him, which was reassuring, and the Frenchmen had kept their running gear in Bristol order, which made his own job light. He lashed the brace and sheet to leeward so that the sail would catch the wind as soon as dropped, to be trimmed as soon as maybe. After only a couple of minutes Worm joined him and declared the headsails were free for running up, and even better, they would not need to cut the bow lines to the shore. They were light grass warps with their bare ends not far beyond the bitts. To free her head to swing would take them only moments.

"Well done," said Gunning, who had joined them. He looked aloft, returning Ashdown's wave.

"Right," he said. "All ready, Mr Bentley, sir? All ready, Worm? Now, the two of you. Cast off the bow ropes and sway that jib up, and sheet it hard aback. Now go like lightning! Go!"

He went back to the tiller and hauled it hard a'weather, up on the larboard side. He secured it with a hitch, then took an axe. He heard the splash as the bow warps hit the water, then watched the great main course drop down. It hung for a moment, flapping damply, then filled. The yard creaked as it followed the pull of Bentley's tethered brace, and the brig trembled. The sail was fairly useless until sheeted, but it caught the wind and blew her sideways, tethered as she was by the quarter. Ashdown came sliding pell-mell to the deck to ease and haul and trim, while up forward the big grey headsail jerked up the stay, then went up with a run as Will and the black man stamped aft with the halyard.

"Hard aback!" roared Gunning, and his roar of exultation mixed with a different roaring, from the shore. There was pandemonium. The bolder spirits surged down into the water and tried to reach the bow before it swung too far, while the quicker raised pistols and muskets and loosed off a fusillade, without much chance or hope of striking a good target. Some were beside themselves with fury, landlocked sailors without even a cockleshell. Only one of their ship's boats had been put overboard, and that was still moored docilely alongside at the chains. The smaller one was on the deck, on chocks.

As the ship blew round parallel to the beach, with Ashdown and Will now at main sheets and braces, London Jack Gunning cut the last warp with a roundhouse swing, and she jumped forward like a hound let off the leash. Then he leapt back to the tiller, whipped off the hitch, and eased it has he felt the ship make steerage way. "Let draw!" he cried out to the Worm, who let fly the weather headsail sheet then ran across the deck to seize the lee. The breeze was stiff, but almost dead astern, so the old man did not have to haul much weight. Meanwhile, the main was set up to Will's satisfaction, and that of his helpmeet.

On the beach the uproar was extraordinary. There were probably no more than twenty five men, but their intensity of rage, the backdrop of sheer cliffs, the wind blowing down the western walls and then across the sand, made a natural speaking-trumpet. Some of them, in the gloom, were positively dancing, jumping, screeching, waving their arms about — like Frenchmen, as London Jack contemptuously put it. Some even threw rocks, while some fired muskets, loaded, fired again. They were running along the cove, keeping up with their escaping home, and the cove was coming to an end.

Their humiliation pleased the English sailormen no end. As they tried to clamber up the jagged rocks before the eastern wall rose sheer and impassable, Ashdown and London Jack shouted jovial obscenities, which Worm completed with a superb flourish and two banshee screams of "Merde!" and "Oh revoyer!" Pale moonlight spilled through a gap in the racing clouds as the vessel cleared the beach-head, eerie punctuation to an eerie scene. Their last sight of the defeated was black silhouettes on a pale-white beach, no longer prancing but just standing there. And then the cloud-gap closed, and the only whiteness was ahead of them. It was the whiteness of the tumbling seas beyond the protective funnel of the bay. Four men, two sails set, and as they felt it they realised: it was blowing like the seven bells of hell.

"Bloody Maria," said Jack Gunning. "We'd better rouse them Frenchies, Will, it looks serious out there. Worm! Ashdown! Get that mains'l hardened home a bit, it's slacker'n a parson's penis. No belay that and wake those Frenchmen up, the idle bastards! God, Will, there's a bastard blowing up!"

"Aye," said Will. "It's mostly from the West, an'all. Damn! We've got to get back against it, damn, damn, damn!"

"Why we want to go that way?" asked the Worm. "Why beat into that, it bloody kill us all, we got no crew. Go with the wind, we get to Kingston, eh? You crazy?"

Three pairs of eyes regarded him.

"You're in the Navy now," said Ashdown, not unkindly. "You don't argue with the officers, my friend."

"Not even when they *are* crazy," added Gunning, smiling. "If Will here says we beat ourselves to death, we beat ourselves to death. Mr Bentley, that is. 'Sir.' You understand that, you black old Mr Worm?"

There was doubt in the old and open face. Maybe fear. Will made a gesture with his hands.

"We have to go West, Mr Worm," he said. "Thank you for your opinion, and thanks for all the help you've been. But Ashdown is right. You're in the Navy now. We have to take you West to meet your captain, Captain Richard Kaye. He and our fellows have been shipwrecked there, and we have to go with aid and comfort for them. Now Mr Gunning, enough of conversation. The sails we have are a disgrace, and we must see to them, immediate."

As if to emphasise it, the brig caught the first gust clear off the open sea. She staggered, rolled, and began to broach hard round. Gunning put all his strength against the tiller, dragging it to weather.

"Get that bastard heads'l sheeted!" he roared. "And stiffen up the main. I want the tops'l too!"

He gave a shout of laughter.

"Let's take our saviour to meet Slack Dickie Kaye!"

Chapter Four

Slack Dickie, since the *Biter* had come ashore some days before, had become in fact less slack, and with a vengeance. There had been insubordination — driven, in the Navy way, by drink — and he had shot a man. The ball had struck him in the forehead, half an inch above the eyebrow line, and should have killed him. A heavy ball, a lucky shot, and only fifteen feet between them. But Slack Dickie's powder had been damp, he had not dried and cleaned the barrel out before he'd stuffed it, so the bang was more a fizz, and Patrick Strafford had woken later on to fight and drink another day. It was a lesson; but not a very good one.

Slack Dickie, though, Captain Richard Kaye of the Royal Navy, had been hardly in the mood for anything when he had reached the shore. The men had made way for him politely to walk across the thwarts to make the bow and step ashore with leather shoes still dry, but he had hardly noticed what he was doing. He moved rather like a man half-dead with misery, as if something quite overwhelming had befallen him. It had. Dick Kaye had lost his ship, and more than that, his fortune. He stood in the soft, hot sand and looked out into the green-black Caribbean, and he could see a splintered shaft of mast half-cocked and floating on the water. Beneath it, many, many feet, was silver in great quantity, and gold perhaps, and coins and doubloons almost uncountable. And all was lost. Forever.

They had rescued two boats when *Biter* had gone to bottom, or two boats, more exactly, had rescued them. While the boatswain and the two lieutenants had moved everything to get some food on board them, some water, powder, balls, the captain had been frantic to bring treasure. He had been beaten by sheer necessity finally — there was hardly room for all the men who could not swim (the large majority) let alone life-sustainers and other luxuries, and the boats had barely had an inch of freeboard between the two of them. Most men had held the gunwales or been towed on ropes.

On shore, all mustered, the ship's company of the *Biter* was announced as being about two hundred men. It was not Kaye's way to be exact, and it was not Jack Gunning's to keep his sense of humour under check. He had muttered audibly "Ship's company? So where's the bleeding ship?" but for once no one, however much they enjoyed the captain's discomfiture in the normal run, had even raised a smile. Kaye did not notice anyway. His face was forever turning out to the sea, which by now was blue and smiling, with swells diminishing almost by the moment. He had his hand upon the shoulder of Black Bob, his little slave-boy, as if for comfort. His big hand, in fact, was halfway around his neck, a living collar, stealing human warmth.

Sam Holt took charge, and separated out two watches. Jem Taylor, boatswain, was to have the one, with Tommy Hugg as deputy, and the coxwain, Sankey, would take the other, aided by Tom Tilley. Will wondered where that left the two lieutenants, and indeed John Gunning, who was the unofficial master of the ship. But Sam, he guessed, already had a plan, and he was prepared to wait to hear it. The captain was not mentioned, but acknowledged with a brief salute from Holt, which he returned. He was the captain. He was above all this. He was slack.

"Right, men," said Holt. "Break into watches, with the idlers, marines and petty officers falling in on me and Mr Bentley here. Rat Baines, you shall be the go-between, and I don't want to see too many bruises growing on him, do you hear, you bastards? Now, laugh you may do, but I mean it. Rat Baines is my very useful man."

Even Rat Baines joined in the laughter then, but they knew the message was a real one. Baines was not so much exactly hated as despised, but he had his uses sometimes, so they must not cripple him. As they split off to make two small crowds, Sam waved the three marines, their officer Arthur Savary, and the cook, armourer, sailmaker and carpenter to join him and Bentley. Mr Black, the fat-arse purser, hovered on the edge. No one asked him for anything, but he knew his place among the gentry, as he would see it. He steered clear of big Jack Gunning, though. Their animosity was all to do with drink, and prices...

When all was set up, Holt gave a bow towards the captain, who nodded in return.

"Thank you, sir," said Holt. "Now, gentlemen — and marines, of course! — I feel that speed will be our saving, here. We have some few hours left of daylight, and we cannot waste it. Our first necessities are these — find water, find food, make fire, check and clean and dry our armaments, ditto what powder we have brought ashore. The boats need emptying of anything at all we've saved that's useful, then launched to pick up floating lumber before it waterlogs. I have counted half a dozen cases, bundles, puncheons, and more should float up any time. We freed as much as possible on to the deck before the *Biter* foundered, and we must not let it float away or sink. Mr Taylor, Mr Sankey, split up your men as you see fit, and let us get a rustle on. Mr Raper, it is up to you to make your cooking fire, and Mr Purser, your job to scavenge some vittles. Nay, do not make that face at me, sir. We'll have no lazy bastards here, what say you, men?"

As a rabble-rouser, Sam had no equal, Will allowed. The jokes at the marines' expense, the targeting of the pig-like purser Mr Black, brought them together like a clockwork toy, eager to work and pull together, and not to split and bicker. Only the surgeon, Grundy, had not been named, and this was by intention, also. He stood behind the captain, in shabby black, and merely looked pathetic. This was the message: if you have pains and injuries, if you break a leg, look not to Grundy for alleviation, he is useless. Grundy had his case in hand as ever, but its rescue was not a badge of honour, and all hands knew it. It might contain some drugs and ointments, even a scalpel or so, but the chiefest of its value was for him, and him alone. It contained his alcohol, which Grundy needed as much as life itself. But that provided comfort of a sort; for if things got too bad, someone could knock him on the head, and this booty would be shared...

When the men had scattered, the conference got down to tacks. Sailmaker and carpenter were set to plan a makeshift encampment before the night came down, while Mr Gunner collected up all weapons and salvaged shot and powder, and set out to test and make all workable again. Each officer was expected to sort out his own firearms — what armourer would dare to state his doubts on their abilities? — which later led to Patrick Strafford's bonus of continued life. Another mouth to feed, but he was a good man at heart, Kaye sentimentally averred. Wrongly, too.

Will, Sam and Gunning agreed amongst themselves to call Ashdown into their company, because, as they told the captain, he was "a local man, as near as dammit, our only man who knows the island." They asked him for an assessment, first, of any dangers in the area where they were, and if they needed to post guards immediately. Lieutenant Savary, to give him his due, had already got his soldiers fettling their muskets, and indeed Rob Simms, their keenest shot and most useful man in all emergencies, had already loosed off one ball, the acid test. It had caused the crew to jump about like lunatics, and scattered flocks of birds to rise from trees all round them, which was taken for an exceedingly good sign.

"We will not starve, then," said Kaye, complacently.

Ashdown was loath to voice words that might be perceived as critical, but he did say, obliquely: "It could be more than birds we flush out, though."

"God, man," said Kaye, "be not so miserable. What mean you; lurkers? This place is like a wilderness. I doubt the nearest house is miles away."

Ashdown nodded.

"Aye indeed, sir. But not house exactly. There are Maroons in this stretch, it is known for them. Our gunshot means they will not be unaware of us, I guess."

"Aye," said Kaye, sarcastically. "And they would not have watched us sailing in, you think? And sinking. At least now they know that we are armed."

It was a not invalid point, so Will smiled in agreement. But added: "Fact is, sir, that we need to have all guns ready as soon as ever possible, and cutlasses and knives issued, do we not? What Ashdown means, is that we will not be alone for very long. Wilderness or no."

"By Christ," said Gunning. "So how many of them, Jack? These Maroons — they are runaway slaves, is that so? Why do they allow them to exist?"

"Because they cannot do no other," Ashdown replied. "They were much more numerous in earlier years, but they have treaties now. Live and let live. And divide and rule to boot. The Eastern men tend one way and the Western men another. Sometimes the Easters will fight for the planters and earn money in tracking down runaways from the plantations. Other times they fight the Westers, or fight amongst themselves, as do the Western men. And then again, sometimes they raid an outlying plantation as in the old days, just for the hell of it, may be. They are not tame, these Africans."

"They are savages," said Richard Kaye. "My pa has told me all about them. Black bloody heathens of the deepest dye. If they should try it on with us, we'll chop them up for dogmeat. Let them come!"

This caused a quiet air of discomfiture, and Holt said laconically to Ashdown: "How many then? The captain says we'll chop them up. Could make dogmeat out of us instead?"

Ashdown licked his lips.

"It is not my place to say, sir. But some of the... ah communities, encampments... some of them have numbers in the dozens. More. Like villages, in the mountains. Damn near impregnable. Then there are smaller bands. They roam about. White men upon the roads are... well, let's say in danger. Let's say — to the Maroon men — they are fair game."

This incensed the captain.

"You are talking like a coward, sir," he snapped. "We are British men, and white. We must strike out for the nearest settlements, the planters' not the savages', or failing that march straight to Kingston or Port Royal. Or will you tell me now there are no roads?"

Ashdown had not flickered at the insults. Kaye was an officer, of course. A gentleman.

"There are roads, of a sort, sir, yes. And Spanish Town is nearer than the other two, and it's the biggest, but it's some days of marching without animals. The roads are... well, Connemara comes to mind, sir. Even an ass would balk at some of those boreens."

"Quicker by sea, then?" Bentley asked. "Some of us could sail round to Port Royal. Not many, though."

"I'm game for that," said Gunning, suddenly. "What say I take an officer or so and Mr Ashdown here and sail round for reinforcements and a ship? Come on, Capting! That makes sense, don't it?"

"We've got two hundred men here," Kaye said testily. "All the Maroons in kingdom come could not overwhelm us. We'll march."

"And they haven't got a boot or shoe to bless their feet with," said London Jack. "They're sailormen, not bloody waggoners. Why not split the difference, then? We'll go by sea and you can get some volunteers to try the rocky road. We'll have a wager on it, shall us, Dickie? I'll give you five guineas if you get there first. Or at all, for that matter! I'll lay another five you'll get eaten on the way!"

Sam, through devilment or what Will could not guess, put in his hapence-worth.

"You must leave the bigger boat though," he said, as if judiciously. "I've got more than half a mind that we'll get down to her and take some more stuff off. She's crammed with valuables, ain't she just?"

Kaye's eyes were on to him like arrows.

"What? Get stuff off of *Biter*? But she's in a hundred foot!"

"Sixteen fathoms by the lead," Holt agreed. "But there's more hamper showing now unless I am mistaken. What is the tidal range round here? Do you know, Mr Gunning?"

The answer was immaterial. Kaye's nut-brown, slightly bulging eyes were reaching out beyond his nose. He took a half-step towards the water. Indeed, the bare broken end of mast, tethered to the spars below by tangled cordage, was angled up towards the heaven like a sea-mark. And as they watched, a bulky wooden box burst to the surface. There were floatables all round, and the yawl was going after them, one by one.

"Hell's teeth," breathed Kaye. "They swim down for oysters in these parts, don't they? Ain't this where they dive for pearls, down in the lower depths? Hell's teeth..."

Will and Sam had only vaguely heard tell of such things, but Gunning knew, inevitably.

"Over in the Gulf of Honduras," he said. "Or maybe Nicaragua, I can't remember, but they do it all the time. Those black lads can hold their breaths for half an hour and go down a cable's length! Tom Hugg can swim, Capting, for all he's like a bleeding whale. Jem Taylor ditto, I believe. And there'll be lots of lads among this likely lot, won't there? When I come back I'll lay good money on it — you'll have the Spanish treasure up! We'll all be rich as Mrs Creasey is!"

The struggle in Dick's mind for a decision was ended by this proposition, however slim it rang to Bentley and his friends. He gave a nod of masterful command and took Sam off to check over the jollyboat, drawn up at the water's edge. The yawl, offshore, had six or seven men on board, and a pile of rescued gear. She was clearly the ideal vessel for the salvage job.

Work went on apace, onshore and off, and the morale among the company was exceeding good. Geoff Raper, the one-leg cook, had a fire blazing, six feet long between two rows of gathered rocks. Black had broken out some salt beef and flour, and the carpenter had constructed spits of springy greenheart to roast things on. As he had thought to bring two axes and an adze ashore with him, so Raper had rescued two iron pans and a variety of spoons and trivets. The armourer had dealt out powder, checked and remixed it in his black arts way, and Simms, marine, had tried and failed to shoot a bird, before Savary had told him off for wasting precious powder. He and his fellows, though, had brought back various exotic fruits, which they had tasted, all unknown, and luckily for them had not been struck down poisoned. Some of the sailors said it was far above normal shipboard fare already. Sam Megson, half-witted like all the Corkhead breed, declared they'd landed on the "Paradise of Eden."

Within some few hours they had a good camp up, rough wooden shelters with roofs of woven leaves, and lookout positions facing cleared areas that were long enough to give good warning if they should be attacked. Mr Purser, under fear of death perhaps, had been lavish in his doling out of barrelled meat, and Raper as always had conjured marvels up. He was marvellous to watch himself Will thought, prancing and hopping around the fiery pit, hurling food and imprecations everywhere, sweating like a dervish king.

Gunning was getting restless, though, fearing the light westerly might die before the jollyboat was under way, so he, Bentley and Jack Ashdown stuffed down their vittles hurriedly and prepared to leave for Port Royal. They took meat and biscuit in generous amounts, but water remained a problem. The scouting parties had found nothing close to camp, and had been forbidden to wander far until they were armed and organised, so they took two bottles only from the number Taylor had had filled up from the scuttlebutt before the *Biter* had gone down. All three guessed that they would find water along the coast, and in any way, if the wind and conditions answered to their hopes, they would be in port before things were desperate. The jollyboat was pushed off stern-first and the sail was hoisted smartly, and they were under way. Will felt foreboding as the people stood and watched them, because a silence fell which was somehow ghostly. But when the mainsail had filled and the sprightly little vessel heeled and creamed along, he had a sensation of well-being, as a sailor will at sea.

As the sun began to lose its heat, the prospect was in ways a joy to contemplate. The island was extraordinarily beautiful, white strands, grey cliffs, and a background of verdant green. From out of that, steep mountains rose, purple and misted, with a crown of clouds on some of them. Bentley, unaware of it, let out a chuckle, which made Gunning raise his eyebrows.

"Well, you're an easy one to please," he said. "Tell me what's so wonderful and I might raise a smile myself."

"Pardon," said Bentley. "Just a private thought. Megson had it right, perhaps. It is a sort of Eden. Maybe reminded him of home, I guess, as he's a Corkhead."

"Corkhead?" said London Jack. "And what the hell is that?"

Bentley laughed.

"From the Isle of Wight," he said. "Do not ask me why they call 'em that though, no one knows. But it is lovely, and very green, and Saint Catherine's Down is like a mountain, I suppose. To a Corkhead!"

"Mr Ashdown," said Gunning satirically. "We are commanded by a king of lunacy. Jump now, if you can swim. Sadly, I cannot..."

***

On the beach, as night came down, the well-being and good humour hung together passing well, and far longer than Sam Holt and Taylor, who were naturally allied by sense and circumstance, had expected. Geoff Raper's food was consummate, Captain Kaye allowed a brandy ration from the one small breaker they had brought ashore, the mild weather reconciled the people to the idea of sleeping on the ground, and Sweetface Savary's marine soldiers took up guard duty on the outskirts without demur. Savary himself, though womanly in looks and the object of much rough desire from the seamen most desperate in their longings, had proved himself as manly, and no soft touch. He gave his orders firmly, and generally was obeyed. He also, as of habit, took his place at his soldiers' head, as it were, and encouraged them in their duty.

The night, by English standards, was a noisy one. As black as pitch except when the moon showed through the high and milky cloud-cover, it was full of cries and shriekings that sometimes struck as human but more usually did not. When the cooking fire had died down and the brandy-glow worn off, some of the sailors began complaining. Taylor and his giant boatswain's mates, Toms Hugg and Tilley, having circulated, reported that some had the horrors, as sailors often did. Rat Baines was spreading tales of ghosts and goblins, backed up by the carpenter, known as a miserable sort of sod. The surgeon, Grundy, whose other supposed duty was to be the *Biter*'s man of God, merely had the shakes. What the men wanted, Jem Taylor said, was a fire, big and noble, to drive off the demons crowding in.

Kaye, at first, said no — on the grounds it might draw unwanted attentions on them — then thought again and said, why not? If they had not been seen or heard by now they would never be, and if they had to fight, well let it happen soon. The men were well, and fit, and fed, and happy, and it would be a bloody rout. In truth, his thoughts were otherwhere: he wanted to do a sortie soon, he was certain they would find an easy road to Spanish Town or Kingston, and Ashdown's tales of savages were all my-eye. "God's sake," he said to Holt and Taylor, "the man is Irish, isn't he? And a papist rogue to boot..."

While he was expounding this, the embers of the cooking fire (with no permission given yet) began to flare. Sam turned to go and bawl them out, but Kaye, as slack as ever, waved him to forget it.

"What matter, when all's said and done?" he said. "Keep them happy, keep them warm. They'll follow better in the morning when we strike inland."

"Captain," Holt started, but gave up. How tell this man it was not the way to keep them disciplined? Jem Taylor shrugged a shoulder, unseen by Kaye, and Holt sent him to keep an eye on things. He and the captain sat, with Purser Black, for courtesy invited to the inner circle. The surgeon could have come as well, for the same reason, but he had merged into the darkness with his bag. Even when the flames were bursting up into the sky, throwing white flames and red all round the encampment and the nearest trees, he was not seen.

As the fire grew, so did the men's exuberance. Their noise turned into singing, there were impromptu dances, and the shoutings grew obscene. Kaye was unimpressed, and even told Sam off for being so jumpy for so little reason. It was drink, though, Sam was certain of it, and after some while this was confirmed by Taylor. Kaye remained dismissive.

"Drink?" he shouted, in the boatswain's face. "What mean you, drink? We brought one small keg ashore and I have doled this night's share out. Do you think those people are magicians?"

Where liquor was concerned this was quite probable, in Sam's experience, but Kaye had hardly come up the normal way, 'mongst normal men. Sam and Jem knew drink could appear from anywhere — or apparently from nowhere — and in a shipwreck would be the only true necessity in seamen's eyes to guarantee continued life.

"What is the state of them?" Holt asked the boatswain. "Are they ugly in it? Do we have control?"

"We have sneaked all blades well out of sight," said Taylor. "Blades and firearms, except their working knives, I guess. But there is a faction growing that I do not like. Ayling and Thompson may be at the heart of it, and that loudmouth one, Pat Strafford. They've been scuffling with silly Sam Megson, who stood up for Ratty Baines when he snitched some brandy."

"Stood up for the Rat? By God he really is an idiot, isn't he?" said Sam. "Maybe that's why they call them Corkheads, nothing more!"

"But there's others joining up," said Taylor. "Carver, Sweeney, McGuigan and that lot. Tom Hugg's watching them and Tilley's gone to fetch a podger from the yawl. There's shouting that they're going to run for it."

"Bah!" said Kaye. "Run where? At least if they get butchered we'll know there's niggers out there, won't we?"

Holt was on his feet. He pulled a pistol from inside his coat and checked the pan.

"There's only powder and a wad in this one," he said, cheerfully. "I thought this might happen and I didn't feel the need to waste a ball, or life. Come on, Jem. Leave it to me, sir," he added to his captain. "It won't be anything."

When he reached the fire, though, things were nearly on the cusp. Within the crowd of men, mostly unmoving, was a smaller band of — what, revellers? Or villains? Troublemakers, certainly, and all too clearly drunk as monkeys. Si Ayling, a good man in the general way, was bare to the waist and sweating, and in a fighting stance. He was yelling blood and thunder at a man called Jennings, who was standing over the prostrate form of Megson, who had a bloody face.

As Holt arrived it took a turn for worse. Jennings reached behind him and produced his sailor's knife, short and dangerous, from his belt and showed it to Si Ayling's face. Who leapt at him, not an instant's hesitation, and tried to club him down with his fist. More sudden blood, and a cry of rage from Ayling, who clutched onto his opponent, and the pair of them went down. This raised another squawk, from Megson newly squashed, and a further rush of men into the middle. More than a dozen fighting, and a riot on the break.

Sam, who could think as fast as any man, whipped out his pistol and discharged immediately. The effect was instantaneous, but sadly not sufficient. The bang and powder-flash cooled down half the brawlers, but only half. In fact Sweeney and Carver, not noted for their brainpower, began a charge on Holt himself that could only end in death by hanging if they landed blows.

They did not, though, for Tom Tilley flashed into the firelight at the same instant, running from the water's edge. He had an ash stave with a metal end in one enormous hand, and his first swing tore open Markie Sweeney's upper lip and scattered broken teeth. Tommy Hugg jumped in from the rear, with only two enormous fists for weapons, and bore McGuigan to the ground. The excitement of a roughhouse spread, and exhilaration began to take control. Some twenty men were fighting, more knives were coming out. Toms Hugg and Tilley stayed within the thick of it, but Lieutenant Holt, joined by the boatswain, stood on the fringe and watched. The vast majority shuffled in unease, fighting manfully the urge to join the fun.

"What best to do?" asked Sam, of Taylor. "We can't bring it down by force of arms. I have another pistol loaded, but it's got shot in. No point in killing for the sake of it. In any way, it might incense the rest."

"From what I heard, sir, some of them want to run," Taylor responded. "Grass being always greener on the other side. Mebbe when they've traded blows enough they'll bugger off. Is that too bad an outcome, do you reckon?"

"As long as they don't damage Hugg or Tilley," Sam Holt said. And they shared a laugh.

It might look more serious than it was, but it did indeed look serious. Sam wondered idly where they'd got the spirits from, then suggested to the boatswain they might be best occupied in hunting out the barricoes and staving them. That way, at least, this could be the last drunken night. Before they could start, however, Slack Dickie played his hand. He emerged into the jumping firelight with a horse-pistol in his hand. He was not a bad shot, Dickie, and he favoured the hand-held cannon. If only, thought Sam, with contempt, for the satisfying bang it made.

He did let out a creditable roar, though, which cut the row down briefly, and for a few seconds there was a pause, which struck Sam as rather wonderful in the firelight, like the representation of a holy revelation in a painting of the classic mode. Bloody, sweaty, panting men stared ruggedly out of their little circle for an aching moment at the visitor from an unknown world. Big, and clad in blue, with head held high and a bloody great firearm pointing straight into the heart of them. Pointing at Patrick Strafford, in fact — a smallish man, but very virulent — and pointing to the purpose, very much.

"Stop this drunken lunacy, you stinking bastards," Slack Dickie yelled. "Or I'll kill the lot of you!"

It broke the spell, and Pat Strafford, apparently enraged, took a step forward, and his fist was raised.

Kaye pulled the trigger without a second thought, but there was, Sam noticed, not much of a satisfactory bang. More a snap, and then a fizz, and a discharge from the barrel-end of a great gout of dirty, whitish smoke, veined with bright red flame. When Strafford fell to the ground — not poleaxed backwards but with a slack-kneed forward slump — even he looked surprised at being hit. There was another moment, this time of pure silence, then the noise burst forth once more. Holt, with a sinking heart, pulled out his second pistol. Bloody Kaye, he thought. He'll be the death of all of us some day. And it could be now, quite possibly.

But Strafford's henchmen, assuming he was dead, had other things in mind. They saw Holt's gun, they guessed the captain could produce another, and in any case they had their reason now, clear-cut and golden. They turned as a body, pushing through the shipmates bunched all round them, and ran out of the firelight, away from the sea, towards the trees and rising ground.

"Stop! Stop!" roared Kaye. "I'll see you hanged, you villains! Stop them, you bastards!"

None of the bastards tried that lark, none of the bastards lifted a finger. Even Hugg and Tilley were happy to let them go, although they did not care to make it obvious. The other men stopped shouting, and many of them assumed a sober look, respectable as aldermen. Within seconds the crashing sounds of undergrowth died away. A shout of "Who goes?" from an outlying marine guard, a filthy imprecation in response, then nothing else.

"Stand down, you lubbers!" shouted Taylor. "Tommy! Tom! If anyone else is inclined to run, you will break their legs, please. Captain's kind permission. The rest of you get sobered up and get turned in, before we come amongst you with a whip."

He turned to his captain, mildly.

"There, sir," he said. "Riot's over. Do you want that we should tie them up? Any of 'em?"

But Kaye, job done, was looking for a drink himself, and a well-earned rest.

"Damn them," he said. "Just bed them down and keep an eye till daylight. And get a couple of them to dig a hole for that man there. What's his name again?"

Taylor grinned from ear to ear at thought of burial, for the corpse was showing signs of life already. He answered "Strafford, sir" however, in case Slack Dickie should be upset at his lack of prowess killing mutineers, and tried to keep his face straight until the captain turned away. Holt went along with this arrangement.

"That was impressive, sir," he said, as they walked back to their positions. He saw Lieutenant Savary moving in to join them.

"Aye," said Kaye. "That nipped it in the bud, and properly. Ah, Mr Savary. We've had some runners. Did you not see them? You should have shot them, man."

There was concern on the sweet face, but minor only.

"We had heard the shouting and the guns, sir. We thought they might be in pursuit of islanders. And they were unarmed. I'm sorry, sir."

"Ah well, no matter," Slack Dickie said. "Sankey. Get me a drink, man! And Mr Holt here, and Lieutenant Savary! Hot work, but satisfying!"

"Do you not wish I should pursue them, Captain?" asked Savary. "Although I guess they'd only disappear into the woodland further."

"The hell with it," said Kaye. "They'll come crawling back if they get hungry, and I'll maybe string one up to teach the rest their manners. We'll hunt them in the morning while we're out looking for that road. But I doubt we'll see a hide or hair of them again. They'll be gone and soon forgotten. Good bloody riddance to them, too."

They did see some of them again, however, the next afternoon. Markie Sweeney was found first. His severed testicles were stuffed into his torn and gaping mouth. Perhaps the knocked-out teeth had been an open invitation...

Chapter Five

Deb Tomelty's new life among the blacks of the central hillsides was a confusion, a relief, and not at all what she had imagined it might be. For a start the people she was taken in by were not warriors, or "Maroons," they were very far from warlike, and for the most part they were women. It was two days after the escape from Sutton's plantation that she arrived among them with her fellow escapees, and she was consumed with many sorts of terrors, not least the way they might look on her. She was white, and they were black. They were slaves and she had been a household servant, due to get her freedom in some years or, more likely, attract a master-man with money and become his dame, or failing that, his whore. And injuries notwithstanding, she was exceeding beautiful.

Worst, in her anticipation of the way they'd treat her, was the fact she could not speak their language, although her grasp of Kreyole was coming on apace. In fact, to her astonishment, she discovered that many of the blacks could speak English very well, including those who had had no words at all in days gone by. As Mabel explained it, when Deb asked her why they would not talk it or respond at Alf Sutton's, it was "because we hate him. We hate all of them. They are white." Deb was white as well, but did not need to make the obvious rejoinder, because she knew already. In the days since she had seen the black men tortured by Sutton and his surviving son, and been burnt and injured going to their aid, she had been numbered among the slaves both by white men and by black. Mabel had tended to her injuries, fed and washed her, and when the last reprisal had come, and Sutton and Siddleham, his lordly neighbour, had attacked and killed and driven off a group of twenty, maybe more, Deb had gone with them because she could not stay and hope to live. When Siddleham himself had smashed down off his horse crossing a gully, she did not stay to succour him, a white, although she had tended Kaia's brother till he died. In the slaves' eyes it was the saving of her: in the planters' a warrant for her death.

The community she stayed with in the foothills were not slaves and were not Maroons, as Mavis told it to her, but runaways. They numbered thirty or so, and they lived by selling food, not thievery or predation. Even on the plantations, some planters gave slaves a small amount of land, usually inferior, and one day a week or so to cultivate it. The women in particular could coax any vegetable or fruit within the island's range to grow like wildfire, and took up the role they had in their former lives. On market days they were allowed to sell any surplus they might have beyond subsistence needs, and toured nearby plantations or set up a market system for slaves less fortunate in their husbandry.

Why run away then, Deborah wished to know; while assuming it was a love, or need, for freedom. Her new-found friends — Mrs M, Rebekah and Kinji — did not laugh out loud at her, but found it half-amusing, even so. Most of them had been driven out by jealous white foodstuff-vendors, who were resentful of the unfair advantages the women had. Which were? Free land to cultivate (in that they did not have to rent it, like the whites), free time to cultivate it, freedom to sell it for a profit. And, naturally, the ability to undercut white peddler's prices because, as slaves, everything was provided by their philanthropic masters...

They were seated in a clearing quite high above the coastal plain when Deb learned this, and to her it was a tranquil idyll. The four of them, joined now and then by Mabel, who was following her little son in his explorations, were bathed in dappled sunlight as the breeze moved the palm fronds up above them, and were sucking small fruit contentedly. She found it hard to envisage the actualities of being "driven out," but believed them when they described the threats and blows that had convinced them it was time to go.

"White women mainly done the damage," said Mrs M, "but if it was a worser beating needed, then their man would finish off the problem. That why Rebekah got no teeth. Show, gal!"

Rebekah was a lovely woman, Deb considered, but she had wondered why she never spoke. Now she drew her lips back to reveal completely empty gums, and an ugly hiatus in the structure of her upper mouth. She stuck her tongue out just a little way, and it was red and scarred. She closed her lips and smiled.

"Mark you," said Mrs M, "woss black man done that hurt. He got... favour... off the seller lady. More sell, more favour. She not as pretty as Rebekah, but she earn much money."

"Rebekah," said Deb. Because she could not think of another thing to say. "Is that her real name?"

"Can speak for me self," Rebekah said — and Deb blushed scarlet. Rebekah smiled, forgivingly.

"They call me that when I get here," she said. "My mammy call me by a 'nother name but I not remember him. They sell my mammy to another man the day we come from Congo-land, and my sisters and my brothers too. My father die on ship, so I got no family anymore. 'Cep Mrs M now, and my friends and Kinji and so on. They best people. No trouble now we livin' here. No man, no trouble. Ain't that so!?"

The women laughed and Deb joined in, and truly, she felt safer with no men. She had left one of them dying — Sir Nat Siddleham, if she understood his name exactly — and she regretted that, but he would have killed her anyway if he had not gone down. And his sons were vile, although meant to be gentlemen, and her master Alf Sutton was even worse, as was his one surviving son who had sworn — as all the others, come to that — that he would fuck her when he had the chance, and she'd be grateful, even more so since she was so burned and ugly. She kept her thoughts of Will Bentley brief these days, because she knew that he was lost to her for good, whatever part of the land or ocean he might be upon, but she wondered, in the sweetly-scented sunshine, if he would want to fuck her still, and she knew he would. And she rushed it from her thoughts, her heart quite crushed.

There were men in the hillside camp, of course — camp or community, their formal word for it was town, it seemed — but it was the women's world, which kept it safer from attack. There were two old men, called Alfred and, strangely, Toad, whose role appeared to be to keep the fire burning, and there were young male visitors with links to some of the women, who all went coy when Deborah tried to probe. She thought there must be another camp nearby, where the menfolk lived, or perhaps they kept on the move for fear of being apprehended. All were runaways of some sort, but she understood the women were not hunted as routine, whereas the menfolk were. The women had their uses, of course; they were a source of produce that plantation slaves could buy or barter for, and sold stuff of finer quality to the planters' cooks.

Ten "items of Alf Sutton's property" had run from his plantation with Deb Tomelty the night of the attack, but Kaia's brother had died, and two of the other men (with the slave names Flight and True) had melted into the darkness not many miles and hours later. Goanitta and Mildred had continued on their flight, as had Mabel and her little son, whom she loved but could not bear to give a name because he was Alf Sutton's, who was old enough to be his grandfather at least. Marge and Missy were the other two (the Suttons delighted in their naming scheme) and a lugubrious old greybeard man called Dhanglli, known even to his fellow Africans as Dangle. He was greeted by Toad and Alfred as a long-lost brother, which Deborah supposed he might well be.

For the first few days after the escape, Deb assumed that the Suttons and the Siddlehams would do anything to track them down, and the women agreed it might be true, especially her fellow escapees. But it was by no means certain according to Rebekah and Mrs M, because there were dangers facing white men when they strayed too far from their plantations. One of the favourite things the black men did to get their own back was "pick off" lone white travellers if they should meet them on the road, or if they strayed into the woods. The whites had militias — each man had a duty, it appeared, to do so many days and weeks of patrolling and of training — but they were difficult to raise and organise, because it cost the planters time and cash, and put them into extra danger. Then there were the "wild Maroons," who were armed, and dangerous, and very prone to fighting the wrong fight.

Deb looked at Mrs M quizzically, but the old black woman chose to smile rather than answer. Deb questioned Kinji and got but little out of her, and Goanitta, from her own plantation, filled in. She used fast Kreyole, but Deborah got the gist quite easily, and answered in the same. This pleased the women, and she got a sudden kiss from Mildred, who was normally standoffish and straitlaced.

"Them white man make a treaty," said Goanitta. "Them Maroon work for them white man and them black man do get pay. Track down and kill some runaway, take head back and get plenty wine and silver. Maroon and white man they all same bad. Some time black man forget him rule, though. White man militia run through them tree and say 'How do, my nigger?' and Maroon go chop 'em up. Bad black man, see? Maroon him bad, break treaty. Very bad."

The grins of all the women told the story very well, and Deborah also thought it sounded rather fine. She nodded slowly, and they watched her smile.

"Bad nigger, see?" said Mrs M. "Fight wrong fight. It keep Mr Planterman away, though, these country parts not safe, they wild. So maybe they do not come for you and other garl and men who run away that night. Or if they come, they come in many strong, and that be many bad. We got spies though, ain't we just? White man like big bloody elephant, you know?" She made a trunk and flapped an ear — Deb laughed acknowledgement: she had seen pictures. "We see an' 'ear acoming and we go. We vanishes. We spirit us away."

In later conversations, in passing days, she learned about the country to which she had come, although it soon became apparent that the runaways themselves, or all the slaves indeed, knew very little of the English structure under which they lived and worked and suffered. They worked for plantations and the work was hard and heavy. So hard that few of their menfolk lived much beyond six or seven years, except the ones who went over to the masters earliest and most fully, first as overseers then slave-drivers or a kind of vicious "bloodhound" force to beat and even kill the slaves who could, or would, not accept their grinding lives. Even outside the harvest times the work was never-ending, as the canes exhausted land with fearful speed, necessitating constant clearance and expansion, the digging of new rows for planting, and turning, and manuring, and digging in. Then, there were dwellings to be built, not for themselves but for their masters, who needed great houses to make them feel at home in this accursed island, and great houses took great labour. Unluckily for them, many of the Africans were exceeding skilful, in making bricks, and cutting trees, and shaping wood, in every craft the planters had to have. Unluckily for them, it was not a way to avoid plantation work either, because it could be done when sugar work was not the great imperative. When they were not killing themselves cutting cane or in the boiling house, they could be killed constructing palaces for their lords. Slaves were expensive. It was a constant cry among the masters, Deborah knew. But they killed their men in seven years or so.

The women's work was not so harsh, although as constant, and the white men had high hopes of them as breeders of new labour. But on this island at least, it did not work like that, as Deb had learned from Bridie back at Sutton's place, and others too. Slave women produced no children, almost, and those that were born rarely lived more than several minutes. Even among themselves, and certainly not to a white girl, however trusted, they did not go into this. But Deb knew that roots were used, and plants, and what they hinted at as *obeah*, or *obi*, as far as she could hear the words. When they wanted to, they could all use a Kreyole she could not clearly understand. But they did not conceive, or killed their babies in the womb. Or smothered them. That was the fact of it.

Mabel had a child, though, although he did not have a name, and he was almost white. Alone one afternoon, wreathed in aromatic fire smoke, Deb dared to ask her why, and Mabel gave an answer, of sorts. She looked at Deborah, then looked away, then back again. Her eyes then filled with tears, which overflowed and poured down either cheek. She turned away without a single word, and left.

Deb's whiteness was a problem, though, as was her beauty. Among the women it was nothing, they liked her for herself, and for her transparent equating of her self with theirs. She worked with them, slept with them, ate with them, communed with them. She was not seeking to find another, better role or place. But as her hair grew back to cover the worst of scarring on her scalp, and as her facial scars faded almost to nothing, news of her presence and her beauty was clearly spreading far outside the "woman's town". Men started visiting — the first ones led by Flight and True, who were roundly abused for it by Mildred of the icy eyes and fiery invective — and their studied casualness was soon replaced by a growing impudence. Some were not mere runaways, what was more, but were Maroons, and saw themselves as warriors, and wore their ragged shirts and trowsers in a different fashion from the plantation men she knew. One had a leather belt, another a flowery bandanna. But the difference, mainly, was in the eyes. These were not slaves, their hauteur said: they were fighting men, and free. They were Windwarders, the women told her, from the Blue Mountains up in the east where sugar was too hard to grow and white men, consequently, had no interests. They were interested themselves, however, in Deborah. She was white, and had been vilified by her masters, and had run away, and thus, potentially, she was a Black Man's Prize. Or Whore.

Deb Tomelty, who to herself was only Deb, whose breasts were merely breasts, whose face felt only ordinary, had been made aware that she was beautiful to men from an early age but still, when she thought of it, did not know how it worked or what it really meant. Her eyes were clear and brown, her face a perfect oval, maybe, her hair had grown as dark and lustrous as it had ever been, her teeth were white and even, her body neat and lithe and firmly resilient, but inside her head she was a hatter-girl who had caused misery to her mother and then run away and seen her best friend killed because of it. She had used men's perception of her beauty to make a living, as it were, to stay alive, but she took no pleasure in their attentions, and never had done. Until meeting Will Bentley — who himself had come to ogle her at Dr Marigold's gay house — she had never dreamed that fucking could bring pleasure, and had never had the faintest inkling of love. She had loved him, and did love him, and so much the worse for that. If they ever met again he would not remember her, why should he? To Deborah Tomelty, beauty was a jest. These black visitors, half preening, half meek and humble in the presence of her glowing skin, were an irritation, and a growing fear. She wanted no man any more, unless it be William. She was no longer even sure of that.

Then one day, late into the evening, Deb had another visitor whom she recognised immediately could somehow do her harm. He was tall, extremely handsome, and he was bursting with the energy of youth. He was lean, his features finely made, and his ragged trowsers and open, flaxen shirt gave him a rakish charm that was piratical. Flanked by three stone-faced older men who were clearly his subordinates, he was confident, also; his eyes met hers and sparkled with frank pleasure.

Deb, suddenly, was frightened. He struck her as a young and charming animal. Very young, and very beautiful, and as carefree as she herself had been. But across his shoulder was a long, old-fashioned musket, and at his waist a military cutlass that had been broken halfway up the blade then ground into a wicked point, honed razor-sharp at top and bottom. It was a tool for killing, nothing more, for killing and intimidation.

He stood and stared at her, and there was pleasure on his smiling lips, boyish pleasure, and Deb blushed, unable to prevent herself.

"Hah," he said, at last. "White girl, greeting. I am Captain Jacob. You can be my woman. I am Jacob Tsingi. Captain."

Deb Tomelty stood in silence, and she wondered what to do, or what to say. In a clearing in a wood, in a foreign land, in dripping heat, in the midst of friends or savages or both, she surely did not know. The man in front of her, the lovely boy, was staring at her, his eyes deep and black and shining. His expression did not change, but the faces of his acolytes were wreathed in smiles now, anticipating pleasure. Mrs M had made a sharp sucking noise, between her teeth and lips, though Marge and Missy were round-eyed, which Deborah took as signs. The silence lengthened, until the boy was disconcerted. His ease was turned to tension by degrees. If he spoke again without her having answered, he would lose face, and everybody knew it. The thing was critical.

At last Deb spoke, and her tone was soft and gentle. She hoped Will would forgive her if she took his name in vain.

"I have a man already, sir," she said. "We are betrothed. I am sorry."

She hoped she would forgive herself for this. She hoped more that it might turn the trick.

But Tsingi's tone was harsh.

"Where is 'e then? This man of you? I see no man."

The noise from Mrs M grew louder, and Mildred was suddenly upon the scene as well. She stepped up to the men and talked hard and angrily, in a tongue of Africa. The acolytes spoke back, were silenced angrily by Jacob, who then went at it violently with Mildred, who as violently came back. The other women of the camp appeared, and formed a ring around the argument, and sometimes emitted little cries, responding, Deb imagined, to some point.

Then abruptly it was over. Mildred and Tsingi had gone face to face, both shouting, then she had turned away and made a gesture. The four men had stood defiant, but some agreement had been reached, it seemed. They formed a phalanx and strutted out, shoulders back, heads high. Deborah found that she was shaking.

There was silence for a good a long while. Then Mrs M began to suck her teeth, but with a different cadence. Mildred nodded at the English girl, but her eyes were cold.

"He eastern man," she said. "Him father Colonel Treatyman. Him no right be here, see, gal? But I think him do come back."

"Think him?" said Mrs M, scornfully. "We know him come, gal-Deb. Captain Jacob got the sniff for you."

Chapter Six

Their stolen brig was called the *Jacqueline*, and the wind that met them outside the secret bay was half a violent gale. It took them dead astern and pushed them east, and the untrimmed ship rolled and wallowed like a sow in farrow. She had one headsail up, and a sagging main course that badly needed sweating up and bowsing home. Gunning was at the tiller and he was struggling. *Jacqueline*, one-masted, ill-served, was playing "woman games" as he grimly called it. Will Bentley needed hands, and quickly.

He went himself to rouse the Frenchmen, and he had a knife and pistol in his hands. They were awake and their eyes were showing fear or anger, either striking Will as quite appropriate. He cut their leg-bonds first, and dragged the cloths from out their mouths, upon which one of them vomited noisily over Bentley's shoes. No matter for that, though — there was water coming overside enough, and increasing, to wash off anything in no time at all. He poked his pistol into first one neck and then the other with calculated brutality, and said: "*Je suis capitaine. Vous devez obéir moi*, understand? *Ou je vais vous tuer.* Understand? *Entendu*?"

One said oui, the other said yes, sir. Then all three of them were swept by a curling sea, which drenched Will's pistol as he had not seen it coming. The English-speaker's wrists were already cut free, but he did not try to take any advantage of the useless firearm. The danger now was natural, and all three understood it. They must work the ship, or maybe founder. Will sliced through the second Frenchman's bonds and said tersely: "*Aidez avec les voiles.*" It occurred to him that they would both have knives. It occurred to him that both might need them.

Ashdown was at his side.

"The jollyboat, sir," he said. "Just up ahead. We need to pick her up."

"We can't," said Will. The anchored boat was almost at the line of surf. The Jacqueline was bearing down on it at ever greater speed. "We'll make do with the Frenchmen's cutter and the skiff. We cannot try and stop her now, Jack."

He meant the cutter tied alongside, not the boat on chocks, but he became aware that she was battering the *Jacqueline*, and also filling rapidly.

"Ease off her painter! Range her astern with the skiff or we'll lose her too."

Both he and Ashdown jumped across the deck, but probably too late. The cutter was half-full already, and solid water was breaking across her bow. The painter was like an iron bar, but as Will's knife moved to it, Ashdown touched his arm.

"Sir! She might not sink! She'll maybe go ashore, sir! The Frogs could get her!"

Gunning's voice burst in from aft, like a foghorn.

"I need sails trimming! I'm losing steerage! Lieutenant, bugger you!"

Will saw one opportunity. And maybe two.

"Ram her!" he hollered back at him. "Mr Gunning, sink the jollyboat! Sink our jollyboat!"

London Jack, fortunately, seized the thought instantly, and had control sufficient — whatever he claimed — to swing towards the anchored boat. It was swinging wildly on its cable in the squall, and presented its full side-length at just about the best moment. *Jacqueline* smashed into it forward of amidships and stove in its larboard side with a tremendous crunch. The jollyboat was trodden under on the roll, but better still, the cutter lashed alongside hit the wreck hard enough to burst its own stempost and open the bow strakes like a broken mouth. As the planks sprang outward and the sea poured in, Ashdown deftly cut the painter with his knife.

" Let no man tell you God is dead," said Bentley, both relieved and blasphemous. "Jack, He must be on our side!"

"Bollocks," Ashdown replied. "It was the Devil's luck..."

Clear of the land both assessments proved unlikely, for the wind was freshening by the moment, and it was blowing more from the north than due westerly, which had been its set under the shelter of the island shore. Their first task, with the Worm and the two Frenchmen, was to set up the main course properly, run up a second headsail, then set the topsail, possibly reefed, above the main. Worm, after the work on deck was done, slipped aft to veer out more line for the dandy skiff, which was snubbing too short and taking water, but was generally riding very well. In this sea, this short-handed, it would be a job indeed to get her back inboard and stowed if they should be forced into an attempt.

Once all the canvas they thought feasible was set and drawing, Will joined Gunning at the tiller to talk of cases. The more they got off of the land the harder it seemed to blow, and the more nor-westerly it became. Not good for getting west along the coast, not good at all for getting west then north to reach the *Biter* men, not even good for getting back to Port Royal. With one mast down and no hands to speak of they could hardly claw to windward, and while the French sailors were docile enough they could hardly be trusted once their ship was not in immediate danger of going down. Below decks would be guns and swords and God knows what, and they could not be watched like hawks forever. And they had their seamen's knives.

"First off we'll wear her round," said London Jack. "With your permission, sir. Then we'll harden up to see how much of westing we can steal. There's a stay already rigged between the foremast stump-top and the main pole head, and I'd like a sail on it if it be man enough. Get Ashdown to check it over, sir, then use the Frenchies to help him up aloft and bend one on. Without more canvas fore-and-aft we'll be nowhere, fast. We'll end up in bloody Nicaragua. Long haul back to Dickie that would be, even if the weather ever changed. Where's that long black streak of turd the Worm?"

This was said with affection, which increased when Will told him he had sent the man below to rustle food, and even coffee if available. Jack Gunning's eyes grew dreamy — given his constant battle to stop the unbalanced ship broaching to — and he expressed a desire for hot coffee that transcended even alcohol. Will could believe it, for this once. He too would have gladly killed a priest to taste the bitter bean.

"We'll wear her first, without him," Gunning said. "What betting that she'll go slam hard around just as he's coming up the ladder with a steaming pot, and he'll drop the bloody lot? Men!" he shouted. "Stand to your stations, I'm coming round. Mr Bentley will tend the jib sheets as he is the lightest — I pray you, tend 'em, sir — and Mr Worm will do the most useful work, for he is making coffee down below! Now — prepare to wear ship!"

Short-handed it was a wondrous job, and the two Frenchmen were a sterling asset. They knew where each line ran, they knew each belay point, and they conveyed the information as if all the seamen shared a common language. As they came round on to the wind they could feel its weight the better, and it made them work as brothers, as the alternative to brotherhood was God knew what. They could not come far onto the wind with the hopeless rig, but all felt that they were doing right and heading in the direction best desired. The skiff swung round astern of them and headed the rolling seas without desiring to drown itself, and the driving spray, if almost constant, was very warm and comfortable. Then there was coffee, and cold pork and sweet potatoes.

It did not do them much good though, and Will and Gunning were very well aware of it. Their heading was way too far to southward, and in that they had no choice of any sort. They had a staysail set, they reefed the main, they got an outer jib up, and the Frenchmen were great experts on the tiller, while the English were more used to a wheel on such a vessel. But they were blowing south, into the open Caribbean, leaving Dick Kaye, Sam Holt and all their fellows ever farther to the north.

Then there were the French to deal with. Fine seamen, and fine souls. Chain them below? Toss them overboard? Keep them up on deck until they froze? Or trust them?

They were the enemy. They were honourable men, whatever London politicians might peddle to the people. They would want to get the ship back. Their ship.

And suddenly, the Caribbean night was coming down.

Chapter Seven

Dick Kaye's determination to find a road to Kingston, and to run his deserters down, had faced much competition in the night from thoughts of lifting treasure out of *Biter*, and in the morning this new obsession grew apace. By the time Cox'n Sankey roused the captain and his pet from their tarpaulin slung between two trees, Holt had already been out above the wreck in the yawl with Bosun Taylor, and the report he brought was fuel on the fire.

"You can see her clearly, can you?" Kaye asked, excitedly. "And there's less water than we thought? Good God, Sam, we'll lift the treasure yet! Good God alive, man, this is marvellous!"

Holt shook his head in irritation. The captain's boyishness, as so often quite misplaced, was unusually irksome in the circumstances. He could see the wreck (as had been possible when she had sunk) but she was perched, it now appeared, on a coral outcrop that the leadline might have missed, to give them a false reading. To Sam, though, she seemed still beyond the diving range of man. There were cases and barrels caught up in the sails and rigging as they had risen from the decks where they had been placed before the foundering, and it might indeed be possible to dislodge some of them so that they would surface. There might be food unspoiled, they might even retrieve hardware of some sort. But gold and silver did not float, however buoyant their containers might have been.

"No, sir," he said, as patiently as he could bring his voice to. "Not lift the treasure, we're still talking twelve or fifteen fathoms, maybe more. No one could get that far, then they'd need to get inside the wreck and find the stuff and bring it up!"

A sort of growl of impatience came from Richard Kaye. He was sitting on a fallen tree-bole and his face was already dewed with sweat, although the sun was scarcely high.

"Oh, there are ways!" he said. "Christ, Sam, sometimes I find you downright womanly! Maybe more you say, but maybe less, as well. If we can see her we can get there. Men can swim, and we have ropes. There's cordage everywhere, we can cut it off the floating hamper. When men get in they take an end with them, and lash it on and give a jerk and hola! Up the treasure comes!"

He was like a little child, thought Sam, in some despair. Everything was easy. He had lost the ship, they were stranded, and no man knew how and if they could get back again to the bosom of the Royal Navy. A dozen crew or so had run, Bentley and two more had sailed off into the night on nothing but a hope and prayer to bring salvation, and at any time, perhaps, they might be attacked by slave escapers whose keenest joy, he guessed, would be to get revenge. They were white, they were virtually unarmed, they had little food, less water, and no shoes or boots to march in. They were sitting ducks just waiting for the fowlers to arrive. And Slack Dickie fancied hunting treasure...

At this moment, while he was marshalling his objections for the next verbal foray, Black Bob was seen advancing, with a makeshift tray. Between them Sankey and Geoff Raper had mustered up a breakfast for their lord, which filled Sam's heart with gloom. It was good — fried meat, a certain sort of flat-bread concoction, fresh fruit, and even coffee. The sort of morning meal, within its limits, that told the captain everything was fine, and normal; dandy. Behind Kaye, by the cooking fire, Sam could see the men in ordered lines, also receiving sustenance from the cook. Raper was a wonder, no doubt of it, although a hopping rather than a walking one. But with this captain, and these men, he might also prove quite fatal. Corkhead Megson's cry came into his thoughts: Paradise of Eden. It was not likely though. The worm was in the bud. Kaye's next sentence confirmed all fears.

"You see?" he said. "Here's Black Bob with a goodly feed. Everything is champion, Sam, and for God's sake don't try and spoil it. Smell that coffee! Bob! You are a princeling, sir!"

Although invited to partake, Sam walked away disconsolate. He saw Sweetface Savary emerging from the bushes, and he had a razor and a glass in hand. They stood together looking out across the sparkling green Caribbean, and Sam milked him for his thoughts. Nothing had been seen throughout the night, the soldier told him, neither sight nor sound of either friend or foe. Just strange, disturbing noises, which he guessed were normal island sounds.

"It's not like home, sir, that it's not," he said. "And I don't trust it to be as peaceful very long. I'll need some sailors, quickly, to take over as musket guards. My men must get some sleep. Can you select some for me, please?"

After breakfast, after Hugg and Tilley had mustered all their men in two watches once more, with details to search for food, fuel, water, the captain called Holt to make up a conference, with the boatswain, carpenter, Henderson the gunner, Lieutenant Savary, Dr Grundy and the purser, Black. As expected it was not so much a sharing of opinions, though, but Kaye's airing of decisions. The sun was climbing, the heat was rising, and his lust for useless action knew no bounds.

"Gentlemen," he said. "Lieutenant Holt here reports we have a golden opportunity. The sea is lower, and the *Biter*'s lodged, it seems, upon a bed of rock. With diligence, perhaps a modicum of luck, we can reach her, and we can take the treasure off. Likewise items of less valuable a nature, but nonetheless welcome to our enterprise for that — like beef, pork, beer perhaps, and bottles, kegs of powder, maybe shot. Even if we cannot kill sufficient food on shore here we can provide with comfort for ourselves, we'll have the wherewithal to live. We can get canvas up an'all, and rope and nails and things. We can build a proper camp."

Sam was not going to argue, however infuriating was Kaye's dishonest gloss, but he did allow his face to say a lot. Henderson the gunner, an acid man who knew his own importance, did not avoid a sneering note.

"A proper camp is it, sir?" he said. "I'd say we need a proper fortress, and that right quickly, too. I don't know how much powder I can save and get to work if salt and damp have done their business, and I don't see how we can hope to get it up off of the wreck. What if there's swarms of black men in them hills? Savages?"

"We *will* build a fort," said Kaye, as if he'd planned it all along. "And you, Mr Henderson, are the man for that. Mr Carpenter, I confide you'll take that in hand also, and work side by side?"

The carpenter, whose name was Venman although never called as such, made a shrug. He would do anything, if ordered; except enthuse. If he had rope enough, and wood, and something he could cut it with, then building shelters was a bagatelle, and he was content to have Henderson in charge, so that if anything went wrong it could be the gunner's fault. Despite all this, Henderson was pleased to have him as a companion. Mr Carpenter was a streak of piss, but he did magic with a hammer and some nails. Taylor told off his mates to select helpers for the craftsmen, while the search for firewood and water carried on. When such organising was well in hand, the captain ordered the boatswain back to talk of salvage.

"Mr Taylor, there is a rumour you can swim," he said, and Holt watched the boatswain's muscles tighten. "How many of the people can, and which ones best? I am fired up to get the yawl on station."

Before Taylor could answer, Sam put a blaster on.

"Hold hard, hold hard! I beg your pardon, sir, but I need orders here. We have a party of deserters, sir, who may be armed. We have a hinterland that's thick enough to hide a herd of elephants. Mr Ashdown insisted yesterday there would be natives here, or Africans in any rate. Escapees, sir, Maroon bandits from the plantations. Surely we must investigate? We must find that road of yours, sir – your first and best idea!"

On Kaye the use of flattery was guaranteed, as Holt had often proved before. The road to Kingston or Spanish Town had been deemed too dangerous by Ashdown in fact, but had been the captain's own initiative. Reminded of it thus, he could not bear to give it up. The boatswain, who read Sam's intentions clearly, put in his pennyworth.

"You are right indeed, sir," he said. "What should Ashdown know? If we can reach it we will be secure, surely? I say the road, for certainty."

The logic was impeccable — as balderdash. If they did find a road it would probably be rather more a track. It would be impassable without beasts to carry them, and each bend and gully would be a perfect point of ambush. In case Kaye should work this out, Sam became more truthful.

"In any way, we have to know, sir," he said. "We have to see if there are lurkers out there, and if we are strong enough to hold them off, and for how long. We have to run down our own mutineers and bring them back to help us or be hanged, and if we do discover a road, find out where the nearest white men are, and in what strength. Who knows, there might be a militia garrison. There must be such a thing, in this ungodly country."

Kaye nodded, all his deepest thoughts confirmed.

"Aye," he said. "There will be. There will be a road, and there will be our countrymen, with arms. You will go and find them for me, Mr Holt, and you may take a small body of men with you, whom you may choose yourself. But Mr Taylor here, and me —"

Holt interrupted. Daring, but his time was very short.

"With your permission, sir. I really need Taylor to come with me. He—"

"No, sir! He is a swimmer and our finest seaman! I have hopes that he will get men down into the wreck!"

This was a test of character and no mistake, thought Sam, his anxiety overcome by his amusement. If Jem Taylor were susceptible to flattery, an'all! The finest man forced to lead the plunge to certain death...

But Taylor said politely, and with supreme irrelevance: "I have a pair of leather shoes on, sir." There was a pause, then he continued deferentially: "For walking on the roads, sir. And through this forest. And half the men can swim, sir, or at least a goodly smattering of them. And Tom Tilley handles boats as well as I do, or even better."

"The shoes are not a light thing, sir," said Holt. "I have shoes, Jem has shoes, the marines have boots. Probably no more than six others in the company, save for fat Black the purser. Would you have him come with me? If the Maroons were cannibals he might serve as bait, I'll grant you."

It was a good joke, much appreciated, and Black was no longer in the vicinity to make objection to it. Kaye conceded the argument, but insisted Taylor should help prepare the yawl and persuade the men that the diving was a workable idea. Meanwhile Holt talked to Savary and won the services of Simms, the smartest of the soldiers, who not only had boots but had a musket, sword and bayonet and was a master of them all. Kaye, on an evil whim, wanted Holt to take Grundy along with him (who had shoes but nothing else of any use to any man) and made it clear that he would not mind at all if the surgeon did not come back, for any reason in the world or none. Sam, who feared the captain might get on his high horse, came up with the argument that the surgeon might be needed if the diving men should come to any harm. More spuriosity, but Slack Dickie chose once more to fall for it. Truth to tell, with gold in prospect he was in a sunny, sunny mood.

"Aye, aye," he said, "it is a point well made. By George, their lordships must pay him for something, when all's said. Now Taylor, and Mr Holt, how best to do this other thing? Give me considered thoughts."

It was deemed sensible, for the first forays at least, to keep the number in the yawl a minimum. Although the weather had been in a changing mood, with constant threats of squalls and rain, it was calm enough for sea-bathing as at Brighton this morning, and the boat could be rowed out by three or four without an effort. Kaye had to go, of course — only a spice-apple on a stick could have made him more like someone on a holiday — and Grundy was forced to cower on the bottom-boards with his precious box, a picture of dismayed incompetence. Tilley, a man of quiet humour when the humour took him, treated his role as second choice of diving master with easy affability. He had no objection to forcing sailors to drown themselves on the captain's whim, if that is what it took to lead a quiet life: indeed, he thought it shaped up as something of a lark.

The "divers" he had chosen, with Taylor's assistance on the shore, were four in number, and too young to feel regret, as yet, for having "volunteered." Each was slim and lean, and thought anything was better, as a fact, then crawling round in fetid undergrowth tearing trees up and building shelters. On land they would be sweating. Offshore they would be cool and comfortable, could enjoy the feeling of the water on their bodies, and might even, Tilley hinted, find brandy in the wreck that they could get a swig at. Their names were Manton, Collins, Jones and Macintosh. Jem Taylor and Lieutenant Holt watched from the shore as they paddled out towards the *Biter*, and hitched a painter to her floating stump of mast. Jem waved a hand to the little black boy in the stern sheets beside Slack Dickie, but as usual, cowed Bob did not respond.

"Well," said Holt, "they have the luck of it I suppose, Jem. Let's pick up our party and go and sweat ourselves to death. What sort of snakes and creepy crawlies do they have out here? Without number, I suppose. Maybe East Sussex ain't so bloody awful after all..."

Five minutes later, with Rob Simms and a sailor called Sam Hinxman, who had no boots but claimed his feet were soled in iron, as indeed they did appear to be, the pair of them set off. Up ahead was forest, green and black, and beyond that, before they lost sight by plunging in, tall stony mountains, shrouded in high cloud. Further along, indeed, the mountains seemed to have their own local storm, which they watched race along with black rolling clouds and spectacles of fired lightning. They agreed the Caribbean islands were a most unusual place. And wondered how the hell they'd ended up there...

Chapter Eight

Out on the yawl, Kaye's euphoria did not last very long, although his optimism did. Above the wreck, things looked beautiful, and beautifully easy. The water was so clear that every plank could be discerned, and looked close enough to touch. Even Black Bob, aroused momentarily from his normal stupor, reached out an eager hand to break the shining surface of the water. He was surprised when he found nothing under it but sea. Kaye laughed.

"Well, Bob! What did you expect? We have to struggle for what we get in this world, boy! And you have never had to struggle, have you?"

The four young men dipped in their hands as well, and marvelled that however hard they stretched, the prize did not come close enough to touch. They did not see it as insuperable, but were anxious to get overside and bring the treasure up. The treasure being liquid in their minds, most probably. Grundy had not yet worked this out. He was morose as death.

Tilley was already organising. He had obtained light line on shore, and had it stretched and coiled. Between them he and Jem had estimated the smallest depth they thought was possible, and marvelled that any man should think it feasible to dive. Gunning had said that pearl divers in the Gulf survived depths almost mythical, but Gunning was not here now, and Gunning would say anything that suited him. Tilley's role, in any way, was to facilitate, not to argue, so he had brought rope and idiots. Although they were clamouring for precedence he chose Collins, whom he estimated had the smallest lungs. When he failed, the next man could do slightly better, Tilley thought, which would keep the captain happier for longer. Collins stripped down to his raggy drawers, which led his shipmates to some hilarity. As if their drawers were any less destructed, when it came their turn to show.

It was when he balanced on the gunwale smiling that Collins had his first clear doubt. He had the light line round his waist, Tilley with the coil in his hand to save his life if need be, when it suddenly occurred to him that this might be insane. He opened mouth to protest, and Richard Kaye, in realisation, bellowed at him like a bull. Collins jumped, lurched, staggered, lost his feet and went in with a mighty splash. Kaye, jerking on his safety line, damn nearly cut the lad in half, and he surfaced shouting with the pain, then choking with the swallowed water.

Tilley reached overside and lifted him inboard as a mother might pick up a little child, observing mildly: "Not much blood drawn, luckily. It brings the sharks from miles around."

Collins threw himself onto the bottom boards like someone in a play, and Kaye, enraged, booted him quite heavily. Not in the stomach though; he did not want to destroy his lung control for later. Tilley, the pragmatist, undid the line and signalled the next smallest man, John Manton. He presented drawers to view — but no more laughter — and presented self for tethering with far less enthusiasm than Collins had done. Black Bob looked terrified, and Surgeon Grundy picked his nose. Kaye took off his coat. The day was getting sweltering.

"Don't horse about," said the captain, bitterly, when Manton stood ready on the side. "And I'll thank you, Tilley, for no more nonsense about sharks. They do not have them in these parts."

No one believed, but none could argue with the lord and master, and anyway the blood of Collins seemed not to have attracted any. It was, indeed, only an angry weal around his waist. Manton took courage, took an almighty breath, then plunged overside feet first. Which was hardly very logical, as he rather quickly found.

Unlike many sailors he could swim, but it was not a skill he would win prizes at. Just below the surface he kicked and struggled manfully as he tried to turn his head and body end-for-end, but by the time he was pointing to the *Biter*'s deck his leg was tangled in his safety line and there were bubbles escaping from his mouth. He kicked mightily with both feet, starting to move down below the surface, but before his heels were three feet under the bubbles had become a white volcano. Next instant he was end-for-end once more, and his gasping, bursting face shot through the surface. Thrashing in a panic, he grabbed at the gunwale, missed, slipped underneath. Again it was left to Tilley to provide the crane to haul him out.

Slack Dickie had a face like thunder as Manton lay in the bilge and retched. Macintosh though, bowing to the inevitable, got to his feet and began to untie his britches-waist. Tom Tilley held a hand up for a pause.

"We need a method, sir," he said. "With your permission. Drowned rats ain't going to get no treasure up."

For a long moment there was no sound inside the yawl but panting, while the captain took this idea in, and Tilley put his seaman's mind to the problem. There was a grappling hook in the bow, and he indicated that the surgeon should pass it back to him. Grundy blinked, his disconnected thoughts a thousand miles away, and Kaye bellowed: "The grapnel man! That bloody iron, by your feet! Lift it back here!"

Grundy, it transpired, could not lift it, which Kaye and Tilley thought was good. It was indeed a heavy one, a boarding tool shipped in the yawl to act as an anchor, but which a normal man could lift, if not a so-called surgeon. It was unwieldy though, and Macintosh, getting the idea, eyed it dubiously. It would take him down all right; but would he get back up again?

"Sir?" he queried. "That don't look safe, an' beg your pardon, sir. That don't look safe at all."

"Bollocks," said the captain. "We'll put it on a line and when you're down there you can hook things on to it and we can haul them up right handsomely. What's your objection, man?"

"I'd rather get down to the bottom on my own," said Macintosh. "That is all, sir. I might get caught in that, and then I'll drown."

To general surprise, Kaye accepted this without an argument. He even suggested they drop the hook down first so that Macintosh could pull himself to the bottom hand over hand. Tilley unbent its short and heavy rope and replaced it with the lighter coiled line. Then he leaned across the gunwale, studied until he'd worked out the best spot, and lowered the grapnel down until it reached the *Biter*'s deck. A few jerks here and there until it found a place to jam, then all was ready. Collins and Manton took an interest now, feeling half-deprived that they'd been tricked out of their turns. They made it clear that they'd be ready if and when Macintosh made a dog's breakfast of it.

He did, but not so speedily as they had. He dived overside head first and seized the line about five or six feet under — ignoring the way his loose and tattered drawers slipped off his buttocks up to the thighs and almost to the knees. The laughter on board was easier this time: everyone was urging on their man.

Macintosh did very well indeed, but the thing was hopeless, realistically. By the time he was down twenty feet, perhaps, his movements seen from above were jerky, with his legs thrashing about to almost no effect. He would not give up, though, and struggled on and on. All those on board save Grundy, who was indifferent, were holding their own breaths for him, and the strain was pretty near unbearable. Time was standing still. Each man could feel a drumming in his ears.

And then the diving man gave up. There was a convulsive movement below them, then a mighty blast of bubbles and they saw him rising, thrashing arms and legs like some machine. It felt like ages before he broke the surface, and as he rose his tortured lungs gave up the fight and he breathed in, taking down an enormous gulp of seawater. Then he vomited, and shouted obscenities through his racking gasps. He would have sunk perhaps but Tilley took him by the hair, then by the neck, then underneath the shoulders and then into the boat. There was water pouring from every orifice it seemed, from ears and mouth and nose and eyeballs, but Macintosh was triumphant.

"I can do it, sir!" he gasped. "I can do it, sir, it's easy! I've got the way of it this time!"

Tom Tilley thought he was a clown, but the other sailors, who knew no better life than vying with their shipmates, and Captain Kaye who maybe knew no better anyway, took him gladly at his word. Kaye asked Grundy what he thought — if any damage had been done — and Grundy, naturally, declared the man as fighting fit. When the captain suggested a drop of medicine from his box Grundy went pale with apprehension, but Macintosh — who perhaps had no knowledge of the surgeon's cure-all — declined in any way, with a convulsive shudder.

It was Jones's turn to go down next, and he was determined to make the last man look a booby. He stood on the gunwale for what seemed an age, filling and emptying his lungs, which looked, indeed, to be a good size. He was a Welshman, brought up in the mountain country, and his chest was very deep. When he was ready he nodded briefly and dived in very cleanly, thrusting downwards with his legs. He did not kick, but pulled down hand over hand, apparently tireless. On board the yawl the men started to be excited. Perhaps they would see treasure after all, and soon. Captain Kaye began to grow a grin.

Did not last long. Without a signal of distress, Jones was on the up once more, reaching above him, looking to the surface, and kicking madly with both legs. As he got close, air was bursting from his mouth, and when he had grabbed the gunwale he gasped great gouts of air and let out wheezing roars. He tried to pull himself on board but could not without aid, then lay as if exhausted across the thwarts. His lips were tinged with blue.

"How far?" asked the captain. "You were almost there, I think? Did you touch the deck, or nearly?"

Jones did not reply, but his shipmates all pooh-poohed it. They could do better though — and would. Manton and Collins clamoured for the privilege of being next, and Kaye chose Collins, on the principle of strict rotation so that each man could recover. Collins was full of pride this time, now that he had a rope to pull himself into the depths by. Tilley, who had watched the last man like a hawk and done his calculations, placed a private bet on with himself. He won it easily.

Collins came up shamefully quickly, although he had got farther than his first time down. John Manton crowed less about his chances then did even better, and Macintosh claimed to have touched the deck before his lungs insisted he let go of the line; a statement that raised Tilley's eyebrows. Out of bravado, perhaps, Macintosh suggested they should bring the grapnel up and tie it to the next man going down, like a plumbline. That would end the wasted effort kicking and pulling, speed up descent, and give incentive to cling longer on. Jones, whose turn it now was, did not like the plan at all — and did not need it, he insisted. If Macintosh could touch the deck, then he could dance a jig on it. When he returned to surface, there was a small amount of blood from his left ear, but still no sharks. And he had reached the deck, he said, and Kaye apparently believed him.

He had not, for probably it was impossible. Each man, for the first two hours or so, got down further every time, improving his technique of holding breath and saving energy, but neither the divers nor the watchers from the yawl could tell with any accuracy how far away or close they were. Kaye kept insisting that the tide would surely drop soon which would make it easier, but if it ever did, it was not enough to measure by the *Biter*'s drowned mast. Kaye, naturally, had not boned up on Caribbean tidal ranges, which were sadly negligible. And although each man got down deeper for their first few dives, each man grew tired as the time rolled on. When they called a halt for dinner and a midday rest, all four of them had swollen eyes, sore throats, and thickened tongues. All four claimed they had reached the deck. All four were lying.

Kaye found, and forced, two more men, called Bell and Jolley, to join the diving boat after their dinner, but Bell got stomach cramp on his first attempt and almost drowned. Jolley was rendered so terrified by this that he could not leave the yawl unaided, and when he was shoved overside, roughly, by the boatswain's mate, he let out a heartrending scream and swallowed half a gallon. Which fired up the others to greater efforts, to prove their superiority. Later, Bell and Jolley made some proper dives, but never really got the hang of it. Sweat ran, frustration grew, tempers were getting frayed.

"It is boys that do it in the Gulf," said Tilley idly at one stage — and instantly regretted it. Kaye gave him a dirty look, because they had no boys, just men, and then the penny dropped. Tilley's regret grew a hundredfold and he wished that he had bitten off his tongue. Black Bob, who for once seemed almost tranquil, was trailing fingers in the water, unconscious that he was the focus of attention.

"It's worth a try," said Kaye, and the men just gazed at him. "Bob," he said. "You can swim boy, can you not? You aimed to swim away at Port Royal, you faithless bastard."

The little African glanced up, surprised, not realising what was going on.

"Strip off," said Kaye. "It is not a hard thing, Bob. Just hold your breath and down you go. Then you'll find treasure, and I'll give some to you. There! Is that not a handsome thing I do?"

The boy, whose grasp of English nobody knew for certain, still did not appear to understand. His eyes, though shocked, were not yet full of terror — but it was there not many seconds afterwards. Kaye went to him, and lifted him up by one arm, and said again: "Strip! Strip, sir, down to your buff. Do you need a whipping, sir? Now do your duty!"

The men were all uncomfortable. No one liked this thing about the captain and his pet, it was an idea that disturbed, obscurely revolted, them. The boy was pretty, well enough, and many would have liked a go at him themselves. But the captain was a gentleman, and should behave. This poor boy was a plaything, he was helpless, he was a little child. Now his eyes were bulging from his head: he had worked out what his master had in mind for him.

"No, sir!" he stammered. "No swim lord, sir! No swim!"

However guarded were the people's faces, Kaye could feel their disapproval very well. It incensed him. He was galvanised.

"Whey-face bastards," he said, generally. "Don't sit there, dummies, there's treasure to be got. The child can swim, he is a bloody native, ain't he? Bob — I charge you — now you must pay me for your keep."

Black Bob began to cry, and then to scream, and Kaye smacked him hard across the face. He stripped him efficiently till the black boy stood quite naked, covering himself from all the seamen's gaze, then jerked him up by the wrist towards Tom Tilley.

"A light line," said Kaye. "Tie it round in case the bastard swims away. Oh you, ungrateful!" he shouted at Black Bob. "It is not a lot I ask you, is it? You will enjoy the swim!"

Bob could swim, it transpired, but try as he might, threatened though he was, he could not get himself underneath the water for more than seconds. He came up kicking and spluttering, and tried to avoid Kaye's repeated blows. After several attempts, the captain dragged him back on board and threw him down among the sailors' feet.

"I'll go again, sir," said Macintosh. "It looks like..."

"Me, too," said Jones. Kaye quelled them with his eye.

"Tilley, haul up that grappling hook. I'll get the bastard down there, malingering little toad."

A grim silence descended on the yawl as Tilley hauled up the grapnel hand by hand. Black Bob was not looking, had no idea what might be happening. Surgeon Grundy, similarly, appeared to have no clue. He sat in the bow, full-dressed despite the killing heat, a look of dreary blankness on his face. He held his box much like a talisman, a comforter. But he could not open it and drink, he knew that well. He was suffering.

"I shall not tie you to it, toad," said Kaye to Bob, as the hook came inboard. "Unless you fail me. Just keep a grip on it, that's all, and down you'll go, like clockwork. We've all been to the deck, look at all your fellows. It will be easy."

Black Bob had slipped into his normal mode, of just not understanding. His eyes were blank, his face was neutral, he allowed himself to be stood up on the thwart as uncaring as a wooden doll. He did not any longer cover up himself. He was indifferent. Tilley cleared the line tied to his wrist, and lifted up the grappling hook to him. Bob merely looked at it, uncomprehending.

"Take it, you fool!" snapped Kaye. He seized the black boy's fingers and closed them around the iron shaft. "Hang on to it and Mr Tilley here will drop you down. Breathe in, boy! Fill up your chest! Hold your breath!"

He had both hands on it and had taken a breath, but whether he knew what was going to happen next was anybody's guess. He stared wide-eyed at Kaye, and then Kaye pushed him overboard. Bob disappeared in a splash, and immediately shot up again, frantic and thrashing arms and legs. Tilley grabbed the rope to stop the grapnel going down, and Kaye pulled Bob roughly from the water by his arm and punched and clouted him.

"Hold it, you bastard, hold it, hold it!" he screamed. "Once more now boy immediately, and you will hold it or I will wring your neck, d'you understand?! I'll strangle you! No! This time, we tie it on!"

"No!" wailed the black boy. "No, sir! No! I will hold, sir! I will not let go!"

Kaye lifted him without a moment's pause, slammed his feet onto the gunwale, and pushed the grapnel at him, so that he took the shaft in both his hands.

"Breathe in!" he roared. "That's right, breathe in! And hold it, stupid boy! Hold it!"

The faces of the boatswain's mate and all the seamen were a stony picture, of anger and disapproval they dared not express. Kaye, triumphant, tipped Black Bob overboard, letting out a "Hah" as he went under with no massive fuss. Staring downwards he said "Hah" again, and the others, almost with reluctance, followed his gaze. In the crystal waters Bob was dropping like a stone, clutching the grapnel like a cuddle to his chest.

"You see," said Kaye, complacently. "I knew the fool could do it."

Although he had the line in hand Tilley let it run free, and it went at amazing pace. Bob's lifeline, flaked next to it, whipped overboard at equal speed, and the sight became mesmeric. Even Grundy watched it with his sickly zombie eyes, and his pale tongue licked his lips. Then, with a grunt, Tilley stopped the grapnel rope, then the other one.

"He's off," he said. "He's gone down far enough."

"Shit!" shouted Captain Kaye. "He's let the bastard go! Good Christ, he's almost there, an'all!"

In the pale sea below them, Black Bob was writhing and twisting like a hooked eel. He was rising to the surface but not swimming for it, and bubbles were pouring from his face.

"Christ, he'll drown! He's drowning!"

Tilley passed the grapnel rope to other hands and began to take up the lifeline slack at speed. In a couple of seconds it tautened with a jerk, and he could see Bob being dragged upwards by his leading wrist, head sideways, mouth open, but fewer bubbles now, hardly any. Men reached over the gunwale to seize him when he surfaced, but Kaye moved sideways, keeping clear. His face was a strange mixture, of anger and concern. The hand came first, on the lifeline, then Tilley grabbed the arm, pulled him on board, and checked the lashing had not destroyed his wrist. He rolled Bob over, bent him double, and lifted him by his skinny hips. Water gushed from him, and he gasped, and choked, and coughed — and then he wailed.

"Bah, there's nothing wrong with him, the article!" said Kaye. "Grundy! Open your casket, man! Some medicine for the boy! Your best!"

The surgeon's eyes flashed out such horror — genuine, not feigned, — that several of the men burst into laughter. Grundy made no move to open, until Kaye raised a fist and shook it at his face. Then, beneath the fascinated eyes of men who had never seen inside the magic box, he worked the lid up an inch or two.

"Higher, man!" shouted the captain. "It is no bloody secret, sir. It is a bloody sawbones box!"

They caught a flash of saws and blades and clamps, but very little more. The surgeon's hand darted inwards like a striking serpent, to come out with a bottle in it, square and ridged and black. He pulled the cork and made to take a swig himself until the captain half-exploded. Grundy smiled sickly, stammering, "a test, sir. I am not sure if it—"

But Tilley whisked it from his grasp, and cupped one huge hand beneath Bob's head.

"Open mouth, child," he said. "A drop of brandy's what the doctor orders. It will have you on your feet again instanter."

Black Bob, however, was far gone. His eyes were open, but they were reddened, bulging, with a mass of angry veins across the whites. His tongue inside his mouth had been bitten, and one ear was dribbling a thin red fluid, mainly blood. He was still gasping, but his cries had ceased. As the bottle approached his mouth he was panic-stricken.

"No, no," said Tilley, kindly. "It will not hurt you, boy. Good medicine."

Bob arched his back, but Tilley slopped in a good quantity, which slid past his tongue and down his throat, with extraordinary effect.

Bob folded up then arched again convulsively, with a cough like an explosion, then a gush of vomit from deep inside of him, which although nine parts seawater caused the men to jump and roar. Bob, convulsions over, then began to scream, high-pitched and piercingly. Grundy darted forward and snatched his bottle back, and Kaye leaned down to give the screaming boy a hearty clout across the face. He then picked Bob up bodily, and planted him, naked and howling, on the bow. At which instant, everybody heard a shot, which stopped them in their tracks. Black Bob's wailing was suddenly the only sound.

"It's the lieutenant, sir!" said Manton. "Look, on the beach! It's the lieutenant, with a gun!"

It had been fired to attract attention, and Holt was waving with vigour now, for them to come ashore. As far as could be seen he was alone, and he was shouting, as he might well have been for some time past. But Bob was still screaming, balanced on the prow, and Tilley took his arm in case Kaye should toss him overboard. He also slipped the painter from the broken mast and told Jones, Macintosh, Jolley and Collins to ship oars, and Bell to bob aft and take the tiller. Dick Kaye did not demur, and moments later they were leaping for the strand. Holt's face, when he saw the naked, battered boy in the bottom resting on Tilley's knee, drained of colour. He was horrified.

He was also, Kaye realised, quite alone.

Chapter Nine

Seeing the naked boy, seeing the bedraggled sailors in wet underdrawers, Holt knew before the forefoot touched the sand what Captain Kaye had done. He was enraged, he was beside himself.

"What in hell?" he roared. "Good God alive! Captain Kaye, sir — what in hell?"

Kaye matched his anger instantly.

"We have almost got the treasure up!" he snapped. "You have not got anything, or anybody. Where are my men, sir?"

Collins had unshipped and hopped lightly off the prow into the water. Holt saw the grapnel and the fathoms of wet line, and his horror grew. Bob's colour was still peculiar, and his ear was bleeding freely.

"I heard him screaming!" Holt shouted. "I saw you strike him, sir! I fired my shot to stop it, sir!"

"Where are my men, sir?" Kaye's eyes flashed fury at his lieutenant. "It was not you that stopped it, sir, do you not think that! This child is useless. Such a song and dance. Now he feigns hurt, and you are taken in, you namby! He is the scion of an inferior race, do not you understand? He has lost my treasure!"

The silence from all the other men was almost palpable. To be caught between two angry officers — angry at each other, both like exploding bombs — was an awful nightmare. They knew not where to look, they dared not make a sound, they knew not what to think. Though all, in this instance, were on the side of Holt, and anti Richard Kaye. They did not even dare to unship the other oars and pull the boat up.

"I repeat, sir," Kaye ground out. "Where are my sailors? What have you done with them?"

"Tilley," said Lieutenant Holt. "Pass the boy out. Now, sir! Move! And gentle!"

"Tilley!" roared the captain. "How dare you — oh, to hell with it. Go on, go on. And get this boat stowed, for the sake of Christ! It is a bumboat for a shoreside slattern whore!"

He clambered through the oarsmen, across the thwarts, as ungainly as a guinea hen. By accident or design he kicked Grundy in the face as he went by, and Grundy did not dare to even squeak. As he jumped ashore Holt stepped aside, and they did not share a glance. Tilley jumped over the side with Bob in his arms and walked him up to the lieutenant. Sam reached out to touch him and the black boy shuddered.

"Where are they, then?" said Kaye. "I charge you answer, sir! Has there been a massacre?"

In a way there had, but not as Kaye had feared. At that moment there was a hallooing closer to the camp — all other men had steered well clear of the party on the beach — and Hinxman was seen loping from out of the nearest trees and underbrush. Although he had been running he was hardly puffed, and he swung a bundle from one hand that looked not unlike a pudding in a cloth. Behind him a few moments later Bosun Taylor and the soldier Simms appeared, much more soberly. They carried nothing, and Taylor had a sort of haggard air. Great heat, great clambering, great care? At that distance it was hard to tell.

"Hah!" said Kaye irascibly, as if disappointed that some tragedy had not befallen them. "Here are the laggards. You found nothing, then, did you? Another jolly wasted goose chase."

Holt was still stationed close to Bob and Tilley, fearing even that the boy might die. He had opened his eyes, though, and was lying easy in the giant's arms. "There there," said Sam. "You will be all right, boy. You will be all right."

Kaye, with a look of frank disgust, gave his lieutenant up for lost and summoned Taylor up to him. The boatswain was panting slightly, his face bright with sweat. It had cuts and scratches also, as did his hands and arms. His shirt had several rents.

"So?" demanded Kaye. "Report, sir, as your lieutenant is not disposed. What did you find, and why the pell-mell? Is there a road? A garrison?" He gave a short, dismissive laugh. "Or only bloody savages? Did they frighten you away?"

Grundy, who had been climbing from the boat, made a sudden noise. He was perched, ungainly, on the gunwale at the bow, his black box balanced with him.

"Sir," he gasped. "Good God, sir, what is that?"

The pudding-cloth that Hinxman held was dripping from the bottom, and the bottom now was stained with spreading red.

"Christ, man!" snapped Kaye, in horror. "What have you done? What is that there?"

"It is a shirt, sir," Hinxman replied, in a half-witted way. "It is McGuigan's, sir. His head's in it."

It could not have been the shock to his humanity, for Surgeon Grundy had none, as everybody knew. But he slipped off the prow, and cursed, and then let out a genuine scream, as his black box slipped as well, and splashed into the water.

"God's bones!" shrieked Grundy.

"Oh hell," said Holt. "This is revolting farce."

To bring the final curtain down, Hinxman let go one corner of the pudding-cloth, and McGuigan's severed head rolled on the sand. It hit Grundy's box and he kicked it sideways, and snatched his most precious up and hugged it to his meagre stomach. Tilley laughed, then quickly cut it off.

"Sorry, sir," he said to Holt, who was, indeed, outraged. "I thought to hear the surgeon tell us he was malingering. McGuigan, sir."

"Oh hell, oh hell, oh hell!" said Captain Kaye. "Is this the worst, Sam? Have they killed them all? Are there hordes of them?"

"We only saw them flitting in the shadows, sir. They did not attack, so maybe there aren't many. I told this man to bury poor McGuigan, sir. I left them to complete the task and came to give report."

Hinxman was aggrieved.

"I did, sir. Bury 'im. I thought Cap'n would like to see his nog for proof, like." He looked at Kaye. "I buried Markie Sweeney, sir, he was the worst. We found him first, and they'd spent more time on him. They'd cut his bollocks off and stuffed 'em in 'is gob'ole, sir. Very Christian, I don't think!"

Inevitably, unbidden, the *Biter*'s company had come down the beach to hover and to watch. But Holt was still outraged with Hinxman.

"I said to bury him," he gritted out. He was panting with suppressed anger. "You are a savage, Hinxman."

Through shock or not, this infuriated the captain in his turn. He stamped across to Tilley like a pouncing cat and smacked Black Bob across the face, a ringing blow. The strange irrelevance made everybody gape.

"No sir!" he snapped at Holt. "We are not the savages! It is this vile object and his ilk! Black savages, murderous criminals, apes! We are surrounded, sir, and you choose to show pity for this boy! I should have drowned him while I had the chance, an unwanted puppy!"

Holt's face was white, the scar tissue from his battle injuries on Shoreham beach glaring through the sweaty sheen. His lips were trembling with the effort of keeping dumb. His hands were gripping and ungripping uncontrollably. Sweetface Savary, the officer of marines, chose this moment to try and break the spell.

"Sir," he said. "I beg your pardon, sir, but had we better not form up defences? In case these..."

Kaye switched his fury on to him.

"You mean you have abandoned watch!? You mean your men have left their posts!? By God, Savary, I'll have your hide! By God, sir, this is dereliction!"

Despite his prettiness, Savary — as he was proving every day — was in no wise short of backbone. He neither twitched nor paled or clenched his fists. He looked calmly at his captain's congested face and replied, "My men have abandoned nothing, sir. They are on constant watch, as ordered. There are three of them, sir, that is all. Is three sufficient for your purposes? The stockade is hardly ready yet, is it?"

This bordered on being insolent, and some of the sailors cringed. The weight of their officers in a public falling-out was crushing them. It was not right. It was not bearable. Indeed, to most of them, it was unknown, undreamed of.

Slack Dickie Kaye had a choice to make, and for once he made the right one. He stopped shouting, and got a grip upon himself. He stepped back from Bob and Tilley, he found focus for his great frustration. He took a breath, through open mouth, a breath both deep and shuddering. He cast his eyes at the men ranged round him up the beach, then looked beyond them. And there was no one at the stockade workings, not even Mr Henderson or the carpenter. But the need for work had been proved as overwhelming.

"Good man, sir, Mr Savary," he said. "You correct me and I swear I'm in the wrong. For sure your men are on the guard, and they shall have my men with them presently. Mr Holt, sir, find out the gunner and the sawdust man and get this work back under way. Far as I can see we are still open to attack, which is not acceptable. Ah — Mr Henderson. Excuse the irony, but what year do you propose completion?"

He was back in charming mode, and all the men relaxed. But they were fired, too, because the case was serious. As if to make the point a larger wave rolled in, broke on the shoreline, and moved McGuigan's head a foot or two, washing the sand off one side and depositing more on the other. Jem Taylor, all distaste, picked it up gingerly by its tarry pigtail and rewrapped it in the bloody shirt. He gave it to

Hinxman with a dirty look but no further comment. He raised his voice.

"Hugg, where are you man? Ah. Quit skulking and get these bastards on the move. Tilley — oh..." Tilley still had Black Bob in arms. Taylor looked to Holt for guidance. Holt, convulsively, plucked Bob from Tilley, despite the black boy struggled for a moment.

"There there," he said, awkwardly. "You'll be all right with me, my boy. There there."

Kaye again chose to take the gentle path — although his chief lieutenant might be seen as shirking his most pressing duty — and led the petty officers back up the beach. The carpenter had joined the gunner while the sailors, aware the fun was over, were spreading back towards their undone tasks with urgency renewed. Taylor, Hugg and Tilley assumed their roles as guides and organisers, letting it be known that a new type of zeal was expected, with fist and rope's-end as encouragement. Rob Simms, who might reasonably have expected to get a rest, was detailed with his musket back up the beach to join the guards, two more reliable men called Bamford and Nuttall were armed with horse pistols and cutlasses to aid them, while Savary took a roving brief, carrying a spyglass as well as armaments. Mr Grundy, bereft once more of any company, mooched up to hover in the purlieu of the sweating purser, who was trying to impose his will on Raper: who ignored the pair of them with a humourous contempt.

The work, though, positively romped along. It was a case of digging holes and trenches to receive cut sapling-boles, using the metal tools that had been brought ashore, and hard wooden spades that the gloomy carpenter had fashioned with his adze. Some of the seamen, as to the manner born, could do things with an axe or knife that made the unfeasible an achievable reality. By nightfall there was a ring of stakes, driven deep enough to withstand all but the greatest shock, with the tips pointed so sharp, and rendered so hard and durable by plunging in water-fire-water, that even the most doubting of the Thomases were looking proud of their own vital part in it. There were gaps still — the final form of ingress and leaving points had to be decided — and a second row of stakes, and earthworks, were also planned. But a celebration fire was lit this night, not dampened too much by a sudden violent storm of rain and wind, and while they were outside the stockade enjoying it, no sly Maroons, invisible though their blackness would have rendered them, crept in and laid in wait to cut their throats on their return...

There was still drunkenness, however, which infuriated Kaye and puzzled even the less-naive warrant men. It was not as vile as previous, no bloodshed, and naturally, nobody this time chose to run into the waiting wilderness. In the morning came sore heads and ill tempers, but the work began again before the sun was up and very hot, and the men were sweating soon enough to leach out the poison through their pores. Raper, as ever, served a hearty breakfast, with meat today, snared by half a dozen of the men who had fed themselves and families all their lives outside the towns and cities of the homeland, until, indeed, they had been snared themselves to serve their lord the King. There was water too, sweet and plentiful. Not all the *Biter* men had wasted the day before.

Kaye, if he felt shame about Black Bob, did not give a hint of it, although Sam discovered early that they had not spent the night together. The captain had told off the boatswain to "look out for" the little boy, as one of the few men Bob did not hold in mortal fear, and the boatswain had tucked him up beside him in his own place behind the stockade walls. At breakfast Bob kept close to Taylor, never looking at the captain, and Kaye, unusually, did not make a thing of it. Sam did speak to the little boy, without a firm response but evoking no sign of loathing or of terror neither, and when he touched him lightly on the hand by way of reassurance, the hand was not snatched away, despite it was withdrawn quite quickly. After breakfast, when the captain told Holt and the boatswain to join him on an expedition with Tilley and Lieutenant Savary, Bob was left to help Geoff Raper, with Purser Black in nominal command, and Surgeon Grundy, presumably, to oversee his spiritual welfare. This was a standing jest: the dreadful Grundy as shepherd to the *Biter*'s flock of lambs.

Kaye's expedition, it turned out, was a reconnaissance. He wished to see the area Holt had surveyed with his own eyes, to form his proper judgements for himself. Tilley and Taylor were his muscle — and would fight a savage hand-to-hand if need be — the marine lieutenant was his firepower (whose uniform in any way would scare a black man half to death), while Holt had been already, and thus knew the land. The treasure not forgotten, Kaye had ordered the best of his six divers — Jones and Macintosh, aided by John Manton — to take the yawl out to the wreck again, with Hinxman, who had proved himself a savage and whom Kaye therefore thought highly of, to keep them in control. To Holt this smacked of total madness, but he did not care to say so, nor was he in any way surprised. On land, the ordering of the marine guard and Bamford and John Nuttall was in the hands of Simms, at Savary's suggestion. There seemed no harm in this.

As they forced their way through the undergrowth Kaye, sweating like a pig already, explained his salvage thinking thus to Holt:

"They will not reach the wreck but they will not malinger and will train themselves to get a better depth each time. Hinxman is not an officer or a warrant — although he will be after this if he does well — so he will let them take their ease so long as he knows there's no one there to overlook him, which should encourage them. We are not so desperate for time now as we know we cannot just strike out for Kingston willy-nilly, and the fort is coming on apace and will be invulnerable. Even if Bentley don't come back at all we can be self-sufficient, and when we return I'll see what has been achieved at the wreck, and maybe send some fresh men down. It is like gunnery, dear chap — practice makes perfect. We do our reconnoitre to make our lives secure — and the men keep at the proper hunt! What think you? Good?"

This is a marvel, thought Samuel, almost tiredly. He is concerned, merely, with the safety of his lust for wealth. If we do *not* return — he is too dull to work it out — and if the Maroons out there should be in numbers — we are dead men whatever, and however long it takes. Dead men, but rich, if Kaye should have his way! He said bitterly: "I do not think men can go down that far, sir, however great the intention and temptation. And already the savages have cut off three men's heads."

"Three? Oh yes, Si Ayling, I had forgot. Pity that, he was a good man, wasn't he? If I have got the right one in my memory. Still; only three. There can't have been so many of the negers, can there?"

Savary, with curtained perspiration running from beneath his wig, gasped: "But more disappeared than just the three, sir. There was that fat man with the limp, and at least five more, if I recall it."

"You do," said Holt. "I think eleven ran, all told. The fat man is Mick Carver — is, or was — and there was Chris Thompson, Seth Pond, Joe—"

Kaye cut him off by bellowing.

"Enough! Enough! You are such detractors, you love the black side every time! If they were massed out there you would have seen them, they would have took you too! Those other men have run, that's all, they are deserters, not breakfast for the niggermen! And they'll come crawling back, I'll wager you. As soon as they grow hungry and they see a savage with a knife. Well, what say you? Do you have proof of any kind? Or merely sour minds and mealy mouths?"

Sam had seen black shadows in the undergrowth the day before, but he was quite unsure how many, or what they signified. No point in arguing with this stubborn man; and he was not prepared to make things up. Indeed, he hoped like hope that Kaye was right, that the runaways were still alive and should stay so.

"No, sir, no proof," he said, and Dickie preened. "No proof at all."

"And you are wrong about the diving, too," said Kaye. "Ain't that so, Tilley? They'll get down to her before we return, would you say? Or very shortly afterwards?"

Tilley, whose feet were not as hard as Hinxman's, was suffering like hell. But he was not as dim as Hinxman neither, so he told his captain what was desired and expected.

"Ho yus, sir, yus indeed. We damn near done it yesterday, and they is fresh today, as fresh as daisies." He sighed. "I only wish as I was with 'em too..." He sighed once more, but Kaye remained indifferent. "Aye," continued the sweating giant. "Sam Hinxman is your man, sir. If anyone can do it, Sam can. He'll think of something and they'll jump to do his bidding, believe me. Beg pardon, sir, he is an evil bastard, Sammy is. Oh, he'll get something done."

Five hours afterwards, as the shoreside party emerged out of the underbrush and back on to the beach, they saw what Hinxman and his willing lads had done. They had a clear view past the stockade, and Kaye had his glass in hand, and they heard shouts and screaming from across the water. At a few hundred yards the glass was sadly not necessary, as they could see with naked eye a shape burst from the water and then flop back again, with a renewed caterwauling so high-pitched it had to be a little boy. It had to be *the* little boy as well, they all knew that, and hared off to the water's edge, sweat and exhaustion all forgotten. Kaye, beside himself, danced with fury and bellowed so loudly that all noise at the fortress earthworks ceased. When the yawl's bow grounded on the sand some minutes later, he made his intentions so apparent that Hinxman cowered in the sternsheets, a full boat's length away and wishing it was far, far further.

Black Bob was lying on the bottomboards, in watered blood and vomit. Naked once more, he looked half dead, but he was sobbing as if his heart were broken. Manton, Jones and Macintosh were shamefaced, as were Bell and Collins, who had rejoined the diving crew. Sam Megson was on there too, shifty and repentant. Jesus Christ, thought Sam Holt wearily, all the dummies on a jolly-out.

Dick Kaye restrained himself from shooting them, but when the bow had been pulled up on the shore he laid into Hinxman first with words and then with fists. That Hinxman had started it was not in doubt, although Kaye did not bother to enquire, and if Hinxman had cared to make a fight of it, he would have killed or crippled his captain with two blows. His every part was muscle, and his eyes were hot and small, a bull terrier's. That there were limits to his stupidity was proved, however, by his reaction to the beating. He stood face up to the captain, and his arms hung by his sides. He never closed his eyes, even as each blow landed, and even when his nose was split almost into two he did not raise a hand to touch it or wipe the blood away. As on the day before, a crowd of quiet men had formed to watch this punishment, a semicircle whose ends were in the sea. The others of the boat's crew stood in the water, facing across the yawl from either side, hands resting on the gunwale, silent, hopeful. For all they knew they would be next. Thank God Slack Dickie was so fat and weak, they no doubt thought. By the time he'd knocked down Hinxman, he'd not have strength left to disturb a pudding skin.

When Hinxman — still showing raw intelligence — decided the time was ripe, he collapsed onto the strand as if unconscious, and lay still for a few kicks to the face. Bosun Taylor, meanwhile, had gathered Black Bob up and waded to the beach some feet from the activity. Holt joined him, and the two of them walked through the avid crowd back to the fire area. Grundy and Purser Black, seeing maybe which way the wind was blowing, approached them cautiously, each movement of their bodies studiedly obsequious, to gabble out the expected tale: it had been Hinxman's doing, they had been powerless to prevent it, they had no authority to directly order him to cease. All true maybe, but what the hell, thought Sam; poor Bob, in this ship's company, was doomed. As the surgeon tended to the boy's external wounds, he made his mind up. He talked to Taylor privately, and the boatswain agreed, with great relief, a sort of quiet joy. He went and made some preparations.

They carried Bob out from the camp when Grundy had done with him, and in a quiet clearing a half a mile back from the beach, they sat him down and Taylor talked to him. The little boy trusted Taylor, as no other man he knew, and as he listened some life came back into his eyes, some sparks of animation. They had seen some men, explained the boatswain, some Africans, some blacks, lurking in the forest. Yesterday for the first time, and then again today. They had not spoken — they were the white man's enemy — but it was certain they were there, and waiting.

"Black Bob," he said, and Bob listened, expectantly. "Black Bob, boy — would you like to go?"

Perhaps he did not understand, perhaps he could not believe them, but Black Bob seemed confused. His eyes showed hope, then fear, then disbelief. Taylor, touched almost to tears, took him in his arms and whispered comfort in his ear. Sam, also deeply moved, watched from a little distance, and held his breath. He willed the little boy to understand their good intent, their urge to help, to save him.

And he did. He cried, he clung onto Bosun Taylor, he laughed, he babbled, then he cried some more. They showed him the bundle they had made up, the food, the water, a square of blanket, clothes, and they led him deeper into the brush, towards the area where the Maroons would be. Bob, recovered, found the rising ground no problem now, in fact he outpaced the men with ease, despite his feet were bare and theirs were shod. On the edge of the thickest scrub and woodland, they stopped and stood. It occurred to Holt for the first time that they were in truly mortal danger. He had a sabre with him, and one pistol, while Taylor had a thick black stick. This morning, in this very spot, they had seen men moving in the undergrowth — but there had been more than the two of them then, and they had carried guns with ostentation.

"Christ, Jem," he said. "Soon as we spot them, we'd better cut and run!"

The boatswain smiled tightly.

"Get ready then," he said. "For I can see one now."

Sam's mouth went dry as he saw what Taylor saw. Not fifty yards away there was a black face peering through the bushes. Another then appeared, six feet away from it. And then a third. The boatswain put a hand into the small boy's back, propelling him.

"Now, Bob," he said. "Look you, there are your friends. Now then, Bob, you go to them, before they eat us up!"

The boy hung back. He looked over his shoulder at Sam, then at Bosun Taylor for further reassurance. Taylor, with an effort, wiped the fear from off his face. The need to run was urgent.

"Go on, Bob," he said. "Don't hang about, lad. You don't want to get me killed, do you? They're your men, boy. Your friends. Your people. Go!"

Four men were visible. They had stepped out of the bushes. They were dressed almost like whites, except more ragged. Torn shirts and scraggy britches. One had a gun, one had a cutlass, the other two had clubs. They were silent, threatening.

Holt stepped forward.

"We are here in peace!" he shouted. "We are not your enemies! We have a friend for you! A little African that you must help! Look after him!"

The ragged men stepped forward, and Holt and Taylor back. Bob remained unmoving, but a cautious smile was on his face.

"Go on," said Taylor. "Go on, Bob. Your own kind. They are your people! Go!"

Suddenly, Bob made his mind up. With another backward glance, he ran forward, his bundle in both hands. As he ran he shouted something, which the white men could not understand. But it was filled with wild elation, and the blacks moved to meet him, and it was time to go. Holt and the boatswain turned and plunged into the undergrowth, down the hill. Behind they heard voices, but not shouts. For a moment, in a hundred yards or so, they stopped to listen. There was no sound of pursuit.

"Christ, Jem," said Holt, "we've done it! We've saved the poor child's life! Jesus! Can you guess what Slack Dick will say! Jesus!"

"Sir," said Taylor. "Sir, I do not give a cockerel's bollocks! It's done, sir, and no one can gainsay it! We have done right by Black Bob! At *last*!"

"Amen," said Sam. "Amen to that. And no one more deserved it... He has gone back to his own."

Chapter Ten

Honourable men or not, the French sailors on the *Jacqueline* threw in their lot with Bentley and his people with a will. They were called Chrétien Perrin and François Imbert and they both hailed from Saint Mâlo, in a place they called Bretagne. "Petit Bretagne," Perrin said to Bentley one morning, "and you are from the big Bretagne. We also 'ate ze French."

They had spent a bitter night together in the crippled ship, and the brotherhood of seamen was urging very strong. Bentley was not too naive, however, and Gunning, who was at the tiller, kept giving him the warning gaze. They were French, they were the enemy, they could not be trusted, even for a moment. This thin-faced man, though, in desperate need of shaving and with a glittering eye, had an easy charm it was hard to not respond to.

"*Je ne comprends pas*," said William. "*Vous dites que vous hassez les Français? But vous êtes Français tous les deux. N'est-ce pas*?"

Perrin stubbornly stuck to English, as stubbornly as William practised his French.

"No, no, not at all," he said. "I tell you, Petit Bretagne. We even 'ave a lingwidge of our own, like yours from the Pays de Galles — you call that what? From Wells?"

Bentley laughed.

"Wells is in Somerset," he said. "*J'ai un oncle prés de cela. Non, vous voulez dire Wales*." He wished to spell it, but that was beyond his knowledge. He laughed again. "*Un pays où les hommes baisent les moutons, on m'a dit*."

Both Frenchmen's eyes popped in amazement.

"What?" said Perrin. "You say – baisent les moutons? You mean – ferk ze sheeps?"

"Alleluiah!" said the other. "*C'est dégueulasse*!"

"What are you saying, skipper?" Gunning demanded. "My old lady's Welsh!"

"It's dirty minds," said Will, all disingenuous. "Not mine, theirs. Baiser means to kiss, far as I know!"

"You know nuzzing zen," laughed Perrin. "But I think zat is not true, hein?"

"Me neither," said Gunning, quite won over. "My old lady ain't Welsh, neither, for that matter, sir. Just thought you ought to know that for a fact. Now, Frenchmen or Bretons — get up that blistering mast and help out Mr Ashdown and the Worm. I want to set more sail, and I want it drawing, comprenny vous?"

With the deck deserted, Gunning and Will fell to serious discussion. The bad weather had left them in the early morning light, and the wind had gone round fair at last. William had managed several star sights, and both of them were expert at dead reckoning — Gunning, ever modest, to the level of a genius, he said. They were heading nearly north at present, and hopeful of a landfall before night, or very early in the morning. In the last days they had moved little, except dead to the lee, more or less due south, using the diminished rig to jog along as near hove-to as possible. Hard work and tiring, but it was over now, and they were cruising more like the old King's yacht than a cripple, or an armed foreigner, or anything at all to do with real, unpleasant life. London Jack, ever the pessimist, expected by the hour to be sighted, then sunk, by a Guarda-Costa rogue, or worse, captured by another Frenchman who would take them prisoner without the option of becoming servants to Senõr. But hour followed hour, and the horizon remained clear, the sky bright blue and cloudless, and the wind out of the south and elegantly sufficient for their purpose or desire.

The Bretons, whether they really despised the French or not, were more than happy to be on board a British vessel — as *Jacqueline* now was — and worked as well as anyone could want from seamen. They had pointed out the arms caches, including, they insisted, the most secret ones, and the captain's special wine and spirit stocks, and freshest food. They had not complained about the constant vigilance upon them, nor being shackled up to sleep when the weather had permitted such a luxury, with Imbert, a rather modest man of only about eighteen, seeming quite heartened to be taken for a threat. They had both said also, in English and in French, that they would sign Navy Articles if it should be so desired. Strange patriotism, opined London Jack one night to Will, but not unusual, they both agreed. It made Will think long and sadly of Céline, who had saved his life, and probably been hanged for it. A patriot to France, a friend to England, and an enemy of war and humbug everywhere.

When they raised the coast of Jamaica next day, a pale smudge rising from the misty morning, they began to wonder what they would find. Both Gunning and Jack Ashdown — who knew the coast quite well — had noted mountain peaks and other landmarks, and taken bearings right along the shoreline till the day they had hit upon the *Jacqueline*, so knew roughly what they were looking out for, and roughly when they saw it. They had moved too far eastward, but not by many leagues, and they had a good set, and offing enough, to sail a handsome course nor-westward that would bring them to their fellows. They passed the cove where they had taken *Jacqueline* at about ten miles off, but were not much tempted to go and take a look at their abandoned French adversaries. They wanted Captain Kaye. His face when he saw what they had brought him would be worth a quart of brandy...

Thinking that, Will thanked his lucky stars and Providence that Gunning had shown no wish to fall on the brandy that they had on board their prize. As usual when the going had got hard, the London man had proved his worth in trumps. But how strange, how tragic, Bentley thought, that at other times he would go mad for it, would risk everything to get his head at bottle or at bung. How strange that he would always risk his own life, but stay sober long enough to save another man's.

There was brandy on board the *Jacqueline*, in great supply, and wine, and strange liqueurs. No beer — apparently the French eschewed such piss — but beef and bread in plenty, and pork, and onions, and dried fish and pickled cabbages. And small armaments and powder, carriage pieces and round shot, chain and grape, and an armoury of swords and cutlasses that would equip a hundred men. No cargo though, and no great room for it. She was a privateer most probably, or maybe a message boat, or a link in France's naval chain that one day was due across the North Atlantic to wrest all prizes from the English Crown and planters. Perrin and Imbert, closely questioned, were convincing in their lack of knowledge, although Will could not believe entirely what they said. Like it or lump it, though, according to them she was a petty armed trader, and not a Navy ship at all. There were no papers in the captain's cabin that Will could find; which meant that they were hidden well, or the French commander was conscientious, and had them safe onshore with him.

"What matter, what the hell?" said Gunning, as they mulled it over. "She's ours now, and she is a very proper little ship. Once we've got a foremast up again and got a rigger on the job, we've got a better ship than my old *Biter*, in some ways. Is she ours? We've taken her in war — is she our property?"

Will laughed.

"Oh you, Jack! You say you are not a Navy man, but I'll bet their lordships disagree! In any way I am, and I'm in command here. No, she is not our ship, she is his Majesty's, she is a prize. If you *were* an officer, indeed, you'd be entitled to prize money, but you ain't! Maybe it's time to bow to the inevitable!"

As they approached the shoreline Ashdown climbed to the truck to use a spyglass, and after an hour or so of gazing he hailed that he could see the camp. There was a fire, there were pale patches that could be canvas, and there was some sort of compound, or a wall. Will questioned him at length from the quarterdeck, but Ashdown confessed that he was stumped. Gunning went aloft with another glass, and the younger Frenchman swarmed up to cling to the bare pole beneath Ashdown's feet. But patience was the order of the day. Until they got closer it remained a mystery.

"It's a stockade!" yelled Ashdown finally. "It's a bloody fort! We've come to the wrong bay, sir! If they've got big cannons we'll be blown to buggery!"

Consternation flooded Bentley. He gazed at the shoreline, but from where he was saw nothing. He checked the skyline and was sure they'd made it right. The Worm, at the tiller, was unconscious and indifferent. To him, it was just a lovely sail.

Gunning shouted down: "Don't fret, Mr Bentley. There isn't a cannon built can shoot this far. Stand in as you are, sir. We'll soon see better."

Aye, thought Will. But what if there's a French ship hidden? A man of war?

He dismissed the thought. The coast was long and pretty straight beyond this bay. No creeks, no inlets, no hiding place. Christ, he told himself impatiently, it *must* be them! What sort of bloody fortress?

"Mr Gunning!" he shouted upwards. "What sort of fort is it? Is it built of stone?"

Then François Imbert cried: "*En bois! Espèce de pallisade!*"

"Oh shit!" Will shouted, overjoyed. "They've built one out of wood! We go in, Mr Gunning! Come down and lay on sail!"

There was another conference as they got closer, but that was easy overcome. Almost inevitably they found an English ensign in the *Jacqueline*'s flag locker, and they ran it to the highest point they could. They ascertained that the fortress had no boats to come and fight them with, they recognised the *Biter*'s yawl — that had scurried to the beach from where it lay at anchor just offshore — and they knew no guns or powder had been lifted from the wreck to lob metal at them with. That only left the possibility Kaye and his cohorts had been overwhelmed and the stockade was filled with warlike Maroons who would wait until they walked up the beach then set upon them and cut them down. None of them, for a moment, believed it.

They did proceed with caution, however, as they made the last approach, with Ashdown standing at a loaded swivel gun in the waist, a slow-match in his hand. It could be ranged onshore if necessary, but could also sweep the deck. Perhaps this would be the moment for Imbert and Perrin to refind their loyalty to King Louis once again...

Not a bit of it. The anchor dropped, sails idle, Will and Gunning stood on the foredeck in ostentation, and perfect peace. As the onshore breeze swung the vessel round its cable, they walked back to the stern. And Captain Kaye — more cautious than they would have given him credit for — then emerged from a gateway in the wood stockade and waved in jubilation. They heard his "Halloo!" faintly through the breeze, and then more men poured out and joined him and Lieutenant Holt in striding to the water. By this time Will and Gunning were in the skiff, which Worm had drawn close astern and bailed out in the past half-hour, and pulling hard towards the greeting party. Worm and Ashdown stayed on board, and Perrin and Imbert had allowed themselves once more to be wrist-bound. They were nervous at the prospect they would meet a Navy post captain, but not very, to tell the truth. Within the strange lights of seamen everywhere, they were considered shipmates; or even friends.

Slack Dickie Kaye, Will, Sam, Taylor — all of them — were frankly overjoyed, and did not try hard to dissemble it. Within minutes tales were passed, joint admirations expressed, and seamen organised to go out to the *Jacqueline* to bring off essential stores and the Frenchmen and the Worm. All three of them were looked and poked at, and found not wanting in any great essential, with Worm in particular thought a marvel. News spread like forest fire of his gigantic age, and he regaled them with wild tales of seamanship and slavery. His was the only black face in the camp now Bob was gone, and oddly, it was some half an hour before Will noticed this.

They were drinking wine and eating sweetmeats in a circle — Slack Dickie fell upon life's new-found luxuries with amazing gusto — and the histories of the last few days were being swapped. Dick had received a quick inventory of the French ship's treasures and crowed at the details of her cutting out, while Will and Gunning were most impressed at the spiky fortress that had sprung up in the wilderness of sand and scrub that was the foreshore. It was only when Gunning inquired after Maroon attacks, and Kaye let out a laugh and mentioned a captive, that Bentley clicked.

"A captive? What, you mean they've— Oh, good God! Where is little Bob?!"

Kaye was delighted.

"He's got back home to Africa!" he cried. "He's gone back to the people that he came from!"

Will was gripped by foreboding. He sent a look to Sam, most quizzical. Sam shook his head, attempting to reassure.

"The captain's right," he said. "No, no, not dead, Will! He esc— we let him go to them. There were black men in the bushes, and he longed for them, so we let him go."

"*You* let him go, not *we*!" said Captain Kaye. "It was not I, Mr Bentley, although I would ha' done if I'd thought of it. Nay, it was Lieutenant Holt's idea alone, and I applaud him. I had had good service from the child, but all good things, you know. He has some skills will stand him in good stead among the lusty savages, you must take my word!"

His humour was lascivious, and it made Will shudder inside himself; but he was glad the boy had gone, indeed. When he heard later, privately from Sam, what Kaye and then his cohorts had put him through before he got his freedom, the relief intensified. The details of the diving attempts were horrifying.

The salvage was not over, though, and now he had the *Jacqueline*, Kaye's enthusiasm knew no bounds. His plan was this, he told his officers: the carpenter and sailmaker would complete and rig the new foremast, all spare hands would finish off the stockade, and musket men would cover them from land attack at all times until the work was done. If they lifted much from off the *Biter* wreck then well and good, but if not, then good also. They now had a ship — small but handy — and tools, and food, and arms, and shot and powder. When she was fully seaworthy they would set sail for Port Royal, to turn up there in triumph to a heroes' welcome. A prize, and two prisoners as well! They would be admirals!

"She won't be stuffed with gold, though," Gunning said. "Although she will be stuffed with Frenchmen, if you should desire it. Why take back two when we could have forty-odd? War prisoners not merely look good to the loyal populace, they can be ransomed. Who knows, some of 'em might be rich!"

"Explain," said Captain Kaye.

"They can't get off the beach where we cut out the brig from," replied London Jack. "We left them naught to sail on, and according to our friend Old Worm, only a goat could get up out of that by land. *He* did, but then he is a goat, don't doubt it. They're stuck on the beach with little food and no main armament, just muskets and their swords. We scuttled our jollyboat and one of their cutters as we buggered off, and they're ripe for picking. And on our way home, as a benefit!"

"Hhm," said Captain Kaye. "That interests. That interests indeed. No treasure, but a ship and prisoners. It is a gratifying prospect."

"There might be gold as well," Will put in. "Well, at least as much a chance as getting *Biter*'s..."

Kaye ignored the jibe, but smiled a little.

"Go on, then?"

"According to Worm," said Will, "the Scotchmen are alive. He's seen them in the forests round about. He found their boat disabled on the foreshore when he ran off from the French. They have gone inland, and they'll have their treasure with them, won't they? The bags they took off of the *Santa*. Find the Scotchmen, find some silver, find some jewellery and cash."

Kaye's eyes were dreamy.

"Find them, hang them," he said quietly. "Justice is done, and the nation's treasure's saved. Glory, we really would be admirals..."

Over half a week, the work forged on like lightning. The riggers rigged, the builders built, the divers — well, the divers risked their lives to no advantage that anyone but Kaye could see. Two men had eardrums burst, one was blinded for more than half a day, but then recovered, and one man shit himself spectacularly, naked at thirty feet. The depth attained did get better though, gradually and day by day, and some of the younger men began to find it awful fun. They vied for who could hold his breath the best, they vied to win the brandy prizes Kaye doled out (through Purser Black, who made a tidy profit although the liquor was lifted from the *Jacqueline*), and they vied to find efficient ways of getting down. Some held rocks, some tied them to their wrists and trusted in their quick-release bends, some hauled themselves down anchored, knotted, lines. Tom Tilley, sometimes Tommy Hugg, oversaw the operations from the yawl, and saved lives when someone needed yanking up. They also measured depths-achieved, and set up a wild hallooing whenever another fathom mark was passed.

For some reason, which increased the competition severalfold, the young French seamen François Imbert was the best. He was a shy and timid man, who hung back two days from volunteering, and was only taken in the boat at first because the captain thought that he might run if left on shore. Perrin had finally admitted that he was a gentleman of sorts, with money vested in the *Jacqueline*, although he still denied that he was Navy, or an officer, so was exonerated from any fear of running or of treachery by the giving of parole. He had pointed out that Imbert was not foolish, and would go to any lengths to avoid being butchered by "les Noirs," but Kaye had grown up with servants, so trusted no one of their class.

Imbert suggested tentatively that he might try and dive after yet another volunteer had ended up half-conscious by too much daring and too little breath, and he made his point by taking an enormous lungful, and holding onto it. At first the Englishmen observed him with the mildest curiosity, but as the seconds passed, the interest grew. One of the lads sucked down some air to give him competition, and when he burst it out again, Imbert was still impassive, still inflated, and showing not a single symptom of distress. They had no watch nor sand glass for an accurate assessment, but when he at last began to throb, his cheeks to puff, his facial muscles and his neck to twist and clench, it was already a phenomenon, a wonder. On shore afterwards, to their messmates, the sailors claimed three minutes, four, maybe even five. Balderdash indeed; but it was almost double the next best English time.

Thereafter they took their cues from him, and watched to learn fine points of his technique. Seven fathoms was passed, and after two more days they made it slightly under eight. The highest level of the sunken hull was at nine fathoms and a half, give or take a foot or so depending on the tide, and by the time the *Jacqueline* had two masts once more, and yards, and sails all bent on and ready, men had started to believe it could be done. François Imbert, who spoke enough of their language not to be hated out of hand in the fine old English way, became a shipmate to be proud of, and a kind of mascot known as Frank or Frenchie Amber. After all, he was like to earn them money; lots of it.

Came the day, though, when Slack Dickie said they must set sail. Among the divers this could have caused a mutiny, except they were certain they'd be back because their captain was a greedy bastard, just like them, and they had begun to love him for it. The non-divers needed less persuading, because now the backbreaking, grinding, sweating work to build the stockade was finished — they were bored. Kaye had not kept them short of food or liquor, and there were fights and racing matches to fill in the leisure time, but without trenches to dig and trees to cut and mantraps to fashion, there was little else. No — Little Else would have been another matter, as some wag quipped. Little Else or Middle Meg or Big Boozy Bertha herself. Toms Hugg and Tilley put the idea about that there was quim at Kingston and Port Royal, and inelegant amounts of it — black quim, brown quim, Spanish quim and English. And jugs of rum ad libitum.

Sam and William, as befitted the sobersided element, quizzed Kaye about the wisdom of abandoning such a stronghold, in case somebody took it over. He scoffed at this idea, and not without good reason. Why would anyone want to live upon this beach, he asked? The stockade was defensible, but what had savages to defend? And contra whom? And why should any ship put into here again, ever, did they think? It had nothing, not a harbour, not a field, and water a good haul way, even if new people should ever find it. All that was visible of the *Biter* wreck was a floating end of old topgallant mast, and they could cut that off an'all, if it so pleased them. There was treasure down below, but no one knew that except themselves, and even they could not at present get to it. At present, though, he emphasised. They would return.

"We will return to get the silver, and will track down and get those Scotch Lamonts as well," he said. "We'll trap them as a bear is trapped by honey, we'll let them know somehow there's money to be had. They will not keep away, will they? They are incapable! And then we'll catch and kill them."

His bitterness towards the Lamont brothers interested Will and Sam, as did his lack of animosity towards John Gunning. London Jack had hit the bottle the day the *Jacqueline* had come to shore, and had drunk himself insensible for four whole days. Since then he had been incapable, and murderously ill-tempered. He had beaten Surgeon Grundy with a broken oar-blade, kicked the purser till he was black and blue, and almost drowned Rat Baines for sneaking mouthfuls from one of his many bottles. However gross his actions, Slack Dickie had indulged him, with a smile.

While the stockade and the beach were cleared of every last thing that could have been of aid or use to anyone, Gunning had lain down in the beating sun and groaned or farted, sometimes both at once. He had been loaded into the yawl, swung on board with a tackle from the mainyard, and lain down to sleep the day away beside the binnacle. The anchor was weighed, the sails were set and trimmed, and the *Jacqueline* achieved a bit of sea room then headed east. The weather was glorious and the breeze was fair, and Kaye was jubilant.

"Heigh ho!" he said, to Will and Sam. "Off to Port Royal and that heroes' welcome! Banquets, celebrations, the *bon ton*!

"And the gels, boys. Oh, just think of it, my lads! The gels! Heigh ho! God bless 'em..."

Chapter Eleven

Deborah, who had always had a tendency to think that life would turn out better in the end, began to realise in her third week at the women's town that her ideas were, once again, proving rather quickly to be wrong. As she weeded and tended with the other women, listening to their conversation across the rows of papau and cassava, laughing with them as they scratched and pricked themselves preparing pineapples for the market, her mind turned often to her Stockport home, and her lost mother. It occurred to her that her Ma had known that she was leaving before she had herself, and had known, moreover, why it had to happen.

Because her father was a beast was the apparent reason, because he was cruel to both these women in his life, unbearable. But no. Really, it was because Deb knew that all she had to do was run, and all would turn out well. Her father was a bully — therefore, find a man who was not. Her employment making hats and caps and bonnets was a job that drove hatters mad (a half a joke and more than half a truth) so it seemed obvious the remedy was to leave. In Stockport there was only hatting really, unless one wished to work for half the pay, which was half of nothing to begin with, so clearly the road to freedom was the road away. Friend Cecily was a like-minded girl — Deb's mother said they shared the same rose tinted spectacles — so one day they upped and left. Whatever else her abandoned mother would have had to say about it, Deb realised at last she would not have been surprised.

Sometimes the guilt for this, this lack in her, this failure to realise what her actions might lead to, Deb found almost overwhelming. She stood upright in the violent sunshine, unconsciously holding a rough pineapple with great tenderness, as if it were her mother's face, and felt the sweat run down her cheeks like tears. Missy was near her, and Goanitta, and she saw they were neither sweating nor suffering her mental agonies. Not for the first time she felt envious of the fact that they were slaves. They had been torn from their homes and families, and it had not been their fault. As she had got to know these women, and she had clicked into their language and their way of thought, they had talked to her of home, of their lands across the sea, and she had tried to understand their pain. She wished that somehow she could say sorry for the death of Cecily.

They were not slaves now though, Missy and Goanitta, and that was their touchstone, the single thing that gave them meaning to themselves. It was here the complications piled up, began to bear down on Deborah's understanding. In this camp, this "woman's town," they were neither slaves nor free, not Maroons nor — it was dawning on her — nor any thing. If they had a name in this island paradise it was "runaways," and if they had a future it was precarious. They grew plantains, cocoa, avocados, corn, their skills were wonderful, and their menfolk visitors cleared ground for them, protected them, looked out for them, and largely stayed invisible. They protected, then they hid. They were not free either. Nobody was free.

Mildred was Deb's most incisive informant, although she appeared to like the white girl least. She came and went from their secret area deep in the woodland more like a man than other women, and according to Kinji and Rebekah, she was a "sort of" man, she was a warrior. Getting explanations of this from the girls was difficult, because laughter was their self-defence, and Mrs M, when Deb appealed to her, sucked her teeth and spat into the fire. But Mabel, when she was around, would sometimes be forthcoming, and Deb learned much from her, if not this vital point.

"No one on this island free," she said one night, her nameless boy-child sleeping in her arms. "We come from Africa in chain and slavery, and most we dies like that. Us woman in this town we left alone by white man, we left alone by black man, but only 'cause we got some use, see gal? White man grow sugar cane, sometime him little coffee, indigo. We grow him food he eat, and feed his niggers. Sell it, keep all happy. If him got sense, he grow him own food. Him got no sense."

"But you are free then, in some wise or other?" Deb asked, uncertainly. "If they know you're here and let you sell your products? And if they let you be?"

Mabel laughed.

"Until it suit him other way," she said. "Until his own niggers tell him we take their trade away, so we got to stop. Anyway, who say he know we here? He know we somewhere, white man, but he never find us, can he? If you go walkin' gal, you ever find your way back here? No think so."

Mrs M, who had been listening across the fire, spoke low in a language Deb could not follow, and the conversation, apparently, was at an end. Mildred, however, at other times, sketched in more details that moved slowly, in Deb's mind, towards a murky whole. The mass of blacks upon the island were held as slaves, she said, but some were allowed some freedom, of a sort, and some had taken it by running to the mountains to become Maroons. This had happened, she said, "since time began," and challenged Deb with her cold eyes to challenge that. Over the years the Maroons had become a terror and a danger to the white man, there had been wars and massacres, there had been triumphs and disasters. The greatest of the leaders had been a witch called Nanny, who lived in Nanny Town to this day, except she was a spirit, maybe, now. She was the *obeah* woman, said Mildred, a lady of the science. With her great guidance, the white man could not win.

It seemed to Deb, although she did not say so, that the white man had won already, hands down. So she made a non-committal noise, and was rewarded, to her surprise, with a smile.

"White man cannot win, I say, but I not say black man win, though, do I?" Mildred said. "Black Maroon win treaties with the white, and black man live in peace now, of some sort. Maroon have own towns, have own fields and cattle, have Captain this and Colonel that, and get to see the gubnor once a year to get one present and tug one hat. Not free, maybe, but white man not free either, eh? Maroon force treaties, white man pay him money. And in this town, in other little town like this, we also free. We not Maroons, we not free, we just invisible. We run away like you and Mabel do from your place, and no one know us."

"Free or not free, though? You can't be both...?"

"White man free, white man not free. Same thing, maybe. You tell me which."

"But what are *you*? A Maroon? A warrior? Rebekah said—"

Mildred clicked her teeth. Finality.

"Tssst! Rebekah said! You go sleep now Debbeerah." She laughed. "You free go to sleep, you not free talk all night. You understand me now?"

Deb listened to her chuckles in the hot and noisy darkness.

***

It was the return of Captain Jacob Tsingi that brought the major complication, and compounded it. Whatever Mildred had said to him and his companions on their first visit to assess the new white runaway, he made it clear by his actions that he would not keep away. His reappearance came within five days, and it was ordered, Deb supposed, to look accidental. It was not.

She was stacking yams in a shady corner with Marge and Kinji, and it was the Africans who saw him first. They were chattering in Kreyole, all three, and as usual Deb was sweating, they were not. She waved both arms above her head to move the air around her, and pulled out the bosom of her cotton gown to cool her breasts and stomach. As she did so, Kinji squeaked and grabbed at the cloth to cover her again, pointing with her elbow and her eyes. Captain Jacob was silent in the shadows, silent but not alone. His older men were with him, his bodyguards as Deb now understood. When he saw that she was looking, his face broke into a sunny smile. He was like a schoolboy.

"Miss Debbeerah!" he said. "I give you greeting! I come to see this man of you. I come to make him offer."

Although she wondered, with a pang, how he had found out her name, Deb found herself responding to his open smile, and his absurdity. His acolytes were looking glum, as usual, and the contrast was endearing. His energy was astonishing, his features shining like a sunbeam, his tight-curled hair as springy as fresh mountain fern. Beside her, she felt Kinji and Marge responding also. Kinji, indeed, was opening like a flower. She was of a size and age with Jacob, and of a beauty to compare with his. A beauty far more fitting, Deb believed, than she might be supposed herself to have.

"Sir," she said. "I thank you, but still I am betrothed. And my man would not take any money for me. I am not for sale."

Her mind was whirling at these concepts, she was breathless all at once. Men had paid for her before, but never in this way, never to be a sort of wife. But she was certain, she had entire knowledge, that this was what was happening. This young man did not want her as a whore; there was no question of it.

The only question was: what would Will Bentley have thought if he could know? Her stomach swooped in sudden sickness. Christ, she loved him, and Christ, it was all hopeless.

But he would not take money for her, certainly. He would not sell her, no.

"Where is he, then?" asked Captain Jacob. "How long you have to wait? What sort of man should leave him woman wanting in the woods? Come live with me, Miss Debbeerah. I got house in town. I got no more wife than you."

Her mind came back to earth. This boy was sweet and silly and she did not want all this. She would drift away from Will eventually, she knew that blighted love must die. But she would not run away from it. Not yet.

In any way, this was a dream, merely. She had known this youth for less than half an hour, added up. He was some sort of prince, maybe (she had some vague ideas about Africa herself) and he had a gun and bodyguards. She was a runaway, a runaway with scars. Of course she would not end up as his wife. She would be a whore again, this time a black man's whore. Involuntarily she gestured towards Kinji, then flushed with shame. Kinji had a man, who visited already. Christ, thought Deborah. I am thinking like a prostitute or a pander...

"My man is a sailor," she said. Her voice was low, and wobbled. "He is a navy man. He has had to go to sea. He will soon be back. I am spoken for."

Oddly, the situation changed, although the black men in the shadows did not move. Jacob had lost his smile, and the atmosphere, in an instant, was oppressive. Deb was compelled to say some more.

"I am sorry for it, sir," she said, although she did not mean that, precisely. "But these things are... Maybe in your life..."

She tailed off. She did not know these black people yet, these Africans, except that they could be quick to anger. Indeed, she feared she had upset her friend Kinji already.

Two of the stonefaced men stepped forward. They were in ragged trousers only, but wore cutlasses at side. One's hair was grizzled, brindle-grey. The other man was bald, and only had one ear. He said harshly: "Captain Jacob say come. You come."

"No!" said Deb. It was an exclamation. She was shocked and fearful. The baldhead man took another pace, aggressively.

Beside her, Deb heard Marge give a little groan. The grey-haired man pulled out his cutlass from his belt.

"No!" said Deb again, this time a note of rising panic. And Captain Jacob shouted something at the men, and struck one of them open-handed on the shoulder, with a shocking crack. The forward movement ceased. New silence fell. Jacob was in the shadow still, but Deborah saw him smile.

"I go now," he said. "I come back again, when you think about all thing. You tell your man I buy you off him. Maybe I kill him."

He laughed suddenly, as if that were a joke. Deb's mouth was dry, her stomach trembling, as he faded into the woodland with his acolytes.

Chapter Twelve

Post Captain Daniel Swift, to tell the truth of it, felt like a pirate when he saw the vessel down to leeward. A pirate, and a disgruntled one. His ship, the *Beauty*, was a wreck, and the irony of her name, which had long amused him for such an ugly and unhandy tub, was doubled by the actual beauty of the craft brought into focus through his lens. She was a slaver from the makeshift housings on her deck, and a certain hangdog air about her hamper, and unless he was no seaman, she was not under much command. He snapped his spyglass closed, and spoke to his chief lieutenant.

"By George, Anderson," he said. "We could have her if we wanted. Could we not?"

Anderson was a man he liked to twit, because Anderson was beholden to him as few men were. Anderson was brutal, and Swift had seen him killing on the most slender provocation — and made it clear that he was keeping mum. His strange grey eyes had bored into the soft brown ones, which had softly cringed with knowledge. Captain Swift would keep the brutal secret, and keep it like the grave. Unless. And when his former first lieutenant, Madden, had been slaughtered by the Moors of Sallee, Swift had promoted him, to be his officer and slave. Daniel Swift had difficulty with subordinates, although he still assumed perversity in others, not himself. But he had learned enough to know that some men would give no trouble, and that Anderson was such a man. He liked to twit him, though.

"Well?" he said. "Will you vouchsafe an answer, sir? Shall we run her down? It is a sloven, is it not, a veritable shit-basket? But surely those are French colours she is flying? Surely she is an enemy? Legitimate."

For the sake of self-respect, mayhap, the lieutenant did not answer, despite the case was clear. The ship to leeward may have been French indeed — her lines and rig suggested it — but she was not flying any colours, she was scarcely flying any useful sail. He clapped his telescope up to his eye, and he stared and pondered for much of the next minute. And then he said, "Aye, sir, French for half a sovereign, although it is not an easy sighting. Everything is very slack, though, bunting not excluded. That would argue she is a Johnny Crapaud. She is armed, though. I have counted nine guns."

Swift laughed. Most guns on slavers were notwithstanding, when it came to fight. Near port they pointed inboard, mostly, and at sea were more for show, to keep off low pirates looking for such pickings. It was low indeed, he thought, to rob a slaver. In the normal way, he would have rather gone to hell.

"No need of guns," he said, laconically. "The stink's enough to keep a Christian off. But she is slack, sir, slack indeed, you have the right of it. Maybe they're dead, maybe she's a derelict. But her hull looks champion, her masts and yards are good. It is not black men's ghosts we want, Mr Anderson, is it? She is a ship. She is an enemy, and French. It is our duty."

The *Beauty*, that he was sailing now, was slowly foundering. Not in any haste, despite the pumps were manned for hours every day, but slowly and inevitably, it was terminal. She had had hard usage in the Straits, both in terms of weather and of action, and had fired many tons of iron, absorbed the shocks of many detonations, as well as she was old. It was understood the Navy in the Indies would accommodate him with some replacement if they could, but Swift, as usual, had his own ideas. His hope had been to take a prize and sell her privately, if that were possible, a vessel and her cargo too, at best. But there were certain legal factors, even in wartime. A slaver, derelict, might be the answer to a prayer...

"Call all working hands an't please you, Lieutenant Anderson, and prepare to beat to quarters," he said. "She looks an easy touch, but that could be a counterfeit. I will address the officers in my cabin in fifteen minutes."

As a fighting unit, the *Beauty* was an efficient ship, whose men had grown used to the vagaries of Swift's command by long, hard usage. A tight ship was his watchword now as always, and over the years his company had refined itself to people, in the main, who were prepared to knuckle down, to fight like demons, and to swallow hard punishment however unfairly given out. Dan Swift did not see it is as unfair, and despised anyone, man or officer, who did. His remedy for any resistance, real or imagined, was to crack down ten times harder. Six years ago or more there had been a mutiny in his frigate *Welfare* which had been the consequence of failings by his officers, but not of him. Swift had learned his lessons well. He was the ruler, his company and officers the ruled. All decisions were his own, all those who tried to give advice were suspect. If he had a sentimental feeling, it was this: Post Captain Daniel Swift thought his men must love him. He was a very happy man, who had seen the chiefest of the *Welfare* mutineers writhe and wriggle to their deaths on Admiralty hemp. Before too much longer, was his dream, he would track the others down and kill them too.

Even from the windward, when they ranged up to her, the slaver stank like hell on water. It was not just the usual slaver smell of shit, but shot through and overlaid with worse. The sharp sweetness of corrupted flesh, the reek of death that caused the chest to clench rather than breathe it in. Swift's sailing master, a youngish man called Dorrint whose enthusiasm for seamanship was worth its weight in gold, made a pass under full canvas but kept too far off to please his captain, who wished to get a look on board of her. When Swift, flashing with anger, roared at him and raised a fist, he saw that Dorrint was white and gagging. Swift laughed instead.

"You are too nice, sir, far too nice," he said. "For God's sake use your kerchief to block up your lady nose. Now, heave her to, I beg you. Bosun! Three boat's crews. Immediate. Mr Ireland!" (To the second lieutenant) "You take one of them, and Pardoe" (the senior midshipman) "another. I will take the first myself. Mr Anderson, lie off of us a little way — Dorrint's niceness notwithstanding — and bring her alongside if I require it. Bosun! Bestir yourself, you bastard!"

Leading from the front was something Swift had learnt, and something he now revelled in. Not just because his people adored him for it, so he felt, but also because he found excitement in it, and it fired him. On board this filthy slaver he would see the truth himself, and it would tell him what to do for best. Shit, blood, corruption — they were material in their own way. He would have a picture to turn to his advantage, all first-hand. But as they drew alongside, even his conviction wilted. The stench, close to, was little short of horrible. Indeed, he could not force himself to breathe. And half a dozen of his own boat's crew were sick, straight overside.

So Dan Swift climbed on board himself, before the lot of them, and balanced on the rail and stared. His large and hook-like nose was raised defiantly, he forced himself to take a lungful, even as it occurred to him that pestilence, quite possibly, had caused the devastation laid out before him.

Devastation, it seemed, was the only word. Before his men and officers had joined him, Swift had counted a hundred dead, then dropped it as irrelevant. There were bodies everywhere, some naked, some in rags, some well forward in the state of rottenness. There were men, not so many women, few children. Around the steering wheel there was a pile of bodies, and hanging from the spokes a man who might just possibly be alive. Aloft, the gear was clattering, the canvas loose and useless. For the first time, Swift noticed falls, dangling from the lower yards. The boats had gone. The ship had been abandoned. Ireland and the midshipman, Pardoe, were beside him now, both speechless. It was left to a seaman to voice the next discovery.

"They're all black," he said. "They're negroes, sir. The white men must've gone."

In the event, this turned out as untrue. The boats secured, all the men on board were set to searching for some indication of what had led to the disaster, for some sign of life. Swift drew his cutlass at the first mutterings of disaffection, and swept it like a scythe around his shoulder, deliberately targeting the nearest scowling face. He told them, with contempt, that he would lead the search, and any man who would not do his best might jump overboard, for all he cared, and swim back to the *Beauty*. What's more, he added, the sharks were good and welcome, for he cared not for cowards, or backsliding men. Moving aft, he did not even pick his way with care, but scuffed through blood and matter. However, he did have shoes on; which his men did not.

They found some white men, only two, and clear signs that there had been an insurrection. One had been the captain, by the look of it, and his throat had been cloven quite in two. He lay beside his berth, in nightshirt, and beside him, hacked and cut to pieces, was another man, in half a formal outfit that argued he was an officer also. Around him lay a half a dozen blackmen, mostly almost naked, whom he had killed with pistolet and cutlass before he had gone down. Help may have come too late, Captain Swift deduced, because some of the slaves had gunshot wounds in their backs, as if fired on through the cabin door. As Swift nudged one corpse with his foot it wriggled, and a large ship's rat came out from under, red in teeth and snout, and looked at him accusingly. He kicked at it but it moved off sluggishly as if to show that it was fully sated.

The decks above were filled with corpses, but the scene in the slaves' "accommodation" was too vile almost to be believed. Dead men and women chained and unchained, piled and twisted everywhere, in all manner of secretions. Swift brooked no niceness from his people now, but drove them to shift and searching like a man possessed. Hatches were flung open, the makeshift cages and creations on the upper deck were pulled and smashed down to reveal their secrets. There were hundreds on the slave ship, Africans of several different shapes and races, and they may have been dead as much as several days. The order went out to toss them overboard if they were not shackled, and soon the grim game became more jolly, as the white men warmed to it. When the sharks arrived, it revealed itself as possible to make them jump for morsels — say a little girl, or boy. As night fell so did the wind, and the temperature went up. It was then there came a revelation.

Ireland, the second, presented himself to the captain, and he truly looked a sight. He was a well built man, with shaven head, and he was in a welter of sweat and filth and blood. He had been giving orders merely, not deep in the dirty work himself, but he might as well have been toiling in an abattoir. His eyes gleamed out of rings of grime.

"I beg you, sir," he said. "The men need water. We must return before men die."

Swift stared at him. If he was thirsty, why the hell not drink? It clicked. No water butts. No open barricoes on the deck. But by the poop-break a mass of staves and rings.

"Good Christ," he said. "They smashed the water up before they left! What, everywhere? What, have you checked below? Bastardy!"

In truth, Swift was impressed by such a level of revenge and planning. But even if the whites had taken water for themselves he doubted it had got them very far. Slave ships needed mighty crews — for mutinies like this among some other reasons — and it was unlikely the boats could have held them all, and if so could have carried drink enough to see them safely through to land. The nearest Carib islands were a hundred miles and more, and the weather was a killer even on board a ship with shelter and room to move. What's more, with the captain dead and at least one other educated man, what chance they could perform the navigation? The chart was still spread out in the cabin, with compasses and rulers lying on it, there were others in their shelves, no sign of frantic searches. What island, anyway? English, French, of Spain? Truly, the smashing of the vessel's water was an act of malice, merely: of desperate revenge.

"Signal to Mr Anderson," he said. "Have him lie alongside us and we'll switch over crews. No reason that we should suffer only while those smug bastards smile along. Tell each man to chuck three more niggers over then they can have a spell. For myself, sir, I could use a shit and wash."

Later, when the ships were snug and easy in a total calm, Swift stood on his quarterdeck naked save for cotton drawers while his sailors sluiced him down with buckets — another habit he had picked up in the Straits. Still a most lordly man when dealing with his people, sometimes rough, often peremptory, he had some notion that such displays of his normality (as he saw the word) would lead them further in their regard for him. That and the fact, of course, that despite his lack of height he was extremely muscular, and beautifully scarred. Whatever else they might think about him, he was convinced they saw him as scorning danger, however impudent. Certainly, until they had got used to it, his bathing filled them with some sort of wild emotion…

Across the water half a cable's length away, the replacement men ("smug bastards"), made more vigorous by the taste of brandy and the evening cool, went at it like beavers to clear the filth away. They pulled down the pens and shelters, they rigged the pumps to sluice water everywhere, they hurled corpse after wretched corpse into the maelstrom. It was said that sharks could smell a slaver from a hundred miles away, and if proof were looked for then this was surely it.

By dawn, it was reported that the ship was clean. All bodies gone, he queried, and Anderson gave him a quirky smile. Aye, all dead ones, sir, he answered – but sixty seven live. Next question — what do with them?

Swift thought and talked it through at breakfast, then for some time afterwards. The breeze had risen very light, and Pardoe and the boatswain, Pollard, had gone on board the prize to get her under way and keep her handily in station. Swift listened to the clanking of the *Beauty*'s pumps — the sea was damn near flat, for Gabriel's sake! — and wondered how he could make the slaver his. The captain's papers, found still intact and locked up in a box, had confirmed that she was French indeed, and that was good. Better that the escapees had not seen fit, or been able, to take the paperwork. Even if these men were ever seen again, the ship, except in memory, need not exist. She was named *Cybèle* above her rudderpost, with a distinctive figurehead at prow. A job for chisel, axe and adze. The men who had abandoned her, Swift confided, would be a job for sun and wind and water — lack of it.

"Tell me again, Mr Dorrint," he asked his sailing master as the breeze blew through the open cabin windows. "Which is the nearest land, and who has hold of it?" He laughed. "As far as one can trust in that, these warlike times."

Dorrint tapped the chart in front of him with his pencil. It was of the West Atlantic, with the curve of islands bowed out towards their course. The *Beauty* was, apparently, poised at the very middle of the chain, with north or south to choose from. To Dorrint and to Anderson, however, it seemed obvious. Dorrint traced his pencil lightly north and west, to where Jamaica nestled beneath the rump of Cuba.

"Well we know that this is ours, sir," he said lightly. "We have been blown a good way south by recent weather, but it sets fair now, by look of it. Now that one there is French, I think, and that and that one, but sneaking through is nothing in the normal way."

Swift seemed distracted. Then said suddenly: "We could take her to a French one." He touched the chart. "Martinique. Is that the closest, Mr Dorrint? How many days to there?"

The airy cabin was a peaceful scene, bathed in slanting sunlight, but Dorrint looked uneasy, and unsure. Swift did not wait for answer, but carried on.

"'Tis said," he mused, "that some French islanders will trade with us, illicitly. Antigua I have heard of as a touch. What say you, Mr Anderson? Should we try Antigua?"

He kept it light, so that they could not know if he was serious. But his hard eyes bored into the lieutenant's soft ones, and Swift was gratified to see him swallow, nervously.

"Well, as to that, sir..."

"But she is a navy prize, sir, surely?" put in Dorrint; scandalised, perhaps. "I mean, sir," he went on, less brashly, "well, surely... What, sir — sell the slaves back to the French?"

Swift's eyes were as cold as steel, and grey, and deadly. Dorrint tried to hold them, but he quickly quailed.

"Beg pardon, sir," he muttered. "I misunderstood."

"No, sir," said Swift. "I doubt that." He smiled, but it was not a dazzler. "No, sir, they can be damned inconvenient these laws, what? They stand between a man and honest wealth."

Dorrint and Anderson both laughed then, at the cue, and their laughter was relieved. The idea had been sown, however, which was good enough for Daniel Swift. He called a steward to them and ordered coffee and a glass of brandy to round things off. All three had coats on, two blue one black, but he suggested they should all go shirt-sleeve order, to match the glory of the day. All sat again, and let the mood grow mild.

"Prize money," Swift began again, at last. He sighed. "Ah, it can be such a damn long time a'coming, can it not? And such a meagre thing, when spread out to all and sundry. If this ship were a cruiser, say, if we had took her in a battle, well... Anderson, I know that you have woes on that score, man, forgive that I should mention it..."

Anderson was not a very private man, and did not mind at all. At home he was a gambler, and despite appearances something of a whore-man. Not just at home, to say the truth. He'd grown indebted even in the Straits. He sighed.

"If their lordships paid us as they say they will 'twould be a starter," he said, gloomily. "It is more than two years since I received a penny. Mrs Anderson, back in Surrey, send letters that are full of tears and misery. How long since we were fighting Sallee men, sir? I doubt you've seen a brass farthing of that money due. I have not, for certainty."

"Nor I," said Mr Dorrint. "Though I was led to have high hopes, in the beginning. Sometimes it's very tempting, is it not, a bit of trading on the sly? Well — rather tempting." He took a taste of brandy, flushed with his new-found boldness. A small smile crossed Swift's face. Even a licit master's share was very very small.

"But not to France," he said. "You have the right of it there, Mr Dorrint, it would be the action of a scoundrel with no love of King or country's pride. We could not try the French islands, however keen they might be to pay us for their slaves. Sixty was it, Mr Anderson? In good condition they could raise three hundred pound or so, as I believe the pricing goes these times. I am not well up in it, you understand, by any means..."

"There were sixty seven," said Anderson. "One more died at midnight though, which brings it down to sixty six. The surgeon says their hardihood is quite astonishing. All should have died in normal way, he thinks."

"What, sir could we...?" Dorrint broke off. He took more brandy. Swift shook his head.

"Oh no, no, no, of course not," he replied. "The complications would be legion. The paperwork involved... Hhm." He paused, as if in thought. "On the other hand... Well, listen to that infernal pumping, gentlemen. Up to six hours every day and the sea is like a mill-pond. This ship is finished, is she not, we could not chase a duck across a lake, let alone John Frog. Such money could be put to work, indeed!"

Swift sometimes felt very lonely in command. One reason that he hankered for Jamaica was that he had family there of sorts, his loyal nephew, and knew he would find other minds that worked like his. Will Bentley, had he been privy to this delusion, would have been astonished and appalled, but Swift had no inkling of such complexities. He knew where he would take the *Beauty* now, and the *Cybèle* and her stolen slaves, and he thought that he would get away with it. But it was a strain. He thought he had complicity; but what if he were wrong?

"Their lordships wished me to have another ship," he said, "that was stated before I agreed to sail this way. And when we get to Kingston the agents there will — forgive me — fuck and fart about like women at a christening. Two years to get your pay, sir — how long to get a ship? And all the time the teredo and the hurricanes will do their very worst. I say we sail instead for Saint Eustatius, and there come by money. The *Beauty* will be made more beautiful, at least her vital holes will get a damn good stuffing. Now *that* is love of country, sirs, not shilly-shally waiting for a miracle. We'll get cash and get a ship that fights again, not fills up like a sieve at every capful of wind. What think you, sirs? Advise me!"

Swift's nose was in its high position, his eyes glittering with self-satisfaction and belief. He had left these men no option but agree with him, and he'd wager that they did not know to what, precisely. But their confusion was positive, they knew that he was right, whatever his direction. Indeed, young Mr Dorrint was quite fired up.

"Why Saint Eustatius though, sir?" he said, naively. "I do not know the island, except by name. Do they buy slaves from Englishmen?"

Anderson laughed triumphantly.

"They're Dutch!" he said. "They buy anything from anyone! To a Dutchman, Mr Dorrint, there is nothing in the world but florins, guilders, shillings, call them what you will. They live for commerce, and no awkward questions posed. Not that," he added, cautiously, "questions would be difficult in this case. The *Beauty* is a wreck, indeed. Their lordships know this. This is perhaps a fitting way of doing their intention for them, and without causing any pain."

Most elegant, thought Captain Swift. Most elegantly put.

"By George," he said. "What excellent ideas you have, Mr Anderson. Mr Dorrint? Do you agree? Then set a course sir, if you please! Saint Eustatius! Yes, an excellent idea. I will commend you to their lordships, both of you."

I will have that ship, he told himself. The *Cybèle* shall be mine – pourquoi pas! Perhaps a little treasure, too.

Oh, excellent...

Chapter Thirteen

London Jack, inevitably, was as sober as a judge the day he conned the *Jacqueline* past the Twelve Apostles into the purlieus of Port Royal. They had been flying signals carefully, plus a gigantic England ensign, so the batteries, although full-manned and loaded, were silent. Inside the harbour they could see no sign of any navy ship, save an old cutter on the foreshore with her mast down, but a mooring master pulled out towards them with speed commendable, and Gunning began to round up to drop the bower where it had been indicated. At the splash, a swarm of bumboats burst out from the shore, causing such excitement among the people that Will and Sam were forced to organise Savary and his marines to keep good order.

"Later!" roared the boatswain, Taylor. "You'll get your rum and whores, my boys! There's work to do, remember!"

"Bunts, clews, tacks, sheets, halyards!" John Gunning shouted. "Come on, you bastards! Get your arses in the air! Hugg! Tilley! Tell me when it's holding! Stand by to veer some when I gives the word!"

"Aye, sir!" came from forward. "Aye aye, sir!"

"Good God," Kaye said to William, "it's like a bloody pirate ship." He roared at Gunning: "Moderate your fucking language, man! There's brass approaching! Keep down your Thames-side filth!"

Indeed there was a pinnace heading from the shore, a gleaming blue picked out with painted cable at the rubbing band and pulled by black men dressed in white. In the sternsheets, under an awning, sat two officers in blue and bright-work, one with a leg that stuck out at an angle.

"And get a tackle rigged," continued Kaye. "It's that bloody cripple, Shearing. Well, he'll have no argument with us this time, I do believe. The *Santa*'s gone and so's the treasure, and the Spaniards can whistle up their arse before they can blame us."

They had talked it over "to ad nauseam" as Holt had put it jokily, but for Kaye it needed constant repetition, to reassure him nothing would rebound. Shearing would be told the simple truth — that they had sunk the *Santa* as per orders, and under a black flag to hide identity — and that the *Biter*, too, was gone. The capture of the *Jacqueline*, he hoped, would be the big new interest point.

In the event, to Dickie's great relief, Shearing's pinnace provided its own distraction. The second figure in the sternsheets was Lieutenant Jackson, shaky and bleary-eyed, and apparently rather drunk. While Shearing, perched in a sling, rose with easy grace to land upon the deck on his good leg, Jackson spoiled the effect by slipping as he clambered across the bulwarks, to be grabbed by Kaye and Bosun Taylor and stopped from rolling overboard. Shearing cast off the sling and stood steady as a rock until Dickie was clear to take his proffered hand.

"Captain Kaye," he said. "I confess that every time we meet it is a carnival. Forgive my clumsy adjutant, and tell me, pray, what ship is this?"

"Captain Shearing, sir. I have pleasure to report, she is the *Jacqueline*, latterly a private cruiser for the French. No wealth to speak of, sadly, but below in irons some forty captured men, including Captain Bethany, who has surrendered but refused to give *parole* for good behaviour. The ship was damaged, sir. We have re-rigged her, after a fashion, but she needs grounding, urgent."

Jackson, now properly on board, walked as steadily as he could to Captain Shearing and handed him his crutch. It was in polished ebony, with silver trim. Jackson, by contrast, was a sloven, both eyes shot through with blood.

"But your ship is called the *Biter*," said Shearing, mildly. "Pray tell me what you've done with her." He stopped, glancing about the crowded deck. "But can we go below, sir? It's like a swarm of bees. I imagine we can talk in privacy, if this vessel has a place to sit?"

He said this without malice, and a minute later they were in the cabin — cramped but comfortable — while the peddlers, pimps and prostitutes continued their trading on the deck. Sam, in a passing whisper, expressed to Will his admiration of Shearing's style. No sort of stickler, but he had a natural way with men. Let's hope some rubs off on Slack Dickie, he indicated.

The mood within the cabin took a grimmer turn, however. Shearing made himself as comfortable as he could, Kaye took the next best seat, Will and Sam stood up in deference to Jackson, who had to sit, or fall. Once settled, Shearing launched in without preamble.

"Well, sir," he said. "Explain yourself. We have been visited, I must tell you, by a representative of our Spanish allies, and the tale they told is... strange. The *Santa* was beset by, they think, the ship that had been seen before, but this time they scuttled her and then flew off. The Spanish chased, and there was action of some sort in which they came off worst, although they hedged about that circumstance somewise. The upshot was that the marauder – crippled, they insist — slipped off into lucky night, and they could not come up with her no more. She was, however, the same brig, British built, and she flew the skull and crossbones. You, I take it?"

The noise outside the cabin was riotous, even jubilant, and the mood inside contrasted strongly. Bentley studied the calm, keen face of Shearing; it gave nothing away.

"Yes," said Shearing. "I said the skull and crossbones, Captain Kaye. Your sense of humour or someone else's? I would be pleased to have an answer, sir. My only comment would be — old-fashioned, don't you think? The Bloody Red, the Jolie Rouge. For mercy's sake!"

Kaye laughed.

"A little something we ran up, sir," he said, levelly. "You had made it very clear the Navy must not be involved. And we got clean away, and it was in daylight, the lying rogues. We dismasted one and outran the other rotten. Apparently, it did the trick. They have no proof, I understand it, sir? No evidence?"

"Go on," said Shearing. "I am listening."

"And let me tell you, sir," continued Kaye, "they can look for *Biter* now for three eternities and they won't find her, that is guaranteed. She is no more. She is on the bottom. Sunk."

Lieutenant Jackson, given his condition, shocked them by speaking then. Only Shearing did not look surprised.

"And with her all the treasure, I suppose?" he said. "Well, if that is a triumph, you must pardon me."

His voice was light, but very firm and clear, not slurred or muzzed by alcohol at all. But having spoken, his relapse was complete, his chin down on his neck.

Kaye said defensively: "We did fight off two Guarda-Costa, sir. That is to say, two pirate ships by any other name. If that is not a word too old-fashioned for Jamaica ears."

Shearing smiled.

"Do not mind Jackson," he replied. "He suffers; leave him be. Your achievement, sir, is understood, believe me. It is a pity, that is all. To risk so much to get so little. Had you been found out and captured it would have caused a war. Instead of which the Navy's lost a ship. As well as all that coin and specie."

"We have lost a wreck, sir, and got a better hull by far," Holt put in. "The *Jacqueline* may be small, but she is sound, unlike the *Biter*..."

He tailed the sentence off, realising what he had done. And Jackson, who if drunk was far from in a coma, lit on it like a homing bird.

"She was rotten, was she?" he asked, in a cutting voice. "We had heard the rumours, sir. So the bottom dropped out at last, did it? Very heroic, I must say."

"Fiddlesticks!" snapped Kaye, with a more than respectable imitation of an honest man traduced. "We fought a hard action against two Spaniards and took a weight of metal at close range. If *Biter*'s bottom had been suspect she would have gone down like a stone!"

"What did she sink like, then?" said Lieutenant Jackson. "A ball of fluff?"

The two men faced each other like angry dogs. Shearing glanced at Bentley's face then Holt's, to read a true opinion. They had no expression. They had served with Kaye too long. Slack Dickie turned to Captain Shearing.

"I find this abominable, sir," he said. "Hoy off this junior immediately before I call him out. My ship was well-found and excellent, I recommended her to the noble lords myself. She sank from stress of action and we nursed her almost to the beach. A short sea-mile more Providence, and the treasure would be for the taking now. And some may still be, sir. If you would only call off this insolent attack."

Will took a short, sharp breath. Was Dickie going to give away his great secret from simple anger, then? He believed he could get the treasure up, even if no other man on earth agreed. But cash had given him new-found craftiness, it transpired. They almost goggled when they heard the next.

"Sir," continued Kaye, "forgive my choler. You must allow the charge is rather impudent, if insolent might be, in fact, a word too strong. Truth is, sir, there is another part you do not know of yet, which could still lead to riches. And as Mr Holt says, the *Jacqueline*, as prizes go, is pretty fine. The matter of the prisoners, an'all. She was a private ship, sir. Who knows what ransoms might come in the question? The French-held islands are not poor, I understand?"

Captain Shearing moved back and buttocks in the wooden seat, easing the discomfort of his crippled frame. It was getting hotter in the cabin now the ship was anchored, and he licked his lips.

"You surprise me still, Captain," he said. "Surprise me further with a drink, I beg of you. Lieutenant Jackson, do me the honour, sir. I fetched a bag of limes and such from my own little garden as a token for good Captain Kaye. I stowed 'em in the sternsheets and forgot. So kind?"

As Jackson trotted off — an ungainly trot, to say the truth, a sort of staggering — Will called a steward and instructed for water, sugar, glasses and a jug. But Kaye wasted no time in waiting. He told Shearing of the disaster with his prize crew, how they had skipped from off the *Santa* when the Guarda ships had come on them. And how they had taken several bags of silver, gold and money in a handy skiff. The *Biter*, after hot work in the fight that followed, had had no chance at all to run them down. Shearing blinked sweat from out his eyes and rubbed them. He looked as if he could not believe his ears.

"Let me test you, Captain," he said, at last. "Do you tell me your prize crew, the men you put on board the Santa to guard and keep her, took a skiff and made off with the booty? Good God, sir, how was this? Good God, sir, were they renegades?"

"Three Scotchmen, sir. Did I not mention that? I had them down as villains from the first, but in the event they showed brave enough in taking the treasure ship in the first engagement, so I had to put my trust in them. Circumstances, and the weather, left me nothing else to do."

Will was savouring Slack Dickie's way with truth and lies when it occurred to him that the Scots had come from Jamaica in the first place — run off the island, according to Jack Ashdown, for heinous, filthy crimes — and Shearing, just possibly, might know of them. Maybe that was the reason Kaye mentioned no names. But no recognition came; why should, indeed, so grand a Navy personage know such scum? Slack Dickie piled on words to keep their herring red.

"They had some Spanish men alive with them when the ship was taken, what is more," he said. His tones were mournful with disgust. "It seems they slaughtered them. Cold blood. But when we found that out it was too late. They were overside and off, shit from a goose. They had the skiff prepared and ready on the Santa's blind side. It was a wicked plan, but neatly executed. As they will be, one hopes, if God is willing."

Shearing fixed Kaye with a steely eye.

"And the good news, then, is that all witnesses are now disposed of, I suppose? The Scotchmen killed the Pedros, the *Santa*'s on the bottom, so is the English 'pirate' ship." He sighed. "I will give you best in this, Captain. At least there should not be a war. Ah, Mr Jackson. Good man. I think my mouth has turned to mule dung."

The frail lieutenant had come in with the captain's steward, with the jug already full, and glasses bearing slices of tropic fruits. The drinks were poured, the healths were given, and all the men drank gratefully. Lieutenant Savary, of marines, came in and took a glass, but he seemed pale, distracted, in some way. Will saw a thin dew of sweat on his brow and upper lip, and wondered if there might be trouble brewing on the deck. Savary, however, made no comment, but merely sipped his cooling potion. He left soon, but he did not hurry out. Shearing, refreshed, was more friendly when he spoke once more.

"Come on then, Captain. Spit it out. How might all this sorry saga 'lead to riches,' as you put it? It seems to me as if everything is lost. The only riches is a little captured ship to make up for a big one, and a hope of ransom for some forty Crapaud peasants you claim are aristocracy. When did they get fresh air last, incidentally? Men die in Port Royal if they stay below too long, even French peasants. If the heat and rats don't get 'em the stench will choke them pretty soon."

Jackson put in: "Or perhaps they'll crush to death. Forty? On the orlop of this cockleshell? They'll be wilting like wax candles."

Kaye was a picture of irritation and contempt.

"You say so, sir," he said. "I say they are the enemy. If they are sweltering, they should have stayed at home. No matter — in the matter of the treasure I will tell you this. One of the men we have on board here has seen the Scotchmen and knows where they are lurking. They are in the west part of the island, and from what I have seen of the terrain, they will move nowhere very quick. My proposition is we go and seek them out, and bring them back and hang them, and there's your treasure, pat. And what is more, the final witnesses are gone. These three Scotch, and their two accomplices, one Miller and one Morgan, are all that's left alive to speak badly of our Spanish enterprise."

"But they have a boat," said Jackson, thinly. "And Hispaniola is an easy sail away, or Cuba."

"In a skiff?" said Slack Dickie, acidly. Jackson was not abashed.

"They sailed away from *Santa* in some sort of storm, not so? While your ship was prevented from a chase by the same weather, I believe?"

"In any way," said Will, feeling somehow sorry for his hapless commander, "they do not have a skiff no more. Ha' you forgot it, sir? I picked up Worm when he was sailing it."

Shearing was on the verge of laughter at the Punchinello show.

"Gentlemen! Gentlemen!" he remonstrated, good-naturedly. "This is verging on unseemly! What have worms got to do with it, pray God? I must remind you, there is a war on, sirs! Worms? Whatever next!"

Sam said judiciously: "It is a man, sir, not a worm or snake in actuality. Just very, very thin and wiggly. A black man, sir, that we thought might be a spy. Lieutenant Bentley and his fellows found him drifting in the skiff, which he had stole, apparently, from off the Scotchmen. He claims to be a hundred and indeed he has the craft of many years. He must have, for no one else of us has give those bastards worst!"

" Nay," said Jackson, back on acid. "But the Maroons down to leeward will, believe me. If those rogues have gone ashore there, they'll end up in the cooking pot!"

"Fie, sir!" Captain Shearing's rebuke was genuine. "Mr Jackson, enough." He turned to Kaye. "They are not cannibals, the black men, sir, nor yet entire savages. But the lieutenant's right thus far: The Leeward Maroons, while not so wild as those to east of us, will hunt them down and kill them willy-nilly. The only thing that could save them would be armaments in great profusion, a lot of fighting men — and luck. Believe you me, sir, if they had treasure when they came on shore, they will not have it now."

Kaye opened mouth for a denial, but caught the glance of William and of Sam. Even Dick could see the value of discretion. And doubtless, thought Will, he had another consideration, on the opportune. If the authority in Jamaica thought the treasure must be lost, then let it be so. And when Dick found the Scots and got it back off them — it would be his! Will half expected salivation.

Kaye did not salivate. He nodded, as if convinced by better judgement.

"Aye, sir," he said. "I bow to greater knowledge. But that disheartens somewhat; that the treasure should be back within our grasp and then be lost again. But forgive me, sir, I thought the Maroons were our men now? There have been treaties, surely?"

Shearing nodded.

"Aye, that is true, sir. But treaties can account for less than nothing, though. The Leeward men are sometimes biddable, and make part of their living tracking runaways for planters and the Assembly, so perhaps the word might be put around. The Governor might be persuaded to offer some reward if the specie is substantial, I suppose. What think you, Mr Jackson?"

"I think that they are savages," Jackson replied. "And some have never signed, have they, far down in the West? In any way, I would not trust Maroon men with a twisted groat. Consider Siddleham, for instance. Have they tracked down his runaways? I think not, sir. They are savages, merely."

The name of Siddleham struck into Bentley's ears with an unexpected clamour. Siddleham was the planter, Sir Nathaniel, who had first revealed that Deb was on the island, employed as a servant by his neighbour, Sutton. He had called her whore, had boasted, indeed, that his own sons had been involved in the scene of violence that had injured her. Will was sickened and exhilarated, all at once, at the prospect of some news of her, any news.

"What?" he said. "Have they run away? Sir Nathaniel's slaves and servants? But what of—"

"Hah!" Kaye bellowed. He gave a shout of laughter. "We remember him, sir! He had kind words to say of Bentley's little fancy piece! And have they run? Well, serve him right says Will, I'll warrant you! Eh, Will?"

Shearing was staring at him, his face a picture of distaste.

"Captain Kaye," he said, "this is most unseemly. Sir Nathaniel, I have to tell you, has had a dreadful accident. He is paralysed, and it is feared he might not live."

"Oh glory," said Kaye, quiet and contrite. "Sir Nathaniel. Oh glory be. I crave your pardon, sir, I did not know."

"As how could you, sir," said Captain Shearing, forgivingly. "It is a dreadful tale, that happened after you had gone. Some twenty ran, as I believe, including, sadly, the young English maid. Sir Nat and sons, and Alf Sutton's men, set off in pursuit, and Sir Nat came off his horse and broke his back. As Jackson would have it, the Maroons are much at fault that they have failed to find the runners yet, but I believe he errs. Only plantation blacks have looked so far, and it is early days."

He stretched his spine, and grimaced painfully.

"Gentlemen," he continued, "I am getting very hot, my leg is paining me — the leg that is not there — and I must go ashore and arrange accommodation for your prisoners. But Captain Kaye, and gentlemen, I do congratulate you on your successful mission in the matter of the *Santa*, and despite what I have said, I feel your intention has some merit after all. The treasure would be more than comfortable, but I cannot stress too heavily how delicate the matter is, to keep the Spanish sweet. If the Maroons don't shut those Scotchmen's mouths then you must, nothing is more necessary. You have my permission in this, and my full weight behind you, and you will have a slipway and all the shipwrights that you need to get your vessel right. On shore, I promise you, there will be a right warm welcome, both for officers and men. The word will go around immediate."

He raised a hand to Jackson, who helped him upright with bad grace. On deck the crowds were sparser, and the black boat's crew were still stolid, tethered to the new-rigged mooring boom. Shearing was swung up on a tackle and then down, while Jackson made an ungainly scramble down two pendants from the boom. Salutes from waist and sternsheets, and the black men shipped their oars and pulled very sharp away.

A young black whore came up to William and beamed into his face, so close he caught her lovely female breath. In a kind of agony, he turned his face away.

Chapter Fourteen

The organisation of a berth for the *Jacqueline*, the transfer of the prisoners, the noting and securing of all consumables (and thievables) on board, a never-ending list of other mundane tasks, kept officers and men at work without a break for half a week, in spite of Shearing's optimistic picture of their new life. Dick Kaye, in truth, was spirited away quite early to take up shore accommodation with Mr Andrew Mather, the acting governor, who had a wife and young children, while Holt and Bentley, inevitably, mucked in with the men. The *Jacqueline* was vilely dirty, hot and horrible, noisy, and infested with bugs that both lieutenants found truly terrible until they got used to them (about three days). The yardmen over here were black, but apart from that were like yardmen everywhere, in every detail. They were idle, often drunk, worked imperceptibly if at all, and stole everything that was not tied or bolted down. It was, said Samuel dryly, like being back at home.

Kaye, playing the good captain, came visiting a lot, and systematically cleared the ship of all the creature comforts its French owner-officers had enjoyed. They had wine on board that made the wine on Navy ships "turn green with envy" (Sam again), brandy that was wonderful, and various hams and sausages and preserved things that Purser Black dared not try to sell as they could only ever have had the *Jacqueline* as their source. Kaye was on the lookout for such dealings from the very first, because any profits that were going to be made were his and no one else's, he made clear. But very generously, his lieutenants were allowed to eat and drink...

He told them tales of idleness and debauchery on shore that were meant to make them jealous, but reading between the lines, they guessed his life with Mr Mather was a pain to him, because the family was respectable, the wife prim, the children "little prigs." The whole society, in fact, was not "top drawer" by any standard, he said, not like London, nor even like the best of English country life. The people, even at the top, were denizens of a very little island, pining in the midst of a very wide blue sea.

The common Jacquelines, though, were living by debauchery as far as Kaye could see, and he showed a certain wistful hunger for it. Men gained liberty every night as the chance of running far was laughable, and returned, often bloody, often in handcarts, in states of degradation he could only dream about. There were boys in plenty to be had, and women too if that should be his preference on a given night, but the captain slept alone. As he told it frankly to Bentley and Sam Holt, it was killing him.

"The trouble is," he said, "the maids on shore that I meet are surrounded by their pas and fond mamas, and their brothers and their cousins and their beaus. I only ever see them in formality, in dining-room or on a portico for 'sweet cooling lemonade.' 'Fore God, lads, it will drive me wild! Surrounded by such loveliness, and I may not even touch!"

Sam and Will, for this tête à tête, were seated in the cabin smeared with grease and sweat, while their captain was in knee breeches, light pumps, with a silk kerchief in his hand to dab his lips, and they were tempted to toss him overboard. For their part nights were drab affairs, as were Will's days, however hard his friend should try to break him out of miserable memories. They were at liberty to go and do whatever they should wish, but that, in truth, was very little. Search for Deb, search for information, was the top and bottom of Will's needs and wants, and that was quite impossible for now. Apart from seaman work, they must needs to be vigilant as hawks, at least until the valuables had been taken off the ship and stored. Even their most trusted men obeyed the seaman's law in port — if anything would move then move it must, to become hard cash for drinking or for whores. Will knew that Deb had run away, he knew she was a criminal, and beyond that there was nothing he could learn.

Within five days, however, changes were beginning, and the two lieutenants received an invitation to "dine out," in the company of their captain and Savary, in his capacity as the gentleman of marines. The dinner was at the house of Ephraim Dodds, a planter they had met in the Assembly before they had gone off to sink the *Santa*, and he was a crusty man, who held contempt for everyone except himself, and the English Navy in the most particular. He had invited them, apparently, to vent his spleen about perceived lacunae in their protection of the island, but took time out to rail at females, tradesmen, slaves, and all. There were no women in the party, Mistress Dodds "having scuttled back to the old country these many years ago and damned good riddance to her," and his "best servants" were all white. The black ones ("merest scum") were younger, and had indeed a rather skilful line in studied incompetence. For a while, William could forget his woes, and watch the passing show.

Mather was present, and civilised as usual, but there were other planters whose vileness could be graded by degrees. They were all stout and florid men, wrong side of fifty, whose sole topic was the scandal of living in such a filthy island, in such a filthy sea, and abandoned, unappreciated, by the filthy government "back home" who starved them of money and protection while the French islands wallowed in the lap of luxury. Will could see that Holt was on the verge of hysteria at some of these excesses, and even Dickie's eyes grew sometimes round.

"We are martyrs, sir!" gruffed Dodds at one point. "We are beset by French, by savages, by Spanish pirates of the Guarda-Costa, and we are all alone! We have no proper army here, we must raise our own militia and must pay for it ourselves, and our only Navy ship is yours, that is not even properly in the water! We pay our taxes, sir — by God we do, and through the nose! — and where is the Squadron? Swanning, is where! Swanning offshore so we are told, in case the French fleet ever comes, when they will run off to save their precious ships, no doubt! Fleets are meant to fight, sir, not to skulk! And while they skulk, we are murdered in our beds by nigger savages. It is our tragedy! Our time of martyrdom!"

No point in arguing — none of the officers had knowledge to rebut in detail — so they sank into embarrassed silence. Mather, to his credit, did try to demur, but Dodds, his companion Peter Hodge, and a third reactionary called Martin Newman, were quite prepared to shout him down, or anyone. It was Sweetface Savary who called a halt at last, and it was a great surprise. The mild lieutenant had been rather pale and peaky for a day or two, but it seemed that he had reached a certain point. He put down his napkin, dabbed his lips, and said with cutting dryness: "I do not have you down as martyrs, gentlemen. It seems to me, in fact, that you are in clover here. The slaves outweigh you God knows what to one, and yet they do not rise and slaughter you. They give their lives and labour free, they coddle you, feed you, make you rich — and then they die exhausted. If anyone should bear the name of martyr, it is them, surely? The Africans, not you."

It was as if a mortar had gone off. The planters damn near bayed, and Dodds clenched his fists as if to rise and strike. The noise became cacophony and the young Englishmen could only sit and wait. Savary weathered it with pale fortitude, inside a dew of sweat.

When the worst was passed, however, came the shrewdest jibe. Martin Newman stared at Savary with eyes that shone with venom and said carefully: "How dare you say that, sir, and poor Sir Nat a living rebuttal of your vile opinions? Have you no shame, sir? Have you none at all?"

Savary, who was not a confidant of Will and Sam, had no idea what he might mean, and, flushing, said so. Dodds and Newman jumped on his ignorance without mercy.

"So!" cried Dodds. "Know nothing but accuse at will! That is vile, sir! That is *metropolitan*!"

Even Sam did not snort at this absurdity, so fierce was the attack. Newman added: "Sir Nathaniel is our neighbour, sir! A good friend and fine Englishman who is on the verge of death! Crippled, destroyed, brought down to ruination! *He* is a martyr, sir! He is a martyr to betrayal. By black savages and an English whore!"

"Fie sir!" said Holt, but Will asked quietly: "I beg you, sir, what can you mean by that? Sir Nathaniel, surely... well, did he not fall off his horse?"

"He did!" Hodge shouted. "And this doxy had the chance to save his life and spurned it! He appealed to her from off the ground, white man to white woman, and she ignored him! When he told us, he broke down in tears! White woman? She is a bloody black man's whore!"

Sam Holt said shakily: "Let us have this clear. Sir Nathaniel do live, don't he? You say she spurned the chance to save him. But he is saved."

"He lay there and she spurned him," said Ephraim Dodds. "She ran off with her lover to the hills and left him dying. If the Navy has any use at all, the faintest shred of any honour, you would bring her back in chains, Captain, so we can hang her. We demand it of you. In the name of the Assembly. Go out and track her down. She is a murderess."

Savary's voice was firm and clear.

"It was the slaves who died," he said, "not Sir Nathaniel. You burned them, sir, you planters tortured them to death, we heard the screams. The maiden has killed nobody. If murderers there be, she is not one of them."

The dinner party ended almost speechless, and very quickly after this. Had Mather not been present, it could have turned into a rout, its course, indeed, was unimaginable. But he, although the youngest of the island men, was powerful in personality, and capable of instilling some decorum, if not calm. He engineered it quickly that their mules were brought to door, and fussed and flustered to such effect that the "old crustaceans" could not get a toehold to make it a proper fight. Almost suddenly the Jacquelines found themselves in the balmy and odiferous night making their farewells with absurd politeness, and wishing ahead for further pleasant evenings, God forbid. The overwhelming march of politeness, Sam later pointed out, the sign of modern times, had its benefits, however unreal the process seemed to be.

The mule trip back down into Kingston, and then a boat ride to Port Royal and their berth, were pleasant in fact, and for Sam and Will informative. Savary, who had been quartered up in town, elected to go with them to the *Jacqueline*, as their conversation had put all three of them on a firmer footing than before. As an Army man, and also such a maid-like retiree, he had been at some distance from them since the very first, and disinclined to try and bridge the gap. At dinners in the *Biter*'s cabin he had had the air of sharing few beliefs or pleasures with them, more especially the coarser types (as they guessed he saw it), like big Jack Gunning and Sam Holt, say. But it was Sam's robust congratulations for his treatment of the planting men that seemed to make the difference.

"Good God, man," Sam had said, as they left Kaye and Mather at the plantation gates to go their separate ways, "I must say admiration for the way you dealt with them. What antiques, eh? What gargoyles! I thought that bent and gnarled old bastard was going to burst of anger, or have your bloody head off with an axe!"

Savary, tiny and quite peculiar on his gigantic mount, smiled wanly. Although the moon was low as yet, it was not precisely dark, with stars blanketing the skies. The mule was dark brown, with great shining eyes, and exuding health and life. Lieutenant Savary, by contrast, was somehow sickly.

Will said quietly: "I thank you for your defence of Deb. You do not know her, I believe, but you know our story. I met her once, we loved, and I believe I love her still. Now she is hurt, and hated, and she has run away. I must find her and protect her, and I do not know how. There, that is the truth of it, Lieutenant. I am sorry that we have not spoke before."

Sam, if tempted to make comment on the words "protect her," kept silent for once, and Savary, indeed, made no reply directly. They jogged on down the stony roads, absorbed in their own ways by the strangeness of it all. At last the soldier said: "I have noticed, sir, that you and your friend here use first names for each other. I would take it as an honour if you would call me Arthur. Although Sweetface, I suppose, will do if need be!"

It was agreed — Arthur, not the nickname — with pleasure all around, and they chatted for some minutes about family things, and backgrounds and so on. Savary, not surprisingly, was not a rich man, and his father was a reverend, which meant, he said, that he was actually a pauper. It was normal, they agreed, for the non-inheritors of well-off families to go into the Church, the Army, or the Navy, but poor Arthur was thus second-generation indigent, a very heavy load. To finance him, his mama had had to sell her meagre heirlooms.

Sam, shrewdly, wondered if the Church connection was the source or reason for his "unusual views," and Arthur did not pretend for an instant that he did not understand. He flushed and then, more oddly, gave a shudder, that almost grew into a shake. He stopped his mule, and gripped the saddle hard. His upper lip was beaded.

"Are you unwell?" asked Will, reining in beside him. "I thought that earlier you..."

Savary took a deep breath. After a moment he flicked his rein and the mule sauntered on.

"Not quite well more like, I think," he said. "Mosquitoes on that damned beach I guess. They never ceased attacking me." He almost laughed. "My soft and lady skin again. For a man who wants to be a general, it is a curse! Or is that another of Sam's 'unusual views'?"

There was no side to him, and now they all shared laughter easily. But Sam was not to be sidetracked.

"No but Arthur. For a man whose job is predicated on keeping Frenchmen from the planters' shore and negers from their throats so that they can make their fortunes easily, you say some funny things. I haven't heard you praising Crapaud yet, but you gave Dodds short shrift on martyrdom. You said he was in clover, did you not? And worked the slaves to death for profit."

"Well, it is the truth," said Savary, although a shade defensively. "Mistreatment is so iron-bound they must import them all the time, they never cease. Slavery is a man-killing exercise, a machine. That is abomination, surely? In this day and age."

There was a hint of the holy in this which made both Will and Sam uncomfortable. They were believers in the normal way, they supposed, but the *Biter*, an unholy ship, suited them both admirably; the surgeon, Grundy, was meant to be their pastor, which seemed to say it all. Most sailormen, indeed, shied wide of this most thorny subject. Out in the wide stormy oceans, out in the lonely watches of the night, out in the wastes of death and degradation, a deity was difficult to grasp. Especially a God of love and mercy.

Savary went on: "My father is a man of God, and in some ways I am not — you know sons and fathers. But on this thing he is hot, and over years I have tended to agree with him. He even had a public clash with Bishop Berkeley that nearly cost him his stipend. He called the man 'unchristian' — and nearly ended as the people he was aiming to protect!" He saw their faces, uncomprehending. "Berkeley wanted a new law," he said. "To make beggars into slaves of the general public for a term of years. A harder form of the workhouse, or transportation. Or the press gang. Useful, but scant to do with God, I do believe."

"Ah," said Sam. "The press gang, there's a thing. Vile, outrageous, and as efficacious as a paper pisspot. If slaves work no better than a pressed man, I begin to see what you are driving at, Arthur my friend."

"But surely," Will said, "the Church says slavery is within religious laws. Black men are heathens, idolators, their very colour is the mark of Cain. With the best will in the world, they are not capable of suffering the way that white men are. Well, that is what religion seems to say. Is that not so?"

Both Savary and Holt had stopped their mules. They were on a bluff, overlooking Kingston harbour. The moon was higher, and the vision beautiful and calm. Borne on the gentle breeze from the interior, they heard a distant screaming. Which could have been, indeed — anything at all. Sweetface began to shake again. For a moment he was panting.

"And you believe it, do you, Will?" he asked. "Ashdown is a Catholic — or maybe was — and he says it is insanity, balderdash, plain lies. He quotes John Cary, the Bristol merchant. 'Every person lives by every other. The liberty of the subject is vital to the nation's wealth.' Something on those lines, in any way. Ashdown has the quotes, not me."

"Ashdown?" said Sam. "What, Jack Ashdown, our man on board? What does he know of slavery?"

"He was a fugitive, though," said William. "He was deported for some reason from this island, was he not? Oh no, I've got it. He had failed to make his fortune and he shipped home poor. We picked him up from Coppiner's press hulk in the river. So what knows he of slavery, Arthur?"

"He knows much of many things," the marine replied. "You should try to talk to him sometime. I know he is not an officer, but he is long-headed and by no means rough. He *was* deported from the island, although he tends to hide it if he can. He was an abolitionist."

Will felt a little sore that this pale, slight thing should be telling him to speak to Ashdown, as if the fact he was a common man stood in the way of intercourse. He was hurt, indeed, that Ashdown had not identified himself and Sam as confidants. Sam, in fact, was looking at his face.

"Mayhap it was the religious thing," he said. "We are not God-fearers, let's face it, Will. Perhaps Ashdown sensed that in us!"

He was not serious, but Savary appeared to think he was. And he demurred.

"More like, I fancy, the way you think of slavery," he said. "Or the way he thinks you think, maybe. He caught me reading a Quaker tract and he asked, then told me, many things. In particular he found it... er, amusing might be the nearest word, that black people cannot be held true Christians, whatever their beliefs. Did you know that up and down the eastern colonies of America only true Christians can keep slaves? Not Jews, not Mahometans, and certainly not blacks. No man of Africa, of however many generations creolised, can own a Christian servant, never mind a slave. Ashdown found that ironical — good Christians alone can keep men in servile barbarism. Perhaps he assumed that you, like Captain Kaye, like any Navy officer might be supposed to do, took a similar orthodox position. It is in some way, sirs, your duty, after all."

When they got back to the *Jacqueline* they lit up lamps, and sat in the cluttered cabin and drank and talked some more. Ashdown, said Savary, knew he was in some danger back on the island, and hoped to go anonymous as far as that could be. But Jamaica was a land of fragments, despite its small complement of whites, especially now absent-landlordism was so very rife, and most of his activity had been in Spanish Town, so he had hopes to be unrecognised.

"As long as those Scotch devils keep their distance," the lieutenant said. "They dealt in slaves, and theft, and crime of every dye, and they will not forgive him for informations laid by him against them. He paints them as the very worst of men."

By this time, in the early hours, Savary had to go to bed. For a long time now he had been wilting, and although Sam twitted him, it quite obviously was not at all to do with drink. He was growing paler in the pale candlelight, and fits of shivering and sweat were coming on him. There was no surgeon on the ship — Mr Grundy had gone off days ago, and God alone knew where — but there was the French captain's bed, which was good enough for anyone save Slack Dickie Kaye. They had to help him in it in the end, with some concern, and buckets and some towels near to hand. He went straight off to sleep, which reassured them, and they sat and talked some more about what a pleasant man he had turned out to be.

It was a pity they had not got to know him earlier, they agreed, for a good companion on a vessel was a precious thing. He had seemed so frail, so womanish, so unlikely on a fighting ship or in a uniform. But not far below the softness, it seemed, there was sterling steel. They promised themselves with pleasure, turning in, that they would catch up on their losses and get enjoyment to the full.

In the morning, though, Lieutenant Savary was very sick indeed, and the boat's crew nearly made their craft take off like a duck in flight to get across the harbour to the Kingston medicos. It was too late. At twelve o'clock the nurses stripped him, and at quarter past they took his blood. By night time he was delirious, but next morning he was raving, and when he calmed down they took more blood, dosed him with alcohol and mercury, wrapped him in hot towels, then in cold. For another day he swooped up and down, in and out of delirium, and by alternatives screamed and shivered, burning hot or freezing. On the morning of the third day they applied more leeches, and he died.

It was the beginning of a minor epidemic...

Chapter Fifteen

In Deborah's camp in the hilly woods, her life became progressively more difficult. She had quickly patched up her row with Kinji, and her willingness to work hard ("like a slave" as she almost put it in her English way one day) slowly brought the hard-eyed Mildred round. She proved herself particularly effective with the bees, which surprised her as mightily as it surprised the Africans. She would open nests quite fearlessly, and something in her movements — or perhaps her body smell, as Mrs M insisted — appeared to settle them. They let her rob them of their honey as if she were a benefactor, and somehow that is what she came to feel. Sometimes she could prod and poke around for half an hour without a single sting, and she could extract bees from her hair and clothes as happily as a monkey picking fleas.

She could not go to the markets, however, or even leave the camp for any distance with the other women, for fear she might be seen and her presence reported back to the whites. Deb found this irksome, and her frustration grew. Their camp was small, their tilled fields just a tiny patch in a fecund wilderness, and what is more, there were no white people at all for miles around. In any way, why should she be betrayed to them by other Africans? She was one of them, surely? She had thrown her lot in with the runaways.

Mildred, co-confidante with Mabel as the days went by, was a clear-eyed mentor who found Deb's position sentimental. There was no question, no such thing, as a general loyalty, she said, and why should Deb think there might, or ought, to be? For generations people had been torn from different parts of Africa, from different tribes or groups and races with different religions, beliefs and languages, and in Jamaica the planter men had fought to keep them separate.

"Some try make us into Christian," she said, "because they think that make us feel the same. Then others say we must not speak to your God, because we learn to speak English then, and with the one same language all of us, we go to plotting, we go to rise against you. Then some other say we got speak English, all black from all part of the Africa, so we cannot plot because all white man understand us. Maroon chiefs too they make same order. All Maroon speak in English now, whatever part of Africa them from, so no confusion, no knife in back in night. Best thing, dear Debbeerah, you trust no one, see?"

She laughed, her cold eyes touched by light.

"Not even me, gal, that way safe. You trust not even me!"

But Deb did trust her, and she learned her lessons well. How the Maroons were hated by some other blacks, how Maroon towns made their living hunting down plantation runaways, how they received payment for each pair of ears or head as proof they'd kill a runway or (in some enlightened quarters) more money yet, plus a bonus for the miles they'd travelled, to bring one back alive. How, like the whites, they tolerated runaways who did not join their formal bands, because they were useful to them. As go-betweens with slaves on the plantations, as middlemen for selling Maroon produce, and as providers of some food and vegetables the Maroon lands could not grow.

"It is very funny thing," said Mildred, with not an ounce of humour in her voice, "the Maroons don't trouble us if we are useful to them, and the plantation slaves are grateful for the food we sell them likewise. Likewise white men too, who pretend we are not runaways, and not exist even. And then some small thing change, and all come slaughter us. Them Maroon, them plantation bastard, them plantation slave. They send men, and dogs, and horses and they shoot and chop us up. We must not be betrayed, Debbeerah. That is why you not go out of here."

Deb was not stupid, and she knew that there was something else, that Mildred was willing her to understand. She did not, and Mildred, with a noise between her teeth, finally began to spell it out.

"Your wanbe 'usband," she began. "Your lickle Jacob. Tsingi. He is Maroon."

Deb waited. No further forward, but she could feel tension in the air. Mildred clicked her teeth once more.

"He young, he is a captain," Mildred said. "Wha' you think of him? Him Daddy is a colonel. Colonel Treatyman."

Deb was uncomfortable. She knew all this already, but in truth she did not know how to answer any more. She loved Will Bentley and knew she would not see his face again. She felt lost and lonely among her newfound friends, she felt as much a prisoner as she had felt with Sutton and his filthy sons. And Jacob, despite his arrogance, despite his most unpleasant bodyguards, was young, and beautiful, and above all, free. If he was a captain of Maroons he would have a town somewhere up in the West, in the Blue Mountains, she believed.

As a captain of Maroons he must have some agreement with the whites, be free in his associations, be free to come and go. Be free to marry her — or at least to make her concubine — a white maid and a runaway. Or not? She did not know, of course, she knew absolutely nothing. But Mildred did. She was waiting to be asked.

"Mildred," said Deborah. "If I should go with him... Would I be all right? Will he... look after me?" She felt a pricking in her eyes, felt tears begin to well and flood. Mildred's face was honest still, her dark eyes sombre. "I do not want to go," said Deb. "I do not want to go, Mildred. I have a man, an English man. And I am white."

Mildred nodded, very slowly.

"Yes, you are white," she said. "For us that no problem. If you was black and Jacob was white, no problem neither, white man fuck black woman any time. But black man not fuck white woman, see? Black man who fuck white woman he end up dead."

"Oh," said Deb. "But... But I thought Jacob..."

What did she think, what had she thought? She did not know. But if he asked her...?

"Problem is," said Mildred, "he done tell you now already. Whatever you say to Jacob in the end, he got have you, gal. We have hear him ask you, him men have hear him tell you. You told by Jacob, so you got to do it, see? He say you go be his woman, so you go. Unless your man can save you, Debbeerah? And he can not, I think? Can he be here today? Tomorrow? Maybe tomorrow is too late, who know? Maybe tomorrow, maybe the next day, but someday soon. If you be here, if you not go with your one man — you go with Captain Jacob. That the truth."

Deborah was aghast. She felt the earth in front of her was opening.

"But you said... you said he would be killed. What — would the white men kill him? The planters?"

"Who can say? Maybe the planters, maybe some hothead. Maybe the women in Maroon town. We much good at poison, maybe that go make you sick and die."

"Me? But—"

"You, him, what matter which one, or both? White men like kill him, then have you afterward. Black girl like kill you, then have Tsingi. Maybe no one die. Maybe Maroon town strong enough, white men cannot find the way. Maybe Nanny put science on Tsingi, Tsingi cannot die. Nanny can do this. Yes, Tsingi will not die."

The picture was emerging, in Deb's mind. If she went with Captain Jacob she would surely die. White woman and black man was the great taboo, for Africans and English just the same. But Mildred was saying, or seemed to be, that Deborah had to go with him, whatever. She breathed in deeply, and felt already dead.

"If Jacob asks me... if Jacob tells me I must go and I refuse him, what can he do? Will I be... carried off? Will he set his men on me?"

Mildred said calmly: "He go want revenge. He not steal you because white man would hear, there many white man spies and such thing cannot go untold. White men would hear and they would get up force and go and kill him. Even Nanny cannot do everything. Your Uncle George, your King man, mighty powerful. He send soldiers, sailors, across the sea."

"So he will not kidnap me? And if I go with him, I will be killed, be poisoned? Mildred. Then surely I must stay?"

The black woman held her eyes until Deborah looked down. Then Mildred sighed.

"He will have revenge," she said. Her voice was sad. "He will tell bloodhounds, it his only way. You run away from your planter man, with Mabel, Goanitta and the others, you hide here with us. Jacob will tell them where you living, he will tell them how to come. It is Jamaica way, Debbeerah. They will burn our crops, and burn our huts, and rape and maybe kill us. Mabel and her little boy. Missy and Goanitta. Marge and Kinji, Rebekah and Mrs M, old Dangle and the other greymen. They will not take me. I will go to the westward, to the Cock Pits or beyond. There is a man there I have heard of who has no truck with neither white man nor Maroon. I will go and be his woman, I will join with them and fight. Him name is Marlowe."

They were sitting in a clearing, and the light was going down, and Deb had a strange conviction that much of what Mildred was telling her could not be true. She thought of Jacob's laughing eyes, his open face, and she did not think he would be capable of such betrayal. Betray her, maybe — she was a special case, difficult for all of them, including herself — but not the other women, not the Africans, his countrywomen, allies, friends. She convinced herself that Mildred had a course mapped out somewhere, beneath the surface of the seen events, that she would not tell and Deb could never know. But in the end of all, it left Deb with the decision, on her own.

To go with Captain Jacob into...what?

Or to sit here with the women and her bees, and to think of Will Bentley as a prisoner thinks of freedom, when the sentence is not even started yet.

"I have told you truth," said Mildred, as if she read her mind. "We will be betrayed."

***

Although Lieutenant Savary was the first to die, he was not the last one of the people by a sad long way. In Kingston and Port Royal it came as no surprise, in especially as the *Biter* men had been sleeping in western woods and on the shore, where at dusk the flying things could be swept from the fetid air in handfuls. Back in harbour they had thought to have escaped scot-free, but that was not what old Jamaica hands had known. Savary's odd symptoms were not odd to them, nor was his sudden and pain-racked death. By the afternoon that he was buried — quickly, quickly as the tropics gave no quarter on the dissolution stakes — several more of the people were showing signs, and those that were not were panicking. It seemed to hit the strongest first, after its taster on the pale thin frame of Sweetface, and both Toms Hugg and Tilley were soon down on the main deck of the *Jacqueline*, that had been stripped and scrubbed with vinegar and vim. After them fell Simms, a man of iron will and indomitable soul, silly Sammy Megson, thought immune from everything for his lack of brain, and John Manton and Seth Jolley. These were the ones that Will knew very well, but there were others also, in an increasing throng.

The two lieutenants, who had been moved indeed by the death of Arthur Savary, found themselves taking charge and almost overwhelmed. At sea in such an epidemic there was nothing to do but sit it out and hope, but in harbour they expected it to be a little better, at least for medicines and help. In fact the Navy establishment — Captain Shearing, Lieutenant Jackson and a half a dozen subordinates — were less than useless, and made it clear (or Jackson did) that they were acting by set policy, not any sort of slackness. As he explained it, with a scented handkerchief pressed to his mouth when Will accosted him, such outbreaks could spread through an establishment and bring a whole operation down. They could have black men to nurse in plenty, black women to clear up shit, vomit and corpses, and the retired Navy surgeon who lived just out of town might come and give advice, for payment. Jackson smiled his thin smile at Bentley.

"He is a drunk, of course," he said. "Truly, sir, it is the Navy's greatest curse. What do you say to that?"

His bleary eyes were bloodshot still, and he was no more steady on his feet. But his question appeared to be a challenge of some sort, another gauntlet down from this most argumentative of men, so Will said nothing. He had taken against Slack Dickie very clearly, had had his spats with Sam, so Will decided he must play the mild well-mannered one.

"It is unfortunate," was all he said. "My men need a surgeon or a medico. But I can see it is no fault of yours, sir. I thank you for your exposition."

Not good enough for Jackson.

"But you have a surgeon, do you not, sir? His name is Grundy, a frequenter of the gutters, I believe?"

First Will had heard, but he did not rise to the bait. He raised his eyebrows in interrogation, still politeness personified. It riled Lieutenant Jackson somewhat.

"Aye, sir! Are you unaware of it? He moves from drinking den to ale bunghole and makes an arsehole of himself. There, sir! If your men need doctoring, why do you not call him back?"

Because we are better off without him, Will thought but did not say. Chilling though, that the grubby sanctimonious little man, their surgeon and arbiter with Almighty God, could not even keep his troubles quiet when he had a whole town to hide away in. It explained his absence at the burial of Sweetface Savary, though. Poor Sweetface. He and Sam had sorted through his papers and found him linked in loneliness with his father in Staffordshire, whose letters were both passionate and destructive of the cause his son fought in. He did not approve of killing, for a start, and was determined that slavery was a mortal sin. Which left Arthur, as Sam had put it in his caustic, sympathetic way, "with little indeed to take much pride in, stationed in the black heart of the trade."

There was no chance of moving men ashore, or rather off the propped up hull of *Jacqueline*, for it suited the Assembly better to keep "infection pits" at distance. She was being refitted on the hardway outside Port Royal, where lived only blacks and whores and wrecks of people in the normal way, and where the chance of illness spreading to the town itself was thought of little moment. Jackson said bitterly at one point that "the pity was" that she was beached. Otherwise, they "could have took her out to sea and saved us from all suffering."

But he did send slaves in plenty to do "coarse caring" and the "clearing up," plus a regular stream of undertaker's carts to take away the most unlucky ones. For some days no one died, although nineteen were sick, then Tom Tilley went, that struck both Will and Holt as very hard indeed, followed by Megson, Seth Jolley and last Rob Simms. Which meant the marines were now two men, without an officer. Watching the immense frame of Tilley being winched ashore, manhandled, almost dropped, brought frank tears to Bentley's eyes, and his companion's. They watched him buried that very afternoon, bareheaded in respect.

Slack Dickie was not at the burial, although he had put in an appearance for Savary's, and London Jack turned up just as the box was going in the hole, and near fell in after it. Not from an overwhelming grief, despite he had appreciated Tilley as a seaman, nor yet from drunkenness, because he was now over that and swore, with unshakeable unawareness that he lied, that he would never take a drop again. But he was clearly very ill, and almost lost his footing at the sandy edge of the enormous hole that Tilley needed. Sam and William were terrified in case he had malaria, but it later revealed itself as the effects of his four-day drinking spree as usual, for which reprieve Sam threatened to stand him a breaker of fresh rum.

Slack Dickie, afterwards, was the subject of their conversation and here the big man had some fascinating news. The captain was, he said, in love. They laughed so loudly that he winced, and the island reverend, hovering in the background of the cemetery for a tip or human intercourse, threw them a dirty look. But Sam and Will were fair to getting uncontrollable, so moved out into the road to town and followed the gaggle of Tilley's shipmates who were heading, doubtless, to praise his memory at the shoreside ale and spirit taps. It was a lovely day for walking (or for burial), and the air was clean, and fresh, and warm.

"Nay, but 'tis true," Gunning insisted, when they badgered him to say it was a jest. "I know he likes boys' arses but we've seen him with rude women many times an'all. Have we not?"

"Bow to your greater knowledge," Sam joked, while Will acknowledged it was so, why make an argument?

"But love? What, real, aching, weeping love?" pressed Sam. He glanced at Will as if to say some more, then thought better of it.

"Look, some men are incapable," he said. "Some men love any woman, every woman — not just you, John, neither! — and some men have one love only, and that's unusual, and some others have one love only and that's themself! And Dickie, *surely*, is the leader of that camp? He is the king, the godhead, he is the Great I Am! Does she love him, this woman? Is she a Bedlam case, a whore? She can't love him! No woman can! He is a fat boy, overgrown!"

Unseemly laughter from a funeral group, but they could not help themselves, despite Gunning's sickly state. Dick, it seemed, had met this woman in the way of business — "not that business, sirs! No, not that style of business!" — while "ferreting about to do his father's will." By which he meant that Kaye had been mingling with Jamaica's highest in the hope of "learning how to buy a plantation to sink his family's money in and lose it!"

This gave them pause for thought, although it did not surprise them much. Their private mission, agreed as secret in the very highest degree between the captain and lieutenants, was clearly not that secret any more. They could only hope Kaye's indiscretion had not gone too far or been taken very seriously.

"But how would Dickie find Jamaica's highest?" asked Sam, skating over it. "What would he do? He is staying with that Andrew Mather, isn't he? Surely too sensible to be taken in. He is a sourpuss."

Will said: "He is the Governor. Leastways, for the moment he is standing in. He must know people, mustn't he? Everyone, I guess."

"Aye, so," said Gunning. "And Dick's had letters from his Pa. There's letters, incidentally, at the Navy offices. Surprised that Jackson han't brought them down to you. I got two dozen." He rubbed his eyes, as if to clear a pain. "I'm not a bit surprised," he corrected. "The man's a poison toad. I told him they were all from my different wives, to shut him up. Not so funny had he known it was the simple truth. Oh boys, I will be in trouble if I ever see old London town again."

They pieced it out as thus: Slack Dick had gone from house to house with Mr Mather, from family to family, making himself known. At first it was presented as courtesy, showing the Jamaica planters that the Navy cared for them, and by that token the government at home, but they had cottoned on quite quickly, those with any brains, that the young man had another motive, or maybe one or two. First he made it clear, said Gunning, that he was up for better company than Mather (which was appreciated universally he said, and understood), and indeed better by far than that of Dodds and Hodge and Newman and their ilk. He was backward in coming forward on the "delicacies," (that is "the Sex") but – *quelle surprise* — London Jack was not, and a bolder element emerged with heartening speed. These young men, Gunning said, were the "usual country thing," smelling of "horse and mule shit, with mud up to their elbows," but a few of them had sisters, and they were really "rather gay."

Both Will and Sam found this peculiar from their drunken London friend, because his tastes ran for a different caste entirely, they well knew. And when pressed he said he found them "milk and water, with too much of the church about 'em for my taste." He stopped, and grinned, and then continued.

"But I have to say, sirs, some of them are very bold, considering their positions in society. A couple of them fairly set their caps. And I'll say this for friend Dickie too, the one he chose seemed to be the richest one by far, and if he married her quite like to get a lot of land, instanter. I don't know how the law goes on this island, but her father is a racing bet to die."

Her father, when they teased it out of him, was none other than old Siddleham, who was lying crippled in his bedroom like a king, John Gunning said. His estate was half as big as London, his older sons were playboys and quite giddy, and his eldest daughter Marianne was tall and stately and the brightest of the bunch.

"But in truth she is an idiot," he said. "She went in tête à tête with Dickie, she played her spinet for him, they went long walks with mother as a chaperone around their gardens that were laid out by a man from Kew, and God blind me for a liar if I tell you not the honest truth, now they are in love. I ha' seen them at it, sirs, even the negers in the sugar canes can catch them kissing and stroking hands, while Mama, so she pretends, cannot. It is revolting. I fear it drove me to break my lifetime rule and have a little drink!"

This was strange for Sam and Will to contemplate — Slack Dick in love — and they found it easier to tell themselves he might be doing it for a motive, ingratiating himself with the island's powerful to further his father's clandestine plan. But there was stranger still when they got to the Navy rooms to pick up letters, for among the pack for William there was one from Uncle Daniel Swift, and its contents were a bombshell. They were sitting in an airy outer office drinking lemonade, Sam puzzling over the one short note that had been his total store, and Will did not even try to keep it secret. He could see no purpose, and no chance.

"Well this is monstrous, Sam!" he said. "My uncle is at his mad old tricks again! Listen — and this is naught to do with me my friend, I promise you — the rogue states baldly that Kaye's Pa has offered me his daughter's hand in marriage, and he has been so bold — so *bold*, the impudent old swine, so bloody *bold*! — as to accept on my behalf! 'The twenty thousand I mentioned is confirmed!' Oh, is it!? Is it indeed, Uncle!? Good God, Sam — whatever shall I do!? He says I am betrothed! To your Felicity! Whatever shall I do?!"

"She's very ugly, Will," said Sam, and his voice was tight, despite himself. "You told me so yourself. But twenty thou...Good God it is a fortune, Will. It is a ransom for a prince. I would be very tempted, truly, if it were me."

"Oh fiddlesticks!" said Will. "This is no time for your stupid jesting, Sam! He's on his way, and he already plans to spend the dowry as far as I can see! I've to join with Kaye and find an estate and lay the groundwork down for when he comes, and he says the money's piling up extremely high! They're serious, Sam. These madmen are all serious! Swift's on his way to here, and he's going to set us up as planters! We'll have black slaves!"

"Hysteria," said Sam, "hysteria. Perhaps you'd better take a stronger drink than lemon. My letter's much more sensible. Your new wife will be very smart, Will. I envy you."

"Enough! Shut up, you idiot!"

"It's very short, as well." He read: "Mr Holt, I am overlooked constantly. I will do nothing. Nothing. I need a knight on a great white shining charger. Do you know of one?" He sighed. "It's not even signed," he said. "It's a thing of beauty, Will, is it not? It's poetry."

It's mad, thought William.

Neither of them, in truth, knew if to laugh or cry...

Chapter Sixteen

The contrast between their lives on the *Jacqueline* and their new lives as island socialites could not have been more stark. Shortly after their return from Tilley's burial, they received a message from their captain to attend him that evening, early, and "to be in finest fig." Gunning had gone off to God knew where before their expedition to the Navy rooms, but would not have been invited, it turned out. The island "tone" apparently, thought him an ill bred lout.

"Finest fig!" said Bentley in disgust. "Good God, Sam, how does he think we're living currently? Our very clothes must smell of death and vomit."

That was true, as the vessel had a constant reek, despite the washings-down with vinegar and the burnings of leaves and herbs that the "nursing crew" did constantly. There were thirty eight men ill by now, and the detritus of their sickness, when cleared up from the decks, was merely chucked overside to rot. The good news was, she was due to be refloated in a day or so. One way of getting dockyard men to work, it proved, had been to make them want to finish expeditiously. Even the undertaker's men had been complaining.

"I've known it worse at sea," said Sam, philosophically. "My clothes might stink, but they're dry at least, and I've got the salt stains off most of 'em. In any way, according to friend Jack, the island bloods all smell of dung themselves. And people sweat a lot out here; you mean you haven't noticed?"

That was true indeed, as they had remarked on after their awful dinner time with Ephraim Dodds and friends. There was an odd formality which Kaye — the only one of them with real knowledge of the gentler classes — had sniffed at with upper caste contempt, that made the planters – bluff farmer-types who should have known much better — dress up as English gentlemen and therefore smell quite dreadful, a mixture of stale perspiration with pomade and unguents, constantly slathered and renewed. Sam hoped frankly, though, that Dick's new associates were of a different order, and that there might be girls, indeed. Despite the difficulties, they both scrubbed up quite creditably, and were rowed across the harbour looking rather fine.

They met Kaye at the Assembly, and took the usual hired mules to their engagement. It was not very far, but Slack Dickie was nervous, and insisted interminably that they were "on their best behaviour." The estate that they were visiting was that of Sir Nat Siddleham, he said, which came as no surprise at all, and it was most important that, et cetera, et cetera. Will and Sam shared a smirk across the jogging saddles. But were consumed with curiosity to see their captain's "love."

The house was at the top of a long rise, and it was magnificent. They were met by grooms and servants in full livery, with the young male members of the family at the top of a broad flight of steps built from imported granite. Behind them, like a second rank, were three daughters, ranged in height and age from right to left. Captain Kaye strode up the stairs almost proprietorially and slapped the eldest of the Siddleham sons across the shoulder before shaking hands with the other two. Bows to the ladies, then the presentation of his "friends and fellow officers," who were both suitably impressed. Marianne, the oldest maiden, watched everything with a quiet smile, while the younger girls, Lucy and Elizabeth, had a tendency to blush and giggle. They were fifteen and fourteen, and Lucy took a shine to William on the instant, and let it show. He was "so small and neat and beautiful," it was reported back to him in days to come. She had confided in her grown-up sister, in strictest, *strictest*, confidence. Slack Dickie passed it on.

Lady Siddleham, who was something of a personage, attended the small party in an enormous withdrawing room, and fussed around her "boys and gels" to put the guests at ease. More black men in ostentatious livery — one was bare chested and wore puff-thigh pantaloons like a Turkish slave — provided drinks and sherbets, and she made small talk as efficiently as any landed dame at home. Sir Nathaniel was mentioned in polite low tones, as "indisposed," so could not greet them for the moment. Which considering they knew he was paralysed and crippled seemed to understate it, rather. Understatement about the "small, informal dinner, for which apologies" followed quickly on. It consisted of three different courses of exotic meats, and fish and sweet things. Strangely, towards the end of it, a white man in overseer's garb appeared at the doorway, and signalled to a footman, who spoke to him and then approached the oldest Siddleham, whose name was Jeremy, and whispered in his ear. Two minutes later, after talking to the white man, Jeremy spoke softly to his mother and signalled his brothers to follow him. It was quickly done, and the maidens were flustered by it. But Lady Siddleham was unconcerned. She was a plump, still woman, with a soft, untroubled face, and she smiled now vaguely at her guests.

"You must excuse my sons," she said. "There is some disturbance on a neighbouring estate. They will be absent for some little while, I fear."

"Mother?" said Marianne, sharply. "Disturbance? What estate? It is the Suttons, I suppose?"

The vague, untroubled smile again.

"Yes, dear, naturally it is," she said. And to the Navy guests: "We are cursed with Yorkshire neighbours. I swear they are worse out here than they are at home. There was a murder there quite recently, one of the sons who was something of a natural, if I may be so frank. An idiot of some kind, I fear he did vile things to the animals as well as to the blacks. No taste at all; execrable."

"Mama," said Marianne, rather severely. "Such ribaldry is not perhaps appropriate with the young ones here."

Elizabeth and Lucy collapsed in giggles gratefully, and the Navy men put on a great display of "not at all, charming, charming, think nothing of it, Madame." But Marianne, whose features tended to severe, turned the talk on to less heady topics — and of far less interest to her giddy sisters. The better types of neighbour, she revealed, had "thinned out" dramatically during the worst years of troubles with Maroons, as the visitors may have noticed. Captain Kaye had most certainly, she said, looking at him with a smile of open admiration. To which he responded fatuously that he liked "to keep his eyes in motion perpetual — it is a captain's way!"

"That is why the governor at present is that awful little man Mather," put in Lady Siddleham, earning herself another glare from Marianne. "The proper man is in England while his wife indulges in the vapours, and his proper deputy — well, he sadly died last week, the fevers recently have been very bad. So far you have been lucky Captain, I believe? Long may it remain so. The air here is a foul curse."

The toll of *Biter* dead was currently eleven, with nearly forty ill, but Slack Dickie airily (or politely?) agreed with his hostess. Will guessed he really did not know, and reflected that "it was a captain's way!" Marianne, however, still judging the conversation as not quite *comme il faut*, suggested that the officers might care for a stroll in the garden, to see Mama's latest blooms and innovations. Although Lady

Siddleham's face lit up at this, she noticed instantly that the two lieutenants were hardly overwhelmed, which fitted well with her younger daughters' predilections. Kaye and Marianne shared a little smile, as if this was engineered, and accepted readily when Mama suggested the three of them should go alone. In England, even Sam knew, this would have been beyond the Pale, but in the Caribbean — well, was anything? For himself, he was relieved. The girls were young and empty-headed, but at least they were not flowers! On the girls' part there was absolutely no problem: however lovely William might be, he was far too old, except for maiden dreams. He must be one and twenty if a day... Sam was in his dotage.

Boys, young men, or "beaux," though — yes, they were at the forefront of these young ladies' minds. They prattled on about the island "escorts", or rather the sad lack of them, and how the "life" out here was enough "to make one shoot oneself." It was a tragic round of education (governesses and special tutors), recitals of the drabbest, drabbest music in Spanish Town and "Kingston Come" (as they called it wittily), and formal visits to any wives and daughters who had not risked the French and sailed back to the better life at home.

"Indeed," said Lucy, covering her mouth archly with her fan and looking at Will through upturned eyes, "if it were not for the hanging of a nigger now and then, I think that we might *die* of boredom!"

That it was said for some effect was plain to see, but both Will and Sam were shocked, and let it show. This caused amusement, and a laugh that bordered on malicious.

"Lah!" said Elizabeth. "Your faces! You don't think blacks are humans do you, sirs? We *live* here, sirs — we *know*!"

They were seated in a kind of observing room, with one wall open to the vista of the sea, and the view was beautiful. The Caribbean ranged from azure to dark green to black, with white horses but no sail in sight. It would soon be dark, night would drop like a sudden curtain, day's heat would turn to aromatic milk, delightful. But the girls had sensed their target, and they went for it at a charge. What was pain and ugliness to these unworldly Navy men was meat and drink to them. They were sophisticates. It was their lovely fun, and innocent.

"If you wish to charm the ladies on this island," said Lucy, almost primly, "you need to try a little...ah... *navigation*, Master Naval man.

Being kind is not the start of it. Black persons are not just slaves, they are our enemies. They bear the mark of Cain and they live only for ingratitude. You must hate them, sirs. It is imperative."

Will did not know what to do, or think. A picture of his own sisters slipped into his mind, little Martha and mature Lal, and he tried to imagine them speaking thus of any human beings. Or indeed so indiscreetly to any strange young men. They had servants on the home farm, and dealt with village men and women in the normal way, and for all he knew they might even dislike them: more probably were indifferent. But he did not need the memory of Sweetface Savary to recognise these statements as a perfect fright.

Sam tried for lightness, but did not achieve success. He shared a glance with Bentley, and his face was tight.

"While bowing to your long experience," he said, "I must be allowed to differ, if I may. I cannot lay claim to any great piety, but black men are human beings, still. Black men and women. In England some say that slavery per se is wrong. Is sinful."

"Lah!" said Lucy. "And what do they know? Black people *like* to be slaves, Lieutenants. And unless you are *anti*-pious — which God forbid indeed — how dare you talk of it as sin? Our men of God out here harbour no such delusions, believe me, and they live in the thick of it."

"In any way," said Elizabeth, "in England they do not have slaves, and I have been there so I know. They have poor people in plenty, which we do not, and they are even worse in some ways, they smell so very badly, but... but..."

"You are prattling, sister," said Lucy. "You have lost your gist. And we do have poor people, have you not noticed them in town? But the truth is, sirs, we must be cruel to be kind. My father says for years and years and years we treated them like humans, like princes even, and they bit our hands. We watch them, sirs. If beaten and abused they almost flourish, if treated kind they steal and cheat and run. All our harshnesses, if harshnesses they be, have been forced upon us by their own behaviour. There is nothing on earth my father would not rather do than to be kind to them, but he truly cannot. They do not *like* it, sirs; that is the honest truth."

Neither Bentley nor Holt, in honesty, had given much deep thought to slavery, although they had skated round poor Savary's views in the days after his death, but both were cast down by these girls. They knew negro sailors, who turned up in ships across the world, they knew the Worm, they knew Black Bob. Kaye's treatment of that small boy had caused them much discomfort, and his treatment at the vicious hands of the Lamonts and other members of the *Biter*'s crew had filled their hearts with horror and bright rage. But these maidens were so sweet and dainty, and naive. Even the slaves they knew in myriads they did not include among Jamaica's poor...

"You do not think I'm prattling, do you, sirs?" said Elizabeth, determined to recover her position. "We can even kill our slaves, it must be right, it is the law. We may kill them and dis... dis... chop them up. And they have brought it on themselves, believe you me."

Lucy smirked.

"Dismember them," she said. "That is what my little sister wants to say. We can dismember them. If it proves necessary."

A vivid memory of screams, and a reek of burning flesh, came into Bentley's mind, and he could tell from Holt's face that he had reached there too. The sweet sudden darkness of the Caribbean night was filled with sudden dark forebodings.

"But... why?" he asked. "Why ever in this world should—"

Lucy was almost irritated.

"Not for pleasure indeed, sir," she interrupted, snappishly. "You do not believe such things are done just for amusement, I confide? On this island, sir, slaves are our livelihood, each one costs upwards of forty pound. It is done for correction, when absolutely nothing else will do. Is that not obvious?"

"Most efficacious," Holt said, dryly. "They do not err again, for certainty. Once dismembered."

The younger sister giggled, but Lucy was on her high horse.

"Would that were so," she said. "You may laugh, Miss, but think of poor father." She turned her face to Will and Sam. "A slave man was executed for a foul murder and the slaves rose up and ran away," she said. "Poor father joined the hunt to bring them back to justice, and they brought him down from off his horse. The slaves call such things *obeah*. Their heathen magic that they brought from Africa. So the executed man did err again, sir. There!"

"Lah," said Elizabeth, dismissively. She was the younger, but she did not believe such magic talk. "Next you'll be saying, sister, that Nanny is the English slut. She did it really, sirs. The English whore that run away as well, carrying the baby of a dirty slaveman dog. Pa asked for help from her and she spat in his face. Nanny is their witch-woman. Their *obi* dame. Some slaves say the whore is Nanny, now. They are so very, very silly."

There was a pause. All but Elizabeth knew the atmosphere was tense. Will's mind was rigid with this new information. Sam said carefully: "It could be said the troubles were caused not by the slave but by the execution. And that the others rose because..."

The two girls were staring as if he were quite mad, so Sam, to calm things down, shut up.

Elizabeth said: "It was the Suttons, that is the only good part. Ammon, the one that died, was a terrific beast. Otherwise, they would have tracked them down, I guess. Bloodhounds would have gone into the hills and slaughtered them, English slut included. But it was only the Suttons, and they have not got the money. They are going under soon, Mama says. They are going bankrupt."

"Sadly," said Lucy. "That is not true, lieutenants. Well, they may be going bankrupt, but it is not true about the tracking down. My brothers have been moving heaven since that day, but to no avail. They have gone off to the middle somewhere, and no information has yet come back. Fie, Lizzy, how could you think we would not get revenge for Pa if there were any way? The truth is, sirs, the birds have flown, and they have gone to roost. It may be that we never will find where."

The Siddleham boys did not come back from the Suttons' place before Captain Kaye and his fellows went, but this was not considered strange by the lady or her girls. Alf Sutton and his surviving son had entered into a regime of confrontation with their diminished crew of slaves, with Seth, the son, visiting wild and brutal reprisals on them, especially when drunk, which sometimes lead to minor riots. Alf Sutton, like an avenging angel on his huge black mule, would round them up like cattle with a long stock whip, while his son and their favoured drivers — black slaves themselves who had "made good" — would wade in with shorter whips, and fists and clubs. If things bid fair to getting out of hand, the Siddleham brothers could be quickly told, and would go to aid the Suttons with delight. They often came back bloody, even the youngest who was but a child, and hardly sober. It was a simple pleasure.

Kaye had heard about these neighbours, and their precarious existence, while walking with his loved-one and her Ma, and showed his interest very clearly, as he reported to his friends while riding back to town. The Sutton place was running down, he told them, the family very, very "low," and it seemed to him that it was ripe for picking. Both Will and Sam thought this was premature, as judgements went, and neither was the slightest bit surprised at his impatience. They were more cautious, though.

"I hope you did not make an offer, sir," said Sam. "'Fore God, Captain, I don't think you should risk your father's money on a whim."

Kaye laughed at this clear criticism, and accepted it. Not at all, was his reply. He was testing the waters only. But the place was clearly worth it — for the Siddlehams were sniffing, too!

"What?" said Sam. "They go and help them sort their troubles out and all the time they look to buy it? Don't sound very honest to my ears."

"Bah, honest," Kaye replied. "It is business, Sam, nothing to do with honesty. In any case, it is the Jamaica way. Miss Siddleham — Marianne — was very frank. She said I could do worse than swooping on the Sutton place — but I could do better, better by far. One advantage though, and she said this herself, I was not angling for it, one advantage would be proximity. I would be next door to her. Now ain't that passing sweet?"

"Oh, wonderful," said Sam. "Correct me if I err, though, but you are a Navy captain. You live next door to no one, in the way of things. And anyway, what is this 'I'? Have you forgotten your sainted father? And satanic Daniel Swift!? Our brief is to reconnoitre, is it not? Not to find you a country seat next to your lady love! What say you, Will? Or shall I call you Mr Silence?"

Will, indeed, had hardly spoken for an hour, and Sam knew exactly why. He had been struggling with a sort of horror, a deep pain of loss renewed and mixed with jealousy. Elizabeth had said that Deborah — rather, "the English slut" — had been carrying a slave man's child. It might mean anything, he did not know. It might mean nothing. He was lost in pointless agony.

"What?" he said. "What lady love?"

Kaye found that funny, and gave a shout of laughter.

"Aye, be not so bloody saucy!" he told Sam. "Be not so bloody impudent or I shall strike you down to gunner's monkey! But I think she is, though, I must confess — and she says, friends, that there is money out here to be made. For once my Pa, it seems, has got it right! With Marianne's guidance — Miss Siddleham, that is! — I think we'll bring it off."

"We were meant," said Bentley, forcing himself to play a part, "to be as silent as the grave. You will put me right, sir, if I should be wrong?"

"Good man," cried Kaye. "You would shame an advocate! And rest assured, it is a secret still. Marianna and Mama are souls of discretion, and Miss Siddleham says her oldest brother — that is Jeremy — has a business brain that would make his fortune anywhere. She will talk to him about it soon, and then we will return. I tell you boys, this night has been a gaysome night for me, indeed for all of us. It has put us on the path to... well, to riches, anyway. I shall write my Pa this very night, or maybe in the morning. There is money to be made, friends. There is not the slightest doubt of it."

A black man's child, thought William. My God, can it be true? But Deborah. I love you. I wish, I wish, I *wish* I knew where you might be...

Deb Tomelty, within two days, knew where Will Bentley was, because rumour from the white world to the black was fast, and subtle, and very likely to be true. She had heard after the burnings that a Navy ship had landed in Port Royal from England, and in her heart — sense and logic notwithstanding — she had been certain it was his. Now she had it from her women in the woods that a fair-haired young officer, small and strong, and "with a face of suffering," had been mentioned at the market by the Siddleham household slaves, a visitor with two other blue-clad men. She suspected the "face of suffering" had been added by Kinji off her own romantic bat, and Deb was grateful for it. But it made the shadow of Captain Jacob loom very large.

She knew where Will Bentley was. But she feared she could not get to him.

Chapter Seventeen

By the time nineteen Jacquelines had died — including Tilley, Simms, Megson, Jolley and the divers Jones and McIntosh — the epidemic had run the worst part of its course. There were still more than a dozen ill, and some of them would not recover fully it was thought, but the ship was now refloated and virtually re-rigged. In some few days she would be fit to put to sea, which meant that Kaye had a fight upon his hands. He had to get "the cripples" off his boat, (as he put it with his usual charm), and Lieutenant Jackson, at the offices, was having none of it. Bentley, much against his will, was forced to witness the confrontation.

"There is much work to be done," said Kaye, when he realised that Jackson was minded to block his reasonable request. "I have to sail along the coast with the greatest expedition, and damn well you know it, sir. I cannot sail, and search, and doubtless fight, with my main deck a'cluttered up with sick and dying."

Although the argument was in its infancy, Kaye was beginning to lose his temper. Which suited Jackson admirably.

"Now Captain Kaye," he responded, with reasoned calmness, "I cannot undertake the rank impossible, not even for a man I admire as much as I do you. Men are always ill in Kingston and Port Royal. Good God, sir, even Captain Shearing is at present indisposed. And I am in an absolute command here, naturally. I'm sorry. We do not have accommodation for your sick."

Slack Dickie's eyes, Will thought, were taking on a bulge. The windows were all open, the blown-in air was sweet and mild, and Will, of a sudden, felt a pang for Hampshire, and the smell of rain-soaked grass. He had a vision of Deborah, at his side. They had made love in Surrey, first, not Hampshire: but either one would do. He noticed sweat on his captain's face. This place is hell, he thought. We have come to hell for England.

"God damn it, sir!" said Kaye, "I must insist you find some, then! Captain Shearing was adamant: I must sail west to seize those Scotch and win back the treasure they purloined. I would remind you, sir, the case is urgent. Captain Shearing fears that they might blab. That they might reveal how we sank the *Santa.* He said it might mean war."

No doubt at all that Jackson was enjoying this. Lined face and bleary eyes, a picture of some sort of misery, were lighted by a subtle hint of pleasure. A captain, young and sprightly, determined to do his duty with vigour and efficiency, being faced down by a mere lieutenant who looked only fit to die. Bentley, younger yet than either of them, viewed Jackson with a fearsome lack of sympathy. For once his fellow feeling was with Kaye.

"Well, that is all quite true," said Jackson. "It perhaps might have been foreseen." He was bordering on the insubordinate, so stopped that line. "But sadly, Captain, the fact remains. For the present, I can only—"

Kaye slapped his large and meaty hand down on the table, making a solid bang.

"When is Captain Shearing fit?" he demanded. "When he hears this, I swear he will overrule you. I swear he will be minded to..."

"To what, sir, make sick men well again? Would that he could work that on himself. He suffers from his battle wounds. He spends many days in agony, every year. Weeks, even. Would you have me haul him out for you?" A pause, just long enough before Dickie exploded. "I beg your pardon, sir. I overstep myself. Forgive me, I hold the captain...his suffering affects me very near."

Kaye was defeated, and he knew it. He held out both hands, as if to raise a globe, or bowl, then dropped them to his sides. Will put his oar in, emollient and polite.

"Sir," he said. "We are most sorry, most cast-down, to learn that Captain Shearing is unwell. Please convey to him our very best when you should see him next. But perhaps it is possible that you might give some hint, some estimation, as to when we might transfer our men? Almost any quality of accommodation would be the equal of what they are fixed in on the *Jacqueline*, and we are assured the disease is well beyond the infecting stage." He tried a minor jest, to lighten it. "Why, sir, even Surgeon Grundy has returned. We would leave him to look after them in any place that you might find, naturally. In any place however mean and comfortless."

"Aye," said Kaye, lighting on his lieutenant's method. "Or even better, sir — we could take him off with us. Make Port Royal into a better place!"

Strangely, the ghastly old lieutenant responded with a laugh, and his smile, even for Slack Dickie, grew less acid. But backing down completely was not on the cards, nor ever could be. He shuffled papers on the desk in front of him, and let out a heavy sigh, as if of real regret.

"Ah well," he said. "I can make no promises, that's not in my power. But I have one place — 'tis very vile, mark you — aye, there is one... it used to be a stable block. Grundy would stay, you undertake? Mm, now that is..."

"Or go," said Captain Kaye. "Whichever suits your pleasure, Lieutenant Jackson." He swallowed. His pride, among other things. "My case is critical, sir, or I would not be so importunate. And please convey my wishes and condolences to Captain Shearing, as Lieutenant Bentley has suggested. His illness is a present pain to me. Great credit to you, that you are so extreme solicitous of his good comfort."

He positively glowed with false sincerity, and Jackson glowed with pleasure as he lapped it up. He did not believe it for a single instant, all three of them knew that. But his victory was signal, and complete. A greater-hearted man might have called enough, but Jackson liked to savour and prolong.

"Nothing quickly, mind," he said, "and nothing certain until I have completed my inquiries. But in two days or three — no, four or five or six more likely. Well, Captain Kaye, you have my word it shall move as quickly as may be, you have my word. Mind — I would not do this for anyone, you know. It is just that Captain Shearing is most anxious that we get that treasure back. Such a pity that you lost it in the first place. Still..." — his eyes gleamed — "still, Captain Shearing believes you did your best..."

They were content with that, they had to be, although Kaye bitched bitterly as they left the Navy Offices. Had he not been in love, he implied in almost as many words, he would have gone and got a bottle of Madeira and a whore. Maybe he said it as a test for William, to see if he was shocked, but Will merely smiled. He understood.

That led them to a conversation neither could have ever dreamt would happen, where they skated round the pain and theme of love. Slack Dickie made it very plain that no such thing had ever come his way before, and it had thrown down his confidence in reason's power, or that of rationality. He waxed lyrical on Miss Siddleham's great beauty, her purity, her modesty, her calm intelligence, inviting Bentley to agree at every turn. Will, at a total disadvantage in that he understood completely but was somehow hurt, enjealoused, by the easy path his captain had in front of him, was prepared to concede that it was hard — yet wonderful — yet unlooked for, a great bolt from the blue — because he felt it all himself. Except, of course, that Deborah was the acme of sense and beauty not Marianne, whom he found merely rather angular. Talking of which:

"Do you know," Kaye said, "I even feel such sort of stuff for poor Sam now. He says he loves my skinny sister, and I know Papa confides she'll go to you. It's split my sympathy! I pity you because Flip is so awful, and I pity him because I could not bear the thought of Miss Siddleham in another feller's arms and nor can he my sister, most of all his friend's. And then there's you and that pretty little whore. You cannot really love her, though, can you? She is a Spithead Nymph."

"But I do," said Will. His voice was brittle, but his heart was burning, and the pain inside his gut was physical. A Spithead Nymph. And now a rebel's mistress. If he did not find the truth out soon he thought that he might... what? Die? Impossible, ridiculous. But the pain was like a knife.

Kaye was studying his face, and on his own was unaccustomed gentleness. They had reached a point close to the waterfront, a vista of spectacular beauty, and Bentley could see that his brash and foolish Captain had reached some human understanding. It was a signal moment, and had he not felt as miserable as sin, he guessed it would have heartened him. No. It did. Between them was a surge of something like complicity. They stopped talking, and together watched the blue-black busy water. They shared the pain and joy of love.

That evening, there was another dinner at the Siddleham estate, that had become the focus of society for the Navy men. A crippled father notwithstanding, the sons and daughters were determined to enhance their social round, which all had told the officers, individually and collectively, was the greatest single problem of their island life. They were English — they said that there was no such thing as a Jamaican, not a white one, anyway — and they were in exile of a sort. They lived here, they had made their lives and future here, they had been born here all of them: but they longed for "home." For the daughters, London fashion was the aching void, for the mother, horticulture in a proper climate. The young men hated the island life completely. Stink and disease and death, no easy women except slaves, nothing to do except to hunt and drink. To the Englishmen, this sounded much like life at home for rich persons (save the colour of the portable females and the prevalence of death) but they agreed that they did not really understand.

They did meet people at these dinners who were not so vile as Ephraim Dodds and his associates, although the "oldsters" were often present for protocol, and because those with wives could parade them for the satisfaction of Lady Siddleham (whose nose should be long enough for looking down on lesser mortals). There was a sad lack of men about their own age, and women even more so, and the men who did come tended to the loud and loutish in their eyes. A fellow called Charlie Tennet was the best of them — aged about twenty five, red-haired and full of energy — who loved hard drinking and would hunt anything that moved, and kill it with amazing relish. He had a couple of friends, one dark and taciturn called Blair, the other, Dimnock, a sort of idle prattler who was quite harmless notwithstanding, so far as they could tell. Between the nine of them they passed the time away without much pain, although Kaye hardly left the ambience of Marianne. Jack Gunning, again for protocol, was usually invited, but everyone preferred it if he remained invisible, which he did with great efficiency. Neither Will nor Sam, when they discussed it one night, had any idea where he spent the time at all.

The middle-aged planters, with Mather at their head, moved in and out of conversation with the Navy men, and Marianne indeed — who knew now of Kaye's interest in island estate — often steered them into proximation. The consensus was, without Kaye admitting precisely what his plans might be, that seafaring men in general and Navy in particular were exactly what the island needed. Historically, they said, a fair proportion of the most successful settlers had been sea captains, and the reason was not difficult to find.

It was for Kaye, perhaps, but they were pleased to elucidate, and Will could almost see him preening as the flattery piled on. It was a question of control and discipline, they said, a question of planning ahead for all eventualities, then throwing it all up and working out a new path to salvation. As when a storm should break at sea or, likewise, the myriad disasters that could beset a planting man. Disasters such as what?, he wondered. Well, rebellions, wars, acts of piracy, slave revolts, hurricanes, earthquakes, eruptions, outbreaks of violent illness, sudden death, new laws and taxes willy-nilly from a government in London that frankly, rankly, did not care or sympathise — need they go on?

"We must anticipate from day to day," said Andrew Mather. "From hour to hour, minute to minute sometimes. Each time we plant we kill the land a little so we must constantly extend. Across the sea the government hits us with booms and slumps with no warning or redress. We must know money, and markets, and capital returns, and if we go back to England for whatever reason — usually our wives and children, frankly, cannot stand it for very long at any given time — we must find factors or agents to control it all who will not, we hope and pray, enrich themselves and bankrupt us. Oh it happens, sir, it happens with appalling regularity. Is that not so, Ephraim?"

Old Ephraim Dodds was happy to confirm it, but Jeremy Siddleham and his brother — and the younger men — raised clandestine eyebrows and made many secret signs. Miss Marianne herself tapped a finger rather boldly on Dickie's cheek and told him, not too loudly, to discount the carpings of the "disappointed men." And Dodds himself was prepared to admit he hated the life, and everything about it, and would go home like a shot except he hated England more.

"But at least it ain't full of niggers," put in Peter Hodge, and Martin Newman added, "Nay, nor yet your wife, Ephraim! At least the blackmen dunnit answer back!"

Mather was impatient with this prattling, imagining Kaye to be a more serious sort of man. He drank more wine, offered his glass up for a refill to a footman, then said across the table: "What I mean, sir, is that you captains have a wide diversity of skills. In some ways, black slaves are like your common sailors. They are stupid, clumsy, servile, but extremely devious. If forced they can work exceeding well, but will take any opportunity to spoil or destroy. Even the ones you know have brains between their ears pretend that they are incapable of picking up a fallen stick, and however much they smile, you know they hate you."

Kaye whistled.

"Were you ever a sea officer, Mr Mather? That is remarkable as a picture of a tar. You must ha' sailed for England, surely?"

Mather smiled with satisfaction.

"Nay, sir. The army is my expertise. I am colonel of militia here." He nodded. "That is another thing. All of us must serve the island in some way, it is a first necessity. Your naval skills would serve you there as well. Discipline, control, and the use of firearms! You will be a planter born!"

Holt, who had been listening to this with fascination, asked a question that he knew the answer to already. He found this whole society bizarre.

"Sir, may I inquire... I take it black men cannot serve in this militia? It is entirely designed to keep the black man... in his place?"

Dodds spluttered, and his colour rose. Something to do with "disgust" and "madness" and a "bloody farce." But Mather's smile grew broader and more liberal.

"No indeed, sir, you are very wrong. We do have negers under arms, both trusted men and free, and very good soldiers they make too, some of 'em. 'Tis the uniform they like, sir, just like the peasant of whatever creed or colour. A bit of scarlet, maybe a bit of braid — and a cutlass and dirk as well. Most satisfactory."

Kaye turned a sneer on Holt; perhaps to chide him for his mistaken superiority. But Sam knew the truth he wished to reveal, because he had heard it from Jack Ashdown. He smiled a little broader.

"And English servants, I suppose? And Irish; you have a lot of them out here."

Ephraim and his fellows set up another grumbling, and Mather's face took on a clear disdain.

"Not Irish, no," he said. "We cannot trust the Papists, sir. There is a history in the Caribbean of the Irish siding with the French. St. Kitts, Bermuda, Barbados — wherever trouble comes the Papists will turn coat. It is a constant worry for us. We do not give them arms, or let them carry them, indeed."

Martin Newman, from his position with the crustacean element, laughed jovially.

"Fair play though, Andrew. The French shit hot molasses in case their Protestants throw in their lot with us, their Huguenots. Proof positive for me that our dear Lord is not a Catholic, whichever way you test it!"

"In any way," said Dodds. "If you treat a nigger right, he'll be as loyal as a beaten dog. By treating right I mean you work him till he cannot lift a hand against you, and if he does, you whip him till he bleeds." He turned to the three officers, leering. "Best thing about the nigger is," he said, "he's black. When you see a black you know that he's a slave and treat according. And if he runs, he's got nowhere to hide. Except among the other blacks, and they're all slaves ditto, so he can be found. They're better far than white jail trash, in that way. You don't even have to brand 'em like a beef."

The young women that Sam and Will turned to sometimes as a relief from views like these — which more and more they found discomforting — were rarely any better, was the painful truth.

Escaping from the planters on the tails of Slack Dickie's coat when he went communing with his lady love, they often found themselves in conversations with bold maiden visitors, who seemed to think all Navy men were impressive, and most fearful smart. They wanted to impress, even the youngest, because Kaye was a catch in every way, and they hoped that they might win him, somehow, from Miss Siddleham, who every one of them could tell a tale about (but surely would not, lah! the idea!) if forced. Kaye was handsome, with those lovely hazelnut-brown eyes, and clearly very rich. There was a hint from somewhere, also, that he was a lord, or duke, or somesuch, and in any case, one day he'd be an admiral, wouldn't he? Mr Bentley, surely, was a peach, and Mr Holt, sardonic and forbidding though he be, yet had a wicked twinkle in his eye that some of them found peculiarly exciting. And then there were his wounds! That thin, pale, scarry face! It promised mysteries unimaginable...

Determined to impress, and yet the tales they told were little short of horrifying to Sam and Will. At one dinner party for the younger people only, one maiden — demure, peaches and cream, an artist with the fan — sat beside her brother who was almost unconscious from too much drink, and told how he was an expert, when sober, with all sorts of island beasts, a true magician.

"Heavens!" she said. "One day as I was riding in a carriage after him, I saw him rope a female from twenty feet away, just by throwing out a noose from off his horse! It dropped across her head and did not even snag her ears, then he drew the knot just so, and did not choke her, which a lesser rider must certainly have done. He pulled her five miles like that, at quite a trot, right back to the house she'd come from. And funniest of all, the master was displeased beyond belief! She had not been running, as Tony thought, but going to the market!"

"What?" asked Will, uncertainly. "It was a heifer was it? Or a sow, or what?"

The others at the table stared at him round-eyed. Even drunken Tony struggled to sit upright, and opened bleary eyes.

"Sow?" he slurred. "That's rich! It was a nigger, wa'n't it? I thought she was on the runaway! A heifer? Hey, that's a funny one! A heifer or a pig!"

"But you dragged her on a rope?" said Will. "A human being? But..."

Another young lady, pleased at his humanity perhaps, was reassuring.

"Oh, sir," she said, "I do assure you they are used to it. Where they come from, in Africa, slavery is the normal thing, and we treat them far better than they ever get at home. It may seem hard to us, but it is their natural element, believe me."

"Ah," said Sam Holt dryly. "Like stags in England. They enjoy the hunt. It's what they're bred to."

The maid, perhaps, thought that this might be a satire, but drunken Tony had no such doubts.

"Aye," he said. "Precisely. You understand it perfect, sir. What she really wanted was I should have hied her to the woods and mated her — she was a very pretty piece, as niggers go. Don't gasp in horror, girls, I'm jesting only! But that's the thing, see? However much they crave a mating, we must think of our race. We must keep it pure when all's said and done. There are standards to be met."

Although around the table the agreement to this was pretty universal, red-haired Charlie Tennet spoke for the men, and less politely.

"Bollocks," he said. "Beg pardon, ladies, I am a little drunk, though not like Tony, though — but the way I see it is, our duty is to knob 'em when we can, at every opportunity. The buggers won't breed is what I say, only God knows why, and buying new 'uns off the ships'll bankrupt the whole island if we're not careful. On our place there's half a dozen ginger-nigs and they ain't an act of God, I'll tell you that much. They still die sometimes, though. I think the bitches murder 'em, is what. So making more, surely, is a double service."

The young men cheered, including Kaye it must be said, and Miss Siddleham, as hostess, thought possibly it was becoming too exuberant to be exactly seemly. She set out, tight-lipped, to damp their ardour down.

"You are all like rutting boars," she said. "What would you say if some poor white woman fell with child at the mercy of a drunken slave-man? Would you applaud the coffee-coloured by-blow then?"

The other maids were truly horrified at such a vile idea. They knew it happened, although never in *this* part of the island, never in Jamaica at all, but in French islands, say, or Spanish, or Barbados, where moralities were lax; they knew it happened, but, really, not to girls like *them*. Drunken Tony's sister, though, inspired, made the shrewdest point.

"That filthy English slut the Suttons lost," she said. "She mates with blacks. She threw herself on one when they were burning him, and is to bear his bastard child, 'tis said. Nay, 'tis certain. I heard it from Seth Sutton in person when I met him at the harbour on Tuesday or so. She would mate with any of 'em, Seth told me. She would not have a white man, any way."

"Aye," said other maids. "That's what I heard as well. And her so soon from England. And they say she's almost pretty; for a slut. And she's run off to the hills to breed up little black boys. Her name, they say, is Deborah."

Marianne gazed curiously at Bentley, for Slack Dick had hinted at some connection with this maid of infamy, although he had — from a growing sense of fellow-feeling for his juniors, perhaps – been very circumspect, indeed abstruse. Despite Will's down-turned eyes, however, she could not resist a question on the point.

"My father mentioned, sir," she started. "I do believe... did you not know the maid in London or somewhere?"

Will remembered with great clarity that Deb's name and his had been conjoined in the Assembly building some weeks before, and was sick with shame that he might be prepared to deny her now. But Holt stepped in to turn it gracefully, and raise a laugh.

"Nay," he said. "That was some other slut called Deborah. London is full of them, you cannot step a hundred feet in Cheapside without falling face downward on a Deb. Two a penny, I promise you Miss Siddleham, you ask our Captain there. Two a penny, five a groat, a gayhouse for a florin!"

Kaye joined in the laughter and noted down, Sam hoped, the line to take in future. Will pulled himself together best he could and felt cold steel deep in his vitals. The faces all around him, flushed with drink and jollity, made him want to... what? He did not know. And if she was with child — by anyone, black or white — then what again? He truly did not know.

There was a ball there some days later, although not a very formal one, and for Will and Sam it said everything about the lost society that they had felt and thought. It was in honour of the *Jacqueline* (only four of whose company received an invitation) because Kaye had announced that she was finally to sail. He and the older sons and Marianne were deep in negotiation these days — or conversation, speculation, the two lieutenants had little clear idea — to do with property, planting and such business-things, but he had told them that he would not be gone for long, and had hinted that there was like to be advantage in it, for them all. The oldsters were invited more or less on sufferance, but it was a young affair, and by the standards of the metropolis, an offense to nature and decorum. At one in the morning Sir Nathaniel was taken ill, his nurse announced to roars of interest or indifference, and then the grand dame, the butler, the daughters, and finally the sons found it impossible to penetrate the chaos and get the guests to leave. Not to put too sharp a point on it, it was a drunken rout.

Neither Will nor Sam was very drunk — nor very sober neither — when they climbed on board the *Jacqueline* alongside an inner harbour quay, but both of them were glad indeed to be afloat once more. Better still was the prospect that next day, or even this, they would be sailing clear of this pestilential spot.

They were talking in low tones, Sam smoking a pipe of sweet tobacco, when a lightweight cart clattered to the quiet ship and they recognised the bulk of London Jack. They had seen not a sight of him throughout the evening, and they imagined, would have wagered any money on it, that he was murdered with the drink. Till he jumped down, flipped a coin to the carter, and came up the side as agile as an ape to bid them both good morning.

"Good God, John," said Sam. "Have you been wasting time? I should have thought the only way to live through that grim night would have been to hit the potion!"

Gunning sat, and screwed the heel of his hand between his eyes. His smile was all contentment.

"I leave such tricks to thee as knows no better," he said. "Why drink when you can fuck? I have been busy all the evening."

"Oh indeed!" said Sam. "You've been swiving a fine lady, I suppose! Like smoke you have!"

"Not I!" said Jack. "Why waste your time on milk and water when you can choose the strong, the stronger, and the strongest? Three goes I've had, and with servants, all of 'em. One black, one white and one mulatter. You young lads will never learn, will you? Oh, William — something for you an' all — I've found your little Deborah. Leastways, I know just where she is. Now — is that worth it, or what?"

He might as well have punched Will in the stomach. His mouth was open, but he could not speak. Gunning, with a roar of laughter, reached forward and flipped his lower jaw upwards with a crack. Then he ruffled Bentley's hair with a giant hand.

"She's being hunted by a wild Maroon called Captain Jacob," he said. "He wants to marry her, or something very like it! Her whereabouts are secret as the grave, my lad — except I know them, don't I!? Now! Let's hear your thank'ee for old Jack!"

But before Will had gathered himself together, Gunning became very serious, suddenly.

"Ah," he said. "One other thing. I think Sir Nat is going to know her whereabouts an'all. And he won't be told for pleasure, like. No, not at all. I think the thing is critical, Will. It's critical."

Chapter Eighteen

Sir Nathaniel Siddleham's crisis, however little effect it had on his house guests, was serious indeed. In fact by breakfast-time that morning every medical man in Kingston and Spanish town, save Mr Grundy who was mercifully drunk somewhere, had been conveyed or galloped over to give an opinion and to tender advice and medicine. Despite being bled so heavily that he resembled a bolt of wrung-out flax, Sir Nat did not respond to treatment, and by midday he was dead. First the gloom of bereavement settled over the big house (the slaves, as far as indicated by displays of grief, feeling it by far the worst of all) then the bright flame of vengeful fury. The clamour for reprisals against the Sutton slaves for running were loud indeed: but were as nothing compared with the hatred for the Spithead Nymph.

In the Jamaica way, news spread like wildfire that her whereabouts were known at last, ironically too late to save the dear lord master it was noised around, although the logic of that general opinion defied logic itself. Where the news had come from was never quite pinned down, and even Gunning's informants had known only that she had been betrayed, and not by whom. Sir Nat himself may or may not have been told — again, rumour insisted that the news gabbled after midnight had struck the fatal blow — but by morning the brothers and the oldest daughter confirmed that they were cognisant of the area, indeed the very camp, where Tomelty and her vile companions could be found. As soon as Sir Nathaniel had been sodded, it was imagined, the bloodhounds would be released to run them down.

The *Jacqueline*, in the way of dockyards, was nowhere near as ready as had been promised and reported, so the brothers' immediate assumption that Captain Kaye would be able, and more than willing, to join the expedition was as immediately denied. It was put to him bluntly at the service — which in any way he considered rather disrespectful towards the memory of their father — and his demurral, however regretful and polite, caused upset and reproachful words. Had Miss Marianne added her weight to the brothers' hot demands, Kaye would possibly have cracked, but her displays of grief were more traditional. She and her sisters followed behind Lady Siddleham so heavily encased in crepe that Sam wondered they did not expire from the heat, and after the solemnities they did retire, all the four, to their quarters in the house, and did not re-emerge.

The truth was that Captain Shearing, through his mouthpiece Lieutenant Jackson, advised against involvement in a way that amounted to an order. Any expedition, it was pointed out, was likely to be very bloody, of dubious legality, and far better left to the island men themselves. They had bloodhounds, they had armaments, they had appropriate transportation, they had spies and local knowledge. All that the Navy would add would be a little pomp (which the planters would have dearly liked) and a kind of legitimacy that would in fact be spurious.

So keen were the gentry, however, that the very night of the funeral, a noisy party of the younger planters, with Ephraim Dodd and Martin Newman in tow, turned up on the quayside in two coaches and insisted that they be allowed on board. Dimnock, Dodd and Charlie Tennet crowded into the cramped cabin of the little ship, while the others stayed outside in the care of Holt and Bentley, who had no clear idea of what was going on. It was a pitch dark, moonless night but they could see that the vicious drinking that had started with the obsequies had continued, and was bidding fair to become a rout.

Dickie though, for once, had no intention of allowing his ship to become a slackers' haven, and said so. Told that the Siddleham brothers had sent this deputation he said he flatly disbelieved it, and there ensued a shouting match. But he was in a quandary. It was, in island terms, a tragic and a solemn day, and he recognised that these men were showing grief in their own way, and berating him for not offering to help them in seeking "justice." Jem Taylor and Tom Hugg were told off quietly to keep the seamen all below and to allow no reprisal or reaction of any sort, under whatever provocation.

It appeared to turn the trick, although it took an unconscionable length of time, and the men were put on shore at last, although they hung about the quayside until they were left alone and to their own devices, as if the Navy had washed their hands of them and "gone to bed" indeed. In fact Kaye wanted further drink in celebration, and expounded the planters' proposed mission to capture Deb to his lieutenants so blithely that Bentley's torn emotions forced him to backtrack as hard as possible from the likelihood that any harm might come to her. The island men were drunk, half-mad, and undoubtedly incapable, he said. If the runaways were trackable they would have been tracked 'ere, and in any way, if they apprehended Deborah, her being white, she would merely be brought back for questioning, would she not? As her only crime had been merely to refuse pointless succour to a dying man, then what penalty could possibly accrue? It was a nonsense.

William, quite naturally, was not convinced at all, and turned in to his cot to toss and turn in an agony of undirected fear and impotence. He was still awake well after dawn when a weird shouting broke out on deck above him, and he turned out with the others to see a most odd and shameful sight revealed by long rays of the eastern sun as it rose across the still dark waters of the harbour. Hanging from the main yardarm, lifting gently in the first ripples of the morning breeze, was a pair of ladies' drawers, of a white and flimsy aspect, with ribbons of blue and pink.

Worse still, the watchman had not noticed them, nor any others of the *Jacqueline*'s people. There were dock-workers abroad, carters, drovers and fruit sellers. Once spotted the drawers became the general attention, raising whoops, and cheers, and a throng of lookers-on. They stayed on high five minutes or less after the first sighting, but were rapidly bruited all over Kingston, then the island, as the "Drawers of Cowardice." The young bloods of Jamaica had got their revenge.

***

Mildred had told Deborah that their camp would be betrayed, and that when the bloodhounds came they would rape, and burn, and kill. The most likely betrayer, she had further said, would be Captain Jacob, because Deb had turned him down. But when the raid came she had still not done so, in so many words, although she had told him her man had come, and was living in Port Royal on his Navy ship. She had asked Captain Jacob if he would help her, if he could, instead of having her himself, and save her for her Englishman.

It had been a most strange meeting, and after it had ended, Deb had still not known what the outcome would be. Captain Jacob, away from his three bodyguards, was neither as arrogant nor as frightening as he could be, and in her swoops from hope to misery, Deb felt that if she could talk to him for long enough, he might agree. Whatever else she had learned in all her dealings with men so far, she had learned that powerlessness itself could be a potent weapon. She threw herself completely on his mercy, and knew that her weakness was complete. If he chose to spurn her appeal to mercy, he could use her as he wanted to, then kill her if he so desired it. She told him that she loved another man, who could not aid her in any way whatever, who did not even know of her existence on the island. She asked Jacob — she did not even beg him — to reunite her with her Will or, at very least, convey to him a message.

They had moved into the woods together, with the hard-faced bodyguards almost out of sight. Tsingi had argued with them for some little time, had shouted at them, had sworn and stamped, before they had allowed them to withdraw, and they had kept careful watch, and had had their weapons drawn. Had Deb not been so crushed with desire to succeed, such fear of failure, she might have almost found it strange enough to smile. And when they moved back in to end the tête-à-tête, when they indicated by word and gesture that Tsingi, Captain Jacob, must come, he had still not given her an answer.

"I will think," he said. "I will talk back at my town. It is a pity that you do not want to marry me."

At that moment she almost did. The prospect of a settlement, of peace from uncertainty, a simple pairing with a man, bade fair to overwhelm her. Captain Jacob appeared to sense this, too. He smiled into her eyes, and his smile was kindly, and spoke clearly of regret.

"I will come back," he said. "I will do what I think is possible. And now I go."

But when Tsingi did come back, two days later, the raiding party, by a cruel coincidence, came as well. Black bloodhounds were the leaders of the rout, and they attacked the camp just after dark, in overwhelming numbers. The women were all around the campfire, and there were young men as well, the visitors who came to see Goanitta, Rebekah, Missy, Marge. Toad was at the cooking pot, Mabel was playing with her son, old Dhanglli was collecting twigs. And as the bloodhounds — all fellow Africans, all promoted slaves — burst in from one direction, and Tsingi and his fellows emerged from the woods on the clearing's other side, the Maroons and the planters' hired killers were briefly face-to-face. The hiatus was the starkest, shortest moment, and the massacre began. Tsingi and the bodyguards turned on their heels to melt back into the undergrowth, the women screamed and tried to run, the menfolk — weaponless — tried to make a fight of it.

Mabel's baby was the first to go, spitted on a pointed stick. Mabel tried to save the body and two other bloodhounds ran her through. Toad tried to prevent three men from raping Rebekah and was thrown onto the fire and scalded with the contents of the cooking pot, while two of the young men ran and two more died. In the chaotic darkness beyond the clearing the white "generals" arrived, having been led in a less steep way by their scouts, and Captain Jacob, strangely, blundered straight into their arms. Jeremy Siddleham, Charlie Tennet and Richard Blair all claimed credit for the fatal shot, but it was not a bitter argument. Each played an equal part, they did agree, in the beheading. His bodyguards escaped.

All in all, as a reprisal, it was a splendid night. Nine black slaves dead, and one mulatto pikni, which they buried (they threw it in a ditch, in fact) because the white men thought it might be in poor taste to bring it back with them. No doubt though that the death of poor Sir Nathaniel had been adequately compensated. For other slaves that might be tempted to revolt, it was a useful lesson learned.

The only sadness was that the Spithead Nymph had not been killed, nor even apprehended. They had searched and tortured to find her whereabouts, but the fact appeared to be that she had not been there. No one could tell them, or would tell them, where she had gone, and when she had left the camp. Another woman's name was mentioned, though, a woman who had once been at Alf Sutton's holding and who had also run after the burnings. Her name was Mildred, and that was the extent of the information. It was assumed that they had been warned the raid was coming, and had run to hide together somewhere in the forests. Not so much a sadness, the young whites agreed, as a full-blown tragedy...

Chapter Nineteen

Although the people that had run had been Alf Sutton's slaves, neither he nor his son Seth had been told of the reprisal raid. Firstly, Marianne was adamant that the whore was behind all the trouble and that it was her family's prerogative to avenge their father's death, and secondly, the Siddlehams had plans for Sutton's land, which made socialising hardly on the cards. By the same tokens, the "trophies" from the expedition came to the large estate, and graced the poles and baskets erected at the main gateway. There were severed breasts and ears and testicles, one woman's flayed face-skin with the nostrils cut, and the head of Jacob Tsingi with his eyes put out.

Captain Richard Kaye was the first Navy man to see them and he was, quite frankly, deeply shocked and sickened. He was still pale when he made his hallo to his lady love, and even more put out when she laughed at him for being over-sensitive. It was the normal way, she said, what runaways expected, and what would-be runaways needed to see from time to time to keep them in their place. The assemblies on some islands paid compensation if a slave rebelled against a planter, but on Jamaica this was not so, unfortunately.

"Lah, though!" she conceded. "It would bankrupt our exchequer some years, would be my guess. Deterrence by example is the better way!"

The ladies' drawers incident had been glossed over, if not apologised about nor yet forgotten, and to indicate to cynics that his reasons for refusing to help the expedition had been good, Kaye had sent the *Jacqueline* to sea the very next day, under command of Will and Sam, to shake down the new rigging and check and trim the ballast, while on the shore the Offices and Black the purser had been selecting stores for later loading and Mr Henderson the gunner had been doing ditto with the powder and the shot. Further, Kaye, with his new-found humanity, had recognised that the hunting down of Deb was something Will would not necessarily wish to hear or think about, nor, likewise, Marianne's reaction when she heard of the maiden's escape. He had been told of her infuriated rantings first by Jeremy and Jonathan, then from his love herself. It was a sheer disgrace, and this time the Navy *had* to take a hand in it. Again Captain Kaye, at his bravest and his gravest, reiterated that it was not possible, and mentioned, in passing, the Navy's deep distress at how the ship had been insulted. He congratulated himself, later, that his fierce adored-one had admired him his steel, and had forgiven him.

The pressure grew rather than diminished as the days went by. Rumours began to spread around the Siddleham estate, and were picked up by other planters, Mather, Hodge, Dodds, Newman and the rest, that the reprisal raid had gone a sight too far. To use human bloodhounds and armed planter-men to hunt down runaways was acceptable — although Maroons liked to claimed exclusive rights to tracking down their countrymen and cutting off their parts — but the death of a Maroon itself was a dangerous thing indeed. Dangerous, foul, and almost bloody murder. If not against the white man's law, at least against the treaties, which treaties were the product of dozens of years of slayings and reprisals, and misery on all sides. Jacob Tsingi was a captain, son of Colonel Treatyman, and a young man of whom the Windward people had had the highest hopes. There was talk of compensation, there was talk of white apologies, there was a grumbling for revenge.

Miss Marianne Siddleham, when she heard about all this, was incandescent. For a treaty man to earn his silver pieces (thirty) he had to apprehend white whores not breed with them, she declared, as Tsingi most certainly had done with the slut Tomelty. Maroons were useful if they knew the rules, and the money they could earn was so small that only savages could be impressed by it. What's more, Maroon or no Maroon, he was in reality just a black savage and even God would not heed his fall, which made him lower than a sparrow. And serve him right for presuming he could have such relations with a white, however debased that so-called white should be.

The brothers Jeremy and Jonathan — Joseph being perhaps too young to care — agreed with this, and were prepared to take it further at her insistence. If there was a "grumbling for revenge" indeed, then they should show these savages some sense and manners, and take revenge straight back to them. The camp had got off lightly, they persuaded themselves without much hardship, and they took their sister's point that somehow they had been tricked. That the slut had disappeared the night that they had gone for her was surely no coincidence, and that she was still enjoying freedom while their poor father was rotting in his (unquiet) grave, put fire in their blood.

"What proof have we indeed that he was a Treaty man?" asked Jeremy, in conclusion. "He's just an eyeless maggot now, and no one has come to claim his head. It is probably just the niggers piping up a storm. What care they for life, in any way? It's nothing to them, and it never has been. It's nothing over seas in Africa, and it's nothing here. I do not believe the so-called Captain Jacob can be missed."

They tried once more to get Kaye to pledge some help, but he was not for turning. His ship would be back in Port Royal shortly, tried out and tested, and as soon as ever she could be stocked and fully manned they would sail West, he said. He could not, naturally, go into any details of their task, but suffice to say he was under orders very strict. The thought of lifting treasure — either from the wreck, as he intended, or from the Scotchmen's haul from the *Santa*, as Captain Shearing thought — led him on to money, and the other job in hand. The excitement over Sir Nat's death and everything had pushed it to the background in one sense, but opened up another tempting creeklet.

"I hope I shall not be very long, in any case," he said. "And what's more, I'm more than half expecting my associate will come here sometime soon. You know, Captain Daniel Swift, Will Bentley's uncle. I am confident that we shall do some business, then."

Business, as always, fired up the Siddlehams, except for the dowager and the youngsters, who had not been much in evidence since the old man's death, and very soon the troubles were forgot while they sat drinking juleps and gazing out across the sea. Kaye had received impression, very subtly, that Sir Nat's death had changed some things materially, but he was not certain, yet, what it might precisely mean. There had been hints that "poor Mama" was no longer happy in the place where "dear Papa" had died, and that the younger ladies, Lucy and Elizabeth, were making representations for a large change in their life.

Subtle to the nicest degree, but Kaye suspected the family might be considering some sort of move. What — back to England? To another holding? Out of sugar altogether? He did not know, they would not say. But he — oh subtle, subtle man, how proud his father would have been of him! — had dropped his own hints that such a place as theirs would be the acme of ambition, but indubitably, far beyond all but the wildest financial dreams. And they had responded, by and in degrees, and treated it as serious, as fascinating, as something that, somehow, some way, perhaps... And there had been much archness and fluttering of fan, and blushes from both Marianne and himself, and some not-so-subtle *jeus de mot* about "family properties" and even (shameful!) "in the family way!" And also hints that (in view of such connections as they enjoyed and hoped might naturally "develop") well, hints that money might not be beyond negotiation.

Riding to his lodging late one evening after such a conversation, which had started from a discussion of the failing Sutton place, and how easy that would be to wrench away from them, Kaye was on air. He loved Marianne, and she loved him. The brothers were his friends, and could see the value in a connection. Their estate was large, and rich, and most successful, and he would get a dowry too! As he gave the mule into the care of one of Mather's grooms, he almost gave vent to a little song. He was a successful captain, of a happy ship. He would make a most successful sugar planter, too.

The Siddlehams' conviction that the death of Tsingi would "hardly cause a stir among the savages" was undermined a little in a few short days, when his head, already stripped of the bulk of rotting flesh by birds of carrion, was "stolen" from its stake and disappeared. Had no traces been left behind wild animals could have been held responsible, but the overseers reported much evidence of black magic rituals, that the island whites knew variously as voodoo, hudu, obi or obeah, and the slaves would not seem to name consistently. Its effect on them, though, was signal: many dropped their tools and refused to work despite some beatings, and there was a widespread and general wailing from the womenfolk. It was held, the slave drivers reported, that the estate was under curse.

Cursing, in the house, was certainly the order of the day. Jeremy and Jonathan dressed down their overseers, and Lucy and Elizabeth enthusiastically chastised the household "girls" for disobedience and "mumbo jumbo cheek." When Kaye came visiting, as he did like clockwork every day, he found the place in preparation for the mounting of another raid, this time involving all the planters, not just a scattering to give "backbone" to the bloodhounds. He was asked once more to come, and he said once more he could not. In fact, this time his reasons were compelling: the signal station at the Twelve Apostles had reported that the *Jacqueline* was in sight. The wind was light, but in some few hours she would be alongside the quay and ready to be loaded.

"That is a pity, sir," said Jeremy. "For I think it should be wondrous fun. This time we plan to finish off the job, we'll burn the camp down and we'll kill or chase off everyone who's in it. That includes that damn white whore, who presumably is back again, as she for certain is behind the desecration of our little charnel yard. I wish her joy of the filthy trophy of her nigger-love she got. She's caught the plague for certain if she kissed that maggot-mouth."

Kaye had understood that the Maroons of Jacob's band were of the eastern hills, with small connection to the woodland camp, but it was by no means his place to question. He did feel, though, that to leave the plantation house and women bordered on foolhardy, and, because of love, he said so. He was pooh-poohed.

"Ha!" said Jeremy. "You have been talking to old Andrew Mather, sir!" Kaye feared he might be blushing here, for this was true: the dangers had been none of his own imagining. "Old Mather is a woman, sir! He lost some family many years ago and has not gotten over it! My two overseers will stay and they are white, my drivers are all loyal men, for if they're not they know I'll hang them! Holdings are often left with less, sir, when reprisals must be done. And my sister is a lioness, sir! She is a match for any man, be he black or white!"

Marianne, who had entered the room and heard the last of this, smiled rather thinly at her brother as she let Kaye touch her gloved hand with his lips.

"Indeed," she said. "A very tigress, also, which ever is more fearsome. But Captain Kaye — I must be frank. If you must part from us, I care little what might befall me in your absence! There! I am very bold!" Her smile widened. "But I do beg of you, sir, return as soon as ever possible. In that, there is *no* jest..."

Poor Dick was holed beneath the waterline, and lost. He felt close as a toucher to giving up his commission on the spot to stay with this lovely woman, this paragon! And he did believe she was invincible. When he left eventually to go and meet the *Jacqueline*, the plantation's preparations for the expedition were well underway. This time it had been decided to rope the Suttons in, as Alf had many years experience in hunting blacks, and it was expected that the quarry would be spread out wide. As he rode away, Kaye heard the sound of cane-knives being honed on grinding-stones. The bloodhounds were rearming.

***

The *Jacqueline*, being warped and nudged into the quayside berth, looked sharp and fine for sea. As the sails were stowed the hatch covers were coming off, and before all was secure, the dockyard men were manhandling crates and barrels underneath the tackles swinging from her yardarms. Kaye stepped aboard to the required piping, but the sense of urgency made such ceremony a thought irrelevant. Lieutenants Holt and Bentley gave smart salutes, and London Jack tipped his hat sardonically. They moved below out of the ruckus as soon as may be and Will, with stiff correctness, reported that she was "smart and stable, and in readiness." He did not say so, but his eyes shone for news of Deb, and Kaye — who knew what love pangs were now — strove to put the best shine on the news.

"They went," he said. "They made a raid into the woodland, as I guess you knew. But they did not find her, Mr Bentley. Some were killed, about a half a dozen I believe. But she was gone already."

Will, Sam and the captain stood in silence for a little while, not knowing what to say. Jack Gunning, being Jack, had not come below. There was loading to be done, including magazines. He would not let mere dockside men do that. Will let a breath out, striving to hide the juddering. He was relieved; but feared that there was more to come.

"Thank you, sir," he said. "And then?"

"They are going back," said Kaye. "They killed a Maroon captain, but they do not think the thing is finished, not completely. There has been talk of disaffection, and the idea is, I believe, to preempt them, to get their blow in first. That is... as I understand it."

Will said nothing. Holt said this: "Will she escape? Can she get away? How many men are going?"

Kaye considered lying, then gave it up.

"She did last time," he said. "Mayhap she had a spy, someone who gave a warning. 'Twas not you, I suppose!" A jest, but it fell on stony ground. Kaye sobered. "There are many going. More than last time, and all the white men, too. But if there is an informer surely, she has had a damn good start. I would not give up hope, Will. I would not give up hope at all."

"I wish to stay," said Will. It came out unbidden, and he looked surprised himself. Kaye stared at him as if he had said something extraordinary. Will said: "I beg your pardon, sir. I am well aware I cannot. It is just that..." A note of bitterness crept in. "I beg your pardon. I know you do not consider Miss Tomelty... she is just... I would dearly like to know her safe, is all."

Kaye was not good at being avuncular, but he did his best. He said gruffly: "I understand. I have a proposition of my own. It is most... am not certain Captain Shearing will approve, but... Lieutenant Bentley, I am going to sail tonight, or even *in* the night if she takes that long to vittle up and arm. I want you to stay in Port Royal. And you, Lieutenant Holt. It is a... we have men here, who will need knocking into shape when they are fit again. There is..." He had run out of ideas. And then, a flash of inspiration: "Your uncle, Mr Bentley. Daniel Swift. We must expect him any day, he cannot be long now, can he? I think you should be here to greet him, or rather bring him up-to-date. What say you?"

What could he say? Not so much a surge of joy ran through him, more confusion, and new fear. He could not go hunting for Deb, clearly. In fact, he could do nothing for her at all. Except, if they should bring her back he could accede for her, see that she was treated with the process of the law. Or, just *see* her. Will looked at Kaye in deepest gratitude, but he could only blink.

"By God, Captain Kaye," Sam put in briskly. "That is damn decent, sir, and a rather fine idea. Mr Bentley — you will be very near at hand, whatever happens."

"Aye," said Kaye. "That is another thing. Now both of you, hear this. There is perhaps another motive for my generosity. The Siddlehams are going in a mass, the brothers, neighbours, all those black murderers they call their bloodhounds. They will set out like an army and...and leave precious few behind. Am I clear? I see that I am not. The only guards left at the Siddlehams' will be some drivers, mayhap an overseer or two. There are women there. Old Lady Siddleham, and...the young ladies. Now do you follow me?"

"But is it so..." Will started. "I mean, sir, is it a problem, hereabouts? Surely the brothers would not...?"

Kaye was embarrassed. His hands went out in deprecation, and he smiled.

"In truth," he said, "I must imagine not. But Mr Bentley. You of all people... can surely...?"

"Ah," said Sam. "The fair maid Marianne. Well bless you, sir! I never thought I'd live to see the day! Will! We must be on hand in case of an emergency! Two bold lieutenants without a bed to lay our heads in, and a garrison of sick and hurt! Most capital!"

Kaye said stiffly: "It pleases you to mock, but there you are, sir, what can I say? Your wild imaginings put to one side, it still means you get some time in harbour instead of on that pestilential shore, and you can drink and whore yourself to death for all I care — I shan't tell my sister, nay, not on either of you! For certain nothing ill will happen, but if you did hear aught I would be grateful — it would be incumbent on you, in any way — I'd be glad if you would go and have a look. And remember, it is not just the young lady, as you think, but our investment, also. I may tell you now that the Siddleham estate is... well, suffice to say we have some irons heating, boys. And if Dan Swift do come ashore and you have pissed it all away — well rather you should face him out than I!"

All in all it suited everyone, and Kaye, elated that Miss Siddleham – her sisters and the dowager as well — would be safely overlooked however little they might care for that or think it sensible, called in a bottle and they took a comfortable drink. While Gunning supervised the readying of the ship and everybody worked like veritable slaves, the captain made last visits to the Offices to square his plan with Captain Shearing, who happily was back in harness, and agree accommodation for his two lieutenants. He also bespoke a gig for them, without a crew, in the unlikely event that they would need a hull. In such time of need, it was assumed the ague men in the stable-cum-hospital would be fit enough to pull an oar, or raise a mast and sail at least.

Then Kaye made his last visit to the house up on the hill, and mooned around a little with Miss Siddleham until she was quite sick of him (she told him very archly, with many a pouty look) at which he made his last farewell and left. It was just before dusk that the mooring lines were dropped, much of the canvas too, and the dockyard oarsmen hauled the *Jacqueline* out towards the outer harbour, and past the Twelve Apostles. The evening offshore breeze was not in evidence as yet, so she lay on the uneasy swell for quite some time, her canvas flapping idle.

Finally, grown as impatient as Jack Gunning when there was sea-distance to be made, Kaye gave the orders for sweeps to be shipped, and the little brig began her plod towards the open sea. Not a man on board that did not treat it with relief, however hard the pulling...

Chapter Twenty

With the *Jacqueline* gone, and the planters occupied with their heady plans of vengeance, Bentley and Holt, in truth, were at a loose end. They had been charged to stay by Kaye for a reason that was spurious, or at least fired by a limp romanticism, but they were as out of water as two proverbial ducks. Out of water to the extent they did not even have a proper boat, or proper crew. The boat Jackson assigned to them next morning was lying alongside a wormy Navy hulk, and it would pull or sail all right they guessed, if real need should arise. But it was old and filthy, half full of water, and the sails and gear were locked up on shore.

Jackson, when they asked what they should do — offering, as it were, to be of help to him — chose to pretend that they were idlers and suggested that an officer could find a thousand vital tasks, so why should he suggest one for them? Shearing, looking neither more nor less ill and crippled than he had before, was politer, but not a lot more help. The Offices ran like clockwork when the Squadron was at sea, as he explained it, even hinting that most of the time their duties were more social than strictly military. Or put another way, as Sam said later to his friend, "there's naught to do but drink yourself to death: viz Jackson!" Shearing did point out the *Biter* crew were convalescing, and it would be a good thing to assess their current state and when they might be fit once more to take up arms.

He smiled his easy smile, and added: "Your Mr Grundy is attending to their every need. If I were their officer, that would inspire me enough to go and seek 'em out. If you're quick, you might even find some alive enough to twitch!"

That was a good thought, and when they found the grubby little den they were ashamed in part they had not been before. It was dark, and grim, and airless and Grundy was nowhere to be seen. James Manning and Mart Rosser, two able men they had known as good on board, were the most senior hands of the seven left "laid up" and they said cheerfully that they were "damn near better." The other five would soon be on their feet, they hoped, although Slack and Venables "would never be much use again, if indeed they ever were." In fact Venables, a very young and very pleasant farmer's lad who had been pressed, got on his feet only two days later, then collapsed and died. Mr Grundy, said Manning, was mostly drunk — though never caught out drinking — and it was three black women who kept the men alive. Tommy Hugg, indeed, before he'd been discharged back to the *Jacqueline*, had married one of them!

Mart Rosser laughed.

"Case of having to with Tom Tilley gone," he said. "It took bad air to split them up. Two giant hearts that beat as one, they was, and along comes a mosquito, with a stinger like a midget's prick! Nellie's good though, sterling stuff. She thinks he's married her for ever..."

Good works, though, do not take overlong, and pretty soon the two men were on the street once more, taking in the sights and sounds of old Port Royal, which were rich and varied to the point of madness, but which could not keep Bentley's mind pain-clear indefinitely. The heat as ever was a constant crushing weight as they absorbed the riot of colour and of noise, the ships loading and unloading, the sombre mundanity of the slave pens and the market. These were empty for the moment, but they led to talk of Sweetface and his radical ideas, and how they both, increasingly, feared he had been right, or at least stumbling along the track to great discomfort and to shame. The quays were empty but the sad trappings were there, the chains and shackles, the auctioneers' platforms, the whipping-posts. They found the setting of the island beautiful, the sea a sparkling delight. But it was a monument to beastliness, a most egregious place. And it led to thoughts of Deborah, who was with slaves, or had run away with them again, or was maybe... what? He did not know, that was the worst. He did not know. He had an overwhelming need to find the truth.

They considered visiting the Siddlehams, but without Richard Kaye, they both wondered what there was to say. Although the older sons were of an age with them, they struck the officers as playboys, verging on the wastrel, and the damsels like damsels everywhere — a foreign country, as unlike anyone or anything they could exchange ideas or conversation with as either could imagine. Sam acknowledged that he had met one fine lady who was different — Felicity — who had bowled him over, and she was very rich and idle, like these pampered island girls. Except she was not pampered, and as far from idleness as any coiled spring of Sheffield steel. He then admitted, under Bentley's prompting, that the eldest Miss Siddleham was also short of airs and graces, and about as languid as a colt. The difference being, that he disliked the mistress Siddleham, whereas Will was merely indifferent to Felicity! In terms of ladyhood and Deborah, neither of them cared to go...

Love and manhood had become an urgent matter, oddly, for the pair of them, where a few short months ago it had been hardly thought about, and certainly not a subject for mutual confidence. Will had listened to Holt's stories of scurrility, had disbelieved them at first then realised they were true, and then had marvelled at his friend's vulgarity. One day Deb had swum into his ken, and somehow they had gone to bed together. Not vulgarity, no, the very opposite, he supposed. Then supposed that Samuel was not a careless stallion neither, but just brought up a little different. And now Sam — as Sam supposed — was "in love," as was William. They talked about it as they watched the sun go down over the dark, dark sea, and were both moved by how quickly, in this tropic zone, the world also changed itself so thoroughly.

"Christ, Will," said Sam. "I do love Felicity, I'm sure of it, and yet I've only met her once and you're engaged to marry her! It is a mess, this life, old friend. And you love Deborah and God only knows now how she lives, and where."

Or if, thought Will, strangled by a sudden, aching gloom. But he did not put that into words. He ordered more wine, and hoped that he might find out soon.

It came that night, the first pointer to the truth, and it came in the person of a bluff, ill favoured, lumpy woman who had found out their lodgings — no hard task for a denizen — and was waiting for them when they returned. They were nowhere near drunk, although they had been drinking solidly, and they were even farther from the state called "merry." They had agreed with utter frankness that their lives were passing bleak, and they had realised, with a kind of mild surprise, that they missed the *Biter* — well, the *Jacqueline* — well, their ship and shipmates. Maybe they were drunk after all; or at least, not fully sober. Had either been a singing man, they might have gone for mournful airs.

The woman, as soon as she spoke to them, revealed that she was Irish, because her accent made Jack Ashdown's burr sound almost courtly. She said her name was Bridie Connor, she worked for a man called Sutton, and she was a friend of Deb Tomelty. More than a friend, a messenger. More than that — she brought news that she was safe.

The quarter they were lodged in was pretty low, and she was glad when they told her she must come in off the street, and did not even look at her as though she were a whore in search of business. Sam organised them to the sitting-room and offered her a drink, which was only wine, he said, but all they had. Bridie declined it and all three sat, suddenly uncomfortable.

"Well?" said Will. "Mistress Connor, please? Please tell me everything you know. But Deb is safe?"

"And so she is," said Bridie. It came out in a gabble. "As safe as madcap girls will ever be, I guess. She run off from the savage camp before the last raid and that is just in time an'all, before heading West, and she is with a Coromantin maid called Mildred, who is what the slaves do call a santapee, a sort of holy terror. And Sir. She do say she loves you."

Will swallowed, wishing he had not drunk the wine. He felt dizzy, almost sick, and he imagined it was happiness, or relief. He felt elated, and relieved of a great burden, and really rather sick.

Holt said: "Christ, William. Cannot say fairer, in my book. That is a news to hear indeed."

Will nodded, still speechless, and Bridie added, carefully: "She did not dare to say that in so many words, sir, and did not wish that I should say it, neither, for fear it was not welcome, I believe. But I said I would say it, if she willed or no, and she did not give me nay. She is a dear girl, sir, *cailín deas*."

Will said: "If you see her again, you must tell her — you must tell her that I love her too. I can't dissemble, in all honesty. I hope I do not speak too fresh."

"It's good to hear a class man speak at all, God love you, sir. And talk love-talk, an'all. The bastards that I work for are mere animals. Worse than the lowest *spailpín*, and they are the masters."

"But will you?" said William. "See her again? Where is she, can I go to her myself? God, but I'd..."

He faltered, embarrassed. But Bridie's face held no contumely. A little sorrow, though, and regret.

"I have to tell you, sir, that cannot be. They are heading westward, perhaps for the Cock Pits, maybe far beyond. They know there is to be another hunt, all the blacks know that, and this one has the Sutton men an'all. They are the danger, not the Siddlehams, manhunts are meat and drink to them. Deb and Mildred have to disappear. You cannot see them, sir; I am sorry for it."

Sam, to take the subject off such thoughts, put a surprised look on his face.

"The Siddlehams seem to rate them as mere fools," he said. "They plan to buy them out soon, don't they, Will? They say they're damn near bankrupt."

Bridie laughed sharply, but with no great humour.

"*D'anam don diabhal*, sirs! Sure, and so they would! 'Tis them is near the edge, not old Alf. Leastways, that is the feeling here. All airs and graces, but no bottom to them." She smiled. "I doubt my mastermen are short of money, though. They dinnot spend it, that is for definite!"

Will was impatient with such gossip, and his expression showed it.

"But will she get away?" he said. "I mean, as far as can be guessed. This Coromant, this — Mildred, was it? — why is she with Deb? Why are they going, how are they friends? Please tell me all you can, mistress."

"They worked for Sutton and his son was killed; not Seth, the idiot called Ammon. They were not friends then — Mildred is not friendly in the normal way — but it seems it's different now. Deb helped the black folk. She risked herself for them. She tried to save one slave man's life."

Will looked at her. His face was racked.

"Excuse me," he asked, almost painfully. "There is another man. Called... They killed him in the first raid, and now his... head... has gone. 'Twas said that he and Deborah... I..."

Her eyes were calm and level.

"They called him Captain Jacob," she said. "Yes, it is all known. Alf Sutton's slave men say it is a fantasy, Jacob was a Maroon, more like to be hunting Sutton's runaways and Deb than helping them. The runaways are broken now, no danger if they ever were. The Maroon men are separate, and from the East. They are Blue Mountain men."

"So Deb and this Maroon man... 'twas said that..."

The grey eyes hardened.

"Deb said she loved you, Misterhoney. Is not that enough? Whatever pretext they are giving for a second raid, or to hunt her down, is just a pretext, all a fantasy. She is innocent, as all the others in her camp. They are runaways, indeed, but that has always suited planters has it not? They sell good vegetables and fruits and honey, they put food on masters' tables that the slaves would not grow for them even if they could, because they hate them, rightly so. They will seek and try to kill her, and her friends, and they are innocent. And Deb loves you, sir, Maroon men notwithstanding. Let that be enough."

She had talked herself to a degree of anger. Her nostrils flared.

"They killed another young girl that I knew," she said. "A girl called Mabel, and her little baby son. Not just *her* son, but Alf's or Seth's or crazy Ammon's, what we call a *bakra-pikni*, and no one knows his father except that he was white. They are bedlam, sir, the whole damn boiling lot of them, they need to rot in Hell! You talk to me of Deb and Jacob, and I do not know or care! She loves you, sir, and that should be enough! And the lunatics are after her again, and God knows they should be stopped, for she is innocent. That will not happen, though, for there is nobody that can. So Mildred hopes they'll make it to Marlowe's country, where they might be safe. *Och ochone, ochone...* Truly, sirs, it makes one... oh, God, *desolate*."

Will would have liked to know who Marlowe was, but he did not ask. Instead he said: "I truly thank you for your help, Mistress, it has been... a balm to me, I promise you. And if by any chance you do hear more... or if by any chance you can bring word of me to her... Well, these are our lodgings, you will find us here. Our gratitude would be enormous."

"I know it, sir. I am rather coarse, as your kind goes, but in this you have my understanding. Ach, I have said that very bad. Sir — both of you — I will do everything I can. Deb is a most dear *cailín*, and I pray she will survive. This is a terrible place we've come to, sirs. It is as cruel as Connemara."

When she had gone they sat and watched their smoky lamp for some long time, and mused, and wondered, and agreed that things were looking up, were better, any way, than they had been before. It was agreed, also, that they must go to see the Siddlehams, to put their point of view.

"We have certain knowledge that this new raid is wrong," said Will. "Deb is innocent, the runaways are just runaways, not plotting anything at all, it can lead to nothing but more pointless bloodshed. Whoever took that poor man's head it was not Deb or her ilk. God, I wish that London Jack were here. He might get intelligence, or better still might feed some sense to them."

They did go to the big plantation the next morning, but their success was minuscule, or no success at all. Jeremy and Jonathan were too busy fitting out their bloodhounds (and their greenhorn brother) and refused to listen, however hard they pled. They referred them, with insolent dismissal, to speak to their sister "who dabbles in the strategy of things." Marianne was even less prepared to mind their case, and tried to fend them off with Lucy and Elizabeth, who, she said, would make them lemonade. The nearest they got to the subject was a supercilious explanation that they had been on Jamaica no time at all, and knew very little of the island ways. Or nothing, her long nose seemed to emphasise, as she stared coldly down it.

That very evening, the Siddlehams declared, they would be ready to march into the foothills and wreak their proper vengeance on the blacks. If the white whore was there she would receive comeuppance likewise, and if she and some of them had flown, they would be tracked down mercilessly to the far ends of the island. Justice was hanging in the balance, Jonathan said grandly, and justice would be done, however long and hard the way to it.

In the event they left next morning because, apparently, the Sutton men had not turned up until too late. This time the major stealth employed before the previous strike was deemed unnecessary, because they were going as a throng. If the quarries flew, singly or in numbers, they would be hunted down. The pole left bare by Jacob's stolen head — and other poles set up and waiting — would not be naked long.

Chapter Twenty-One

Black Bob's life, after his release by Holt and Bosun Taylor, had been an overwhelming joy. The five men who had been waiting for him were not of his tribe, nor any close relation to it, but they were from the Bight, and their language shared roots, if nothing else, with the tongue that he had known when he had first heard people speak. They all, as former slaves, had also been forced by their masters to adopt a form of English, and this (although it would have astonished Richard Kaye) he understood almost to perfection, and was fairly fluent in.

Bob's wild elation when he rushed up to them was what overcame the men's suspicion. They were of the band that had killed and mutilated Ayling, Sweeney and McGuigan, and since then had hunted down and killed four others of the *Biter*'s runaways. The two white men who had brought the boy were armed, although only with a sword and stick that they could see, but might have had bad intentions, as why not indeed? White men were the enemy, and white man's retribution was swift and cruel and fatal. Ayling and Co had burst upon them with intent — they had assumed — and had paid the bitter price. But Bob's smile, on this occasion, was enough to melt their hearts. Coupled with his escorts' decision to simply melt away.

There were no women in this band, but they did not care to use the boy as Kaye had done. They totalled about fourteen — the numbers seemed quite fluid — and appeared to be nomadic to a degree, living in shelters in the woods that to Bob's eyes were ill-defined as territory. It was only after two days that he discovered that they had a base in some caves two hours or more from the *Biter* beach, and in these caves had captive Englishmen. The first one Bob saw and recognised was a fat man with a limp, who had used to leer at him from time to time on board, but there were four more, tied up in makeshift bonds. When they saw the boy they set up a caterwauling that was full of hope and dread.

"Bob! Bob!" cried the fat man. "You know me, shipmate! Mickie Carver, the black boy's friend! I've never said a word against you or your people, have I, lad? I've give you tidbits off old Geoff! For God's sake, shipmate, tell them we're good men, tell them to let us go!"

The other men all joined in, and Bob found their pleading fascinating. These big, bold white men grovelling like swine. Before *him*, the captain's toy. Whom they had hunted down, once, and tried to rape and murder. Whom they treated with contempt, and pinched in passing if Kaye was not around. They were calling to him. They were begging. Tears were standing in some of their eyes. Bob's new-found smile broke out again, like sunshine bursting through a cloud. It seemed that he could choose if they should live or die.

The chief of the black men, who gloried in the English name of Chattel (which no man had ever revealed the meaning of, presumably), stood before him and the frantic sailors and smiled a much easier smile. He and his companions also found it rich and rare to see these big white scoundrels cower before a tiny boy. One word, his smile said plainly, and they taste the sword. Bob was their mascot now — an effect he seemed to have on men — and it would please them to do his bidding. Killing white men was a pleasure anyway. A lesson in reverse that they had learned.

But Bob could not decide. He looked at Carver, whose name he had never known and never would have done if not for this, and saw just a fat, pathetic, dirty, sweating hulk. He looked at the others — called Chris Thompson, Josh Ward, Seth Pond, Arthur Ebury, again unknown to him — and saw strong bully-men contorted into shapes of terror. In truth, Bob had suffered at the hands of many on board the *Biter*, most recently Sam Hinxman, on the diving boat. These captured ones, for all he knew, had run from Hinxman and his friends; leastways, they had not been drowning him as Hinxman had, for gold.

"You want the treasure?" he said to them, out of the blue. They stared at him, entirely bemused. "You want me dive down in the sea and get the treasure? You go-long drownding me?"

"No," said Carver. He had no idea, perhaps, what Bob was asking, but he was smart enough to know the answer. "No. Eh, mates? No, no, no!"

There was a chorus of denial from the others, which conjured forth another dazzler from the black boy's lips. Chattel was frowning though; an interrogative.

"Treasure?"

"In the sea," said Bob. "Go make me dive for. Go make me drown. Blood come from lugs till Mr Bosun bring me run away. Not these men, no, sir, they not there. No want them dead, sir, they good men. They go live."

This statement — why he said or thought it no one had a notion — was the sweetest music to the sailors' ears. They gave a cheer, that set up a shrieking chorus from the wild birds in the forest, and Bob cheered with them, like the simple, happy soul he was. Chattel and his cohorts, sick of butchery perhaps, quickly set the white men free, and gave them drinks of water, and a little food. They had already stripped them of any weapon, however small, and the deserters had discovered, while hiding in the woodlands in the last bad days, just how little chance they had of finding help or habitation. In any way, now they knew what Black Bob was on about, they thought they had a bargain counter. In low and rapid English they conferred, then Carver, their elected spokesman, called a private meeting with Chattel and his deputy to talk about the sunken gold, and to explain how they could be of benefit. It would be mutual, was his line: though possibly, that was not his full intention.

Strangely, although they were glad enough to go and watch the treasure being lifted by the solitary yawl, Chattel's band professed themselves, and seemed indeed, to be little interested in it as a thing of value. They moved down to the waterfront with the greatest ease, by-passing Lieutenant Savary's outpost men as if they had not existed, which the sailors thought a laugh. Some of them, in fact, discussed how fearsome easy it would be to give the blacks the slip when they were close enough, and go and rejoin the mates whom they had left such few short days before. None of them, save Ebury perhaps, could see a value in this as a proposition, though, fearing that even Dickie at his slackest might have something to say to them if they returned, and might even say it with a cat o' nine tails. When Ebury, tantalised beyond endurance by the sight of jolly men with bottles, and good meat cooking on a spit, did slip away — unnoticed, as he thought — Chattel's deputy, a quiet pleasant man called Ledermann, followed after him in utter silence, to return five minutes later with his scalp, which he threw at his companions' feet. Nobody spoke about it, then or later, but there was no more talk of running, either.

Although indifferent to ideas of metal wealth, the blacks were much more voluble about the ways of diving to the wreck. Four or five of them had come from holdings in the Gulf of Nicaragua, it transpired — hence the name of Ledermann, perhaps — and they mocked the white men's inability with increasing scorn. It was obvious even from a distance that no one could stay down half long enough, or go down half far enough, and the blacks became more and more impatient to have a go themselves, to show how it was done. And wouldn't *that* have put the cat among the pigeons, as Mick said one night to Thompson back at their makeshift camp. For both had little doubt the blacks would make it down, and up again, if they were to try. It fairly made their mouths water for future possibilities.

When a ship appeared offshore one day, the white runaways were as excited and afraid as the blacks. When she came to anchor and they recognised Jack Gunning on the quarterdeck, though, and then Lieutenant Bentley, their apprehension and confusion turned to fearsome regret, homesickness roared in, an aching desire to get back in the stream of actual life. They watched with hangdog looks the comings and goings from ship to stockade and back, they dribbled at the food and wine they guessed must be on board the Frenchman. She was French clearly, from her lines and rig, and had one mast down and so must be a prize, which made them ache the more. Suddenly, the thought of hot action, smoking guns, fire coursing through their veins, made them see what they were missing. To be a seaman was a dog's existence — except that sometimes, it was the very stuff of life, the very heart's desire. Chattel could sense this in them, with a kind of pity and mistrust. He and Ledermann herded them far away that night, and walked them right back to their hidden caves, and kept them there for two days.

When they returned to watching at the bay, the tenor of the life had changed. The ship was anchored still, but men were hard at work on her, aloft and alow, and more activity was taking place around the stockade. The focal point for them and their black masters, though, was still the yawl moored out on the waters by *Biter*'s sunken wreck. Subtly it was changing, there was more order, method — and more success. One diver in particular, whom none of the whites could recognise, had the knack, or training, maybe just the luck to satisfy the black observers that he was doing right. They made approving noises, grudgingly, and were even keener to show that they could do it better. They took to holding their own breath when he jumped off the diving boat, and grinned and nodded at how well he did.

The white men, watching carefully themselves, noted how their captors could always beat the one successful diver, and still had breath to spare when he burst to the surface like a rising cork. They made great play congratulating them, and slapped their backs, and gave huzzahs, which the blacks appreciated, so far as they could tell. But

Carver was not stupid, like a couple of his friends, and did not set great store by one day using them as docile gatherers of booty. He and Thompson wondered constantly how they could get the weapons, and control. Until that day they flattered and applauded, and feigned civility. They did sound out Black Bob more than once, trying to plant the idea in him that they cared more for his welfare than these ragged types who did not even speak King's English very well, but he did the thing that most infuriated them about negros in general: he smilingly agreed with every proposition and it did not pass his ears and eyes. Chris Thompson insisted bitterly that niggers were just like the Irish and the Welsh — however kind you tried to be they just said yes and then ignored it. Superior as they were as Englishmen — they knew that they were beaten by this smiling, simple boy.

There came a time, though, that the ship was ready, and their feelings as she was prepared for sea were mixed. It was a jolly thing, to see men on the yards, the sails drop down, the capstan manned to haul the anchor up, the headsails backed, the yards trimmed round, but a less pleasant one when she headed offshore, filled her canvas, and picked up way. The black men were content to stand and watch as well, but for less time than the former *Biter* hands, who might as well have been turned to grieving stone. The breeze was light, and it was no quick or easy thing to watch her disappear, and the farther out she went, the more lonely was the mood upon them. Bob, who had avoided the beach while the sailors had been there, joined them after about an hour, and seemed to understand, and sympathise. But Chattel and Ledermann began to laugh and mock at them.

The wooden fortress that the Navy men had built was an impressive structure for a makeshift. The walls were higher than a man, with spiky tops, and inside was a second row of sharpened stakes, angled outwards, with longer, keener points that had been fired and blackened into fearsome hardness. There was a solid square hut in the middle, lightly roofed with withies and palm fronds, and with musket-ports cut in the walls and substantial space all round to aim and fire shots in if anyone should break through the defences. The white men were struck once more with a sense of awful loss. With a stockade like this they could have held off an army. And now, at least, they could hold off the Navy with their new-found allies if they should raise the treasure and the Navy should return. Carver and Co assumed they would stay there from henceforward, or at least that night, but Chattel prepared his little nest out in the woods. They had no choice but to comply, he made it clear.

Around the fire that night, however, Carver and Thompson, aided by the enthusiasm of Seth Pond and Joshie Ward, tried to explain the value of what lay beneath the waves. They could not believe the lack of interest these black men showed, their lack of grasp of the enormous worth within their grasp. They thought perhaps they might be mocking them, pretending they did not know what wealth would bring, but Chattel was finally convincing. They fished and hunted, he explained. They exchanged flesh for vegetables and bread and sweetmeats, they consorted with women in the camps of other runaways and Maroons when they desired it. What benefits would silver bring? Among blacks they had no need for it, and the whites, if they found out, would merely take it all away. Merely? No — they would kill them all as thieves, he said. Thieves and slavemen who had run away.

Carver and Thompson, in the quiet of their sleeping spot, agreed that this was all completely true, so they worked out ways of making acquisition seem attractive. Wealth would buy freedom, they said next time the subject was brought up. It would buy weapons first of all, and weapons were what made the white man strong. And with money they could hide — even white servants on the plantations would hide them out for money — and with the treasure likewise hidden they could bargain the secret of its whereabouts for pledges they'd be free. It had not occurred to them before what freedom, reduced to terms, in fact did mean, and how complicated the getting of it was. Fat Mick tended to even feel a little sympathy for them and their quandary: but that was a passing phase. Thompson, a natural cynic, decided universal guns would be the draw, and carried on on that line, extolling the power they would have if each and every one of them could pour lead out of a musket muzzle, with a brace of pistols to back it at their side. In a minor way, the black men seemed to take the bait.

It was in a minor way, however, for they still appeared to find the sailors' greed amusing. The strongest impression they gave off was a desire to amuse themselves, to relive their early lives across the Carib sea when they had dived — presumably as slaves — to pick up pearls for the enrichment of their masters. Or at least seen others do it while they, as boys, had only watched in envy of the kudos and the expertise. They laughed a lot about it when their minds were made up, and rolled down to the stockade beach as if off on a holiday. Bob had been dispatched back to the caves and there were ten of them all told, plus the whites. Thompson and Pond, both handy men, had searched out useful baulks of wood to start to make a raft or similar for diving from, and Ward had stumbled on a broken-handled adze that alone was worth its weight in gold. But here again the escapers were more amused than anything, spoke to each other incomprehensibly in Kreyole, and split into two apparent searching parties. One lot returned in short order with some gourds of fresh water from a spring they knew, and half an hour after that there was a loud hallooing from offshore, and a light canoe, of reeds or bark or some such material, was seen heading round the point. It was for fishing in the normal way, Chattel told them, and was hidden down along the coast. So why not fish from it to catch the white men's dreams...?

The canoe itself was too flimsy for a diving platform, but between the crowd of them there were skills aplenty to make better things. The blacks had blades and axes, and great knowledge of the sort of woods there were available, and construction started soon on a substantial raft. By the time it was launched the canoe men had confirmed the diving site, aided by the fact that Kaye had not bothered to have the floating masthead stump removed before he sailed away, which gave them not just an easy sea mark, but a makeshift mooring buoy to boot. Before much time had passed, the black men were clamouring to dive.

It was a certain satisfaction to the *Biter* men that Chattel and his stalwarts found the game much harder than expected. They made their first dives more as jumps, with very little preparation, and although they swam down strongly they did not get really very far; maybe three fathoms was the best. They learned fast however, and before very long one two-man team could be seen through the clear water sinking at terrific speed, then stopping almost simultaneously six feet apart on a tilted lower yard close to the deck. As the jubilation grew Chris Thompson, self appointed as an overseer, persuaded Chattel that all divers had to go ashore from time to time, and drink fresh water, and eat fruit. "More haste, less speed," he said portentously, and they appeared to think that made him a philosopher. Chris Thompson, possibly for the first time in his life, began to be a happy man.

The first day was very long, and the next longer. One of the best divers seemed to burst an ear and could not go far below the surface after that, while another swallowed a mass of water and had to be dragged up by the line he had, by luck, been taking down with him. For they had reached the deck, at last, and were seeking things to draw up to the top. First came a fourfold block — no use to anyone but the thought was there — and then a sodden coat that had a doubloon in its pocket... a treasure trove indeed. The next part of the diver's trade was then revealed. They could get down to the roof of the treasure chest, so to speak, but then had to enter what was virtually a water-tomb. Seven attempts, and seven failures. At which Seth Pond began to laugh, and Ledermann furiously beat him from the beach into the water, then had the canoe sent ashore to take him to the raft. Pond, who could not swim, was forced to hug a rock and close his eyes and jump, and when the rock was lost and he was saved, was forced to jump again, this time to get it back. Thompson clashed with Ledermann, Chattel backed the white man up, and the evening was passed in bitterness. Pond, half drowned or more so, had clung on to the underside of the raft until forgotten, and moved around much like a phantom for the rest of that one night.

Next morning there was peace and harmony, and the diving was set fair to carry on. It had become in some way a matter of pride among the black men now, and the whites were hardly like to try and stop them. In truth, three of the divers were gaining confidence and skill, while Ledermann had dredged out from his memory the names of former friends from Gulf days, and some idea of where he might track them down in the west part of the island. Chattel was less sanguine that they might be found so easy, but did not deny "they must be somewhere round."

In meantime, though, the job went on, and on the first plunge of the day a skinny boy called Timba not only reached the deck but went in through the hatch and stayed out of sight until Chris Thompson was almost choking with vicarious fear of drowning. Then there was a double-jerk on one of the lines that were stretched from wreck to raft in permanency, and a sudden burst of air blew sideways from the hatch, followed by the jet-black sphere of the diver's head. One jerk was meant to signal that the surface men should pull up, but it appeared the line was fast. Timba burst from the water like a breaching dolphin though, and, recovered, insisted that they pull the harder. After some jiggling, movement was detected, and slowly a small chest was jerked and juggled into sight. It was heavy, a two-man haul, and they had to take it to the shore to break it open. Chattel and his crew were exceedingly excited by its very weight, but the Englishmen, for the self-same reason, were dubious. It was pigs of lead, and some small ones of iron, that Mr Gunner — Henderson — had collected up.

"Tight bastard," Carver hissed. "Who did he think would want to run away with that?"

The divers were still pleased, however, and paddled out for another try with enthusiasm renewed. Within an hour, two men were inside the hull, and a fair few knick-knacks — almost valueless — had been drawn up. The pattern went on all that day, with diving more successful, and spoils hardly worth the puff. The white men grew disheartened, but the blacks did not. Apparently, they really did not care about the "value" of the treasure.

And then, towards the dusk, a diver shot from deck to surface without a pull on the lifting line. His arm came over the raft side before the rest of him, and he dropped a leather bag that made a metal clinking sound that pricked up every ear. Thompson reached for it, and Chattel nearly broke his hand. It was a bag of doubloons, glittering and shining as if they had never been immersed.

And a shout went up, from off the nearest headland. It was Black Bob, who amused himself these days by keeping lookout.

"A sail!" he shrilled. "Sail ho! A sail!"

The *Jacqueline*, returned, refitted and full-manned for treasure seeking, was heaving round the point...

Chapter Twenty-Two

The second wave of depredations by the Siddlehams and Suttons was swift, and violent, and was bruited far abroad. The raids were done for justice, they insisted naturally, and justice, naturally, was buried deeper and more quickly than the corpses of the people that they overran. They fell upon Deb's old camp and maimed and killed with wild brutality. Mrs M was the oldest woman left alive, and they put her to the sword. The greybeard Dhanglli did not try to hide or run, and was struck down by a boy of seventeen. Then they spread out into the woods all round.

Deborah, who had not been there for many days, still heard of all the carnage as she and Mildred continued moving west. The bloodhounds had intelligence that she had gone and they struck out after her, but Mildred had better intelligence by far and they were always several jumps ahead. Alf Sutton on his infamous black mule was the leader of the most pugnacious thrust, because he had a personal desire to get at Miss Tomelty. Apart from anything else, he thought that having paid for her body not so long before he deserved to get a go at it. After that his son, most likely, then the Siddlehams, then sell her to the bloodhounds and the slaves. He had quite a detailed picture in his mind.

For white men, sadly, the climate and terrain made such well-laid plans more nearly fantasies. In getting on for a hundred years, they had only really conquered the areas that were flat enough and mild enough to take proper roads. However boldly Sutton pushed into the hinterland, he always ended up in bush and wilderness whose boundaries were undefined, but which boasted English parish names as if to make them respectable and real. They struck out from St Catherine, climbed over into St Dorothy, floundered in the badlands of southern Clarendon, then ran into the mountains of Elizabeth. There were tantalising hints that they were getting nearer to their prey, but Alf knew the "natives" well enough to know he could not trust them, and was hard-headed enough to know they were not to blame. Had it been his job to sell such "information," he well knew, it would have been even more expensive, and even less reliable. But determination blind and stubborn drove him on. He was still a Yorkshireman...

For Deb and Mildred, the journey was not easy. They knew where they were going — to find the man called Marlowe — and Mildred said that when they were far west enough he would in fact find them, because he knew of everyone who infiltrated his territory and would need to know their business. She said he was invincible, had not sold out to the white men like most Maroons with their treaties (a word Mildred spat out with contempt), and had no interest in casual butchery so would not just kill them out of hand. Deborah, whose view of men both black and white was more realistic, she felt, thought this Marlowe sounded too good to be true, but she had no alternative that she could see to believing, on the surface, what Mildred told her. Back eastward she was a criminal and a runaway, and her white pursuers did like butchery, or at least employed it as a weapon of control and vengeance. If this Marlowe was to chop her up, she told herself, at least she'd have had a country walk. Philosophy, she figured Will Bentley would have called that...

Deb thought a lot about Will as she and Mildred trudged and lurked across the centre of the island. Now she knew that he was here, she knew also and beyond all doubt that she was tied to him, part of him, and had to fight to gain her destiny. She had received word from Bridie that, however garbled by word-of-mouth transmission, convinced her that he felt the same, was still in love with her. Deb had tried quite hard to convince herself that she had got it wrong, but she could not. She got the messages in tortured English, in Kreyole, and in translation by Mildred from various Akan dialects. And she knew she would have believed it, deep down in her heart, even if they had said it was not true. She found herself from time to time just looking back towards the east, and murmuring: "I love you, Will." She was sanguine that such messaging was as likely as anything more concrete that she could hope to send of reaching her lover's ears.

What she and Mildred did hear, though, with increasing regularity, were tales of murder and depredation by the Siddleham and Sutton hunting crews. It must have been obvious to them very quickly that the people they accused of hiding Deb, or aiding her, were innocent, but it seemed a general campaign of revenge had been decided on, to teach some sort of lesson. Most of the victims were small bands like Deb's had been, neither Maroons nor serious disrupters, and incapable of organised resistance, or even fatal ambushes. What they also heard was that the Maroons who had lost Captain Jacob were becoming infected with the general rage as an addition to their fury over his untimely death. More and more, Mildred recounted, she was hearing rumours of an "expedition of revenge" against the white men.

This interested Deb at first, rather than frightening her, because she was not certain who the targets were. Although she blushed to think what her church would say, she had a hidden feeling that men like the Suttons, and the Siddlehams as well, deserved all that they might get. But when Mildred explained that it would be the people left behind on the cane plantations who would be attacked, she had second thoughts. With the masters and their bloodhounds gone, the knives and axes would fall upon the heads of the weakest slaves, and the women, and what children there might be. They would fall on Bridie also; and Bridie had risked everything for her.

"What can we do?" she asked. "Bridie is there, and I do not want Bridie hurt. Can we get warning to her, Mildred, do you think?"

Mildred laughed, her cold eyes glittering.

"You do forget you man," she said. "He the Navy in the town. He the protector army. Never mind that Bridie, girl. They going for chop up Mister Bill!"

"But he —" Deb stopped. Mildred was right. Will might not be at the Sutton or the Siddleham plantation if there was a raid, but he would be there the minute the alarm was raised, it would be his duty. But his ship had gone, his men had gone, he was...

"I don't forget him," she replied forlornly. "Mildred, can we warn him? Can we get a message back to Kingston? Or to Bridie? Please. Is it possible?"

Mildred rarely answered to such propositions in a clear, straight way. They did not, she pointed out, even know what Colonel Treatyman, Jacob's father, might have in mind. Treaty Maroons used the white men and were in their turn used, she said. A full-scale rebellion was not in the nature of such things. Before moving rashly, she intimated, they should be more sure. Next day, though, after long, hard discussions in a language Deb did not know with some more wanderers that they met, she told Deb that there might be at least a bloody raid. She pointed out again that both the Sutton and the grander place were defenceless. And that both of them, to the Windward Maroons, had Maroon blood on their hands.

"Oh God," said Deb. "Oh Mildred. How long have we got?"

Mildred did not know, but thought it was not long.

"I get a message through," she said. "I go tell Bridie woman through the Sutton housegals. I tell them hurry."

"But when? How quickly can the message go?"

"Him gone already," Mildred said. "Them words they moving now."

***

Chattel and his band did not waste much time in spying on the *Jacqueline* once she had settled down to a routine. They watched with great interest from very close onshore for the first few hours, aware that they were likely to be attacked, and fascinated by the way the Navy men would go about the diving. Chris Thompson, once the ship was seen, had got all divers up and heading for the shore like lightning, all rocks and other heaviness tipped off the raft to lighten her, the strongest men put on to paddling. Some of the black men swam, and the canoe lifted across the water like a wherry in a race.

On the beach there was a conference, with whites and blacks agreed that the raft should be destroyed, or hidden, anything to keep their operations dark. Again Chattel proved his worth as leader. He pointed out that they must have been seen by the lookouts on the ship, and even if they smashed their platform into pieces the fact of its existence could never be denied. Better remove and hide all the long lines they had used (evidence of diving operations), scatter some fishing gear they had onshore across the grounded raft as if they had abandoned it, and lift the cockleshell up the beach and hide it or destroy it. Pond suggested sinking it with rocks, and was looked at witheringly. Even at double fifteen fathoms it would be visible on the bottom as clear as daylight. A raft rigged out for fishing, though, might be believed. And the conference was ended by a flash of light, a rush of smoke, and a dull boom from the bow-chaser. They did not see the shot splash down, but it galvanised them. Within five minutes there was nothing on the beach but the abandoned raft.

They had ample time to take the canoe higher into the hinterland and hide it well beyond a white man's capability, before returning to watch the little brig drop hook. Before she did so, she fired a half a dozen shots into the stockade, presumably to see if any cannon fired back. Fat Mick Carver made a play of despair at this — despair at the folly of the British Navy — which drew appreciation from Chattel and some others of the escapers. Each time another chunk of hard-won fortification sang off into the firmament there was a small ironic cheer. Pond sealed his reputation as a simpleton by remarking, after some long, deep thought: "What bloody fools, eh boys? Our powder would be too wet to go off."

When the ship's boats came ashore stuffed with armed men, the band retreated to a higher and more sheltered point. It was somehow entrancing to watch the sailors crawling on their bellies, dragging cutlasses and muskets through the sand and hoping for invisibility behind each miserable little tuft of greenery. The poor marine contingent — two men now, no officer, no Rob Simms, but still unmissable in red, still deemed expendable by their overlord, Dick Kaye — were almost objects of pity and concern to the English fugitives.

The reconnaissance took the best part of an hour, including the final rush on the stockade amid a storm of whoops and shouts and roars. Then the armed sailors spread out along the beach, each contingent with an appointed leader, and began to push into the woods and foothills, with more zest now they were confident there was no lurking enemy. The lurkers, indeed, moved back and back, with their sense of pleasure not much diminished. Fat Mick and Thompson agreed at one point that the life of an old-time buccaneer might be quite attractive as a half-plan for the future. To have a ship, a base on land, and to pick off easy targets as the mood and opportunity presented...could that be improved upon? At dusk the Navy men went back, worried, no doubt, at how suddenly their world would turn to black, and the Chattel crew trailed them to the beach again, and watched them row out to the ship while a defence contingent went into the "fortress" and blocked and barred the entrance and the newly damaged walls. Possibly for the first time, none of the deserters wished that they could rejoin their former mates. They saw them now, even Pond when Mick and Thompson had got it through to him, as potential targets. The Jacquelines would strain their guts to get the treasure up. Then they would be sitting ducks.

"But there's not enough of us," said Seth, not unintelligently.

"But there's all these niggers," Fat Mick replied. "And there'll be others in the woods, won't there? They'll know 'em, won't they? All we've got to do is teach 'em what's good for 'em. Learn 'em the value of hard cash. And see if they can't get up some sort of army."

"Oh," said Seth. "Oh. Aye. And what then, then?"

"They lifts the treasure, and we takes it off of 'em," said Chris Thompson. "We goes and robs Slack Dickie of his prize. We'll enjoy that, won't we lads? We will..."

The process of persuasion that the treasure should not merely be abandoned was accepted by the Chattel band with surprising lack of argument. It seemed to the white men that the ineptitude of most of the Navy divers when they watched them the next day was a major part of that response. Timba in particular was filled with scorn at the shortness of the time they could stay under, and the elaborate paraphernalia of lines and sinkers that they needed to get down at all. They watched in fascination as first one, and then two and three of the sailors was pulled out in a gasping state, and were loathe to leave the entertainment even when Carver and his men were bored sick of it. But Ledermann and Chattel were prepared to listen as they watched, and were not amazed, but sanguine, at the idea that they might take control again if they had men enough.

"You would be chief man, yes?" asked Chattel, with transparent disingenuity. And Thompson, who was sharp as knives, responded instantly: "Nay, not at all. We need a leader, and we need a black man, and black men will do the diving, for we can't. You will be chief, and we can be your helpmeets."

"Black men do the fighting, too," said Chattel, patting the woodwork of his long pistol. "Black men get more black men, and white man's muskets. Black men can creep in wooden fortress, too. Black men can kill all white man."

They stayed one more night, and in the morning Timba was prevented from taking up position where he liked to watch, and the band of them moved out. There were fifteen or so all told, with the white men careful to behave as less than equals to the others, and Black Bob happy as chief scout, or spy. As they moved fairly quickly through the hilly, thick terrain, the small boy sped and ranged before, behind and round them, returning to report to Chattel and to Ledermann at not infrequent intervals. For once he was looking out for friends, not enemies, and he ranged with confident content.

Then, as he crossed a stretch of barren rock and rounded a bluff on to a small and sheltered plateau facing out to sea, he came across a band of eleven men. Black Bob stopped, and yelped, and tried to run. Five of the men were white, and one of them — tall, emaciated, with pale and curly beard and hair, jumped across at him faster than a spider and gripped him cruelly by the wrist. Black Bob's howl was cut off abruptly as another hand went to his neck. He had found the Lamont brothers. He had come across the Scots.

Chapter Twenty-Three

Black Bob's scream, although choked off, was enough to save his life this time. As he dangled from Wee Doddie's hand, his gurgling screech cut through the Caribbean air like a knife on glass and struck the ears of Chattel and his men. Before it ended, Seth Pond had let out his own involuntary cry, which carried back to the Lamonts and their cohorts in the sudden silence.

"Shut up!" hissed Fat Mick Carver, angrily. "Shut mouth, you fool!"

"Tssss!" went Chattel, sharply. His men, without an order, spread out into a hunting phalanx, and began moving forward, fast and silently, engorged with memories of their lost home, perhaps. Josh Ward and Carver, followed at a pace or two by Pond, went after them, made suddenly aware that they were at a natural disadvantage. The Africans had changed their attitude, were in control. Chattel had cocked his pistol, and his fellows' long blades had now appeared from their concealments — while the whites had only the short working knives they had been allowed when trust had been established. The speed at which they covered ground was, to the Navy men, astonishing.

Around the bluff the Scotsmen's band, although forewarned, had had no time to prepare or disappear. Chattel and Ledermann appeared from out of nowhere, at either end of a solid line of warriors, while Wee Dod and his group could only stand at bay. Dod had two other white men, short and powerful, armed with cutlasses, and some blacks with hacking knives. The *Biter* men, clear of the undergrowth, recognised their foe and were amazed.

"Christ!" said Carver. "It's Angus! Christ!"

"Wee Dod," corrected Thompson. "Not Angus, it's Wee Dod."

"That's Miller and old Taffy Morgan!" said Seth Pond. "I bloody thought that they were bloody dead!"

The balance was without a doubt in favour of the Chattel band. They were close to double the men that they confronted, and they had a gun. There was a hostage in the question, but Chattel and Ledermann were happy in the private knowledge that Black Bob, while a charming trinket, had no intrinsic value to their cause. He would be useful if the Scots thought they would take risks to rescue him, in that they might be taken off their guard that way. With that in mind the Chattels moved forward confidently, and were gratified to see Wee Doddie and his fellows moving back, to halt in the centre of the plateau, no shelter within a dozen yards all round. Chattel approached them frontally from one flank, Ledermann from the other. They came face-to-face two yards apart.

Wee Dod Lamont stared at them through his pale, blank eyes, his face revealing absolutely nothing. Not fear, not interest, not even a spirit of assessment. His face was long and thin as it had always been, his body as scrawny and muscular. Had his clothes not been a deal more raggedy, it could have been but yesterday his shipmates had last seen him, despite it had been many weeks. His right hand hung at his side, the cutlass tip resting on the ground, while his left hand held Black Bob's neck in a casual grip that clearly caused great pain.

"Ho, Dod!" said Seth, and Carver glared and hissed at him. On board the *Biter* the Lamont brothers had been deeply hated men. Now here was one of them at bay, at last a victim not a perpetrator, an unprecedented turn-up for the books. Wee Dod turned his pale eyes on Seth, and did not know him. That was fine by them.

"Drop down your arms," said Chattel, evenly.

"Why?"

"I go kill you."

"I go kill the loon."

The East Coast accent was so strong that even the English sailors could hardly understand what he was saying. The "loon," however, clearly was Black Bob, who cringed and shrieked as Dod put further pressure on his neck. Chattel merely laughed.

"Drop down your arms. Count one two three I go for kill you."

Chattel raised his big old horseman's piece and aimed fairly at the Scotsman's face. The muzzle was not six feet away, the barrel steady as a rock. Wee Dod Lamont was unaffected. His thin lips almost sneered.

"Christ," said Seth, hit by a sudden ray of understanding. "But where's the other two?"

A flash, a plume of smoke, a bang, and the shrieks and howling of innumerable birds. The ball hit Ledermann, not Chattel, who could have pulled his trigger out of shock if nothing else but did not. Ledermann, tall, powerful, beautiful, fell like a broken tree, the smoke from the point-blank shot flowing over him, a moving shroud. Angus

Lamont, just like his brother but a slight shade more robust, stepped from the trees, unsmiling. But his musket had not been fired yet.

"There's aye anither o's," was all he said.

Fat Mickey Carver, the leader of his own small band, now proved his leadership. Before Chattel could make a move, a decision, or even pull his trigger, he stepped smartly up behind him, and clubbed him flat into the temple with the hasp of his seaman's knife. It was a heavy blow, shrewdly aimed, and Chattel staggered sideways, all control destroyed. As Ward and Pond removed themselves from their black brothers with great deliberation to range in with the former enemy, Rabbie Lamont, the third pale, poison Scot, appeared from out the underbrush, his musket already half reloaded. Carver plucked the pistol from Chattel's hand, switched it sharply end-for-end, and proffered the butt to Dod.

"I've brought some handy niggers for you," he said, with rather strained joviality. "And there might be treasure, too."

As Dod pushed Black Bob to the ground, switched his cutlass to his left hand and took the pistol, one of his own black cohorts spoke to Chattel in an Akan tongue. Dod, without a pause, turned and shot him in the stomach. The man screamed briefly, then lay groaning.

"Aye," said Dod, to nobody and all. "Any ither gammers?" And to Carver: "Fit treasure? Or dae ye wint a bullet too?"

Carver, who had gone a little pale, essayed a smile.

"Treasure for the taking," he replied. "Can your slaves swim? Mine can, some of 'em. And Black Bob."

***

The Windward Maroons were well aware that the Siddlehams' plantation and the Sutton place were denuded of protectors as the white men and their bloodhounds rampaged wildly to the lee. It was a not unusual mistake that the planters made. One time in five that they went to wreak revenge and punishment on the stupid slaves, the stupid slaves struck back at empty houses, and boudoirs containing virgins with no protection but to scream and have the vapours. The island history was littered with such disasters; proving to the white men that the blacks were godless savages and to the black that whites were brainless fools. After every degradation a vast militia would be raised, slaves' meagre dwellings would be razed, and the exodus of returnees to good old England would roar upwards from its eternal trickle to a flood. For every white maiden raped and butchered five blacks would be hanged, four families return to the motherland, three prospective settlers change their minds and stay in Birmingham or Leeds. The taste for sugar in the English shires grew and grew.

In the Siddleham estate, the carnage was appalling. The Maroons swept down from Portland and the Blue Mountains not even late at night, and the slaves and workers who got wind in advance took care to disappear completely. A few, perhaps, felt a temptation to warn the overseers and slave drivers who had been left out of the bloodhound pack, but it was overcome, for fear that reprisals would inevitably follow. The white folk who were left — two minor household men, the dowager, Miss Marianne and her sisters Lucy and Elizabeth — suffered in varying degrees before they died, according, it appeared, to how they took the Maroons' tormenting. Marianne, haughty and outraged, was quickly gone, because she fought so wildly that she could not even be raped in any comfort, while the two younger girls excited their attackers with their screaming and were stripped and spreadeagled until they could take no more and then were strangled to cut off their incessant howling. Lady Siddleham, so plump and comfortable, saw what was coming and killed herself and two Maroons with a hidden pistol and a darning bodkin. The menfolk, on the other hand, were merely slaughtered, by knives across the neck.

Three slaves were also caught and killed, two household females taken off as booty, and all the crystalware was smashed and silken drapes and hangings pissed or shitten on. To Mr Mather, when he surveyed the scene in full daylight, it seemed depressingly familiar; he only wondered why they had not burnt the mansion down. And at the Suttons' place the scene was not dissimilar, although the materials were less opulent. All glass broken, all chairs and tables smashed, and two dead slaves nailed to a stable door. There were no women there, but no one knew how many there had been to start with. Except for Bridie Connor, and she had got away. This happenstance, when Mather thought about it, filled him with deep suspicion. She became his major suspect.

In fact, though, Bridie had escaped only because she had gone to give the warning. The network to the West had relayed the message from Mildred at breakneck speed, and it had reached its target — the white woman at the Suttons' place — early on that night. There would be a raid, no one knew when but very soon, as a reprisal on the beasts who had killed Captain Jacob Tsingi, and on their land, and slaves, and property. The final messenger had not known why the plantation dwellers should be warned, because they obviously deserved whatever they deserved, but the message from Mildred — that might have been ignored — was backed up by the name of Marlowe, which was sacrosanct. He had known Mildred in the past, it was relayed, and was prepared to do her bidding and wait to meet her face-to-face for explanations.

Bridie, who was astonished by the quiet, aromatic peace that surrounded the Sutton dwelling now Alf and Seth were gone, nevertheless hurried to Kingston as if her life depended on it. She had no ass or mule but she covered the miles in an almost tireless, rhythmic pace, her bare soles uncut or bothered by the hard and dusty road. She had heard many past stories of the things that bloodhounds and their mastermen had done, and she had no little knowledge of the reprisals taken on outlying, lonely houses and plantations. In truth she had no sympathy for the Suttons and their ilk, less for the high and mighty Siddlehams, but she was no lover of savage men of whatever creed or colour. She had hoped to find a better, fairer life on this green isle than she'd known on the bare and barren fields of her home country, but had been quickly disabused. Violence and hatred were the norm in Ireland; they were the norm here ditto. She was as sickened by the thought of black men killing white as vice versa.

It was not very late when she arrived at Holt and Bentley's lodgings, but they were fortunately there. They had eaten early, and might venture out to take a glass or two if the mood should take them later, they considered. Their landlady let Bridie in without demur, and she clattered up the stairs noisily enough for Sam to have the door open when she hove into sight. They were startled enough to see her, but her succinct exposition had them galvanised. She allowed no doubt that it was serious, she made it clear their instant task must be to alert the acting governor and raise militia.

"When will it come?" said Will. "Sooner, I guess, than later? 'Fore God, Sam, we cannot lose a minute!"

They pulled on coats for sake of protocol more than necessity, and in half a minute were in the narrow street. It was alive with noise and people, and reeked of mud and the detritus of a filthy dockland. Bridie began to hurry off in front of them, but Sam called her back while Will searched for wheeled transport. Failing which, he shouted to the mule man they often hired from, and got two big ones, and a double saddle. Bridie had no ladylike objection, and was thrown up behind Will like a farmer's wife, and gripped him as he beat the mule up into a run. Sam forged ahead and had no truck with slowpokes in the way, hallooing and whipping with brazen determination. Within minutes they were free of the traffic and chaos of the town.

"Which one first?" yelled Sam, across his shoulder. "Ought we to warn the people at the houses? There are maidens at the Siddlehams'. At the Suttons' too, for aught I know."

"They know it all already there," Bridie shouted back. "There might be some daft enough to linger, but I'm doubting it, amn't I? No one will try to save the house at all. Why should they, so? It is the Suttonses'!"

"But what of the people at the Siddlehams'?" asked Will. "Will they be warned? Did you send anyone to tell them to run clear?"

Even through the violent shaking of the mule he could feel the negative of her body movement.

"Who would have gone?" she said. "Why should the slaves risk... Ach, Misterhoney, you do not understand the half, do you? We have to get the army out. Take that road, up to Mr Mather now!"

Sam said: "But should we — must we not tell them? We could perhaps..."

Do nothing, was the truth of it, they knew. However few the Maroon men might turn out to be, they would be a match for two English Navy men with only blades and pistols. What hope they had of saving lives lay in pre-emption, with force brought in. Will kicked his mule up the rocky road to Mathers' house, with Samuel following. They went at breakneck speed.

Andrew Mather was entertaining guests, but social niceties were blown out of the water. At first the Kingston *tone* looked deep askance at the common woman up behind the small blond-headed officer, but two gabbled sentences altered all that. Wives and daughters were packed off to withdrawing rooms while the menfolk roared and shouted — some fired up already with the drink — and sent urgent messages to other militia officers and their men. To Will's surprise their speed and efficiency was of quite high order, and within an hour there were approaching fifty men-at-arms assembled, most with mules, some with asses, and the leading lights with the horses that they used for hunting, in the normal way.

Despite some jostling, the lead was clearly Mather's, and he spoke extremely sharply when Ephraim Dodds began his usual muttering against the Navy men. All the older planters known to Will and Sam were there, most of the younger having gone with the Siddlehams and Suttons on their jolly depredations, but they were robust enough, and had some canny, bulky fighters at their sides. They struck out into the aromatic night with anger and determination, which rose to anticipatory lust for blood as the Siddleham holding came into sight. The pace increased, and the final half a mile or so was taken at the charge. Had the attack not already taken place, it is likely some on the plantation might have died of fright. But, of course, it had.

The rushings and the shouting and hallooing turned quickly into a silence almost stunned. Bridie dropped down off Bentley's mule, looked about her, and slipped into the night. When they reached the Suttons' house an hour later, she was there, dry-eyed in the wilderness. By her calculation, she told Will, the raiders could not be many miles away, might have even been aware armed men had been on the move. Two corpses only, so the rest, she hoped, had made it clear away. Late next morning, Mather announced that Bridie was to be arrested, but changed his mind — Mather was not so stupid as some men on the Assembly chose to say he was — when the Navy officers gave him verse and chapter of the lead-up to the vile events.

On their other information, though, the acting governor was adamantine — and in full agreement with all the other grandees of the island. When they first told him that Deborah Tomelty had raised the alarm about the coming raid — through an escaped Sutton slave called Mildred, and by her through Bridie Connor — Mather had reacted with stubborn outrage. Deborah Tomelty and her ilk, it was insisted, had brought about the massacre, had met up with the Leeward men she had gone off to, and got them to raise a marauding party, and given them the targets to destroy. The deaths of Lady Siddleham, of Marianne and Lucy and Elizabeth, were her direct responsibility, and anyone who argued otherwise was a traitor and a fool.

Will Bentley did so argue, as did Sam Holt. They argued long and hard in the Assembly building, under the troubled gaze of Captain Shearing, and the baleful one of Lieutenant Jackson. They argued that the massacre was done by the Windward treaty men not as a result of the bloodhounds' depredations in the West but as a direct result of the death of Captain Jacob Tsingi. Mather, and Dodds, and Hodge and others of the island leaders denied it with the utmost fervour, and said that Treaty Maroons did not break treaties, it was impossible. And when Marlowe's name was mentioned — Will not even certain that he had remembered it aright — the case was lost.

"Marlowe!" roared Hodge. "You name Marlowe and innocence in one breath? You are not an island man, sir! Your lack of knowledge is a... is a..."

He spluttered off, before perhaps, he said something irrevocable in the way of gentlemanly honour. Sam and Will shared a glance, discomfitted, and Mather, very mildly, came to their aid.

"It is a noted renegade," he said. "A former slave, perhaps — history is indistinct upon the subject — who has disdained treaty offers in the past. He is known to kill without discrimination, black men as well as white. If Miss Tomelty is with him, then she is lost indeed."

"Miss Tomelty?" boomed Ephraim Dodds. "You give the slut a title, sir? You grace her with a token of respect? She is consorting with a murderer! She is of his band! She has led him to poor Lady Siddleham, to the poor maidens Lucy and Elizabeth! The poor, degraded, violated..."

He broke down on a sudden sob, undoubtedly genuine. The silence in the room was positively violent, but Bentley dared to speak.

"It is a rumour only, sirs," he said, quiet but distinctly. "Bridie Connor said only that the warning came through his good offices, because the woman Mildred knew of him and wished that bloodshed should be prevented. Bloodshed from the Windward men. From the Blue Mountains."

It brought only pandemonium. Almost every word that he had uttered was the opposite of what they wished to hear, or would believe. There was shouting for immediate reprisal, for an expedition, for mass executions, for the torture of the savage and the slut. The noise came to control only when a knocking on the door persisted until it could not be ignored. It was a black man, in the livery of the Navy offices. He looked beseechingly at Captain Shearing, but Lieutenant Jackson lurched up to him with an air of angry menace.

"Yes? You blunder in! Yes?"

The servant had a simple message, but it cut into Sam and Will like a stiletto. There was a ship. Off the Palisadoes. A fast gig had come ashore with a dispatch. The ship was called the *Pourquoi Pas*, but she flew the English flag. Her captain was called Captain Daniel Swift. He was preparing a salute.

"Shit and muffins," muttered Sam to Will. "She should have been the Bad Penny, shouldn't she? I think we're going to see some blood. I think we're like to wallow in it..."

Chapter Twenty-Four

The Scotsmen had a salvage crew, and now they had a phalanx of white men to rule and dominate the blacks, which was, they all agreed, as it should be. The man who'd spoken Akan soon died, in satisfactory agony, and Chattel was punched about a little by Wee Dod, man to man, in the age-old way of Aberdeen sea folk when establishing a hierarchy. Chattel, bloodied and bemused, was treated kindly after this humiliation, and told in language that he could barely comprehend that Dod was now his "mannie" and he was his mannie's "loon." One of the other blacks told him later — carefully in English, for fear he might be overheard and similarly shot — that it was not humiliating. The blond-beards were not humans, they were some kind of wizards or obeah men. They could swallow swords, shit bullets, and fly through the air at will. Chattel did not believe: and kept his counsel.

The Scotsmen also had their Black Bob back, and this filled them with a sort of glee that struck truly as inhuman. They did nothing physical at first, but he lived in terror once again, and they took the greatest pleasure from it. Wee Doddie, in particular, could bring the boy to tears, and even make him gibber like a tortured monkey, without a finger laid upon him. From time to time they paid him no concern, with such dedication that the boy began to feel that he was almost free. Indeed, they left him once, deliberately, to see if he would run, so they could hunt him down and punish him. He was alone for an hour, deep in the woods, no sight of any human, black or white. And he sat there, whimpering, and did not move an inch. Rabbie crept up behind him after that, to punish him in any case. He did it with his tongue.

None of Bob's fellows, white or black, could help in any way. Carver and Co, who had not known him well on board the *Biter*, had grown to appreciate his odd contentment and his bright black eyes, and watched with churning stomachs as the Lamonts toyed with him. They said nothing, cue taken from Barrel Morgan and Dusty Miller, who had been with the Scotsmen for an age by now, and knew the rules to stay alive. Chattel and his men, and the renegades who had teamed up with the Scots already, suffered for the boy in their way, or were perhaps indifferent, how could the white men tell? But the boy was suffering, not a manjack of them could avoid sight of that, however much they tried. Had he had a blade, or found a cliff to do it from, he might have killed himself, they thought.

The blacks who had taken Carver and his fellows captive had professed no interest in the *Biter* treasure, but the Lamont brothers were interested in nothing else. They had a camp quite close to the plateau where Bob had been ambushed, and for the first night repaired there with all their new-found cohorts. Not to eat or drink — certainly not be merry — but to fillet them like landed fish for every bit of information that they knew. There was food, of course, and drink, but the purpose was to cement the bonds — slavery, in effect, both for the black men and the free — that bound the Lamont's people. They heard of Kaye's first attempts at diving, of the exodus and slaughter of the other mutineers, of the building of the palisade, the arrival of the French ship with Bentley and London Jack on board, the continued attempts at salvage, and the ship's departure and eventual return. Carver and his fellows praised up the diving boys that they had "trained," spoke of their success, spoke of the iron balls and pigs they had lifted in the chest, cursed Gunner Henderson for that trick, or jest, whatever it might be. Then fell an awkward silence. No money had been mentioned, no silver nor doubloons

Fat Mickie Carver tried for brazenness, and a licked lip gave him away. Angus and his brothers looked at him in the throbbing night, and the fire threw shadows across his bulbous cheeks in a way that might have been amusing. He licked his lip once more and knew that he was lost. Seth Pond — always the first to give the game away — let out a kind of groan. Wee Doddie spoke.

"Fair ussi' 'en?"

Carver tried for courage, now. The Scotsmen could not know, could they?

"Where's what?"

"Fit? Dae wanni fikkin dee?"

Mick Carver did not want to die. He put his hand inside his shirt and pulled out a leather drawstring bag. He opened it to show it inside-out. It was quite empty. And then Mick Carver smiled. It had been his little joke.

"There's the bag," he said. "The nigger's got the money. He thought he was top dog. Well, you've got to humour them, ain't you?"

The black men did not find it funny and nor, apparently, did the Scots. But Chattel was a realist, and produced the coins without a murmur. Angus took them, looked at them, and shoved them carelessly into a pocket. It occurred to Carver that there might be more, hidden on the corpse of Ledermann. Perhaps some time he'd take a look, if the beasts had not scattered the meat and bones too far.

"There's plenty more where they came from," said Seth, ingratiatingly. "Timba got them. He's your man."

Timba smiled, a smile of pride and pleasure.

"I best," he said. "Good divee man. Go get up all him treasure."

The Scots ignored him — it was their method, Carver decided, to listen hard, say nothing, pick their course of action — but they moved on to the current situation, Slack Dickie's return, the renewed salvage by Royal Navy men. Timba, anxious now for more appreciation maybe, poured scorn on "white man divee boys," and said they would not get it if they tried until the moon grew ears. Dod silenced him with savagery, but picked the brains of Carver and the whites, who agreed that Dick was slow, but guessed that he could do it, given time. Except, said Fat Mick, carefully, time was at a premium.

The Lamonts looked at him, eyes level, uninterested. Like hell, thought Mick; like hell.

"Well," he continued, "it stands to reason, don't it? We're the Navy. We got sent out to the Carib to do some sort of job, not play pop and buggery. There's a war on, ain't there? Pound to a pennyworth of shit Slack Dick'll get called back to Kingston. He'll have to leave it. And then..."

He stopped. The three pale-haired men regarded him.

"Fit?"

"And then we carry on. If they've lifted any they'll take it with them, maybe, or maybe leave it in the fort. But they won't have got a lot. They got no nigger lads to do the going down."

Timba smiled, his silencing forgotten.

"Nigger-lads good divee men. Me best nigger-lad."

"Leave it innee for'? Wi'oot a guard an'all? Why shouldee dee 'at?"

Carver felt he had the upper hand. Knowledge was power. But his answer to the Scot was polite, and deferential.

"If'n they took it back to Port Royal somebody'd notice, the lads would boast. But the *Biter* don't exist no more, do she? Even dippy Dickie ain't going to let their lordships know he's got the silver. Is he?"

"So the stuff 'll be there," explained Seth Pond. "Slack Dickie'll..."

The intensity of their pale grey eyes penetrated even Pond's stupidity. He shut up.

Carver said: "In any way, if they've taken it or no, there's still a bloody hold-full, ain't there? And we've got the divers and the guns. And, if they came back sudden-like, we've got the bloody fort as well. Now come on, Angus — we've done all right, ain't we? There's treasure for the picking. And it's ours."

"How far uz it?" said Angus. "Mebbe time we took a wee keek."

"We need more men, an'all," said Fat Mickie. His voice was filled with satisfaction, and relief. "We need more divers, and Chattel here can find 'em for us. We were searching when Black Bobbie blundered into you. Chattel says we'll find some men nearby."

"Guid," Wee Doddie said. He turned his gaze on Chattel. "If ye dinnae, ma wee loon — ye'll be paying wi' yer ba's. Aye. Ye'd best believe."

Chattel did believe. But still he kept his counsel.

***

Deborah and Mildred were certain that their presence was known about, recorded, for every mile they penetrated out towards the West. Although they were lone females they were not molested, and neither did they starve, but they had no clear knowledge if the communication worked both ways, or if they were getting near their goal. They gave messages to be conveyed to Bridie, but they did not know for sure that she had got them. They heard that there had been a "slaughtering" in the East, but they had no idea who had been involved. Deb asked, in English and Kreyole, about white sailormen, or ships, or about the fate of Bridie, but got no significant reply. Mildred spoke in native languages, but said that she learned nothing, either. But she remained confident, she insisted, that if the bloodhounds were still in the hunt for them they were no nearer, and that if real danger should threaten them, somehow they would be saved. Marlowe would find them when it pleased him to. When he was sure, perhaps, the white maiden was no spy.

They were heading for the badlands in the West, beyond the Cock Pits possibly, but they took a southern route to avoid the harshest of the high terrain and the lower marshlands. The way was long and hard, as they had also to avoid plantations and the settled black communities that might betray them, and was inevitably convergent with the path the Lamonts took while striking northward seeking extra men. The Scotsmen's fame — or infamy — had already spread among those blacks in this part of the island who were neither still in servitude nor had "sold out" to treaties that made them "white men's lackeys," and despite their reputation was as hard and evil, the Lamonts had some attractions, too. They were fiercely violent it was said, but would kill whites as happily as blacks, and would win gold for those who wanted it and weapons for those who preferred a short life but a jolly one. They thus recruited many would-be divers, and many more fighting men. They also heard about the white maid wandering the forests. And they wanted her.

Mildred and Deborah, conversely, had heard about the "white man gang," and Deb's first great hopes of succour from them had quickly been dispelled. The news had come first in Kreyole too fast for her to follow, but she had caught essentials that made her question Mildred when they were again alone. The more guarded and elusive her friend's replies, the more worried she became. Surely Mildred was not betraying her?

"Mildred," she said at last. "What is wrong? Why aren't you telling me? There are white men, aren't there? English sailors off a wreck. We must find them, surely? They will help me. They will help *us*! They are my countrymen!"

Mildred's face was troubled.

"Bad men," she said. "All people say they bad men. All people say we must not let them come to us. They go kill or fuck, not help. All people say we see them we must run."

Deb, in her anxiety to talk to whites again, perhaps, to get her feet back on reality, was half aware her longing was leading her to deny things that she knew. She had seen so many acts of beasts on this lush island, acts by blacks as well as whites, that she knew she should believe anything was possible, from anyone. But she felt that if she could just see an English face, could just show back an English smile, all would be explainable, explained, achieved. White to white, there must be understanding.

As luck would have it, though, it was Black Bob who found them, and Black Bob whose warnings she believed. He popped from a thicket one late afternoon rather like a showman's toy, and made both women jump. It was not terror — he was too small, too neat, too fragile to terrify — but a mixture of surprise and concern for his well-being, not their own. He had not come upon them by accident, surely, but — arrived — his whole demeanour screamed that he should not remain. He stood and gaped, as if to speak but struck incapable.

"Eyoop," said Deb, reverting in an instant through countless miles of time and distance, and talking to a Cheshire child again. "Where art'oo sprung from, tha lickle boggart!"

Bob's eyes, in the gloaming, were enormous, full of woe.

"You go!" he said. "They come for you! You go! They kill!"

"Who?" said Deb.

There was a bellow in the undergrowth, a white man's voice, a roar. Bob's eyes changed, they clouded, his face was charged with fear.

"You run! You run! Scotchman go for kill you! You run!"

As Bob began to run himself, an enormous fat man blundered from the woods twenty yards away. He stared straight through the women, seeming to catch the sight of Bob as he darted into the bushes, and to their amazement, levelled a pistol, which he discharged at the area the boy had disappeared into. Deb let out a scream and Mildred hushed her urgently. But they had been seen, no doubt of it. The fat man shouted.

"Angus! Here, man! Here! The bastard has betrayed us!"

He began to limp towards them, as if unsure of which pursuit would be the better one. And they heard more shouting, more crashings through thick underbrush. Mildred gripped Deb at the instant Deb seized her, and they ran towards the far side of the clearing with the speed of utter terror. As they left the space they could hear the fat man hollering, they could hear new shouts, both near and distant. They were running for their lives.

The land between the shore and foothills was wooded, harsh and difficult, with innumerable boggy patches that could have trapped them any time. Their advantages were few beyond the exquisite spur of desperation, though both were lean and hardened by their long days running West. But they had no goal to aim for save for further westing, no safe house or cave or settlement they knew that they could surely reach, nor did they have the least idea of the numbers in pursuit of them. For the first ten minutes they had no idea, even, if the hunt was up, as the greatest sounds they heard were the searing of their own breaths, their footfalls, and the whips and crackings of fronds and branches as they thrust themselves onwards. The only cries they heard were when one or other banged bare feet into a stone, or slipped, or was lashed by swinging boughs.

After some short while, though, they heard loud voices, and a general view-halloo. As far as they could tell, the chase was not directly to their rear only, but spread out and widening. Ahead they had uncharted country, thick brush and clearer land interspersed, and for all they knew an end to cover altogether. Luck alone could save them: they had no other resource to pray upon.

Luck or darkness. Mildred hissed out a hope that night should fall extremely soon, in which case, if the woods did not run out on them, they might yet go to ground or become less visible. But there was no way of telling how soon the dark would fall. The sun was low, but they could not see a stretch of sky enough to judge. And in any way, they were not far ahead; not far enough, perhaps, to find a place that would not be found out by the searchers.

Deb's throat was searing as they burst from the cover and out onto grassy downward hill. Ahead of them three hundred yards there was another, thicker covert, and over to her leftward, a long long way away, she caught a flash of green, with silver waves upon it, which flooded her, unexpectedly, with a raw despair. Then, more to the left but closer, she saw a black man moving in the woodland, black face, black hair, pale shirt. Behind him came another, then she saw a white. And beside her, phlegmatic Mildred gave out a yelp.

"To there!" she said. "Go there!"

She pushed Deb's arm, trying to drive her left, towards the danger. Deb jerked back, pointing with her free hand, and Mildred gasped.

"Straight on!" Deb said. "It's our only way!"

As they crossed the clearing men came from the trees to left and right of them and, for all they knew, immediately behind. They were still out clear, not yet outflanked, but Deb was tiring, her legs becoming leaden. A block rose up within her gorge, she thought that she would choke on it, would have to seize her throat and tear at it to let more air go in. She was stumbling, one knee gave way a moment, then she staggered onwards. To her left she saw a blade flash in the lowered sun, she heard a general clash of shouts and cries. The sense of hopelessness was almost drowning out the pain.

Mildred reached the trees a step in front of her and glanced across her shoulder to make sure Deb was still upright. Her face was in a fierce grimace, her lips stretched over her teeth as she gasped for breath. Beyond her Deb saw the darkness of the forest, then a sight that hit her like a blow.

"Mildr—" she screamed, then shut off as a hard hand knocked her sideways. She staggered, heard Mildred shout, then was roughly seized by the upper arm and pulled out of the sunlight, blinded by the sudden gloom. But a black man's face was close to her, she felt his breath and hands.

"Debbeerah!" shouted Mildred. "Debbeerah! They got us, girl! Debbeerah!"

And they were jerked and bundled deep into the woods. Deb heard a shot, she heard triumphant cries. Hands, hard and rough, were dragging her along.

Chapter Twenty-Five

Daniel Swift's trim vessel was called the *Pourquoi Pas*, but he did not explain the joke to any of the higher folk who saw him as their saviour in Jamaica. She had been called the *Cybèle* when he had taken her in the Atlantic, and also in the affidavit he had sworn before a Dutch advocate in St Eustatius that confirmed her as a total loss. His people, had they ever heard the story, would have been astonished to learn that the prize had actually been overwhelmed and sunk just one day before they'd nursed her into harbour with the surviving slaves on board, but for them — with three weeks of liberty to kill while their own ship, the *Beauty*, was being disposed of — the matter did not arise. Few of them, if any, even connected the new-rigged flyer they joined at the end of furlough with the filthy old slaver tub they had captured. She was a fine replacement ship, thank God, the *Beast* had gone to glory, and Daniel Swift, although a hard bastard, had done them right again. He even broke out gallons of local rum to wet the new ship's fresh-hewn figurehead! Similarly, they did not think to wonder where the rescued slaves had gone, or where, indeed, their share of any prize money.

The slaves had gone, in fact, as part of the splendid deal that Swift had struck with the advocate, Bertius Lahn, and others of St Eustacius's least scrupulous commercial-legal community. They had refined and perfected his simple proposition into a thing of elegance that was acceptable to all, including his lieutenants Anderson and Ireland and the less amenable Peter Dorrint, master. They had sold the slaves for him — slaves they insisted did not in fact exist — and had certified that he had found the *Cybèle*, abandoned and completely empty of human life in a violent storm, then towed her valiantly until another blow had done for her, despite his sterling efforts. His own vessel, the *Beauty*, having been severely damaged in the struggle, they swore on oath that they had paid Captain Swift a certain sum for her, from their own funds, and sold her on to be dismantled (certificate appended).

So the *Cybèle* had been lost, the *Beauty* scrapped, and Captain Swift and company were without a ship or home. However — the *Cybèle* had not only clearly been a legitimate prize but also, more importantly, a derelict he had been forced to board, by law and custom of the sea, in case there still existed persons there on board to save. Sadly there had not, but there had been ship's papers, and the ship, of course, had been insured. As her taking had been not an act of war, nor an act of piracy, her value could be legally recovered once a salvaging deal had been struck with her legitimate owners. And most amusingly, for the Dutchmen, she was insured by Lloyd's of London.

This last circumstance, which meant that no one save for rich gentlemen in England would suffer any sort of financial damage for the loss of a slaver owned by France, their mortal enemy, struck them as rather jolly, more so as the world-wide success of Lloyd's was a thorn and an embarrassment to compatriots back in Amsterdam. But later in Jamaica, when Swift told a (heavily censored) version of the saga to planters at a dinner-party in his honour, he nearly fell into a quagmire. Some of the guests it turned out, desperate to hedge their bets, invested much in Lloyd's, and were horrified to learn the company was prepared to "bail out the Frogs" at the expense of them and other noble patriots. Luckily, he was able to turn it just in time.

To Swift, though, the whole thing meant only this: his associates on St Eustatius, knowing they would draw substantially on a craft that had cost them not a florin (the *Cybèle*), paid the minimal docking and rerigging costs, and "sold" him a non-existent vessel called the *Pourquoi Pas* (the *Cybèle*), to present to the Admiralty at a knockdown bargain price, fully receipted, which remarkably was what they had paid him for the *Beauty*! No money actually changed hands, but the St Eustatians had cash to come from Lloyd's (for the *Cybèle*), Swift had a new and handy fighting vessel (the *Cybèle*), and when he got her back to England their lordships could only marvel at his perspicacity! There was even cash left from the sale of slaves to sweeten his officers and buy rum to keep the people dull. It was perfection, and made him very proud. He could hardly wait to try his commercial skills in buying up Jamaica...

His reception on the island, though, was unusual in the extreme, and extremely unsatisfactory in terms of Swift's beloved Navy protocol. Ireland, who had sailed on ahead in the gig to prepare their welcome, had been told bluntly by Lieutenant Jackson that far from awaiting a salute, they should enter into the outer harbour, drop anchor where indicated, and wait. If they wished to "bang off guns" — Jackson's very words, Ireland swore on returning with the pilot —

that was their privilege. But no batteries would make reply because no orders had been given, nor would they be. Daniel Swift, for once, was robbed of a reply. He gazed at Ireland till his grey eyes glittered, but he seemed incapable of a reaction. It was the pilot who broke the spell. He was a black man, most oddly, not in uniform of any kind, and not in the least degree intimidated by this little ice-eyed officer, quite unaware he had no place or liberty to speak.

"Big trouble pass Kingston Town, sir," he said. "Bakra ladies chop in little pieces. Massas all at six'n'seven. Big slaughter soon. I put you in nice place close to shore."

He turned to Peter Dorrint almost casually.

"Mr Master, sir? You back headsails now, brace foreyard round, go in on starboard tack, we clear them rock off larboard bow then come about off that ol' blockhouse there, see? Hey lookee – 'nother boat come off! Hey! Fellowmen! Man him braces dere! Man him sheet and braces!"

Swift, not used to backing down, took this presented opportunity to stamp to his weather quarterdeck and stand glowering at the small boat winging towards them. The breeze, though light, was fine for her, and she made a cracking pace. As she rounded up at the boarding ladder in the waist his senior midshipman, Pardoe, tried to catch his eye and gabbled: "It is English officers, sir! Shall Pollard salute them, sir? Here, man! Mr Boatswain, saluting party, sir!"

Swift, though, was sick of slackness and such footling about. He stormed across the quarterdeck ready to sear the skin off any other man prepared to make a booby of him, be his rank anywhere beneath that of First Lord itself. His mouth opened in a snarl, then softened into a sudden shout of laughter.

"By Christ!" he roared. "It had to be, it damn well had to be! Nephew! By all that's shameful! It's you that's brought this place to blazes, is it not! Give me a whip and let me flay some hides!"

That he was tickled pink there was no doubt, and that he missed the sombre, sober air of his nephew and Sam Holt was no surprise to anyone who knew him. Swift positively swaggered to the waist and wreathed his sharp features in smiles as they came on board. He went so far as to ignore Bentley's salute, and seize his upper arm and clap him on the shoulder.

"Some sanity!" he cried. "Some sanity among the slackness! What is passing in this damn place, Lieutenant? I have this fine new ship beneath me, and no one gives a fig. A twenty one salute is what I bargained for! What's up?"

"Sir," said Bentley. "I beg your pardon, on behalf of Captain Shearing in command here. He conveys apologies but there has been... Well, a massacre. A terrible disaster, sir."

Suddenly there was shouting from the quarterdeck and con, as the pilot and the master brought the vessel round into the wind and prepared to have them let the anchor go. The mainsail foot bade fair to knock off hats and wigs at least and the three of them were frankly in the way, though not a manjack dared to say it, naturally.

Swift jerked his head however, and they followed him across the waist to the companion-way. Above them all was pandemonium as the *Pourquoi Pas* came to her anchorage. Swift clicked his fingers, and a serving man brought a decanter on a tray, then was dismissed. The captain poured the drinks himself, and they were large ones.

"Well well!" he said. "Well met indeed, young William. And Mr Holt, so how are you; of course you are, you're excellent! What think you to my new ship, then? A prize indeed, eh? I stole her off the French, between the three of us, and the French have paid for her, an'all! More of that later, though! Mum's the word, you understand! She's called the *Pourquoi Pas*, and why not, eh?! Why not, indeed! The people call her Porky Pie, low bastards that they are, and why not for that as well? Everybody's happy though, that I can promise you. And *Pourquoi Pas*?!"

A rap came at the cabin door and Lieutenant Anderson reported that they were lying to the anchor, holding well, and should he order a harbour stow? Captain Swift, without even the courtesy of introducing him, assented with an impatient wave. Then, as an afterthought, told Anderson to "give a go of rum all round when everything is shipshape." His smile grew dazzling as he played it on Will and Sam once more.

"You see, boys? Captain Dan now runs a happy ship! Oh yes indeed!"

The windows were all open and the fresh sea smells blew gently in, but Will's sense of discomfort would be hard to dispel, however much he worked at remembering his relative's strange ways. He had come across in haste to tell of the awful bloodbath, and to convey the island expectation that they, the Navy, were the power and the people who must put it right, and Swift, as ever, was locked up in his own universe. And then, without a step change, he was back. His eyes narrowed, his sharp nose raised up, he looked into Bentley's face and said: "What massacre? What terrible disaster? Come on, boy; spit it out."

With almost visible relief, the two lieutenants began to spell it out. They used broad brushstrokes — the death of Sir Nathaniel after some trouble with a slave band, the reprisals, the awful aftermath — and Swift locked on it like a terrier.

"How many dead?" he demanded. "What — the females quite defenceless? By God, the Afric savages! We must go and cut them all to Hell! But where is Captain Kaye in all of this? He has gone down West already, has he? I do not see the *Biter* here."

They looked at each other. He did not know. Last time he'd heard of them, or from them, he'd been in England still, probably in the Thames. Will's heart was sinking. There was Captain Kaye, and Marianne Siddleham, now dead, there was the Spanish treasure, the *Biter* wrecked, the mutineers, the Scots, and there was Deb. He swallowed. He hardly had the heart for it. He gestured with his glass, and noticed it was empty. Swift noticed also, and lifted the decanter. Will, clearly at some kind of loss, stood up and took it from him. He filled their glasses, remaining standing, then he shrugged.

"You see, sir, it is complicated. Captain Kaye is to westward, but... but he's not seeking the renegades, he is..."

"He is checking on a Spanish ship that sunk, sir," Holt said crisply. "A task we undertook for Captain Shearing. So although he has entered into association with the Siddlehams, as we all have in a way, he does not know of the dreadful murders, yet. He does not know that... that his *fiancée*... that the young woman that he understands is... Well, she is dead, sir. She is slaughtered. With her mother, Lady Siddleham, and her sisters. It is... rather horrible I fear, sir. It is bestial."

Captain Swift's eyes were levelled on them both, his gaze was penetrating. He raised his glass to lips and tossed his head back, to sink it in one swallow.

"Christ," he said. "What, Dickie is betrothed? We had better go onshore then, hadn't we?"

***

The hopes and expectations of the island men, when Swift moved among them and made his assessments and prognostications, rose higher, and faster, than they had dreamed possible. He stood among the ruins of the Siddlehams' lives and happiness, he contemplated the tragic bodies of the ones that they had loved, and he swore that they would be avenged, and quickly. The brothers, brought back helter-skelter from their fruitless ramblings, observed their ravaged flesh and blood with stony faces, then moved to the Navy offices until their home should be remade tenable to plan the next moves against the "forces of the dark."

They told Swift who the villains were — a murderer called Marlowe and the English whore — and said that it would need a major expedition to dislodge and punish them. At the mention of the whore Swift expressed shocked amazement, more so when some details were filled in that the two lieutenants had not "been bothered to vouchsafe me." And more so still when Lieutenant Bentley, white about the face, insisted that the maiden had not been proved in any way to be a culprit, nor was she known for certain to have ever met this so-called renegade.

"Indeed," he said, "our information is that she sent warnings that this outrage would take place, conveyed by a woman called Bridie Connor who you can interview! I declare, sir, that the culprits were not even Leeward men, but government Maroons!"

"A woman!?" shouted Ephraim Dodds, through purple lips. "This Connor is no woman, she is another strumpet, sir, she is an Irish Papist! How do you know these harlots?" he shot at William. "There is whoredom in this, and now we mark it! Is the other one your friend's, indeed? I've hit the spot with that one, have I not!?"

William was enraged.

"Had she not warned us, sir—"

But what? Sam winced. The warning had been too late, in any way. He tried to help his friend.

"She warned us and she said specifically," he interposed, "that the maiden was not with the renegade. She is with another woman only, and they are fleeing—"

"Enough," roared Swift. His eyes were venomous. He raised his head up with a fearsome jerk. He glared at his two young officers.

"Mr Bentley, Mr Holt, you both forget yourselves! We have no interest in such sordidities." He stopped, his nostrils flaring. For a moment there was silence in the room. Then he let a breath out sharply, down his nose. He made a gesture round the company, a sign that they should move things on. "Suffice to say," he added, "that Marlowe is our man, suffice to say these crimes are of the blackest dye. My lords and gentlemen, we must first regroup, we must gather up our forces and make immediate foray. How many men are ranked against us? How well armed? How far away is Marlowe's stronghold, how long to get there? Must we go by land or sea, do we have exact location and if not do we have the spies? Captain Shearing, sir, you are the grand commander here. Do you have Navy forces? Ships? Armaments? How much time is needed before we can go forth?"

The crowded Navy Office room was buzzing with energy and excitement. Jeremy Siddleham, intensely flushed, intensely moved, strode across the room as from a gunbarrel and grasped Swift's hand and pumped it frantically.

"Thank God you're here, sir!" he said, brokenly. "Thank God at last we have a man of action in our midst!"

Other men joined in the congratulations, including grouchy Dodds and his morose companion Peter Hodge. Lieutenant Jackson had a sneer upon his face, but he directed it at Will and Holt when it was noticed, while Captain Shearing, as calm as always, rested on his special chair-arm and smiled sardonically at no one in particular. Swift cleared from out the ruck as soon as maybe, with a fine display of embarrassed modesty.

"An inner group," he said. "Gentlemen, please, control yourselves. We need an inner circle of the most senior, and those with certain knowledges. Captain Shearing, forgive me, sir, if I seem to blunder in upon your purlieus. I bow to you in everything of course, sir, in this matter. And Mr — Mather is it, do forgive me? — yes, Mr Mather; I promise you that this shall be a joint venture, in every way. You command the land forces, I assume? Let us, to begin with, sirs, remove to a private office and put our strengths and stratagems upon the table and correctly ordered out. I beg of you, gentlemen — we must clear the decks!"

There was little grumbling at this, almost to Will's surprise, and he was himself impressed by his uncle's new-found authority. Where once he would have blustered he now had the tactics all in focus, and gave off an aura of genuine command. Lieutenant Jackson indicated an inner room, and made it clear who should or should not go inside. It was Captain Swift, however, who stopped Sam and Bentley from walking in. Jackson's mean features smirked anew.

Although Swift's look was hardly friendly, however, he made it plain it was no punishment. He had another need from them.

"Where is Kaye?" he asked them, when he was sure they were not overheard. "Down west where exactly? I require that you get to him and get him back, instanter. I cannot have him swanning off alone, he is an arrant booby but who bears the weight still of his father's hopes – and mine. I am disappointed in the pair of you that you have let him from your sight. I instructed you to be his brains!"

This was so extraordinary that they almost goggled, but Swift's odd eyes appeared to signify some sort of joke. Suddenly, and even less expectedly, he shot out a hand and clasped Bentley by the wrist. His other hand he put on Sam Holt's shoulder.

"Believe me, my boys," he said, "I am very glad to see you. I have a ship, I have some men, and now it looks I'll have hot work to blow the tedium away." He twinkled. "And when we've saved the bacon of these namby island toadies, my God, they'll break their necks to make rich men of us, we'll have them eating from our very hands."

A sudden shout of laughter.

"Even if," he added, "Slack Dickie's plan has gone awry! To marry a rich heiress — now that would have been a masterstroke, indeed. Poor old Dickie. However does he do it, eh?"

Chapter Twenty-Six

The task set Will and Sam, it seemed to them, was simple. Within half an hour of their interview with Swift they were inspecting the small gig that Jackson had set aside for them, and ordering provisions for their hop along the coast. They had considered taking Manning and Rosser, two of the malaria men who were nearly fit again, but the boat was not too handy and would get along much better without extra weight, they thought. The mast and sail brought from the store were barely adequate, and she would be under-canvassed even for the pair of them. The boat was not ideal, and filthy, and was inclined to leakiness: just what Jackson would have wished for them, they guessed.

It took the best part of a day to get all ready, and the general chaos on the shore was hardly over when they were set to go, so there was little ceremony in their parting. Swift had merely nodded them off when they had fetched up at the Offices, and urged them to sail like demons and to "drag Kaye back with them by the scruff" if need be. Had they not noticed Bridie on the waterfront, they would have set sail totally unheeded. She was lurking in the shadows of a warehouse, as near as maybe to invisible, and they were already setting out when at last she waved.

"Good God," said Holt, who caught the signal. "Bridie, is that you? What do you here, Mistress? Will, grab that post! Shit. There. Ah, that's got her."

Bridie Connor was nervous in extreme. She glanced about as if expecting to be arrested, or attacked. The young men were largely unaware how heavily suspicion was laid upon her still.

"Now, now!" said William, rather fatuously. "No need for this, is there? What is it, Bridie?" He stopped, heart leaping with a sudden hope. "You have not any news, have you?"

She had, but it was not good. She had been contacted in the night, she said, by one of the messengers used by Mildred in the past, and it appeared that the two women had been attacked, and maybe taken. Little clear was known, as neither of them had been seen by the messenger, but the situation was grim. Perhaps Marlowe would rescue them, she said, when she saw Will's face as he took in the news, or perhaps he had already — it was possible. She had hoped that they might have convinced "the new Captain" that Deb was not a traitor. She did not need to study long to understand it was a forlorn hope. But she had thought she had to tell them what she'd heard. God forgive her that it was so sadly garbled.

Though cast down, both thanked her with sincerity, and both pressed money on her. Not for her trouble, but because they knew that she might need it urgently, and soon. Bridie, face strained, tried to smile that thought away, and failed. Indeed, she admitted, she was unsure now where she could safely stay, if anywhere.

Their feelings of foreboding were not helped when they cleared the outer entrances to the harbour and realised that they were in for heavy weather. The sun still shone, the sky was still pale azure, but there was something in the nature of the seaway that alerted them to coming change. The seas were long but getting shorter, or rather were marked by inconsistency, and with increasing frequency the gig's easy, rolling motion as she fled along was altered by a sudden stagger. Although they did not know the Carib patterns well yet, they guessed that there was wind beyond their visible horizon, which was in nature much too close for comfort. Even standing they could not lift their eye-height many feet above the surface and the craft, narrow-gutted, would not have permitted a shinning of the mast even on a millpond.

They had about thirty miles of southing to make to clear Portland to go west, and in their current craft at current speed they hoped that they might do it in eight hours or not much more. But as the day wore on the wind began to freshen, and to head them more nearly from the south. The gig was sea-kindly enough and little water came across the bows, but as she began to work, more started to seep in through her seams. One garboard strake was badly split, and water seemed to grow up from the keelson. Her lack of canvas now became a matter of relief, and by afternoon they had indeed to shorten down. An hour later they were struggling, and the darkening sky had taken on an ochre hue. They took turns on the tiller, and instead of rest the "off-duty man" did duty with a bailing-tin, and almost constantly.

There were isles and islets in the Portland Bight, and before the sun dropped them into pitchy darkness, they chose one they thought might give them some protection with its lee. The seas were steep and breaking by this time, which either indicated shallow water — they had no chart — or maybe rocks or reefs. For their sins they had not checked their anchor cable carefully, having trusted Jackson's claim that all was shipshape, and when they went to prepare it were fairly horrified by its condition. Clearly stored wet, or in a damp part of the storehouse, it opened to reveal soft fibres in the lay, and one point of downright rot. No time for a long splice, no trust in a short, they doubled up a length and hoped the residue would give them scope enough. They had to anchor or stay under sail and ride it out in darkness: the shores that they could reach were much too dangerous for approaching, and the gig was not the vessel to heave safely to.

It was a long, hard night. The wind rose steadily until they could keep canvas up no more, and even in the island lee they were hard pressed not to let the boat fill up. The anchor rope was short, they snubbed and jerked till kingdom come, and neither snatched more than an hour's sleep or so all night. At daybreak the tropic beauty of the island had drained away to something much more near their lives' experience — grey, troubled skies over dark troubled waters, with trees and creepers beating and battering in the violent winds — and the sea beyond the Bight was distinctly uninviting. To Will, however, a lifelong small-boat man, it looked possible; in fact, compared with lying to this untrustworthy hook, bursting with advantages.

"Shit, Lieutenant," Sam said. "Remind me never to sail under your command for pleasure. Talking of which — pray keep her still while I squeeze out a piss!"

They beat out round the point in great discomfort, but once clear of it upped helm, eased sheets, and let her fly. As the sun rose higher the cloud began to melt, and Will began to feel he would not freeze to death in fact. Sam got some sleep, his clothes steaming gently across the lee gunwale, then awoke, bailed out, and let his friend bed down. It was far from easy sailing — both reefs down she was still mighty hard pressed — and as the hours passed they suffered thirst pangs, rationing their water just in case, sore skin from salt and constant movement, and burns around their screwed-up eyes. When the wind began to head them in the afternoon they confessed that they were damn near sick of it, but knew that they must knuckle down, as having no alternative.

"A sailor at sea," said Sam, drearily. "Sometimes I think we're mad, Will. Quite bloody mad."

They took a long board into the open sea when night fell, to obviate any possibility that they would get too close to land, and hoped the wind would not freshen to a fuller gale when they were far offshore. It did not. Will was woken from a slumber by the deeply uncomfortable motion of a vessel in a seaway that has lost her forward thrust. His eyes met Sam's, who was holding the tiller as if it were a rancid sausage or something even less salubrious.

"Gone," said Sam. "It fell off like a stone, Will. Look. Not a bleeding zephyr."

The sky was black and starry, no single cloud in view. The sea was lumps and backwashes, all direction torn away from it. The gig's sails hung down from spars like dun brown shrouds, the mainyard ground and clattered at the throat.

"If I'd had dinner," Sam added, bitterly, "I'd have brought it up by now. Good God, this bloody Caribbean. How I hate it."

By the time the sun was fully up they had been at the oars a good three hours, and their arms and arses were "crying out for mercy." They took their northern heading from the rising orb once the stars had gone, and by midday (or thereabouts) felt they might die of heatstroke or exhaustion. For a blessed hour or two they lay on the bottomboards, shaded by the mainsail they had dropped (largely to stop it chafing to destruction) and told themselves that when they got to shore they would give up the sea and take positions more befitting gentlemen. They laughed, through cracking lips, that they might indeed be delirious, although they were, in fact, quite confident that the land they had just discerned was really there, and not some wild delusion.

When the breeze blew up towards night — offshore, inevitably — they hoisted sail, stripped off their clothes and hung overboard (for safety not together; they were not *so* light-headed), and took a long board to the westward, where they were certain they could see their landmark mountain peak. In full darkness, warm and beautiful, they steered by the stars, bailed a little, and took long turns to doze. At daybreak they could see the coast five miles away, knew almost precisely where they were, and prayed for good landfall and no nasty, nasty shocks. When they entered "Biter Bay" they recognised the *Jacqueline*, at anchor peacefully, saw smoke from cooking fires, and let out a feeble cheer. Two boats were launched to meet them, full of armed men, and led by Bosun Taylor and Tommy Hugg. When they were recognised, the boats' crews raised a mighty yell of welcome. By the time they got on shore, to meet the captain who was waiting grandly at his new table in the centre of the stockade, their ears were stuffed with treasure and success. Slack Dickie's mighty smile, as they approached him, was the final touch. Bentley was sick to his stomach, with anticipation.

Captain Kaye, as ever, was not a man of subtleties. Before him he saw two ragged, salt-stained officers, with unshaven faces, burnt skin, and sauny eyes. If he saw that they bore heavy news he did not absorb it, it did not impinge on his consciousness. Their decrepitude, if anything, increased his own delight.

"Well well, you fellows! What a sorry state you're in! I tell you what! I shall blow you to new coats and linen the moment we get back! Ask me how? My boys — we shall be rich!"

Will was comforted, in some way, by a sense of dislocation, disbelief almost, in this man's odd connection with normal human feelings. He sat resplendent on a salvaged cabin chair, that Mr Carpenter must have spent some hours buffing up for him, and even his clothes were smart and clean and elegant. His feet were shod in polished black, even the sand fearing to stick to them too messily it appeared, although his chair and table were placed squarely in the silver, drifting piles. Around him in more solid piles were ranged canvas-covered bundles, sea stained chests and cases, barricoes and boxes. If even half of it were treasure, Kaye's excitement was explained. It was Will's sad task to bring him back to earth.

His own sense of connection with this man's plight, and his own reality, slid into his guts like cold steel, slow-moving. He was here to tell Kaye that his love, Marianne Siddleham, was dead, which was cruelly true. But his own love might be also dead, or had been captured, and God alone knew by whom, or what the end might be. What comfort might he bring for Kaye, if there was none for him? How could he believe Kaye's love might be the same as his in any way, masked by the fatuous smiling of this bland, round, happy face? How could he believe his own love valid, for a maiden that, in truth, he barely knew. He was abruptly aware of Sam at his side, and Sam put out his hand, and gently touched his arm.

"Sir," he said to Kaye. "The treasure notwithstanding. I fear Lieutenant Bentley must impart some news. From Kingston. From the Acting Governor."

A look of something close to horror flitted over Kaye's face, his eyes snapped wider open as if he had been pricked, or shocked.

"What news?" he said. The look faded as fast as it had come. "Ah God," he said. "Surely not bad news of Miss Tomelty?"

Bentley flinched. It was noticeable. Kaye's eyes seemed flooded with relief.

"No, sir," Will said. "No, sir. It is something..."

Kaye was like a man clutching after straws.

"Has Captain Swift come?" he said. "Has there been a..." He stopped, and licked his lips. "God damn you, Bentley! What is going on?"

"Captain Swift has come," said Holt, to end the silence. "He sent us, sir. He says you must return."

"I can't!" Kaye snapped. "The treasure! What mean you, sir, 'return'?"

No answer to that, thought Bentley, bleakly. The words were plain enough. His body seemed to give an inner sigh. He was exhausted.

"Forgive me, sir," he said. "There has been a raid. Slaves, Maroons, rebels—"

"Savages," said Kaye almost inaudibly. His face had drained bone-white. "Tell me the end. How many killed? They left them unprotected. How many have been killed?"

Will noticed, with superb irrelevance, that the warrant men and sailors who had been close to them had faded like ghosts away. The space inside the stockade walls now held the three of them alone, and treasure piled up high. Kaye was no longer disconnected. Kaye was like a cadaver, his strange hazel eyes the sole thing left about him with a semblance of life. Will shared his pain and horror; it bled into his soul.

"Nine," he said. "Forgive me, Captain. Seven at the Siddleham plantation, two of the Sutton slaves. And... I..."

He had no way to finish that. Had not known, in fact, what he had set out to say.

Kaye said, completely blankly: "But not just slaves, of course. Lady Siddleham and the girls as well. Oh Christ, Lieutenant Bentley. Say that I am wrong."

Will did not speak. His eyes had filled with tears, which came splashing down his salt-caked cheeks, carving furrows.

Kaye said: "Marianna was a tiger. She told me so herself. Her brother said a lion. A lioness. And we left them unprotected. We are all mad."

Jack Gunning came in sight then, through the main opening in the stockade wall, and whooped. He whooped and staggered, then nearly went full-length.

"Hey, bollocks boys!" he shouted. "Drunk again is London Jack, the bastard! Hey, Willie! Hello, Sam! Come to claim your share, eh boys? Plenty more where this came from, if you can hold your breath ten minutes!"

He had a bottle in his hand, squat and black, and stretched it out to them, not noticing yet that Bentley was in tears and Kaye was poleaxed.

"And good to see you too, John!" he said sarcastically. "Don't mention it! Long time away and— Will? What ails you, lad? Good God, my sonner, surely that's not—"

Captain Kaye walked stiffly up to Gunning as if for one moment he might strike out at him. Instead he took the bottle by its neck and pulled it from him, and pushed it into his own wide open mouth, and swallowed, coughed, and swallowed more. Perhaps a quarter of a bottle of brandy burned down his throat. Then he pushed the bottle back at Gunning and stood there, panting. Gunning whooped.

"I knew you'd see the light one day!" he said. "Bad news, is it? Well Pusser Black'll sort you out, Dick. Will — take a try yourself. We can't have King's officers weeping like new-pregnant maidens. Is it the Spithead Nymph? Have you had news?"

The tableau in the blazing sun was quite absurd, and Holt felt it very keenly. The representatives of the civilised world, on a beach in an inferno, in tears, or drunk, or speechless, with their lesser mortals, no doubt, gazing on from vantage points of secrecy, and wondering... God only knows, thought Sam. God only knows.

"Sir," he said, to Captain Kaye. "We are required back as soon as maybe, as soon as ever possible to move. There will be reprisals, naturally. Captain Swift has taken charge and wants to move immediately he can. We were detained, sir. The weather has delayed us. We have brought a cranky gig from the Port Royal dockyard."

Will had pulled himself together, clumsily mopping his face on sleeve and kerchief. London Jack, perhaps more tactfully then he could explain, took himself off towards the gateway almost briskly, shooing men from out the shadows of the walls. But Kaye still stood like an ox at slaughter, as if trying to take in what Holt had just said.

Will added: "There will be a major expedition, sir, by land and sea. Mr Mather will raise a militia force, and Captain Swift has a new vessel, the *Pourquoi Pas*. Quite small and lightly armed, but with a handy force of men. He needs your knowledge and your skill, sir, he needs to play out a strategy, but also he needs more men. The target is a force of Leeward Maroons, and the problem is their strength is not exactly known, nor are their whereabouts. They are led, apparently, by a man called Marlowe. He is infamous."

He ached to say that the island men were wrong, that Swift was being led into the wrong fight in the wrong direction, but he knew that he must keep his counsel. If the expedition failed, that was not his lookout. He was in a position now where orders had been issued, and he had to obey, go with the drift, however false the trail should prove. But in any case, Kaye would want to go back, that was inevitable. Marianne and her family had been killed there, when he was away. It was impossible that he would not return, immediately. And go out on a bloody hunt to seek and kill more innocents. Small wonder that the black men hated white...

"I cannot go back," said Kaye. His voice was shocking, his words more so. He was still white, almost a glaring white, and his eyes were dazed with hurt. As Bentley looked at them, they drifted out of focus, as if he could perceive beyond Will's eyes. Will came close to tears again, which he found difficult to understand, or bear. He had not believed, he realised, that Kaye had been in love. No, not that exactly... he had failed to believe entirely. Failed to believe it could be as real as love had been to him. Somehow, this shamed him, dreadfully.

"But Captain Kaye," he said. He faltered. "Captain Swift and Mr Mather..."

"You two must go," said Kaye, decisively. "You must go back before me and tell them I need time. Good God, man, is that so terrible? We are raising treasure here! We are getting stuff from out the depths that no one ever had a right to see no more! There are black men lurking in the tree-line, there are runaways up in the hills! Are we to sail off and leave it for them, all piled and boxed here on the beach? Are you suggesting that?"

"I am suggesting nothing, sir. But Captain Swift... his orders were..."

"And is he my commanding officer? Does Mather govern *me*, as well as this shit-hole island? Even if we get it back they will take it if we're not careful, won't they, the Assembly or the Navy Royal? Is that what you're craving, Bentley? I must lose everything? I take it you told your precious uncle? I take it he knows all about the sunken gold?"

Dick Kaye was standing tall, and shaking. His face was wild, his expression distracted. Both Will and Sam stood close by him, and neither tried to answer for some time. Then William made the slightest gesture, with his head.

"No," he said. "We have said nothing. The treasure is your business, Captain Kaye."

At last their captain shrugged. He coughed. He cleared his throat. He looked into Bentley's eyes, but his gaze was quailing.

"You of all people," he said. His voice was lowering, almost inaudible. It was as though he had not understood the words. "You of all people, Will, to try to drive me thus. I asked you to look after her. I begged you to protect my... to be help and aid to... my poor Miss Siddleham."

He took a deep breath then, and pulled his shoulders back.

"You go back," he said, more firmly. "Those are my orders, Holt and Bentley. You go back and tell them what you will, and I will transfer this treasure to the *Jacqueline* and follow on as soon as I can secure it." He laughed. "It'll get out anyway, won't it? Perhaps I should bury it, like the pirates used to do! But how to keep men quiet, eh? No wonder pirates got betrayed! Still, we'll get a share this way at least, won't we, though we haven't brought much up yet, in all truth. But the less we brag about the quantity, the more might come to us, I guess. I do thank you, gentlemen, however. For your discretion. I do."

"Sir," said Bentley, "we need another man."

This was unexpected, especially to Sam, who glanced askance at him. But Kaye just blinked, quite at a loss.

"What? An extra man? Well, if you like."

"I want the Worm," said Will. "The old black sailor that we call the Worm."

"Don't know him."

"He is our only black man," Holt said, dryly. "About two hundred years old. Apart from that he don't stand out at all."

Slack Dickie did not see the joke.

"Take him," he said. "Take anyone. Just cut along, eh? Swift lives by keenness. Lay it on thick why I must be delayed. He lives by money, too. You ease the ways with him and I will follow on. Yes, that is best. Go now. Go quickly."

Had it not been so typical, it might have struck as laughable. A four-day fight against the vilest weather, thirsty, hungry, sore, to bring strict orders, and less than an hour later they were to set off again, to do Dick's dirty work for him. They stumped off to see Geoff Raper and have the Worm dug out for them, between amusement and outrage, tempered by their new perception of Kaye's loss and pain.

While the gig was readied and provisioned, while Worm collected up his meagre stuff, they filled up on Raper's food, and washed in glorious fresh water, and stretched their limbs.

"Why did you weep?" said Sam, out of the blue.

"Because I did not know," said Will. "A matter of... He loved her, Sam."

"I know," said Sam. "No need to carry on. And why the black man? With this breeze and this weather, we'll be in Port Royal in two days or so."

"We're going west," said Will. "We ain't going to Port Royal."

He glanced at Sam to gauge reaction. It was directly contrary to their orders. It was mutiny.

"Very good," said Sam, after a moment. "Will you tell me why?"

"I'll tell you why," said Will. "Because I'm sick of it. I find Dickie's love is real and mine perhaps is not. Deb has been captured, killed maybe, or maybe saved or saveable, and I am a few short leagues away and I do not even know. Now I must find out."

"Where will we look? We don't know where to look. That is Swift's problem, and the plantation men's. They say she is with Marlowe, and Marlowe is hard to find. If they could find him, they would have killed him long ago. Will Worm find him? Is that your notion? Why should Worm find him?"

"They will find us. We are not an army. We will not hide from them, they will be curious."

"Good," said Sam. "So they find us and they kill us, or they don't find us and we get hanged in Port Royal when we get back there. Excellent."

William took a draught of wine. The *Jacqueline* still had fine wine on board, which One-leg Raper doubtless stole from Purser Black to please his favourites.

"If we find out where Marlowe is and he *is* a villain, we'll have done precisely what Swift most needs from anyone. We will guide the expedition to its prey. If he is not — and Bridie says that he will be Deb's saviour — well, if he is not, we keep our mouths shut."

"Mouths shut, throats cut... ah well, all one to me." Sam was laughing, but he did so, clearly, from some sort of strange perverse delight. He waved a hand to Raper.

"Hey! Geoff! Another bottle over here!" To Will he added (or to nobody): "If I'm going to my death I might as well go arseholes under."

Will said earnestly: "If we do find him, we'll have Deb as our protection. And the Worm."

"And the Worm, eh? The Roman slave turned gladiator! Will, you are the very acme of military philosophy! But at least he's black and seems to like us. He can be our advocate, I guess." He laughed once more. "More like we'll meet those bloody Scotchmen and they'll butcher us all three! He stole their boat, remember? The Lamonts don't take kindly to that sort of thing! Come on, drink up. We'll forget that other bottle. There's work that must be done."

"You do not have to come," said Will. "Sam, I am perhaps a little crazy, but I've got to go. Please forget it."

"And you'll steal the gig off me, will you? Knock my head in and feed me to the sharks? Is *that* what Worm's for, to be your hired black assassin!? Get away with you, you fool. Let's go and say goodbye to Dickie. Will, I can hardly wait. If you're to marry the maiden that I love, I might at very leastways claim a kiss off yours, when we have rescued her!"

Ten minutes later they were creaming off down southward from the beach. They did not turn west until they were far offshore. The Worm was at the tiller, and he had received news of their plan with equanimity. He knew the country very well, he said. He might catch and kill a little goat for them...

Chapter Twenty-Seven

The way that Deb was taken was extremely brutal, and terrified her completely. She was jerked and torn through the thick undergrowth by a number of black savages that she could not even count in the confusion, with Mildred screaming just behind her. Deb would have fought had she been able, but she could not even kick and scratch. It was as if her arms were being torn from their sockets, her legs knocked and dragged from under her. She smelled sharp sweat, hot breath and heavy swampy odours, and she thought it was a part of dying. Then, suddenly, it stopped. She stood there shaking, with her eyes closed, and jumped to hear a voice she recognised.

It was Mildred. She too was panting, but when Deb's eyes snapped open, wore an almost sunny smile.

"See, girl," she said. "I done tell you, no? I done say he find us, and he did."

They were in a clearing, and all around them there were black men. Savages, Deb had thought when in extremis, but now they looked just like other island men. Except that they were armed, and some one or two had hair much longer than the normal run of slaves. They were not slaves. They were better dressed, in britches and pale shirts, and they were staring with unservile eyes. They looked like the Sutton men who had rebelled, without the residue of fear – in despite the fact that an attack on them was imminent. As Deb took the vision in, they raised muskets to their shoulders and took aim into the woods they had just come from. From within which came scramblings and cries. Pursuit.

One man said: "Hold." The other men held fire. They stood there in a half a circle, like a band of hunters in a formation. They stared down their barrels and breathed easily, despite the running they had done. Deb's breath caught in her throat, and Mildred reached out to her. She pointed.

"It is Marlowe," she said. "I told you he would come. We all right now, Debbeerah."

As she spoke, men came from the bushes opposite, and they were also armed. Deb flinched, waiting for the shots, from either side. There was not a distance between the bands to make avoidance possible. They could only cut each other down. The breath she was holding on to, unknown to her, came out in a long, low sigh. Her lungs and ribs were shaking.

Some of the pursuing band were white, as she had known, but she realised now that it was they only who held muskets, while their blacks had swords and cane-knives. The fat man was in the van, and she could see the sweat sliding down his face even as he wiped it with his pistol-hand. On either side, half hidden still, were two tall, thin men, pale-faced, with meagre beards, and she knew somehow that these were the "Scotchmen" the small black boy had said would kill her. Then more whites emerged, and one of them was also bearded, blond and lanky as a lath. He went and stood beside the fat man, and he raised his right hand, palm outwards, towards Marlowe, as if in a salute.

"Saury tae mither ye," he said. "We've ay come tae get the English hoorie, nae yin else. Sen' her ower here, will ye? And then we'll hie oorselfs awa'. We dinna wish tae cause ye any bother."

To Deb's ears the accent was amazing, but the polite address, the courtly expressions of regret, were even more so. These were the Scots, though, there was no doubt of that. She wondered why they should wish to damage her. On this form, they hardly seemed like killers.

The black commander was as calm as the Scot had been. He left it for an aching length of time before replying. The while, his musket men held to their targets, as steadily as rocks.

"You go now," he said. "The white spy she stay with me. You go now or I have you killed. I go kill all of you."

The words "white spy" sank into her like lead, but Mildred touched her hand and Deb squeezed back hopefully. She watched the white man's face for his response. What could he do, or say? His band was outnumbered, and heavily outgunned. She assumed that he would argue, that he had something else to say.

But he did not. While the fat man showed signs of nervousness beside him, the meagre pale man stayed as calm and courtly as could be. He turned his head leftward, and said to one of the other brothers, "Dod?" Dod nodded, and the head moved to the right. He did not speak this time, but the third Scot nodded his assent.

"Then I wish ye joy o' her, Mister," said the spokesman. "But I hae to warn ye, she *is* a spy, ye ha' the recht o'it on that. Ye'll hae the Bru'tish Navy on your neck fer this dee's wark, I promise ye. Men. Awa'."

The Scotsman turned from Marlowe without another word, as if no musket in the world were trained on his defenceless back, and strode past the fat man and back into the wood. His brothers twisted on their heels, then their cohorts, one by one. In half a minute the marauding band had gone. Until the sound of their progress had faded, none of Marlowe's people moved or spoke. They were disciplined and deadly men.

Deb had studied her new captor while this was going on — for captor he looked and felt like, and he had called her "spy" — and what she saw frightened rather than reassured her. He was a tall man, of extraordinary blackness, as if carved out of ebony, and his air of hauteur, grandeur even, was intimidating. His face also had a sculpted air, with thin lips that seemed incapable of smiling, a high-bridged nose, and deep set eyes that had a glower to them, a kind of inward burning quality. He did not return her look, but had he done so, even for a second, she knew she would have looked away. Numbers and armaments aside, she felt she knew why the Scotsmen and their allies, black and white, had gone away. Marlowe's reputation, clearly, was not a false one.

When the band had gone, though, he did look at her, and his eyes indeed were hard with lack of sympathy. They held hers for a moment, then moved on to Mildred, to whom he spoke rapidly in a tongue unknown to Deb. What he said appeared upsetting, and Mildred's colour deepened, a darker shadow across the natural dark. She replied with vigour, then seemed enraged by his response. The exchanges went on for some good time, until Marlowe turned his back on both of them, and walked away. Some of his men followed him, leaving a bunch of silent watchers to guard the two young women.

Mildred said: "There been a massacre. Back in East. Marlowe think we know why so."

Deb was confused.

"But we warned them," she said. "We warned Bridie. We did know, didn't we?"

"We warn them, and now Marlowe blame us," Mildred replied. "He say we warn planters trouble coming, and they say him do it. He say the Windward men bring it, Maroons. But white man blame him, and go on rampage. They get up army all round Kingston, they plan to march 'cross 'ere and do much mischief. And we to blame."

She read in Deborah's face a lack of understanding. She cooled her anger down. She reached out and touched her friend softly on the forearm, then she sighed.

"We come here all this way," she said. "He think we come to lead the white men to him."

"But we didn't know where to find him! You said he'd find us, and so he did. Can't you tell him we were running too? They destroyed our camp. They killed our friends. Mildred! Can't you tell him we were running, too?"

Her voice was full of tears, and she thought that she might just fall down and weep. Her hopes had been with Marlowe, all of them. He had become a myth, a Holy Grail, a mystical protector. And he was just a man, another man who did not trust her or believe her. How could he think she was a spy?

"The white men would not fight for you," said Mildred. "Marlowe tell them go, they go. I tell him they only want to play with you, or make you hostage, they not really care. I say you just a thing to them. A thing of no much value, but someone maybe pay for you, a bit."

Deb licked her upper lip. It was dry and cracking. No one would pay for her, she thought. She was not worth it.

"He not believe me," Mildred continued. "He said black man is hostage for a white man, not white maid. He say they want you back because you are spy, they want to save you. Marlowe save you because you are with me, no other reason. He know my name and people. He know that I have fought."

The night had fallen not so long ago. Now in the clearing it was almost black. A soft wind rustled in the trees.

"So he will kill me now?" said Deb. "Or what? Give me back to those Scotchmen? What will he do with me, Mildred? Please don't let him kill me, if you can."

"I not think he will kill you," Mildred said. "I tell him you in love with Navy officer, you betrothèd. I tell him he will come for you, when he can. I tell him he in Port Royal, and he have a ship. That is when Marlowe angry. I say Navy man in English ship, and he will come to get you, he is a good man. I tried to tell him, but he think I go crazy, or maybe am spy too. He go storm off, you saw."

A bunch of tree frogs burst into sound, as if to some secret cue or signal to ironic laughter. The noise swelled until it was almost deafening, then began to throb more quietly. I have to say, thought

Deb, that I can see his point. An English man will come to save me, in a Navy ship, but will be a friend. The frogs appeared to have a sense of humour.

"I will talk to him again," said Mildred. "He knows I not betray him, however false our story seem. We go get food now, we go to their town. I will talk this later. Try make him see."

The "town" they ended up in that night was not a town by Deb's understanding, but a transit camp of huts and shelters. There were women there, and a child or two, but it could be abandoned if danger threatened at whatever moment. There were three fires, in a wide spread triangle, but the food was meagre and the atmosphere subdued. Mildred and Deb were shown a place to sleep when they had eaten, then left alone for a long while, aware that Marlowe and some other men were talking of their case, probably disputing over them. The women avoided them assiduously, turning blank faces to any overture, although Mildred tried in several languages, and that night, when it was time to sleep, they lay down side-by-side and felt alone in the noisy blackness. Deb, indeed, would have liked to have held Mildred's hand but did not dare. She thought of Will, and wondered where he was. She gave less credence to the idea he would turn up than Marlowe had, that much was certain. Marlowe thought he might lead an attack. She thought at best he would be helpless to bring aid or comfort, at worst would have forgotten her. She fell asleep exhausted, finally, and had many troubled dreams.

Next day the band moved on, the warriors at least, and Marlowe talked to Mildred much, and Deborah occasionally. He put questions to her through her friend, full of suspicion and distrust. If she loved a Navy man, why was she a runaway? If she loved a Navy man, why was she alone? If she loved a Navy man, why had she become a servant? How could the lover of a Navy man be no better than a slave? How could a white maid claim friendship with a black? Was Mildred in the white man's secret pay? If this Navy man would come, as Mildred had said, how did he know where he would find them?

Later, Marlowe's questioning tended more towards the possibility that bargains might be struck, that Deb's person might be of some value to him and his people. Mildred found this alteration hopeful, she said, as an indication that he believed Deb was sincere. When Deb questioned her on this, not understanding, Mildred was blunt.

"If this Navy man do come for you," she said, "Marlowe can catch or kill him. Hold him as hostage, maybe — Navy man a useful hostage, yes? But maybe Navy man can give him something back for you? Maybe safe pass or something, I don't know. Maybe free pardon, something, yes?"

Frankly, Deborah had no idea, although it seemed unlikely to the farthest end. If Will did come — and he would not, for he could not — he surely had no power to make bargains on the Navy's back, or anyone's except his own. She was sinking into a state of melancholy over this, worse than melancholy, although she had no word for it. She had run with Mildred to save her life, was all. Marlowe was to be the one who would help them. It seemed very cruel that she must now offer impossibilities or be cast out, or die.

"He will not come," she said. "I am sure he will not, Mildred. All this is false. I am no spy, but I have no bargains, neither. We must just tell Mr Marlowe I am not a spy, just a lone maid on her own, a simple runaway. I loved a Navy officer, all that is true. But Will Bentley cannot save me, Mildred. Please tell him, Mildred, please tell Mr Marlowe. It is all a dream."

But Marlowe, whose survival as a renegade depended on great vigilance, as well as many other things, had already set in train surveillance, had posted lookouts, had warned his outriders what he was seeking and where it might appear, if not when or how. In the meantime Deb was treated cautiously but well, and questioned, along with Mildred, about the killing of Jacob Tsingi, the reprisal and who had done it, the Suttons and the Siddlehams, the number of their bloodhounds, their armaments, and a hundred other things. All the women could give in return, save for a few small facts and figures, was the conviction that the white men would come for the rebels, and come in force.

Then, two days later, they were conducted to the shelter where the lead men sat, and Marlowe smiled at them. There was no warmth in it, his features were not any softer, but he did appear somehow amused, at least. He spoke to Mildred, rapidly, then turned to Deb.

"Your man has come," he said. "Not in a ship but in a little boat, and that is good. I going have a talk with him."

***

Dick Kaye was drunk when word was brought to him that there was an envoy from the Scotsmen in the woods. He was sitting on his throne in lonely splendour in the middle of the stockade's outer court, and he was halfway down his second bottle of the day. Jem Taylor, boatswain, had tried to talk to him an hour earlier, and nearly had his head chewed off. All he had had to tell was that the treasure so far raised was on board the *Jacqueline*, that she could be under way in half an hour if need be. But Kaye was no longer interested. As an afterthought, he had offered Taylor a slug from out the bottle, which had been refused. Ah well; not his loss.

Since Will and Sam had gone, since Marianne had gone, Kaye had emulated Gunning in his rush into oblivion. The men and warrant officers had watched with sympathy to begin with, and had carried out their loading tasks, their job of striking camp, without much interest that their commander was intent on blotting out the world. All knew the news from Kingston, all sympathised in some degree as past sufferers from the pains of love and random loss, and all knew that he would "get over it," as they had been forced to do. It was hard to give up diving, but they knew it would be temporary, and they watched with pleasure the amount of saleables that they stuffed down the hold. There were pickings too, of course. It was better than working in a dockyard. Not a man who did not end up with his pockets bulging. Drunk captains do not see much, either: a noble truth.

Gunning's latest session, having run its full four days, was ending when Kaye started his drinking, so the nauseating bond Tom Hugg and Bosun Taylor had expected to build up between them did not materialise, to their relief. Gunning encouraged his captain in the early stages, but found him too morose, too ready to talk of his dead *affianced* interminably, too damn frank about his inner feelings. In any way, the normal reaction to the poison in his own blood was well underway, and within an hour of Slack Dickie hitting the brandy bottle, London Jack was on the point of forswearing alcohol forever, as per usual. Had it not made more work for them, the boatswain and his mate would not have cared a jot; as it was they wondered merely if the captain would follow the slope interminably downwards to the gutter, or have lucid periods like Gunning did. Drink was the seaman's curse, as everybody knew. Provided by their lordships with deliberate intent.

It had been known that "natives" still watched them from the trees from time to time, but it came as a great shock when white men turned up too. The Lamont brothers, like flies to the honeypot, had moved towards the *Biter* wreck after Marlowe and his rebels had rebuffed them, to check if the *Jacqueline* had been called back to Port Royal yet, as they were expecting any day. It had occurred to them, what's more, that news of the captive white maid might be somehow useful. They did not know the circumstances of her flight, nor why the rebel leader had "protected" her, but they guessed it must have some significance for bargaining. They had the recaptured Bob as well, Slack Dickie's little pet, led on a rope these days in case he tried to run once more.

Because they knew the value of the softest option, the Lamonts chose Rat Baines to do their dirty work. They waited until he was doing his — at noisy stool in the fringes of the woodland — and when they surprised him, rubbed his nose in it, so to speak. They sent Chattel up behind him, silent as a snake, to run the blunt side of his blade across the sailor's throat. As Baines told it afterwards, if he hadn't "been at it already — shipmates, I would have shit meself!" He threw himself upright and backwards and Chattel, side-stepping like a dancing master, nudged him into a prickle bush. The Rat, whose instincts for survival were necessarily of the finest, bled, soiled himself, scrabbled at his britches, and stared terrified into his assailant's face — all without a sound. Although when the Lamonts appeared he gulped, indeed, and came close to swallowing his tongue.

The Lamonts, in a line, looked at him with expressions of deep contempt. Baines, all too used to it, smiled humbly back at them while tying off his waist cords then wiping his hands roughly clean on some leaves. Perhaps he planned to offer up his hand to shake. If so, he thought better of it. He began to say hello, but stopped that also. The Lamonts, as ever, were in no hurry to articulate. At last Wee Doddie spoke.

"Go and find yer mannie, Ratty Baines," he said. "Tell him we've got ten dozen men, wi' muskets, knives and swords, and we can pick his people off frae within this cover ain by ain. Tell him we've got some knowledge for him and we want tae parley. Tell him we might help him in the coming war. Tell him we are loyal men."

Had Baines dared he would have snorted, but he was not a stupid man, beneath it all. He knew nothing of "the coming war" so saw no reason to disbelieve it, but he disbelieved the rest, and roundly. They were not loyal men, and parleying, to them, meant selling information, pure and simple. Obscurely, he was aggrieved, proprietorial. Slack Dickie was his captain now, not theirs, they were faithless rogues and thieves and murderers, deserving nothing. Least of all the chance to worm their way back into favour, and a pardon. He wished to see them hang.

"He wouldn't come," he said. "He couldn't even if he wanted to. He's drunk."

Dod's blank eyes bored into him for as long as it took Baines' to drop. Short enough, but time to frighten him to death.

"Fit d'ye mean? Not that mannie, not London Jack. We want tae talk tae Dickie. The captain mannie."

"It is that mannie," replied Baines, almost boldly. "Slack Dickie's taken to the liquor. It's Cap'n Kaye that's drunk." A little pause. "Any case, he wouldn't come, would he? If you've got all these men and weaponry? He's not that mad, is he?" Another tiny break. "If you've really got 'em, anyway."

His courage wept away as the Scotsman raised his hand, but it did not presage a blow, it was a signal. Behind him several men moved into view out of the undergrowth, and they were armed, indeed. Black mainly, but Baines was shocked to recognise Chris Thompson, then Seth Pond. He made a movement with his head, but they did not acknowledge him. Then he noticed a smaller form behind Seth Pond, attached apparently by a rope held in the sailor's hand.

"You've got Black Bob!" said Baines. "Are you alive then, Bob? Well done!"

The small black face appeared to convulse the second that it came into sight.

"Tell the captain!" Black Bob yelled; and was cut off as Pond jerked viciously on the lanyard round his neck. Baines could see him choking on the ground.

"Ye'll tell the mannie that we've got the men," said Lamont. "Ye'll tell him there's a white wumman who's held captive b'the niggers yonder, b'the nigger they call Marlowe. Tell him she's a fine and lovely lady, and if he wants tae save her for the ransom or fitever, tell him we'll lead him there. Tell him it's oor sense ae duty. Tell him he'll need men and muskets and we'll bow tae his command. We'll wait until he's sober, Ratty, eh? But ye dinna need to tell Slack Dickie that!"

Bonhomie from the Scots was more than even Baines could take. The Lamonts' hearts were full of hate and murder. He blurted: "Well he won't be sober by the time we sail, will he? We're going home to Kingston. So you'll have to find your bargains somewheres else. And yer bloody pardon!"

Dod raised his pistol, and Rat Baines collapsed onto his knees. So much for courage, might have been his last coherent thought. So much for bloody sauce! But the Scotsman laughed, and Baines opened his eyes to find himself alive.

Fat Mickie Carver shouted: "That's the way, Ratty! Shite interrupted, shite resumed! He's nothing if not fair, ain't Dod Lamont!"

"Thanks for the fort!" added Joshie Ward. "We'll surely find a use for it!"

The men went off laughing, incautious of the noise they made, and Baines did not await their full disappearance before he hared back to the shore. He had a horrid vision that he was too late, that his shipmates had sailed away and left him there, but little visible had changed. There were men on the *Jacqueline*'s yards, one of the boats was being hoisted up on deck, another was pulling towards her side, not many strokes to go. On the water's edge, Tom Hugg was waiting with a crew to take the captain, and the captain's chair, out to his vessel. Slack Dickie was halfway to the water, not noticeably even staggering.

It took poor Rat some time to make it clear that he had information, because the common tendency, shared by Kaye, was to cuff or ignore him, especially smelling so vilely as he did after his "accident." But in the end Baines shouted out the name Lamont, and then — in the instant silence — that they were here, he'd seen them, he had spoken to them, and they had "Black Bob upon a piece of rope." Hugg was crazy to hear more of the Scotsmen, and if they were armed, but Slack Dickie's brain was fixed upon his small, lost toy. He stood in the water, the wavelets lapping over his leather shoes and stockinged feet unnoticed, and tried to form a question, but only gaped.

"Do they know about the treasure?" Hugg snapped at Baines. "Did you tell them what we were doing here, you little bastard!"

"No!" squeaked Rat. "Nothing, Mr Hugg! I was the soul of all discretion! Though they threatened me!"

"You're a liar, Baines! By God, I'll swing for you!"

"No, sir! On my mother's womb! Treasure was never mentioned, not a word, they wants the fort that's all. They said they'd found a white maid, a fine lady needing ransom who was held a captive. They said that Mr Marley's got her and they could get her back! It was a pardon they was seeking. Oh, sir" (to Captain Kaye) "they said they'd help you. They talked about a ransom, and their duty, and the coming war. They swore that they would aid you, sir!"

And I told them you were drunk, he might have added, but did not. But he felt fully justified in everything. The Scots were murderers and liars, they were not there to offer help, but mayhem. He knew he had done well.

Kaye had his gaping in control, but not perhaps his mind. He took a step through the breaking water and grabbed Baines by the shoulder. Had the captain not been so drunk, and soft about the muscles, it would have been a savage grip. It was intended to be, surely.

"Black Bob," he said. "Did you say on a rope? Is he alive? Is he well and walking? On a rope! The devils!"

There was not a manjack among the boat's crew who dared to dwell on that outrage in case they burst out laughing, naturally — although the Lamonts were unlikely, they assumed, to use a white fancy lanyard round the wee boy's neck, like someone they could mention. Baines twisted up his face in simulated agony.

"Ow, sir! You're killing me! Aye, sir, I swear it. He's on a rope, tied up like a poor sad monkey and they're dragging him away. They can't be very far, sir, but they are heavy armed and there are dozens of them, scores. No, sir! Don't go, sir! Sir, they'll murder you!"

Kaye, like a drunkard, like a man gone mad, like a booby, like an idiot, was running up the sand towards the tree-line, towards the stockade, roaring.

"Lamont! You Scotch bastards! You traitors! Give me that boy, sirs! I command you! Give me that boy!"

The men, as so often with their commander, were embarrassed, and they did not know what they could do. Chase him? No, not. Shout? Shout what? Hit Baines for causing all the trouble? Rat Baines had already worked that out. He had skipped into the water, up to his waist. The waves could wash part of his shame away at least.

Kaye's intention was ridiculous perhaps, but his execution was rank appalling. He was drunk, and fat, and as sea officers went, extremely idle. The sand was soft, deep and fine, and as easy to run in as solidified molasses. Before he had reached the outer wall he had lost a shoe and his wig was half off and sliding down his sweating face. By halfway along that wall, a hundred yards or more before the palm trees started thickening, he was exhausted and moving like a swamp-drowned ox. His face was scarlet, his breath was rasping in his throat, he looked extremely likely to bring on a fatal seizure. To cap off his crewmen's consternation, a black man appeared just then from out the wood, and stood and watched him, unarmed and insolent. Kaye, because he could not go any further in the killing heat, stopped and panted at him. He bent forward, hands upon his knees, and tried to catch his breath and speak. From behind, Hugg watched in an agony of doubt. While from in front of him, the black man half stared, half sneered. But did not speak.

Kaye gasped at last: "That boy, you villain. I want that boy. Tell those Scotch bastards I will have that boy."

He tried another step or two, but his legs would go no further. He was rooted in the sable sand, and each foot, as he tried to lift it, cascaded silver to re-form in shifting piles. His breath now came in raucous judders.

And the black man turned back into the trees and disappeared.

They helped and carried Kaye to the boat, fearing that he might die indeed. He demanded drink, but could not keep even a mouthful down, which saved him, maybe. He huddled on the bottomboards as they rowed out, but when they reached the *Jacqueline* he could get aboard unaided, just. Attempts to put a bold face on it, however, were not successful. Strangely, Gunning looked on with sympathy that was palpably genuine. And when the captain had been seated on the quarterdeck, roused out the crew to lift the boat on board, weigh anchor and get canvas set.

Through his glass, as the ship rounded the headland and set course for Kingston, Kaye could see the shapes of men moving towards the fortress, now forsaken...

Chapter Twenty-Eight

Had Marlowe's men not come to them, it is unlikely Will and Sam could ever have made contact. The Worm, however, whenever gloom appeared to be setting in, had sworn the blacks would come. In any case, he'd pointed out, they could not land, because they could not find a place. The swell around this western part was strong and constant, perhaps reflecting distant winds, and the gig was not a surf-boat. She had a narrow vee at stem and stern, steep bilges, and a low, flat transom. Two men on oars, one man on tiller, would not have been enough. The breaking combers would have surely swamped them.

The place he'd chosen to keep vigil appeared quite random to the whites, but Worm insisted it was the best place around the western tip to be noticed, much used in pirate days to spot prizes making for Cuba or the straits. For better visibility, though, they had to stay close in, which meant backing and filling not far beyond the wave-break line throughout the daylight hours. At night they sailed off farther and hove-to as best they could — not well with their unhandy rig — to snatch some sleep. Their cable was untrustworthy, and probably too short to keep them snubbing safely if they had anchored closer in and all three of them dozed off.

It was not many hours into their first full day offshore that they were noticed, and not many hours after that that Worm spotted the watchers — when they decided, apparently, to be seen. The gig was then let fall offwind to cream in towards the shore, to show their good intent. Two whites, one black, and apparently unarmed. Will and Sam had blue jackets on, but took them off with ostentation when they were at their closest in. Before they went about to keep out of the surf they stood up in shirt-sleeves with their arms outstretched, and shouted, all three on a signal: "Marlowe! Parley! Peace!"

"Lee-oh," said Will and put the tiller down. The unhandy little lug was dropped and dipped and raised the other side, and they gathered speed away from shore again. Three black men were watching now, conferred, and two of them moved back into the woods. The gig took but a short board, then swung back towards the beach to show they were not going anywhere, and they then plugged and plunged about and waited. It was heartening that one man remained to watch. Had they been abandoned, their magazine of tactics might have well proved empty. But as the minutes dragged, than an hour, then another, their spirits began to sink a little. Except for the Worm's. His deep-wrinkled face showed contentment, more so when he whipped his britches down and dropped turds neatly overside.

"Christ," said Sam, in deepest admiration. "I wish I could do that, old one. I've just got bloody belly-ache!"

Shortly after this event, as they were reaching on a parallel with the sands, Worm made a noise of warning from the bow and pointed at the crag that rose out from the surf ahead of them. They saw a craft come nosing round it, under oar or paddle power, more African than English, but not a lot like either, truth be told. There were six or eight men in it, bending to their task with power.

"Shit," said Sam. "Best break those guns out now. Though God knows, if they want our blood no one and nothing's going to stop them, is it?"

"Leave the guns," said Will. "We hid 'em to show willing, now we'll live on hope. What is that, Sam? It looks like some old ship's skiff that's been botched up by apprentices. Hang on, I'll go about. Claw off the surf a little, in case we have to drift. Ready? Lee-oh."

By the time they were settled on the other tack the boat-canoe had drawn much closer to them. Will looked once more, and gasped, and said to Sam: "It's Deb. Oh Sam. She's sitting there. Oh Christ."

"Watch your luff," said Sam. "Don't go in irons, mister. That's no way to show off to a lady!"

"Take her!" said Will, and almost stumbled from the tiller. His face was white beneath his sun and weather tan and he was panting like a dog. Sam smartly took his place and filled the sail again, and looked himself at the young woman. She was sitting rigid in the skiff, at the stern, next to a man, gripping the gunwales with both hands. Sam could not make her features out, but he could see that she was beautiful. He eased the tiller up a little way to get off the wind, then eased and eased his sheet until their forward way was almost stilled. The skiff-canoe altered its course to meet them in parallel and in half a minute was abeam of them, but distant fifty feet. Bentley stood, arms stretched out sideways as before, and shouted: "No weapons! We have come in peace! Oh Deborah!"

He is in a sorry state, thought Holt, somehow surprised by it. I wonder how I'd feel myself, if I saw Felicity. I would hope, at least, for more control. Good God, poor William.

The gig was moving astern now, and Sam reversed the helm to bring her further off the wind, and sheeted in a trifle. He said to Will: "Let's drop the sail. Worm! Bring it down, will you? Then hold her on two oars."

"Will," said Deb, across the water. "Mr Bentley."

That was all, but as Worm and Holt got down the canvas, stowed it in a bundle and shipped two oars, the lovers seemed to drink and eat each other across the sparkling green. Will got out of the way like an automaton, moving forward rather than aft, and Worm settled to his task of keeping her head to sea while Sam sat at the tiller and assessed what the other boat might do.

The black man in the stern sheets stood, and his height was regal, and impressive.

"My name is Marlowe," he said. "You Captain Bentley, of England Royal Navy? Yes?"

Will fought hard to win back his gravitas. He also stood, as it seemed that protocol demanded it.

"I am Lieutenant Bentley. This is Lieutenant Holt. Our man here is called... Worm."

To him that sounded vile; but the Worm smiled happily at the other boat, and touched his forehead with his right oarloom.

"We are seeking Miss Tomelty. She is being hunted by some planters from near Kingston and their men. It is a... it is a great misunderstanding."

The boats were exactly parallel, heading the seas, not moving through the water. The canoe kept station perfectly, but came no closer. Will could barely take his eyes from Deb. He had a dying ache to touch her, to touch her skin. This was the Spithead Nymph, the Portsmouth Harlot, the Black Man's Whore. His mind whirled with vivid, violent images. She was a slut, a murderess, a traitor. She was great with Tsingi's child. She was Deb Tomelty, whom he had lain with first in Surrey, then in a London gayhouse, and whom he loved. He loved her still, and all the stories were of no moment at all, even if they were true, which they were not. He gazed with hunger at her face, to him so lovely, so unbearable, and all the fears and doubts were gone. He loved her still, and wanted her, to touch.

Marlowe was assessing him. He stared coolly at Will, his face without a flicker of emotion. Will felt that he would be a pitiless opponent, if it should come to that.

"We have a warning for you as well, sir," he said. "You and Miss Tomelty, and her friend Mildred. You are all held responsible for a massacre at two plantations. We believe — we *know* — it was neither you nor they. But an army is preparing to come west and you will be attacked."

Marlowe was balanced on the rolling, heaving boat-canoe as easy as a seaman. It was a long time before he answered. Will's eyes strayed to Deborah again. Her eyes were fixed on him.

She was in a simple cotton dress, and her arms and legs were bare. Her hair was still in massy curls, but the face framed by them was now dark brown, berry-like, she was a Jamaica country-girl. It was thinner too, he thought, perhaps she'd suffered much, and the longing to reach out for her was drowning him. He did not care what she had been forced to until now, he did not fear she was no longer his, he had an ache to touch her, that was all. An ache to kiss her mouth.

"Do you have muskets?" Marlowe asked, and Holt glanced at Will, a warning. But Will said, "Yes. They are not for use. They are wrapped in canvas, in the bottom here."

Marlowe said something in a foreign tongue, addressed at Worm, and sharp. The Worm acknowledged with a cheerful wave.

"Sorry, Cap'n. Don't speak that lingo. You could try a bit of French, *purrtettrer*? If you mean the muskets, though, the Cap'n's right. I'm standing on 'em, look."

He bent from off his thwart and re-emerged hugging a sausage of dun canvas, loosely lashed. He put his hand inside and exposed the muzzle of a gun.

"I will have them," Marlowe said.

Will sighed. He would have swapped his grandmother, truth to tell, to touch the skin of Deborah.

"What can I say, sir? We will not fight you for them, and if we did we would lose them anyway. But if I give them, I will probably get hanged. They are the King's."

Amazingly, Marlowe's face of sculpted ebony split into a smile, his mouth a gash of red and white.

"If you swear you will not turn them on me," he said, "then keep. You too beauty to be hanged by Georgie. This woman here she say she love you, you love her."

From the amazing to the ridiculous; Bentley began to blush. Sam, on the other hand, gave a loud harrumph.

"Good God, sir!" he said, apparently to Marlowe. "This is positively Italian! Let us all break into song! You have our word, sir, about the muskets. We promise you, we come in peace. We want to prevent bloodshed, not promote it. Now pray, sir, come and parley, lie alongside and let us talk. And let these bloody lovebirds love!"

There was good humour for a short time, and Marlowe's men did range up close to them, although not close enough for oar or paddle blade to touch. Marlowe was seated once more, and a long old-fashioned pistol with a belled-out end was rested at his side. A man in the bow held a musket ready, and there were doubtless others easily to hand.

"Miss Debbeerah say to trust you," Marlowe said. "What do you say to that? Why have you travel all so far? You two men against many. I can kill you. Tell me about this army."

Will's mind had scarcely got beyond the "trusting" part, or Deb. Marlowe seemed to know, and understand. For a short while the two craft rolled in the easy swell. The sun was very hot, but it was rather pleasant still. There was a long silence.

Will looked at her, from fifteen feet or less. She looked at him, both tried to speak their deepest thoughts and feelings through their eyes. To him, she was smaller, thinner, darker, just the same. To her he was harder, older, lined with care and weather, still beloved.

"Can I go with him?" she said. "Mr Marlowe, I want to go with Lieutenant Bentley. Please."

"Talk of army," Marlowe repeated. "How long before they come?"

"William," said Sam, quietly. "Don't get us hanged as spies, friend. Don't get us hanged by Daniel Swift and Kaye as traitors, will you?"

Marlowe had heard.

"I could go torture you," he said, and Deb gave a tiny cry, and Marlowe touched her lightly on the head. "But I learn nothing then. We scapegoats for the bakra men, because the Windward turncoats kill the bakra ladies. And they kill them because the planter-bloodhounds kill Maroon-chief son, call Tsingi. See, I know all. But what you give to make me safe? How you going stop this army kill me? What you offer for to win this woman back again?"

Will was sickened by awareness. He had nothing to offer, nothing at all.

"I could go take you hostage," Marlowe said. "That some bargaining, two of Georgie's officers and one old skinny slave man, what you think? But you would go fight me, and go die, and dead officer no good to me in any kind. You would go fight me, yes?"

Holt did not give Will the chance to speak.

"Surely," he said. "We would fight like tigers, and surely we would die. Unfortunately, Mr Marlowe, that is our duty. There's no avoiding it."

Deb, across the water, was weeping, and Will was pretty close.

Marlowe said: " I say this, Mr Lieutenant Bentley: I think Debbeerah was spy, she come to lead the men to us and get herself away. Now I believe her, like Mildred say I should. Debbeerah not spy. She your lover-maid. Debbeerah good woman."

Will's eyes had etched the new Deb — face and body, hair and soul — into his brain. Every inch of her was pleading to be with him. The sickness grew.

"She will be safe," said Marlowe. "So long as we be safe. Best for her and everyone you tell white man we not to blame. You do that, maybe you save my life, and Debbeerah's. And Mildred's. And everyone's. If they come we still not die though, maybe. Spirits look after us, maybe. Maybe we fight with demons in our soul. You try stop them, eh? That way the best."

Deb cried: "Please let me go, sir! Please let me go!" And Will said — "Deb."

Marlowe made a gesture and his crewmen dipped their blades in unison and the canoe-boat turned off from the gig and plunged into, then across, the waves. They worked very hard, and flew towards the headland like a gull. The Worm pulled the musket-muzzle back into sight and made a sign at it to Holt.

"He's tall enough and stiff enough, sir," he said. "You like I take a shot at him?"

"What for?" said Sam. "To make a bloody mess much worse? Give over with your bloody jokes, old man. Just stow it."

He turned a helpless glance on Will, then took the tailback of the halyard in hand.

"Come on, let's get this mains'l set," he said. "Fair wind for Kingston, what it's worth. Aye, for what it's fucking worth."

Chapter Twenty-Nine

Captain Daniel Swift, a charming man until, perhaps, you got to know him, had buried himself in Jamaica high society like a teredo worm. His shock and horror at the Misses Siddleham's fate, and that of their sainted mother, had not been feigned, nor had his determination to achieve revenge, and that a fast and bloody one. While Kaye was still away, though, and while Mather and his fellow gentlemen were raising their "great force," Swift went about the business of getting to know the place and its important people. The money in his pocket, and that of Kaye's father back in Hertfordshire, was in the forefront of his mind, and the more he saw of this benighted sugar island, the more convinced he was that they could make a killing. The time was ripe. The money pod was bursting.

The thing he realised most quickly and most keenly about this new found land was that anyone with tuppence in his pocket was a gentleman. Men and their ladies not fit to shine his shoes in England had houses with two dozen rooms, wine cellars full of France's best — and this in time of warfare, note — and enough servants to make a private army. Granted most of them were slaves, but that, to Swift, seemed admirable. The cost of their liveries alone would have seen him bankrupt in a month had Navy pay been his sole fortune, so the thought of paying them as well was anathema. The land was fecund, sugar needed men, and men cost money. Get the men for nothing, and you would be rich. Swift was determined to buy in.

Although the "tone" was low by England standards, the trappings of plantation life were exactly to his taste. Men rode to hounds, and drank, and had night-time societies to assuage the darker appetites of life, while the women kept house in certain elegance, without the rules that stifled normal men at home. The climate, basically, was not conducive to it. While the masters went to supervise, then to meetings, then to Assembly business, then to the courts to hang a black or two, the mistresses stayed in their cool mansions, or were taken out in covered carriages to share tea and sympathy with other coddled dames in darkened rooms. Their health was tenuous, they suffered heat and all the vilenesses of tropic life, and very frequently they were shipped off to spend a month or two in England. The sexes met at dinner not infrequently, and the younger wives would be visited sometimes at night for at least some months — or until their headaches had achieved an epic frequency or a child had come along to knock such new-wed filth out of the picture. Unhappy the woman whose first child was a female, not an heir. Unhappy the woman whose husband was a beast insatiable; or preferred white married flesh to easy black flesh or mulatto, slack married flesh to bouncing, elastic, younger meat.

Even the bound necessities that some planter men resented sounded rather good to Swift. To play a part in government would be a godsend to a man like him. As Justice of the Peace, as Colonel of Militia, as general hunter-down and punisher of wickedness he felt his talents would at last be properly appreciated. Ship captains, it was held by island thinkers, had the running of society in their very blood, and most agreed that Jamaica society was on a modern downward path. Softness had ruined the lower orders, softness had turned the slaves from happy subservients into sullen, savage, malcontents. When Swift expounded his view of Navy discipline, of bringing "proper punishment" back to the island, his companions cheered. At dinner party after dinner party he told his fellows that they should hate the poor, and hate slaves ten times worse. God abhorred the poor, he said, because they had not torn themselves from poverty. Therefore no punishment should be adjudged too cruel, because punishment was corrective and therefore was a kindness and God's will. Swift was not a noted drinker, but on some times in Jamaica he became almost intoxicated by his vision and his rhetoric. And the planters cheered him to the echo. It occurred to none of them, apparently, that Navy discipline, compared with what they used upon the island, had used from time immemorial and would use until the sea ran dry, was the stuff of nursemaids and puling milksops. In Daniel Swift's vision, it was the longed-for panacea.

With the Siddlehams in particular his clear sight struck a mighty chord. At first it had been his sympathy and interest that had appealed to them, and in the aftermath of the appalling massacre, in the funeral, and in the clearing out and clearing up at their devastated plantation home, he had become a well-known figure at their side, and indispensable. A small, hard-set man in dark blue and white, his shoulders back, his nose like a rake into the sky, he gave them strength and encouragement, he became their moral backbone. It was he who pulled them from despair, he who told them of his ideas and strategy for hunting down Marlowe and his murdermen, he who talked about the value of plantation life now that their normalcy was gone.

"We have lost everything, that is the devil of it," Jeremy told him one day, as they stood on a hillside looking down towards the house. "First Papa, and that was hard enough. But now Mama, and all our sisters. It hardly seems worth living any more. Well, living here, at any rate."

Swift, who prided himself on his subtle timing, adjudged it right to ask about profit and loss if they should quit. Was it not, he suggested delicately, a bad time to think of selling, given the war and depressed profits and higher insurances and all the other things?

Jeremy professed astonishment at Swift's knowledge, despite he was neither an island man nor immersed in commerce.

"You are right indeed, my friend," he said, "you have the whole thing at your fingertips. To sell up now would be a strange idea, quite foolish, because the price would not reflect the value. But the trouble is, you see, we are so very... well, disheartened, are Jonathan and I. Joe don't give a fig either way, at his age, he is just heartbroken that his Pa and Ma are gone. But me and Jonathan — well, to tell the truth of it, our hearts are broken, too. Between us two, and this must go no further, mind, well, if the right man came along, with the right money, well, we'd sell up like a shot. Sell? Nay — we'd damn near *give* it away."

Swift — timing again — ended this line of conversation here abruptly, declaring it too depressive to be borne. But he gave Jeremy a warning to be careful how he spoke, in case some man of little conscience might perceive the time as ripe to make a bid, and be persuasive only because the family felt so low. Jeremy seized his hand and wrung it.

"Good advice, sir, good advice," he cried. "Pray God that we can take it, brother Jonathan and me. But the temptation to just sell up and go, to throw the lot away, the years of grief and work and hardship — oh, I cannot tell you, friend. We are low at present, but the future is exceeding bright, our fortune must increase beyond belief, given a little time and energy put in. But where to get that from, how to drag it from our hearts, that's the problem, is it not? We are downhearted, sir, and there's an end to it. I am not very confident we can go on..."

To get them from this painful subject (before he went a step too far) Swift turned to matters military, to tactics, distances, and possibilities for the best achievement of reprisal. He had picked every brain among the island men about the strength and capability of Marlowe and his band, and he had gone to Captain Shearing and his grim lieutenant to double check. The islanders, he felt certain, were overconfident. They were champing at the bit for Kaye to return so that the thing could be set in motion and the victory won. Indeed, over the next few minutes, he felt once more that Jeremy Siddleham thought the thing would be as easy as a mouse-hunt. He could not wait, it seemed, to march out in pomp, find Marlowe, and behead him on the spot. For Swift, that begged many questions.

"The trouble as I see it, sir," he said, "is that we lack knowledge of their whereabouts, these renegades. All very well to push out westward with 'musket, fife and drum' as the song has it, but how do we locate them? Marlowe ain't going to sit and wait for us, is he? He ain't going to come out of the woodland and form up in battle lines for us to run at and destroy? I mean, for God's sake, sir — how do we come down on him?"

Siddleham could see that he was serious, but he still made rather light of it.

"There are ways, sir," he said. "These niggers are not subtle men, are they? We will go in pomp and panoply, with uniforms and drums, if not fifes, indeed! They are like to children, sir, they will come out of the bushes to see the passing show. We can push them, if we need to, right to the far shore. We can push them off the cliffs into the sea."

"Do we have no spies, though?" asked Swift. He did not wish to denigrate, so he kept his feelings tightly penned. "I am sure you have it right, sir, but we do not have much time at our command. At the very least, remember, the French fleet might appear on the horizon, it is always possible. As a commander, I would be happier to set off in certain knowledge that the quarry won't elude me."

This time his eyes betrayed a certain bleakness, which Siddleham took care to read. He sighed.

"Aye, Captain Swift," he said. "'Tis pity that we lack an island network. We have one, of course, but... well, indeed it could be better. Our bloodhounds are efficient, and we can offer bribes." He gave a short laugh. "We have white men from time to time, turncoats, lovers of the pirate life, or of black women, more simply. But most of them we hang, and some are deportees. They make good spies, as they can talk to either camp. There are rumours that the Lamonts are somewhere on the island, but I cannot think it true. Scotchmen, the filthy scum of Aberdeen. They escaped the gallows by the merest thread and a strong hint of corruption, but they wouldn't escape a second time, if they did dare to sneak back. They were efficient spies, though. As well as being rapists, thieves and murderers."

"Ah, Caledonia," said Swift, in mild disgust. "'Fore God, Siddleham, we are beset by races much inferior, 'tis not the blacks alone that bear the mark of Cain." He sighed. "Nonetheless, if we have no good spies, we must make best use of the ones we have, I cannot impress too much our need for solid information. We are not hunting mice, sir, we are hunting a deep dyed villain who is reputed as a warrior. You spoke of bribes. Can I take the liberty to exhort you? Speak to your fellow gentlemen, speak with a purpose. The expenditure of some few guineas, I believe, would pay back its weight in something worth more than just mere gold. I must leave it up to you."

The hard eyes bored into those of Siddleham, but he did not quail. Which heartened Swift most mightily. This man, he felt, was one that he could trust.

***

The Lamonts, at the abandoned stockade, did not waste time luxuriating in their new-found estate. Almost before the *Jacqueline* was finally disappeared they had satisfied themselves there was no trace of treasure left behind, then they began to organise the men, both black and white, into those who knew about deep diving and those who did not. Thompson and Mick Carver retained their positions as masters, with Timba as their jewel, and Chattel was given the task by his "mannie," Dod, of selecting and testing out the new young men they'd persuaded to join them from the hinterland on their journey to the *Biter* bay. He also knew the location of the hidden canoe, and the best water-springs, and he played his cards with notable success. Wee Dod still treated him with brute disdain, but made it clear Chattel was a cut above the others and must be seen as such. This meant a cut above some of the white men also; and when Seth Pond objected, Dod beat him insensible with his pistol-butt. Chattel became part of the inner circle in some small respects. Most notably, the Scots listened to him, and took note. He was a good man for their purposes, they believed. That was enough.

Chattel, the canoe recovered, selected men to build a raft like the one they'd used before (which the Jacquelines had inevitably destroyed), and others to trap animals, gather fruit and plants, and set up cooking places. While this went on he took men out two-by-two with Timba to get a diving crew. Among the lumber left by the English in the stockade as too bulky or unimportant to take away, perhaps, was rope, pig iron and some spikes. A salvage captain could have scarcely asked for more.

Five men were chosen to be the divers, all young, all small, with chests "too little to have any lungs at all" according to the jealous white men who were forced to take a supporting role. Two had English names, two West Coast African, and one — Scrap — that may have been a dog's or a description. Before nightfall on the first day they had reached the sunken deck, and by an hour after dawn the next had brought some silver up. The Scots, however, were not men for a celebration. They took the plunder into the inner fortress; and looked at it. When Fat Mick tried to come and join them they told him coldly that this sanctum was their own, and when, some hours later round the night-time fire, Chris Thompson asked them where the *Santa* treasure was, the stuff they'd sailed away with when the Spanish ship was scuttled, they told him dangerously to mind his business. The two men who'd sailed with them, Miller and Morgan, privately insisted later that they did not know either. The Scots had spirited it away.

Another thing that convinced them of Chattel's true worth was his continued lack of interest in the value of the stuff brought to the surface. Fat Mick had told them early on that the black men were too stupid to recognise a fortune when they saw one, but the Scots had suspected he was up to something, that he had a secret deal, perhaps, with the nigger strongmen. They questioned Chattel craftily about it from the start, and analysed his answers exhaustively, when it was just the three of them, alone. He quickly disabused them of the notion that Africans did not know the *worth* of gold, but pointed out that they were slaves and runaways who could never hope to go back to the towns. Even the poorest white man, if offered some of the gold or silver in the way of bribery, would merely take the riches, then put the black to death himself, or set the weight of planters' justice on him. Which meant bloodhounds, militia, dogs, and death.

"We stay out in the woods, see?" Chattel said. "No work in them sugar fields is paradise for us! We hunt, and sell flesh to the white man, even. We visit the womans in the woman towns, they fuck and feed us, raise up all our kid. You white man think you have one beauty life, you wrong. All you got is hunger for him gold. All you fun is kill him nigger man. We don't want you kill us, so we be you friend. We dive for you. We bring him treasure up. If Navy come we go fight them 'long o' you — or go run, depend on if they winning."

Three bearded faces stared at him. Chattel looked calmly back.

" It good to be part of you strong force," he said. "It fun to rob and steal and kill him planter man and rape him wife and bakra-missy. And when you win all treasure and go move along, we fellow stay in woods. Why you think we want move?"

Wee Dod got off his log and walked up close to Chattel, and Chattel did not flinch or shift his gaze. He was unafraid.

"Ye'll dae fer me," said Dod. "I'm yer mannie, ken? An' ye're ma loon."

They smiled. They understood.

***

The Worm was at the tiller as they sailed across the *Biter* bay heading for Port Royal, and it was in the middle of the night. Lieutenants Holt and Bentley were asleep, peaceful on the bottomboards, and the old black man was dozing, but keeping course as ancient sailors will. The breeze was on his larboard cheek, and if it moved across his neck as the gig slid off her heading, his inexorable hand brought her gently back. The night was black, the air was sweet as milk, the world was all serene.

In any way, there was nothing to be seen on shore that would have drawn the Worm's attention. The fires were all down, the men were all sleep, even the lookouts. The gig, what's more, was a long way out. They had headlands to avoid. The bay, to all intents, was empty. The gig, and three-man crew, sailed gently on.

Chapter Thirty

Slack Dickie, when the *Jacqueline* dropped hook in Kingston harbour, was still as drunk as he had been on leaving Biter Bay, and John Gunning was as sober as a judge. At first the people had found it amusing and endearing to see their slack-mouthed skipper slouching round the quarterdeck, or being led below to sleep the brandy off, but it had palled. One drunk in high position was enough, in any man's opinion, and his inebriation was of a different order from London Jack's wild bouts. For a start he was damned miserable, and on one occasion had been caught out, so Rat Baines insisted, weeping behind the jollyboat. This was not believed exactly — it was, after all, Rat Baines — but like all rumour on every ship grew legs and wings and heart. Far from feeling pity for their suffering commander, the people felt embarrassment and shame.

Gunning, as the nearest man to another Navy officer on board, bore the brunt of it, and wished indeed (though idly) that Surgeon Grundy had rejoined the ship from his supposed duties in Port Royal so that he could have added another well of drunken sympathy. For Kaye, as Gunning told it to Ashdown and Bosun Taylor later, had "took to mewling like some sort of lovesick maid or shepherd swain," and the strangest thing, the most deeply scandalous, was that the loss of Marianne Siddleham was no more the major focus of his misery.

"It is Black Bob he seems to mourn," said Jack, as the three of them shared coffee in the silent, scented darkness on the night that they had slipped their mooring. "I helped him to his berth to save him sleeping on the deck like some damn longshore loafer, and he damn near told me so in words. You'd have thought the Scotch had ate the little neger the way Slack Dick went on. He was babbling that we should have never let him go, that Sam Holt was some sort of heartless bastard who deserved a wicked fate."

"Christ," said Bosun Taylor. "Did I come into it? It was me and Mr Holt that done the deed, in fact!"

Gunning laughed.

"I told you he was arseholes-under. You never got a mention, Jem. You ain't an officer, you see? You don't impinge upon a gentleman like Dick!"

"Did he not mention Mistress Siddleham, then?" put in Ashdown, in his soft Irish voice. "By gob, I was in the stockade when he got the news that day, and you'd have thought he might be going to die there on the spot. I saw him push a bottle down his neck and suck it nearly dry."

"He did an'all," said Gunning. "He took it off of me without a word of by your leave. Mr Black's very best, it was — or put another way, Pure Pusser's Piss. But he seemed to love her fair enough, back then. Though Lieutenant Bentley damn near blubbed as well I must report, and he's hot for the Spithead lass. Christ, men are foolish, so we are."

"I can't see Bentley blubbering," said Ashdown. "He's not a soft-one, is he?"

Jem Taylor grunted.

"He is like blazing buggery," he said. "He's just sweet-natured is the thing. I've seen him slap down Toms Hugg and Tilley side-by-side together in the times gone by. Now *they* was lovebirds in their own sweet way, till Tommy Tee swapped spit with a mosquito, but no one said they wasn't men, did they? Not if they wanted to keep on breathing God's fresh air."

"Aye," mused Gunning. "And Tom Aitch is wed now, ain't he? To Black Nell, and she's a woman, far as you can tell. Well I know she is, for I've rolled with her meself, although you needn't tell him that, if you please! The point is, friends, Captain Dickie Kaye is maybe lost. And any port's the watchword ain't it, in a storm?"

They watched Kaye keenly in the ensuing days, but Gunning had no more converse with him on the subject, although the captain was assiduous in his "following of the spirit." Gunning reported this — although a blind man would have been hard-pressed not to notice it — with a certain self-amused intolerance, as he had "forswore the drink myself," but Ashdown and Taylor, and several others of the crew, were increasingly disturbed. Slack Dickie was a man of very many faults, who could not be trusted as far as one could sneeze, but it emerged that he was held in some affection, if not esteem. There were more drunks than ruptures on a Navy ship, and ruptures were not easy to avoid. Some men died of drink, many were ruined by it, and for an officer it was a great disaster. For his people, too, if he should mistake a lee shore for a sheltered refuge in a hurricane and drop his hook and trice up all his sails. Dickie, in the normal run, was

Dickie: to be tolerated, amused by, or in worst-case cursed and moaned about. This new Dickie was some sort of stranger; a stranger they would give nothing to, and sympathy least of all.

One thing they would give though — they had to, it was in the nature of their trade — was loyalty. When Swift's gig ranged up alongside the entry port back in Kingston harbour, with Dickie white around the gills, and unsteady despite hot coffee by the gallon, you'd have thought he was the Pope for pomp and dignity. Swift clambered up, was piped by men so clean and neat it hurt them, and greeted first by London Jack, in white shirt and dark blue coat as smart as if he'd taken King's commission after all. He begged Swift's pardon for the captain in advance because, he said, he had become the victim of some tropical distemper, which they feared might be the very one that had "killed off half the crew." Swift was a brave man but not incautious, so stayed far enough off Kaye, they hoped, to avoid the fumes of wine and brandy exhaling from his pores and pallid lips, and kept the first meeting down to greetings and expressions of his "urgent hopes that they could get things humming pretty soon." If he suspected Kaye was drunk no matter, for he knew him as a sober man in general, who had made an error, possibly, which all men did from time to time. He passed on greetings from his noble father, and hinted broadly that their private business on the island had been set in train already; they must talk. As the main stow started, Swift was rowed ashore, and Slack Dickie went to bed; without a bottle. Gunning was his guard.

Kaye was struggling, there was no doubt of that, and a lesser man than London Jack would not have kept him off the liquor. Nobody knew if Jack himself believed it when he said that he no longer drank (they did not) but he said it always and with complete conviction, ergo, he thought Dick's desire to get outside a bottle was ridiculous, unnecessary, vaguely nauseating, and was prepared to enforce the rule with utter ruthlessness. When Bentley and Holt came alongside the sleeping *Jacqueline* in their gig one very early morning, he had not touched a drop for countless hours. He was awake though, and staring at the deckhead when Gunning announced them. He was not surprised at their arrival, not moved, not anything. They offered a report, and he listened to their adventures listlessly. It boiled down to this: they had found the maid, they had talked to the renegade, and they believed that all of them were innocent of any part in the recent massacre. They wished to know if he accepted their assessment; he did not care to reach a conclusion either way. Miss Siddleham was dead, that much he did know. And little Bob was lost to him, as well.

One thing did flicker in his interest.

"You met offshore, you say? But could you find this man again, this Marlowe man? Your Uncle Swift is—" Then there came another flicker. "Hold hard," he said. "I sent you back before me to sail down here and report I was delayed! Do you tell me you went off on... Well, bugger me!"

For a moment he seemed angry, pleased, amused. Then his interest lapsed again. What did it matter, anyway? But Holt followed up the thought.

"No sir, sadly, I doubt we'd find the man again." He was rather proud of this word, this "sadly." It was a piece of luck indeed that Marlowe could not be tracked. "That is why they rowed out to us, I guess. The Worm — our black sailor, sir, remember? — our Worm took us to an area he thought the rogues would be keeping overlooked, and so it proved. We saw no beach or landing there at all, in fact, but Marlowe sailed off from somewhere, it was a quite heavy boat. A hidden cove maybe. Maybe even a cave — the rocks are a honeycomb, it's true. Sadly, if we want to speak to Mr Marlowe in the future, he will have to find us out, not vice versa. It is a hider's paradise, Captain Kaye."

***

Next time Kaye met Captain Swift he was stone sober, but his mood was still weak and yonderly. He had gone ashore escorted, discreetly, by London Jack, with the purpose of meeting the Siddlehams. They had had more time to achieve composure now, they had had the funeral, the support of all their friends and fellows through the worst of times, but they all still put on a show of manly grief, even Joseph, despite his careless age. Kaye cried frankly, and Jeremy and Jonathan dabbed their eyes with lawn. But his shuddering was soon embarrassing, and Kaye became aware of it. He wondered if his grief were natural, in fact, and became almost lost in his confusion. Marianne's austere and haughty face — beloved, truly — kept merging with Black Bob's. As touched with misery, indeed, but far more...beautiful. Suddenly, Dick Kaye was dying for a drink.

Gunning took him off from the Siddlehams', on their hired mules, before the decanters did the rounds, on "press of urgent business." It was by pre-arrangement, and it was to be with Swift, in a quiet corner of the Navy Offices. Swift had been picking Shearing's brains on readiness and tactics, and let him know a portion of the concern he felt about striking off into the interior without a guarantee that they would come up with the "enemy." Shearing, naturally, had agreed with Swift that it was difficult, as he had also with the planters' line that it would be... well, not *too* difficult. When Swift had challenged him on this, Shearing had smiled his easy, easy smile.

"I have to live here, Captain," he said. "If I do not back them in their expeditions, my position is untenable. And I expect that you, and they, will find some 'Afric hordes' to fall upon, even if not this Marlowe man himself, if he does indeed exist. You've heard of 'Nanny'? A mythic creature, said to be a woman, revered and loved by all the foolish island savages despite the fact that no one's ever seen her. Ah, but their friends have though, or their friends' friends at the very least, so she does exist indeed, she is as real as you or I. Or, indeed, as Mr Marlowe. *Quod erat demonstrandum.*"

Swift thought such sophistry unbecoming in a Navy man, and let it show.

"Word games are one thing, sir," he said, "but I must do the fighting. For you, and them, and His Majesty the King. I take it hard indeed I have no intelligence, no certainty. I am deploying several hundred men. If they do not fall through force of rebel arms they'll die of the vile diseases on this filthy island, in some probability. I take it hard that I must strike out blind."

Shearing removed all traces of his smile.

"Aye indeed," he said. "It is unsatisfactory, Captain Swift, infortunate. But people have died, sir. Important people. Rich young ladies. The world is full of savages, and it is our duty to destroy and cleanse them. In Jamaica young men come back with black men's heads strung from their saddles, and claim a bounty. It is paid to make the world a better place. It is paid to spread morality, and the Word of God. We are Christians, sir. We behave as such."

Jackson was up to his tricks of insolence, coughing wildly in a corner. Dan Swift looked up to see the doors swing open, and his friend and colleague Richard Kaye step in. At last, thought Swift. Some common sense. He hoped to God he'd picked up something on his voyage to the West. And not just malaria, neither...

With the room cleared of all but the two of them — and drinks ordered, as quickly as might be — Swift clasped Dick's hand (checking his pallor first for infectivity) and gave him the warmest greetings from his father, and as an afterthought, his Mama and sisters too. He asked after his current health (better, much better Kaye replied, remembering what London Jack had bid him say), and how he had been "succeeding in his quest."

This threw Kaye considerably, because for the life of him he could not imagine what the quest might be. The secret treasure Swift should not know about? The march into the West? The hunting of the English whore? The recovery from his loss of Marianne? He was saved by a quiet tapping on the door and the entry of a tall black man in servants' livery. He had brandy and wine, and a jug of lime and other juices, mixed up with soft brown sugar. Gunning had said quite brutally that he must avoid strong drink at any cost, and Slack Dickie wavered for all of half a moment. He saw Marianna gazing at him, and Black Bob's face melding into hers. He accepted brandy and conveyed to his trembling lips. Swift, not noticing, not interested, took a glass of wine, and did not touch it.

With the servant gone, Kaye had worked it out.

"Ah," he said. "Our venture. We gentlemen of property." He felt the brandy sliding down his throat, spreading inside his stomach, and he felt no less bleak at all. "Well, yes, sir, I have had my feelers out. But you understand... events, sir. Events. I must confess I... well, sir... tragedies indeed."

"Pah, tragedies," said Swift. "Aye, sir, of course there have been tragedies. That is why God put us here on earth, we are His warriors, our function now to slaughter people, get revenge. I know you have a personal interest in this one, and I'm sorry for it, naturally, but I sense a golden opportunity for us, very close to home. I have already penned an outline to your father back in Hertfordshire. I have requested that he readies credit to transfer. Do you tell me you have not thought of this yourself?"

Kaye was blinking at the speed of it. He had not seen this man for an age, he had gone through hell and high water since they had spoken business last, and Swift was at it as though it were the only topic to be thought about. He had hardly greeted him, indeed; had scarce acknowledged that there'd been a separation.

"An outline, sir?" he said. "What opportunity?"

"The Siddlehams," said Swift, lifting his nose and staring down it as Kaye swallowed more brandy. "I thought you knew them well? I thought that you were... intimate? Well, do you know they're on the verge of selling up?" He narrowed his eyes, assessing the effect: and found it disappointing, possibly. "Hmph. You do not understand the implications is all that I can think. They are on the verge of selling up one of Jamaica's finest plantations, sir. At a knockdown price. They are prepared, in all effect, to give the place away. To the right man, sir, the right man only. Hmph! And that right man, sir, is going to be me!"

Kaye needed more brandy. The fact he was not surprised confused him, worried him. He had put out feelers, as he had said to Swift, in fact he had had a similar conviction. But it was related to his own unique connection with the Siddlehams, his own bond of trust and intimacy. Good God, he thought, I was going to be wed to Marianne! I was going to be one of them! How has Swift done this?

"Sir," he said. "I had some inkling of it, as a general possibility. Jeremy and myself, and Jonathan. Well, it was only something in the air."

"Haha!" said Swift. "You see, my boy! Strike while the iron is hot. I came, I saw, and I damn well intend to conquer. I have brought money with me — some cash, some credit notes, and I have made it clear to them that I — we — are interested, and will pay in all due haste. Your father will back me, no doubt of that, and the brothers have stressed the need for expedition. Many people offer things, they say, and many things get mired in the bog. London is such a damn long way away, and transferring wealth is never easy. And there's a war on, never forget. Our speed is paramount. Without it, the deal may not be struck."

Kaye — to give himself time for thought, he told himself — poured brandy into his crystal. He swirled it, looked at it, as if assessing a particular variety, interest only, no great desire to taste. But he forced himself, and nodded, mild appreciation. Swift was indifferent to this charade. There was one subject, only, in his mind.

"But we cannot move too fast, sir," said Kaye. "Even if my father is able to make up the price at speed. I do not know the Jamaican system, but there will be legal things, for certainty. There is no society in this wide world, however backward, that does not have lawyers battened on to it."

This earned a laugh, but it was a scornful one.

"Bah, lawyers. The Siddlehams are gentleman, like us. Good heavens, Dick, their father was Sir Nathaniel. If he was a baronet, as I assume, then Jeremy becomes Sir Jem, instanter. We are not in association with London sharks. Trust is not dead, is it, among our quality of man? The only thing I would not trust them for is to hang on for us if someone makes a bigger, quicker offer before we've shook on it."

"But surely, sir, the figures. The yearly profits. God forbid, the losses. I mean, they said that times were bad. Surely we need to see percentages? The books?"

"Oh yes, yes, yes, naturally it will all be signed and sealed and such. I told you, I have spoke to them of it; we went in in some detail. They were unutterable frank. I know the business backwards — and we *must* buy. Look, Captain Kaye — Richard — we will be related in the not too distant future, when my kinsman Bentley weds your Felicity. We are family, man! Do you think I would rush into anything that is not cast-iron sound, and copper-bottomed? As soon as any hint gets out, it will be bees around the honeypot, that is our problem. We must secure it. We *must*."

The spirits were climbing to Slack Dickies' head. This man was like a wire spring, he was overwhelming. And he must be right, indeed he must, for the Siddlehams *were* gentleman, and very fine, and Marianna had been a part of their deliberations over land and money, she had said that many times. It was just... Dick snatched another mouthful from his glass. He had a sudden insight: he imagined his father's rage if it went wrong, if money was spent out on a goose chase. Worse, he imagined his father's contempt. For him. He had said once, to his face, that his only trust in him was to do things wrong. Dick stared at Swift with a sudden, strange intensity. Swift's face was bold, and proud, and aquiline, without a shadow of self-doubt. Swift was completely confident in his own excellence, and in his plan. So should Slack Dickie be.

He said, rather faintly: "We must sign nothing though. Not until we've... not until there ain't no shadow of a doubt, sir. Do you... is that agreed?"

Swift laughed heartily.

"Oh indeed, indeed!" he cried. "Nothing on paper till the Lord High Chancellor's had a sniff himself if you should deem it necessary! But expedition is our watchword, my boy. We must push it very hard. Which word — expedition — leads me rather neatish onto a different subject altogether, that is however, closely bound, nay, inextricably. We have to go, sir, into the mountains, into the West, to slaughter this damn renegade. And while we do it for the common good, we turn it to our favour also, as long-headed men will do. For if we undertake this expedition with expedition — *expeditiously!* — it plays well with the Siddlehams as a firm concomitant. It makes them even more *beholden* to us, do you see? It gives them more *incumbency* to view us with deep favour. Do take my meaning, lad? Do you see that which I'm driving at?"

All Kaye could see was that Captain Swift had worked himself into some minor frenzy of self-admiration by his way with words, which Dick, already rather drunk, could hardly follow, truth to tell. He merely blinked, and waited for enlightenment. Swift viewed him with some irritation.

"Pah," he said. "No poesie in the soul. Look, Captain Kaye, we need to move into the hinterland, and we need to move there soon. If we pull it off, we pull the land sale off inevitably, at the greatest advantage to ourselves. Our problem is, we are heading for the wide blue yonder with blinkers on our eyes, these people have no spies. How much better if we could return in double time with his head upon a stick, this bloody Marlowe. He has killed their Mama and their girls, he has destroyed their heart for staying here, Jeremy has told me so in terms. If only we knew where the bastard could be found! You've been down-coast, you've been far down the West. Was there nothing that you found that could give us the advantage?"

Kaye blinked once more. There was something forming in the liquor haze. He had it.

"Will Bentley has been farther west," he said. "Your nephew and Holt. In fact — good God, sir, they have *spoke* to Marlowe! And the whore!" His face clouded. "Aye, but they both say they are innocent," he added. "They say it was not them."

"To hell with that!" Swift snapped. "To hell with that and all! They've spoke to them?! For Christ's sake, man, why did you not tell me this? Where? Can they take me to them? Good God, sir, this is what we need! Where are they, Holt and Bentley? We must see them! Now!"

Something else came through the fug. Kaye's grip tightened on his glass. He winced.

"Ah, sir," he said. "They cannot take you to him, I recall it now. They met offshore, he came out in a skiff. Well, a hermaphrodite of some island kind, a half a skiff and half an African canoe. They parleyed, then they went ashore."

"They? Bentley and Holt?"

"No, sir. The renegade and the English harlot. They state specifical that they do not know their whereabouts. They think there might be some secret cove. And in any case, when once they'd gone ashore again... well — they could have struck out anywhere."

Swift's face had darkened, and his eyes were bright with anger.

"Shit," he muttered. "Incompetents and fools. Oh shit and degradation." He cried out with sudden passion: "We need spies! Why do we have no spies? White men that shag the nigger gals are best, according to young Siddleham, but they tend to string them up. He mentioned Scotchmen too, some murderers from Aberdeen, but they got chased away. They ship these people off and leave no one to help us, just because they rob and kill! It's rank insanity!"

Kaye knit his brow in puzzlement.

"Hold hard, sir. Did you say Aberdeen? What, Siddleham said— He did not give them names, by any chance... If their name should be Lamont, sir..." For a moment he seemed overcome. "I had them, sir, I had them off that villain Coppiner. But I do not have them now, they are deserters, runaways. And they are traitors, sir, disloyal to the King or anyone. They have stolen... they have kidnapped one of our... my..."

He tailed off, not knowing how to finish. But Swift, his spirits raised then dashed, was now cast down.

"Runaways," he murmured. "In this damn God-hole all useful men are runaways. Ah well, Kaye, they sounded like the men for me, they sounded like perfection on a monument. Deserters, traitors, killers, kidnappers, and you don't know where the bastards are. Ah well. I am not paid to mope. We'll set off blind in any case. A pity, though. They sound like men of steel."

Slack Dickie's brain went from dim to bright in half an instant. He raised his glass slowly to his lips this time, and allowed himself a smile. Men of steel, invincible. But with Swift in the question, and money for the bribes...

"But, sir," he said. "I do not have them, but I do know where they are. I know where they are, and they know where the black man is as well. And the black man's whore. For money they will sell him to us. For money they will sell anything, or any one."

He was thinking of Black Bob. He was thinking of Black Bob, and bribery or force. He heard a voice, as through a mist.

"Where?" Swift repeated. His tone grew sharper. "Where, man? Captain Kaye!"

Kaye smiled.

"We will have to go by sea," he said. "They have a fort, but it is not impregnable. Two days, sir, or three. We will not even have to storm them. No, sir — merely bribery. They will do anything for gold, the Lamont brothers. Anything."

Chapter Thirty-One

The planning and the preparation was the job of less than three days. When Captain Swift had finished picking Kaye's brains, he moved with the speed that made him such a formidable commander. He called Captain Shearing into the room, excluded Jackson, and sent messengers to speak to Andrew Mather, the Siddlehams, Alf Sutton, and some other leading planters. His exegesis was stark: they could find the renegade commander, and they could attack and slaughter him. All they needed was ships, and arms, and men. They had all three.

Will and Sam, when they received their briefing in the cabin of the *Pourquois Pas*, were struck with horror. The Lamonts were the key, Swift told them, and it was due to Richard Kaye they could be found. Both lieutenants almost lost themselves in agitation. These men were criminals, they pointed out, who had — and then they caught Kaye's frantic gesture behind Swift's back, and had to pull their punches, to cover up his own specific crimes. The Scots were evil men, they feebly argued, and dangerous, not to be trusted. To use them might unleash all kinds of savage and unpleasant acts. What was more, Will added, there was little evidence at all of Marlowe's guilt.

Swift's contempt was corruscating. They were behaving he said, worse than Jamaica's namby-pamby men, who at least eschewed such idleness as to say the nigger Marlowe was not a savage murderer, fit only to be strung up and destroyed. The Scots, he said — he liked the phrase indeed — were men of steel. He needed them to do a certain job, as no one else could, that was manifest. And what of evil, anyway — so long as it was evil genius! He needed men of steel, and the Lamonts were the nearest he could hope to come to it. They would contact them now; instanter!

"What, sir, us, sir?" said William, feeling like some sort of foolish schoolboy; and Swift skewered him with those famous eyes.

"No, sir! Us, sir! All of us! We will set sail almost immediate, we will take both our ships, while the island men, led by Mr Mather as their Colonel, will mobilise militia, backed up by their trusty blackhound slaves, and strike out through the roads and woodlands. When we reach the bay where Captain Kaye knows the Scotchmen are, we will contact and employ them. They will direct us to the renegades, we will engage with Colonel Mather's army, and our vengeance will be wrought."

The wind blew gently through the cabin windows, bearing island and harbour sounds that were redolent of peace. Sam said pointedly: "And will you pay them, sir? As criminals unhung?"

"Lieutenant Holt, you border on the insolent," said Swift. "We are here to do our duty, and it ill behoves you to reveal such attitudes. Thanks to Captain Kaye we have a way to come up with our quarry, and I'll thank you not to be so nice. The Scotch men will be pleased to do their duty, I confide. And if they will not, I will have them hanged. There!"

Despite themselves, the lieutenants joined in laughter, although Swift, quite clearly, did not think that he had made a joke. But Sam persisted with his questioning, because, he argued, he could not see why the Lamonts should help, or even be there when they reached the bay. Kaye said that he had seen them moving to the stockade, which surely must be a fine prize for a marauding band to have, why should they leave it? A fortress built for them, defensible, good quarters, water not far off. Bentley exchanged a speaking glance with Holt: no mention of the treasure then, which was the Scotsmen's actual draw. Whichever way though, they accepted Kaye was right.

Will said: "I'll wager we will have to pay them, though, for all that. We know them, Uncle. They are not like normal men."

Kaye added lightly: "Aye, Captain. Cash on delivery, however. We'll pay up when we get Marlowe on a plate. Worth a groat or two, when all is said and done. The boys are right, though. These Scotch are wily coves, more twists than a serpent's coil. Pay nothing till they've done the job, then watch out they do not cut your purse and all!"

Swift's smile was supercilious. He treated them like rather silly boys.

"Ah me," he said. "I see you do not know my method, after all. Never mind. These men will serve me well, believe me, and they will serve my purpose, and they'll do it happily." His nose rose like a blade. "And then I'll hang them, naturally. All three."

This time he did laugh, but the others were less inclined to. He took that badly, growing somewhat angry and impatient.

"God save me, you are blowing hot and cold!" he snapped. "Look, this is the cutting off of cancer, do not you see? We will sail and march on Marlowe and attack him from all sides. It is a reprisal, against men who will not bow to the law, who will not even sign treaties like good honest Maroons! You say he is not guilty, I say 'Pah' and 'No matter anyway — is he not black? Is he not some sort of runaway?' You say the Scotch are also criminals, but so what for that, as well? They can help us do the job, and if it does not work, so what again? What is lost? Something of value or some merely worthless lives? A renegade, a whore, some sons of Caledonia. And between these cabin walls, my friends, we earn a useful gratitude on this island, that will stand us in good stead. Now go about your business, and prepare. I go ashore to settle final details. It is time that we were under way."

Among the other things he did on shore, they found out later, was to go and see the Siddlehams, on the estate he somehow looked on as already being his. As promised, Swift did not sign anything, in spite the fact that Jeremy and Jonathan had had preliminaries drawn up already by their lawyers.

When they seemed cast down, though, the captain seized them by the hand, one after the other, and shook firmly and fervently. They were Englishmen, all three, what need of signatures? The deal was done.

***

The sail from Kingston to the *Biter* bay was not fast, through lack of useful wind, but when the *Jacqueline*, now fully-manned right down to Grundy and the surviving sick-berth men, pulled round the final headland, there was, naturally, no sign of diving activity and not much sign, indeed, of any human goings-on. There was a fire burning, though, and that was deliberate. The Scots, once their lookouts had reported two ships in the offing, had brought their raft and other craft ashore, lifted them by force of muscle, and hidden them behind the stockade in the underbrush. It had been a fixed rule that any treasure brought up was taken inland every day and secreted, so there was nothing else incriminating to be happened on. That the fortress had been taken over was not worth hiding, because the fortress -- without its secret source of wealth -- was merely a handy base and not worth fighting for, in this lonely, useless bay. Let the Navy see they had it by all means: but let them not imagine the sunken gold could be the draw.

The *Jacqueline* dropped anchor first, by previous arrangement, and the *Pourquoi Pas* remained some way away, to be unthreatening. As soon as they were fast, Slack Dickie Kaye got in a boat manned lightly by an unarmed crew (although there were muskets and pistols beneath a loose-draped sail on the bottomboards) and had her pulled into hailing distance. Then he stood up (which proved to the Lamonts at least that he was not drunk this time) and bellowed.

"Ahoy there! You Lamonts! If you're in there, show yourselves! We mean no harm! We can offer you a pardon! There is a matter you can aid us in!"

It was a strange speech, and it echoed back from the trees, perhaps the stockade walls. The air was motionless, and very hot, with hardly any surf to disturb the quasi-silence. Bentley, sitting with the yokelines in his hand, heard words come gently back at intervals. "No harm... pardon... aid..."

For two full minutes there was no response. He could see that Kaye was sweating, it was running out beneath his wig, towards his hazel eyes. He saw him fill his lungs again.

"Ahoy there! Hey— Ah...ah, there you are. Ah."

The last words were at talking level, and Kaye glanced down at Will.

"The bastards," he said, quietly. "Yes, there they are indeed, Bentley. And where's my little Bob, I wonder? Where's my little Bob..."

Two of the Lamont brothers walked out of the stockade and down towards the water's edge. Behind them the third appeared, Wee Dod, with a musket in his hand, but casually, held by the muzzle, the butt-end trailing in the sand. Then came Thompson, and Fat Mick. Mick waved, rather fatuously, but the others all had unmoving, watchful faces.

"I will come ashore," said Kaye. "You need have no fear, there will be no trickery. I come on island business."

The boat sat in the gentle swell, her oarsmen dipping from time to time to hold her station. Kaye gave no further order, so she moved no nearer to the beach. In the heat, the stillness, this struck Will as unreal. Were they to go ashore, or was Kaye afraid? Would the Lamonts allow it, anyway? A fly flew out and settled on his eyelid. He brushed it away, the starboard yokeline bunched in his hand. And it returned.

"Ye can come ashore," said Angus. "If so ye care to. We winna harm ye, Mr Kaye." He took two paces forward, which were mirrored by his companions, save for Dod. Dod just stood, and rested on his musket. He scratched his nose. Angus added: "We've got yer wee black loon."

Kaye made a noise that Will could not interpret, a noise of pain or rage perhaps, suppressed. The Scotsman laughed. He knew its meaning well, it seemed.

"Well, Cap'n Dickie? Will ye step ashore wi' us? Ye're more'n welcome."

"Go," said Kaye, to Will. And "Give way together," Will instructed. "Gently, now. Way enough. Hold water. Bowman there! Ashore."

The forefoot touched the sand and a sailor leapt ashore to take the stemhead. Will kept the oars out, the oarsmen hovering. They could go astern and off at any moment.

But Kaye was not constrained by caution. He gripped the stroke oarsman by his tarry head and used him as a stanchion to project himself forward along the thwarts. In an instant he was balanced in the bow, then leapt lightly to the sand. As he approached the nearest men, Angus stuck out his hand, ironically. Slack Dickie, to Lamont's surprise, took it and shook it, as if warmly.

"If you harm the boy you will be killed," he said. "Apart from that, well met. Captain Swift is on that other ship, the *Pourquoi Pas*. Captain Swift, you may have heard of him; a most unforgiving man. There is an army coming through on foot to join us. We are not seeking you, however, but the rebel Marlowe and his slaughterers. There will be a pardon in it if you do your proper duty."

"Pardon fer fit?" said Lamont, scornfully. "We dinna need yer pardons, man. If'n ye want tae buy oor services ye'll hae t' name yer price. Is it the white quine ye're after? Is there a ransom oot fer her?"

"White what?" said Kaye. "What's that you say?"

Lamont's face was a picture of contempt.

"Wumman," he said. "Dae ye no' speak yer ain king's English?" He laughed. "But come tae think, he disnae neether, diz'ee? The white wumman," he repeated. "The broon-haired quine the mannie's captured. She looks aye worth a baubee or twa."

Kaye understood. Momentarily, he forgot that Will was in the boat a mere few feet behind him.

"For me," he said, "she can— Ah. The woman. Indeed, Lamont. There is an interest in the woman, too. All can be settled, I am sure. But firstly — we must have Captain Swift ashore. I said we would give a musket signal. Do not misinterpret it, I beg of you. But also first — before that even — I must have the boy. Or shall I signal Swift to blow you all to kingdom come?"

Will, reaching for a musket in the boat, could not believe his ears, but Lamont, fortunately, could not either, it would seem. He looked at Kaye distastefully, then beyond him into the bay. Even before a shot was fired in the air the *Pourquoi Pas* was rounding up, to drop her anchor not far from the *Jacqueline*'s. She was rounding up, but hardly under way. The wind was almost nothing.

"He'd be hard put tae," said Lamont, laconically. "It'd tak him a week tae get a gun to bear. And ye canna have the loon, fit dae ye tak me for? Ye can mebbe see him later, an' that's a'. He's fine well, that's a' ye need tae know. He's being well looked after, nae lang wauk frae here. A short wauk where ye'll never find him, neether. But ye can trust tae me, ma mannie, I'm a Lamont. Ye can trust tae me, and dinna ye fergit tha'."

With Swift ashore, and his small body of seamen bearing arms, all parties, strangely, were more relaxed. The Lamont brothers led the Navy officers to the stockade entrance, but the sailors stood outside, muskets and cutlasses ever ready, just in case. The Scotsmen though, had neither reason nor intent to engineer betrayal; their position as profit-takers, in their eyes, was getting better all the time. They had vital information, they had Slack Dickie by his balls, they had a small army and a thick terrain to cover them if things went wrong, they had sunken treasure and a trove already hidden in the ground. Rabbie was like a laird at castle gate when Swift walked in: he offered him brandy from a glass decanter...

Whatever Kaye and Bentley thought, Swift had no opinion of the Scots on moral grounds. He surveyed the inner courtyard of the fortress — just makeshift furniture and piles of small arms and sharpened blades, a few black men looking servile as decreed — and it seemed exactly as it should be. These men had found themselves a place, had intelligence that was theirs alone to sell, and knew how to conduct themselves for dignity and comfort. That they were murderers and thieves was well enough, for if they tried such tricks on him then they would die, and as for the rest of humankind he was indifferent; how much of it was worth the saving? The brandy he declined, but made no sign when Kaye accepted some and drank it greedily. Each to his own, each to his own. He did not even wonder why Kaye was so hungry for the liquor; it was not material to him.

Kaye's eyes had darted round the inner stockade like a tigress looking for its cub. He had moved his body so that he could see all round the inner hut, then had pushed inside it without a by your leave. He saw a table, stools, beds, pistols, pots, a kettle. They had told the truth: Black Bob was in another place. Outside again he took more brandy, despite the Scotsmen's look of quiet condescension.

"Well," said Swift, when Kaye had drunk it down. "The Captain here tells me you can take us to the black man, Marlowe. How far is it, how long to get there, is he well armed, and will he fight?"

Big Angus sucked his teeth.

"And fit's yer offer, Captain? Mr Kaye there telt me you were some hard case, but so am I, and so's ma brithers Rab and Doddie. We take ye nowhere unless ye pay. And swear tae us safe passage hame again."

Swift smiled. He was warming to this man, Bentley could see the signals. He was not surprised. His Uncle Swift was an infamous misreader of men's characters. He moved his eyes instead to Dickie's face. It was haunted, strained, which Will found an utter mystery — or misery, at least. For charity, he thought the loss of Marianne had unhinged him. Perhaps he felt he had a duty now to save the life of poor Black Bob.

As Angus laid it out, it was not the distance to Marlowe's hideaway (or "town") that was the hardship, but the nature of the terrain. Then again, the terrain was passable, with care and guides, but would cost a fortune in dead men. There were mountain paths a goat would think twice about, there were woodland paths that wild boars would walk a score of miles just to avoid — and either of these alternatives was designed with dedication to facilitate an ambush. Men were shot off the mountain tracks with bullets, or spears, or rocks rolled down like thunderbolts from the blue, while in the wooded parts nemesis was silent and invisible. Swift did not bluster or complain, but pondered long and carefully.

"Mm," he said, at last. "So tell me if I've got this wrong. We need to block their paths out to the eastward, and we need to have men enough to lose some as we close in? Once we have them bottled they have nowhere to escape to westward except the sea? But I presume they have a lookout network? No chance that we can come upon them all unknown? How did you find them out, then, and not be cut into little bits and fried?"

"We were hunting someone," Angus said. "The wee white quine. She had a black yin wi' her. Marlowe wanted them as well. For the ransom, mebbe. He ran out to meet them, we met him. She was no' worth shedding blude fer, but some of my blacks can track. We know their town; we know where we can find them. Or them us..." His thin lips formed into a smile. "Ye hae the recht o' it," he said. "We must put them in a bottle. Verra neat."

It did not take Swift much longer to decide his plan. He withdrew a map of Jamaica from his inner pocket and spread it out upon a surface. Kaye, Bentley and two of the Scotsmen moved close to him and followed his finger. Will noted, with some surprise, the glaring scars and mangled tissue, which had never been referred to by his uncle. Swift stubbed a nail-less stump onto a south coast indentation.

"Us here, yes?" he grunted. "And Marlowe must be in those hills and hummocks there? So the bloodhounds and militia must be coming now along this coastal fringe, because that is where the roads exist, is that the right of it? Aye, I thought it must be. And they've come from here, west of Port Royal, to snake down here and — and how long to push through here, in the middle, and then spread north and southwards, to put in the plug? They've got horses and mules, fast Africans on foot, and they will not be bringing cannon, that's impossible, they say. So if they set off two days ago from Kingston, and I now sail round *here* to land, Montego Bay, and then we march due south around the mountain fringes, while you lot and the Jacquelines thrust north — well, in two more days or three from now, as I compute it, all three prongs of us can be turned on to *here*, which is the spot I have agreed with Andrew Mather. And which *you* will tell me, Mr Scotchmen — is in striking distance. Am I right?"

The two Lamonts pored over the map, keeping their fingers off as if they feared they'd give too much away. Swift pulled out a silver box of snuff with ostentation from his waistcoat, took a clumsy snifter with his damaged fingers, and sucked it mightily into his head. He did not sneeze, but blew his nose uproariously.

"I had it from your father," he told Kaye. "Cuban. Who said nothing but bad came from these islands? Well, Lamonts. What of my stratagem? I agree to all your terms, of course. You have my word on that. If I have learned anything, it is to be generous in a bargain, and that way it will work." He laughed. "Especially when the cost to me is less than old Jack Shit, eh! Have your freedom, boys! You're welcome to it!"

Until the blade slides in your back, Will thought, knowing the Scots were there before him. A nest of vipers: the Lamonts, his uncle, all of them. A bloody pool of fangs and venom. And they were smiling broadly, all the best of friends...

"Captain Swift," he said. "There is one hole in the net that I can see, especially as you have mentioned Cuba. Marlowe has one boat at least, for I have seen him in it. Not precisely ocean-rigged, but the straits are not so wide and she may be as seaworthy as all-fall-down for aught that I know. Indeed, he might have others hidden in some secret bay. We did not see where he had come from, or where he went. If we attack him, who's to say he'll not just disappear again? Or fade away, indeed, before we get a sniff?"

May be Swift had thought of it already, may be he had not. But he smiled his broadest smile, clapping his nephew so hard he almost broke his shoulder.

"Excellent, my boy," he said. "But I had thought of that already. That is why when I sail round the corner in the *Pourquoi Pas*, you sail in consort until we reach the area you met him in before. You will lie off or sail close in, whichever you deem best, and try to search out this hidden bay, if it exists, or where he keeps his war canoe. Good God, mayhap he has a little fleet itself! You can destroy it on the ground!"

Will had a swooping in his stomach. Mayhap indeed, he could go ashore. And pick up Deb, and save her. He would take the Worm, and somehow make contact with the lookouts. But Kaye was speaking, and his voice was strained.

"What mean you, sir?" he asked of Swift. "Will Bentley sails in a gig again, or a cutter? You surely do not mean the *Jacqueline*?"

"Oh, do I not? And why not, pray? We cannot leave her here at anchor, can we? And expect her to be still at anchor when we come back? These men might be black, but they can sail a vessel, and that right well, in my experience. Mr Lamont, sir — if we left the vessel here, would you guarantee your cohorts would not make off with her?"

The Lamonts were not noted for their humour, but they shared a smile with Swift. Who then told Kaye he was needed at the head of the shore party from the south, and could not be spared to "merely run a ship." He would take most of the Jacquelines, plus Carver and those other white men, and push up into the interior to a meeting point they would fix upon the map.

"What, with the Lamonts, and Black Bob?" said Kaye, but Swift only frowned at him.

"I know nothing of this Bob," he said. "And I must say I care less. You may take one of the brothers if one of them agrees, but I want two of them at least. No, I will take all three. I do not wish this Marlowe to know we have them as our guides, and at sea with me in *Pourquoi Pas* they'll be as secret as the grave. Your force is vital, man. You will deploy it to block off any exit eastward, from the centre of the island down to this bay. It is a mighty trust, young Richard. Let no foolish fancy get into its way."

Wee Dod was almost kindly, fired doubtless to match this patronising with his own quite subtle insult. He reached out a hand to touch Kaye on the sleeve, smiling harder as the captain flinched.

"Dinna fear aboot the wee black loon," he said. "We hae him verra safe and fast. Ah promise ye he's no' in a state tae run. He's like a wee brid in a cage. But no' sae keen tae sing."

The plan now struck, Swift had had enough of chattering, however. He moved among them like a bundle of impatience, sweeping officers and men before him to the boats. Bentley and Kaye were pulled out to their brig as in a race, fine style, with Lieutenant Anderson of the *Pourquoi Pas*, who had not even disembarked on bringing Swift ashore, urging his boat's crew away from the beach as if there was a hundred pound on it. Still the Jacquelines pipped them, which pleased Kaye mightily, although their boat was lighter, to be sure. Will, though, was indifferent. He would be sailing soon to war on Marlowe and on Deb, whichever way he cared to look at it. He wondered if he could have argued for them harder, for the undoubted fact the massacre at the Siddlehams' was by different perpetrators and for different reasons than those manufactured. But he knew he could have made no difference, and Holt, when they got to talk, agreed.

"It is not justice, it is expedience," he said. "We must hope they are not taken, that is all. And certainly not killed; we might prevent that at least, if it comes to law."

When Will told him of their role as preventive men in the coming operation, Sam saw possibilities of a much more hopeful outcome.

"But we can find them out again," he said. "We will have the *Jacqueline*. We can get Deb off and save her, even if Marlowe will not come. Good Christ, Will, they found us last time fast enough. This time he'll know there is an army closing in."

"Aye, we'll have the *Jacqueline*, which we would make a prison for him, would we not? We are not free agents, Sam, we cannot whisk him off to safety. What do you suggest? A quick sail round to Havana and ask the dons to give them shelter?"

"Well," said Sam, trying for a jest. "They are our allies, meant to be. So bound indeed to give them back to us, not take them in. Confusing, certainly. No great bloody help, though. I'm sorry, Will. I do not mean it to be flippant."

"And Deb cannot come to us alone," said Will, "because whatever else she is, her worth to Marlowe is as a bargainer, a hostage, a safe passage. We'll not convince him that they'd hang her too, I guess." He flinched. "Perhaps they would not, when it came to it," he added. "They have no reason, God knows. God knows that will not stop them, neither. If Marlowe came out to us this time, he'd need to have a reason that I cannot yet imagine."

Discussion, though, was soon cut short by preparation. Kaye chose the best men that he could to go along with him to the interior, and another half or more of the ship's company. Purser Black was sweating soon so hard that the joy of palming off old beef and pork he'd given up as unsaveable even by Navy standards was overshadowed by the constant strain of figure-juggling, and working out proportions of meat, to bread, to liquor. Even fat pursers, it was brought home to Will and Sam, had work to do sometimes that they could not enjoy. Still true, however, that if Black should get it wrong, and the men ran out of vittles on the march, no one could hope to blame him for it, with any success. That honour (taking the blame) went traditionally to the cooks, and here Geoff Raper had unusual luck: one-legged through the steaming thickets was not considered feasible even to Slack Dickie Kaye. So the *Jacqueline* kept Geoff, and other, lesser men became camp scapegoats.

It took both ships two days of sweating labour to have the shore contingents ready, and Swift's last surprise was his order that the stockade should be destroyed before they went, in case it should be taken over by Maroons or other villains, and later cause them trouble. No one cared to argue – least of all Dick Kaye or the Scots, despite both lost their secret storeroom and base for diving operations – and the job was very quickly done. A wooden fortress in the Caribbean was by nature a temporary thing in any way, and first the inner blockhouse then both outer walls gave themselves up to fire with a haste almost unseemly. Captain Swift, perhaps to steal a march, left the firing to Will and Sam's contingent, but it suited them to see the *Pourquoi Pas* get under way before them. It meant that Marlowe's watchers way down west would see one ship heave up into their view then disappear, before the second one pitched up alone, less likely to be perceived as threatening.

Bentley did not order his own anchor broken out until the *Pourquoi Pas* was gone, and until Kaye and his unwieldy battle force had cleared off the beach completely, into the undergrowth. It was some time beyond midday and although the breeze was brisk onshore, they had room enough to clear the western headland with Jack Gunning at the con. Kaye had nabbed Jem Taylor, the marines, and Ashdown — whom he assumed "could talk nigger to the blacks" — but had not even mentioned "taking" London Jack as a possibility. Very wise. Jack had waved an ironic brandy bottle at him as Kaye had left; then stowed it away, joke over, when Kaye was gone. To Will, a very great relief.

As they sailed off, Holt and Bentley gazed back at the beach, now empty of the two hundred men and more who had been mustered there to strike inland and fight like common soldiers, ill-dressed for land work, ill-shod (if shod at all) and deeply disaffected. The two friends did not even answer back with great conviction when Gunning said the Jacquelines would rise up against Kaye and "slice his Adam's apple out" if they got the chance. They were happy only that they were at sea, with, for William, the added hope he might save Deborah. Even the sight of Raper, with his coffee can and his twisty smile, hardly made their spirits very light.

The scene they left was strangely desolate, just littered sand, and scrub, the smoking ruin of the fortress. Somehow it seemed to have an air about it, a sense of dereliction and foreboding.

Only Jack Gunning did not find it ominous...

Chapter Thirty-Two

The ease and beauty of their passage west in *Jacqueline*, the limpid vision of Jamaica in unending sun, had an odd effect on Will. There was not in truth too much for him to do on board the ship, which, undermanned for fighting, was still overmanned in seamen's terms, and unlike Slack Dickie his reaction to the torture in his heart and mind was not to turn to liquid anaesthesia. It seemed unreal somehow, the possibility that beyond that green and lovely shoreline a war was going on, to break out very soon in carnage and depravity. It seemed unreal that he had seen Deb again, still loved her, still yearned for her like a lovesick boy. He had visions of her in a clearing in the trees, her muslin dress, her long curls, her clear brown eyes, her breasts. It seemed impossible that harm might come to her, which far from preventing, was his duty bound to perpetrate. The world was too gentle. It could not be so.

They dropped hook upward of a mile from land at last, because the shore was generally a lee one and Caribbean winds could go from nothing to a violent tempest in a shockingly short time, then they held a conference on what to do for best. Once in the area they had backed and filled about for near two days as close in as Gunning would advise to go, in absence of a detailed chart, and, to their surprise and disappointment, had had no sign at all of watchers on the land. The two lieutenants had taken off the gig alone one time, and had hovered just beyond the line of surf. They had dropped the sail, taken off their jackets, and generally made out as seekers after pleasure, idle and no sort of threat, drifting in the easy waves. To no avail.

Gunning, inevitably, was happy to swing at anchor "till the cows came home." One reason he had never joined the Navy, he reminded them, was because no one, in general terms, had it in mind to "cleave my head in two with some bloody axe." He was a little worried about the chafing to the gear from lying in the swell for too prolonged a time, but "after all I don't pay for the bugger any more!" But he did point out, more sensibly, that it would be stupid, and a crime, for them to go ashore "just on the off-chance you would sniff a bit of tail." Literally a crime, as they were there with battle duties to perform, but stupid, more importantly, as they would be walking blindly into dangers they could not even guess at. Why not send the Worm, he asked? If someone had to get his head cut off, better an old black "who should have died ten years ago at least!"

Will, whose need to go ashore had become a burning ache, could see value in this, and Sam backed Gunning to the hilt for emphasis. As whites they had no chance of catching anything, he said, except a blade or bullet, as much chance as they'd had of discovering the "secret harbour" or the "fleet" they'd spent such fruitless time upon. So in the end they called the Worm to them (not to get his head chopped off though, to be sure) and put the proposition thus: go ashore for us, old friend, and try to track down Marlowe, and the English maid, and Mildred. Tell them if they can come to us, we can save them, all three. Tell them they will soon be overwhelmed. Tell them there are armies from the north and south and east.

The old man smiled.

"You think they don't know already?" he said. "You think Marlowe is blind? He not find us, mebbe, because he's in the thick. I do not think it take me very long, I ready now. You bring the boat around."

In half an hour he was gone, having refused even a pistol so that he could signal his return. A pistol, he pointed out, would earn him death, and anyway what need: "Mister Will" would burn his eyes out looking for him. Back on board they chewed it over endlessly throughout that first night and the torture of the next long day, with the feeling growing in Will that it had all gone wrong, that Worm would fail, that the rebel band were doomed to slaughter anyway. The blackness of the second night, cloud-blind and airless with all breezes died to nothing and the silence total on the sleeping vessel and the shore, from whence no cry of animal or bird carried, oppressed him further till he was almost crushed. Deborah, he thought, was bound to die. He had failed her.

He was asleep at sunrise, though, lying beneath a light covering on deck because of the appalling heat below, and no one woke him until Sam and a boat's crew led by Tommy Hugg was almost alongside the *Jacqueline* once more, with the Worm himself seated in the sternsheets. Will sprang to wakefulness and to his feet, and was hanging over the rail when the old man looked at him and smiled.

"I've seen your Miss," he said. "I've seen her and the black man and friend Mildred."

Will had a swoop of joy. He went almost giddy. The toothless smile beneath him became enormous.

"They will come," said Worm. "All three of 'em. They will be here by the night or in the morning. I must go back shore and wait there on my own. That is the orders. That Mr Marlowe don't trust nobody. No one."

"But—" said Will. "Is she well? Is she—"

Sam interrupted, as if angrily.

"Oh stow it, Mr Bentley, stow it won't you? This man has done a wonder for us all. This man must have some breakfast."

Geoff Raper — not a man to stand round idle, one leg or two — already had the bacon in the pan.

***

Marlowe's confidence, now apparently drained away, that he could sustain a long campaign against the white avengers, had been based on experience, and hope. White men, he knew, came in numbers, in uniforms, and pulled heavy trains of victuals and equipment. Despite long years of practice, they seemed to have little awareness of the dangers of terrain, and little understanding that they would get bogged down in it, that they would be always supremely visible and their adversaries would not. Further, he assumed that his town and its outlying camps were unknown, even as to their general area. The invaders would come pouring through the mountain passes, and across the badlands and the bogs, but they would have no specific goal; they would be entering a swamp without a centre.

At the start of the "invasion," this view had proved accurate. Deb, although she did not want or ask to be, was taken as part of Marlowe's immediate party to watch the first incursions and their consequences. She had no idea how many men he had in his command, because she saw few of them and very fitfully, but the ground they covered was extraordinarily difficult. Despite her leanness and muscularity from her extended existence as a runaway, she was soon exhausted as her party walked and picked its way round mountain paths on the edge of precipices, across ice-cold torrents, and through dripping forests of a glaring green where biting insects could be scooped out of the air in handfuls. She saw small bands of black fighters ambush platoons of black militia, she saw two young planters pulled down off their mules and hacked to death. That night she cried to him, begging to be spared the sight of more such savagery. He told her that if they did not kill they would be killed, and that in any case the thing was in the balance.

Marlowe and his lieutenants had good intelligence in general, but they had no way of knowing how complete it was. They knew a ship had sailed round the island, first spotted crossing Bloody Cove, and they later heard she had dropped anchor in Montego Bay and many white sailormen had come ashore to strike out inland along the course of the Great River. Another force of whites, and their slavemen warriors, had been observed for several days heading west to meet to this army, and another force, mainly white, had been reported moving north from somewhere south of Orange Hill. None of the observers was capable of counting by numbers in the English way, but as the time wore on, they became more tense and dubious. Deb was asked repeatedly to comment on things she could not know — numbers of militia men in the Kingston area, numbers of crewmen on a Navy ship — and the skirmishes became bloodier and more violent, more savage in their toll of men on either side. By the third or fourth day she and Mildred, and Marlowe, were moving back west once more, and she saw some fighters in retreat, not in attack. She understood from briefings overheard, and translations by Mildred, that the three prongs of the "white man forces" were becoming a torrent, a flood, a rising tide they could not hope to stem.

By the time the Worm was brought to Marlowe's presence there was an air of termination about it all, in Deb's opinion. He was brought with dignity, however, not brutalised, and Marlowe recognised him immediately. The Worm, though old, was a negotiator born, a man who did not play politics with facts. He told them that they were being bottled up, and how; he named Swift and Kaye as the force commanders from the sea and Mather and Sutton — both names that Marlowe knew — as the militia-thrust from the island's windward zone. He gave rough numbers — some hundreds in each party — and reported, in answer to Mildred's specific query, that there was a strong force in reserve near Kingston Town, of white men and officers who would come if need be. He smiled his gummy smile.

"Them not leave white womans unguarded this time, Miss. Even planters learn some lesson, heh?"

Marlowe pondered for some moments.

"Why you here for? What Mr Bentley got to offer?" He saw Deb tense, and raised a palm to her, and smiled. "This man say your man

Bentley and him friend lie offshore and not come to join in black man killing. That must be to save you, not me." The smile thinned. "Nor Mildred, mebbe."

"No," said Worm. "He will take all. Not all your fighters, not half Jamaica rebel men, but all of you. He will take you on the ship. Big ship. The *Jacqueline*."

Deb shared a look with Mildred, full of hope. Her guts were torn with longing.

"Lieutenant Bentley," said Marlowe. He said it almost kindly, a matter of vague regret. "Lieutenant Bentley, Lieutenant Holt. They cannot stop them hanging me. Good thought, but him captain not agree, him governor in Kingston, him good King Georgie." He paused. "Say him sorry, but we can not come except for talking. We come in day or two as soon as battle going right. You be at rock by beach, my men go show you where. You be alone. We talk in boats like last time. We find you, then we find Mr Bentley. Tell him, he must not look for us. Now go."

***

The three thrusts of the avenging forces had suffered many casualties, but not in great enough numbers to worry them unduly, Marlowe knew. The troop down from Montego Bay was the most numerous, but until Swift's men had moved quite far inland towards the rendezvous, it had been the least attacked. They had met up with the Kingston force as planned, then with the contingent from the south that Kaye commanded. The total losses among all three were less than thirty, mainly bloodhounds, and the presence of Swift, then Mather, had forced even Kaye to sobriety once more. He had channelled his suffering for Marianne, or for Bob, into a raw determination for revenge.

Mather had proved himself a good commander, and his militia men were useful on the ground, in that they mainly sent their conscript blacks before them when the terrain became most difficult. When the rebels ambushed them, or fell upon them from the heights, the black men suffered and died in place of whites, who being much more visible should have been the natural targets. But the whites had muskets, and could shoot down the marauders from afar — or sometimes their own footsoldiers, which was, in fact, an effective tactic. The more black bodies strewn around, indeed, the more disconcerted the rebel bands became.

There was one set "battle" only, more a bloody skirmish in a large clearing between two woods, which suited the militia and the musket-wielding sailors very well because it gave them a great sense of superiority in arms and tactics. They settled down in banks to fire-reload-fire into the trees and bushes opposite, while some of the bolder mounted men made dashes across the break on horse or mule, whirling sabres and whooping as they dodged the hail of lead from the renegades, in truth more imaginary than real. Alf Sutton, on his great black beast, made one sortie deep into the thicket, and hove back into sight with a thrown dagger buried in his shoulder, although luckily for him it was the thick serge material that took and held the weapon, not his flesh. Another of the mounted planters, even more impressively, struck into the woodland and returned with a black and bloody forearm in his hand. He it was, however, who convinced the doughty warriors that their prey, in fact, had flown. A fair amount of lead in the last few minutes had been wasted on thin air.

It was as the forces spread out thinner and pushed further west that the Lamonts came into their own. They had come ashore from the *Pourquoi Pas* in the first boat with Swift, and had begun their scouting from the moment feet hit solid ground. On board the ship maps had been studied and understood, and the more vicious elements among the sailors had been recruited to travel with them as a kind of escort, cruelly armed. Once the main body of Swift's men were disembarked, the Lamonts and this cut-throat crew moved always ahead to smell out the land, take blacks they found as prisoners to be milked of information, and to let it be known ahead that nemesis was coming. By the time the three troops came together between the heights of Birches Hill and Orange, the Lamonts were ready to bear down into Marlowe's strongholds on their own to find and kill the quarry that was the greatest prize. They had fulfilled their promised duty by leading Swift and Kaye and Mather to the area where Marlowe must have his "town," and indeed some outer hide-outs had been set upon and burned. It was time, the Lamonts agreed, to go off on their own, follow their noses, and to capture Marlowe and the Tomelty. The one, they knew, was a sure reward and possibly a pardon for their many sins, while the other — and her wee black friend — could either be a perfect pleasure to them, or a money prize as well. Ideally both.

Marlowe himself, by a similar reading of the runes, had also concluded it was time to call an end. In his unusual way, he discussed this with Mildred and Deb, as if anything that they might say would sway him in deciding. Looking at his frank and chiselled face, Deb did indeed believe it might. He laid out the achievement of his men, and their options, with clarity and calmness, and said his main intention was that the women should not be harmed. Seeing Deb's confusion, he smiled.

"You came to me for help," he said. "Now I cannot help you any more. Planters come, their soldiers come, your Navy come. I have lost some men, my women and my children run into the woods and higher land to hide away. We can do this. Many places here where white man can not follow. If I take you with us, bakra-lady, they try to chase and so we lose more life, they try long time. That old nigger man say we can go on ship, will be protected. It may be true for you, but not for me. Your man William is on the ship. He go protect you. And Mildred is your friend."

"But he will protect you too!" Deb cried. "The old man said so! You have saved me! The men will kill you if you do not come. Oh, Mr Marlowe, what have you lost, for me?"

Marlowe said: "A few men dead, but not so many as the planter men. A few houses burned, may be some beast. New town to build, new secret place to find. If we fight them too hard they come back and back and back again, like them Maroon wars in the other time. If I go on ship they say they give me fair trial, and then they hang me. Your man is Navy officer, him not the King. King Georgie say that I must dangle. That the true."

Throughout these last few hours, they had been picking through the forests towards the island's western tip, although the direction was unnoticed or unknown to Deb. There were three men with the three of them as far she could tell, but more were always in the background, hidden. Two of the guard, who had guns and cane knives, slashed out a path ahead.

"But I have been your hostage," she said, almost plaintively. "I can be your safe passage now, your—"

"How?" said Mildred. "When you are safe, we are just targets once again, can you not see?"

"But—" said Deb, and at that moment, to her surprise, found herself out in a clearing, in blazing sunlight. Blinded, she made out a black shape ahead of her, beside a gigantic boulder. As the shape began to run towards them it began to yell.

"Get back! Get back in the trees, they're here! An ambush! They have caught us up!"

It was the Worm, and as she realised this a shot came, and another black man took a bullet in the face and Deb heard a scream beside her, which was Mildred. Worm stopped in his tracks, and spun on his heels, still roaring.

"The boat! Mr Marlowe! We must get to the boat!"

The old man, as well as aborting the ambush, had ferreted out the hidden canoe, it seemed, and he hared off down the path immediately. Marlowe, gripping Deb's arm, jerked her after him, and she in turn pulled Mildred. The remaining forward guard ran back bravely past them to cover their retreat, and they heard another shot, and a short scream from inside the wood. As they went past the rock to follow Worm, Deb saw two white men burst out and rush towards her. They were tall and thin, and she thought they looked like death.

It was Rabbie and Wee Dod Lamont.

Chapter Thirty-Three

They must not search for him, the Worm had told Will Bentley and Sam Holt, they must not go on shore, there would be spies to find them out. They had dropped him through the surf with Tom Hugg and three more strong sailors at the oars, had not even stepped onto the beach with him, and had watched as he had disappeared into the trees. Then, through the surf once more, they had held their tongues until they should be back on board the *Jacqueline*, aware the massive boatswain's mate was watching them as he wielded the stroke oar. An hour later, they had called him to the cabin.

"Hugg," said Sam. "Tommy, man... We want to get the ship inshore a piece and Mr Gunning here ain't vetoed it. I want you in the chains with your best leadsman, or you yourself if you should deem that better. We want to jill her to the nearest spot to breakers we can get, then put the cable on a slip, and buoyed, in case we have to let it go and run. We'll need some canvas triced up loose and ready so we can set it at a moment, and we'll need sweeps ready to get her on a tack if the breeze blows foul. We are under way in twenty minutes."

A grin broke across Hugg's broad and ugly face. Apart from taking the Worm ashore, he had been inactive for too many hours. He touched his forehead with a meaty hand.

"Aye, sir," he said. "That Frankie Amber is your man. He can feel the ground along the line like magic, he's as nervous as a cat. French bastard."

They did not feel like laughing so they let that pass, but Will and Sam shared Hugg's relief at action. Within an hour they had the ship less than half a mile offshore, close enough that the *Jacqueline*, occasionally, lifted sharply and heart-wrenchingly and seemed to hover at the point where a wave would break, accelerate, and shoot them in towards the boiling, foamy carpet. Will, at one stage, took himself right up above the main t'gallant yard, clinging to the pole, to gain a view across the trees into the hidden land. It was hidden still — bright green and overgrown — but he was amazed to realise he still found the whole thing beautiful, the breaking seas, the iridescent foam, the bottom below the keel that looked close enough, each other moment, to be touched, and close enough to rise up and smash their bottom out. It was giddying, delirious; and somewhere almost within his sight, his love, quite possibly, was being killed. Had he forgotten?

He had not, completely, and back on deck once more took comfort from the thought that they were as close to shore as ship could be, that they could come up with a vessel putting off from any cove, however hidden, within the shortest time to be imagined. While he had "played about aloft" indeed, Sam and Tom Hugg had readied up the lightest gig on board and moored her at the low point of the waist, watched over by the same nervous Frenchman, François Imbert, who would rather die than let her be dashed into the ship's side by a roguish wave. When Will proposed that he and Sam should stay on deck themselves, and watch out for a signal from the Worm, he was, however, laughed to scorn. As he conceded, it could be days rather than hours before the call might come.

When it did, though, it came on a sudden, in the warmest part of the day, and, most shockingly, it was a gunshot that presaged it. Will had been dozing on the quarterdeck, but the muffled sound, right at the farthest it would carry across the breezeless sea, had him jumping like a man possessed. Sam ran back from the foredeck, and most other men awake were also galvanised. The lookout sang out almost as the report was heard, although he had seen no more than any other man, to tell the truth of it.

"Where away?" yelled Sam, and "Man the gig," roared William. Imbert was pulling in the line already, and Hugg, sweating in a pair of sagging drawers, was urging on his chosen oarsmen to the rail.

"Astern of us!" cried the lookout from the top. "Yon headland, sir! Starboard quarter, sir!"

As soon as the canoe's prow cleared the rocks, it seemed that there was something very wrong. Before the bellowing on the *Jacqueline* died down, shouts boomed across the water, then piercing screams. When half of Marlowe's craft was visible, they saw it rocking violently, and heard a terrific splash, as of someone falling overboard. Will tumbled in the gig with all the others, seized the yokelines, and told Hugg tersely: "Lay into it and get her flying. Come on my boys, oh fly!"

They went leaping forward like a porpoise as a burst of shots rang and clattered round the headland rocks, but Will, urging the vessel onward with his every nerve, saw that the canoe had scarcely moved. There was still shouting though, and a further splash, and more shots. Then, on a sudden, the canoe emerged into the open bay, struggling across a breaking wave. She had a sail up and had caught a puff, an eddy round the rocks perhaps, and heeled steep away from them, showing her bilge, until the breeze dropped light again, and she lay rolling after twenty yards or so. One oar was shipped, but Will saw it slide out of the rowlock and slip into the water, unheeded. The dun sail flapped, the boat fell off the wind, a paddle appeared for a moment above the gunwale, then her stern was to them and Will could see no more. He gripped the yokelines till his fingers hurt and gritted, "Pull, you bastards, *pull*!"

They reached her as she turned once more in a gentle puff, the unsecured mainsail blocking off Will's anxious view as they came along beside her. As automatic as a clockwork man he gave the oarsmen orders — "hold water larboard; easy; way enough" — but he was poised to leap as if held back by springs. Starboard oars were unshipped, hands gripped the canoe's gunwale, and William thought that he might die, so anxious was he. He jumped across, and pulled the sail, and saw the body. But it was not Deb, it was the Worm, and his throat had been cut savagely. He was alone. The boat held no other human being.

The old man's eyes opened then, and caught his. As he spoke, he bubbled blood.

"She might've got away," he said. His voice was thick and curdled. "I think she might've done. God bless her."

***

When Dod and Rab had struck, there had been chaos, and terrified confusion. Marlowe's men had fought like tigers, far more of them than Deborah had expected, and many had had guns. As she fell to her knees — pulled there by Mildred after Marlowe had let go his grip and shouted something she did not understand — smoke and flames had gushed all round her in a cacophony of yells and musketry. Their attackers seemed to be white, the lot of them, and charged out of the wood in what looked like massive numbers. Her impression was that they were sailors, but in her terror they were more like fiends. They had pistols, dirks and swords, they whooped and bellowed like men gone mad. Marlowe's men, the blacks, met them head-on in a mirror show of bestial exuberance. It was a Roman Coliseum, a killing ground.

Had they intended to, they could have murdered Deb Tomelty on the spot. Once on her knees she stayed there for long moments, her face held in her hands, her throat contracted on a scream, her body clenched and rigid, at some sort of breaking point. Mildred was beside her for a second, then was whisked away. Deb gasped, threw out her arms, but did no more, she could not. She saw Marlowe running towards her with a pistol in his hand, pointing at her head. Before she could react the pistol jumped, gushed black smoke and fire, and she had the sensation of a ball flying past her face, which was instantly bespattered with fiery black specks that burned and stank. Marlowe's hip crashed into her as he ran past, whirling her sideways to see him leap upon a white man and drive a knife into his neck. Another white man clubbed at Marlowe with a gun, but he too was overwhelmed and stabbed. Then the white men she had noticed first, the skinny, bearded ones, set themselves at her, and Marlowe was obscured from her sight.

At this instant she caught a roar from the ancient Worm, who was beckoning furiously from a gap in the undergrowth that might have been a path. She was on her feet and running without thought, and burst out of the clearing into the darkness. Suddenly the light was gone, it was blackness cut with vicious shafts of sun, among which she glimpsed men, armed and shouting, rushing at her and away in a turmoil of violence. Ahead she saw the Worm once more, still beckoning she thought, unless he were a demon in a nightmare. Blindly she followed him, brushing against running fighters, black and white, as if she were invisible indeed. When she reached the pathway it was not a path, and the Worm had gone. It was a gap, a rift between two dense bunches of undergrowth, into which Deb threw herself. For a moment she saw Worm again, and beat and burst against the fronds and creepers she seemed buried in. No one behind her, when she checked, nothing in front but a matted wall of greens and stalks and branches. She noticed that her heart was hammering, that her muslin dress was torn almost off her breast, that her legs were running blood. She could hear noise and shouting, but had a roaring in her head that was drowning most things out. And she forced herself forward, she tore and struggled through the undergrowth, she prayed that she might get away.

The clearing came again as suddenly as it had before, and Deb blundered helpless into open view. She was on the edge of a wider open pathway where it became a beach, and on the beach were several struggling men. There was a boat half in the water, its sail halfway set, with some men in it and others reaching across the gunwales with clubs and swords. Deb's eyes met the Worm's, an instant of shock and recognition, then she pulled herself back inside the friendly darkness, aching with what might have been.

What was, perhaps. In front of her, not fifteen feet away, a shaft of sunlight blazing on his face, stood another of the tall, thin, bearded men, and he was blinking. Deb stood still as stone, and cold as ice. He was blinded. Perhaps he would not ever see her. And then Big Angus smiled.

***

There are certain times, when in command of men, that options become unbearable, and desire, duty and humanity can only be at war. Will Bentley, alongside Marlowe's canoe, was two hundred yards from the Jamaica beach, and every fibre in his soul screamed that he should go ashore and search for Deb. He knew the chances he could run her down were low, because the beach was deserted save for a corpse or two, and before him lay a member of his people who needed instant help, that a surgeon only would know how to give. The black man's throat was open, and it was throbbing blood, and he would surely die without attendance. To add to the dilemma — or the joke, as Sam put it later, in the telling — the only surgeon's name was Grundy. No sane man would let him touch their throat in a state of rude good health, let alone attack it with a bodkin.

The fact was that the Worm was going to die, and Deb, with God's favour and for all they knew, might be saveable onshore. Sadly, it left Will with no alternative. They went back to the ship.

It was hours before they could reach the land again — Will, Sam and a stalwart party — leaving the Worm in Grundy's hands, God save him, and the ship in London Jack's. Jack insisted on moving the *Jacqueline* offshore again to keep them safe from stranding, and swore to have her in a state of readiness if they should need her in a hurry.

They picked through the forest with exceeding caution, expecting any minute that they might be attacked. The general direction they needed was not difficult to fathom, even without the Worm to be their guide. They passed two bodies and a lot of broken undergrowth, and a fair amount of blood spilled or smeared on leaf and bole. After some walking they heard sporadic guns as well, and shouting, and the sound of men and horses. Finally Alf Sutton almost rode them down, a rough-hewn colossus on his evil-looking mule. The day was won he said — grandiloquence a little spoiled by his raw West Riding accent — and the "top bastards all are took."

Will's eyes were wide with fear and hope. Sam spoke for him, coldly: "Which 'top bastards' are you referring to, I pray? I will say nothing more, except that they are not our enemy."

Sutton was touched with genuine delight. His sneer became so wide it was an actual smile.

"Tha mun suit thasen fer that," he said. "Ah tell thee only that yon black savage Marlowe is in chains. And my Deborah? My lickle runaway, my maid for seven yur, paid up and signed for? My lickle Deb's been took off by the Scotchmen, 'asn't shoo? I used to know 'em when they lived 'ere, them Lamonts. Ee lads — there'll be some fookin' th'neet, ah tell thee! She'll wish she'd niver run away! Aye, champion. They'll turn her inside aht!"

He laughed, he wheeled his mount, he waved them on delightedly. Ah, simple pleasures, simple pleasures; was there anything to beat them?

"This way, gentlemen," he said. "Tha Captain Daniel Swift has been expecting thee."

They walked.

Chapter Thirty-Four

The "township," when they got to it — huts, fire pits, a midden — was as unlike the scene of a military rout as could have been imagined. Alf Sutton rode on down the "main street" as he had called it, with every line of his body emanating contempt at the "mighty rebel chieftain's way of life." Sam and Will, uncomfortably, noted only signs of poverty and want, with no "citizens," no "prisoners of war," no living things at all save three chickens and a tethered goat. They could still hear noises from the woodland, but that was desultory, and of a triumphant army there was no hint at all.

Alf Sutton stopped his mule and looked down on them.

"Ah said we won, din't ah?" he crowed. "They're gone. They're finished. Women and childer off into the hills like rats, Marlowe off in chains back Kingston way, nowt left to do but mop up scum, which is what we're doing nah, out in the woods. It were easy, weren't it lads? Like tekkin' spice from off a lickle child. These niggers, eh? If I 'ad an 'eart it'd mek me want to weep, 'appen!"

Both Sam and Will, in their own way, felt inclined to weep in any case, but they asked no more questions of this vile, triumphant man. They guessed that Swift would be full of himself also, would be vindicated and renewed in his convictions of superiority. Marlowe was gone, and Deborah, presumably. What would be his intentions now?

Sutton showed them the hut where Swift was sat, guarded by two men from *Pourquoi Pas* with muskets and bored faces, but he did not go in with them. He moved off further down the street to a bigger structure, a large palm-leaf roof held up by trunks, where men were massed and drinking, from the distant sound of it. Through Swift's doorway, they saw him at a makeshift table, smoking a cigar. He too looked bored, but perked up when he noticed them.

"Aha, my boys! At last! What luck? What news? Is your ship all right? Have you many prisoners? We have the bastard, and he would have hanged had it been up to me. Sadly, the acting governor put in his oar, the jumped-up popinjay. He said there had to be a trial, to protect Jamaica's reputation! Have you ever heard the like of that? Jamaica's reputation! Even the nigger smiled, I warrant you. As well he might, with the halter almost round his neck already, I suppose.

Indeed, I'd had the gallows half-constructed when this reputation was invoked."

Will's thoughts were locked on Deborah. He had no words to ask. But Holt said: "How has he gone, sir? Who is escorting him?"

Swift tossed the half-consumed cigar on to the floor and trod it out. He indicated stools brought from his vessel, part of his baggage-train, but neither of them sat.

"Captain Kaye," he answered. "He is there to make the villain walk. I fear that Mr Mather would have given him a horse. I wished to give a whipping at the very least, when my execution plan was vetoed. Their softness amazes me, gentlemen. They tremble at the troubles that they have, they whine to London constantly that they are left bereft, then they put the kid gloves on and wonder why the niggers laugh at them."

Will still said nothing and Sam remained bone dry, struggling with distaste.

"I suppose they will hang him, though," he said. "Due process does not seem too hard a thing, one may argue — except that he is innocent."

The grey eyes watched him.

"You disappoint me, sir," said Swift; but mildly. "If I did not know you for a doughty man, I might think... ah, never mind. It just seems such a waste, is all. My people would have loved a hanging. And they've done sterling work for it."

"Where are the Scotchmen, sir?" asked Bentley. The question jumped out hotly, try as he might. "Are they not hanged as well? Or going back to Kingston? And where is the young..."

He bit it off at that, but he was nearly panting. If Swift knew what the question was — he surely must? — he did not show it. He turned pale eyes from Sam to Will and said, curiously: "Hanged? What, the Lamont men? But they it was caught Marlowe, and brought him in, they achieved when all men else had failed. Far from being ripe for execution they appear to me — and to themselves, I must say — to have won the blessed day. In fact they feel hard done by; not to mince words they feel betrayed. Captain Kaye was not there to confirm it or deny it, but they insisted they had been promised a reward. Not just bright gold neither, but a pardon for their lives, which drove Mr Mather apoplectic on the spot. Another little row, more heated words — he said the King can offer pardons, not Kaye, not me, not even him despite his high opinion of himself. They wanted a reward, he offered them a flogging as criminals unhung who had been deported off the island with no vestige of a right of coming back again. It was I bade them go, frankly between the three of us just to spite him, and I offered them reward indeed. I thought that he would have a seizure on the spot!"

That Captain Swift was revelling could no longer be in doubt. He was making points and scoring points, and included Andrew Mather in the rout. Bentley, in despite himself, could no longer bear it. His gorge was rising as he tried to speak. It came out thick, congested; he was choking on his rage.

"Reward?" he said. "Those men; reward? They should be hanged, sir! They are the most dangerous, they are more— *Oh*!"

"Aye," said his uncle, comfortably. "I am glad that you agree. Those three and their deserter rogues are more deadly than a thousand island men. We must thank our lucky stars that they have gone in peace, we are well rid of them. And when Andrew Mather comes to his wits again I confide that he will thank me, as he should."

"This reward," said Sam quietly, as Will was speechless still. "What did you give them, sir, to take?"

"Nothing of importance, Lieutenant Holt. Nothing that should be greatly missed. They already have the little black boy as I think, and they took the English whore. They brought her in with Marlowe, so it seemed appropriate to take her out again. They took her for a bargaining, some sort of hostage, or perhaps a plaything. What's it to me?"

"But..." gasped Will. "But Miss Tomelty—"

Swift chose to shriek, in violent anger.

"Miss Tomelty!? *Miss* Tomelty? By God, sir, you make yourself ridiculous! It is a filthy little common strumpet, a black man's drab. Do you have thoughts of love still, in your addled brain? You are betrothed, sir, do you forget? It is a prostitute, and neither you nor she can overcome that state. She is gone, sir, and so what? She is worthless; let her go."

Bentley was as pale as a blasted ash tree. His white lips moved, but he made no sound. Sam burst out: "But they are villains, sir. They are rapists who have abducted her. They are murderers."

"No!" responded Swift. "Those Scots are loyal Englishmen! They captured Marlowe and without them we could not have made it out to here, or found him. They have been robbed of their reward and if they want the girl, good luck to them, for she needs hanging too, remember? Have you forgot the Siddlehams? Have you forgotten why we're here? The Scots are villains, maybe — but there are viler men by far on this vile island."

"But Marlowe is not to blame," breathed Will. "Neither Marlowe nor that poor young woman. We told you they are not to blame."

It cut no ice with Swift, and there was no more they could say to him. The Scots had gone, he said; good luck to them. The maid was gone, and who the hell should care? If that was everything the whole damn job had cost them — well, it was riches in the bank. And the death of Marlowe would be the candle on the cake. As to his innocence and the whore's — Good God, it was too laughable to contemplate.

The three men in the little hut had brought themselves to silence, they were finished. They were face to face and failed to see each other's eyes. When Swift tried to fire up his rage once more, that also failed. He merely sounded peevish.

"Now, sirs," he said. "What do you here, in any way? Who minds the ship? These renegades have hulls, as I believe. What precautions have you took to stop them sneaking out and taking *Jacqueline*? How sparky is your guard? There's mopping to be done, there's shore parties to get up, rebels to hunt down. Get back there now and prepare things for the morning; both of you must lead a troop of men. We meet again tomorrow evening, we meet here in this very place, and I expect your pickings to be substantial, am I clear? Or I have to say this — it will be the worse for you. Now, you may dismiss."

"Sir—"

But Bentley's uncle glared at him, pure murder.

"Sir, you *will* dismiss. You *are* dismissed."

They gathered their party and picked back through the dense country to the beach their gig lay on, under guard. All kept keen lookout in the forest, but no human form was seen. Not black, not Scots, certainly no Deborah. They had the whole west corner of Jamaica as their hiding ground. They could, perhaps, have broken further east.

They could, in fact, be anywhere said Will, once in the boat. And Sam, beside him in the sternsheets, sadly agreed.

Chapter Thirty-Five

No sane man, in Holt's joke, would have given a pet rat to Surgeon Grundy to look after, but it was Grundy, on the *Jacqueline*, who had worked a most unlikely miracle. Far from being dead, the old black Worm was in good humour, and almost in good health. When they saw him, lying on a pallet in the waist, both Will and Sam were delighted and astonished. Surgeon Grundy, his glory over, was by this time skulking down below once more, semi-conscious from a shocking head not caused, of course, by drink. He was too ill, indeed, to take congratulations.

"Good God, you Mr Worm!" said Sam to the beaming invalid. "Have you no self-respect, old man? To stay alive in Grundy's tender care — it is outrageous!"

Worm did not look too well, though, that was admitted. His neck was lost in folds of bandage, and his eyes stuck out like burnished sloes. One side of his head was nearly scalped, into the bargain, and three fingers on one hand were broken. He pulled the bandage down to show them his neck (not at their request, far from it) and it was a wonderful dog's breakfast. Grundy had gone at the ragged flesh with a curved sail-needle, it would appear, inserted stitches individually, and tied off each one in clumsy knots no seaman would have accepted on his person even if the alternative was death. Luckily, Sam supposed, Worm could not see them, and his fingers were too hurt to feel.

Even more lucky, Will recognised, was that no major vessels had been severed. Worm's would-be murderers had muffed the job.

Gunning, who had come along to watch the party, smiled with indulgence at these two young Navy officers communing with an "old emaciated corpse," but he saved his broadest smiles for when they moved on from pleasure at the Worm's survival to a hopeless, hopeful questioning. Had the young woman spoke to him? Had Marlowe, had the Scotch or any of their ruffians? In short, had he any clue, any theory, any hint, where the Scotchmen might have planned to go, where they might be found? Truth was, they told him, with affecting pathos — the maid had gone with them, been taken off. They feared for her. They knew she must need aid.

Worm's bright eyes flicked to Gunning's, flicked away, and a sly smile crossed his face. He made to shake his head; thought better of it; grimaced.

"I do not know her whereabouts, sirs, and I am truly sorry for it." The smile returned, altered, it lit up his face. "But look you here, sirs. We have someone on board who maybe does. Ah, now that is something, ain't it?"

London Jack smirked, holding out a palm to pre-empt them.

"She's in the cabin. Slack Dick's, of course, but I confide he would not say me nay."

"She?" said Will. Jack Gunning laughed.

"Aye. She ain't to Dickie's taste entirely, being female, but she is black, which is half the battle, I suppose. She won't share my bed, though maybe she will his, strange things do happen."

"Oh quit your jesting, man!" cried Will. "Take us there! Who is it? What is going on?"

"It's the woman Mildred," put in Worm. "I met her in the woods with them, sir, remember? She ran away with Mistress Deb from Kingston way. She fears they want to kill her too."

Gunning wished to conduct the interview apparently; and it was apparent he had tried his well-known tricks on her before. But the serious-faced young woman they were confronted with held him in contempt and made no shift to conceal it. She asked directly which one was William, and told him directly that the other two must leave. Bentley, although as nervous as a kitten, smiled.

"Mistress," he said. "I have heard much about you from Deb's friend Bridie, and I value your courage and your honesty. I might ask Mr Gunning here to go, but Lieutenant Holt I really need to stay. He is as anxious as I am, I promise you, to aid Deb in her plight."

The danger was that Jack would make a scene, but he confounded them all, including Mildred. He made a bow and turned for the door.

"I am too overbearing sometimes." He directed this mainly at Mildred. "I don't often mean much harm but never mind. I'll go about my sailor things and leave the headwork to these fellows here. But remember, Miss, I took you in. I could have tossed you overboard."

With Gunning gone it was less tense, but Mildred was hardly easy. She was dressed in simple cotton, but there were rends in it, and cuts upon her hands and arms and face. She had been helped out to the ship, she told them, when "the captain" (Gunning) had hauled it further off for re-anchoring and she had thought that it was leaving land for good. How helped? Black men, she said, but of the

Scotchmen's party, who had switched sides and joined up with some of Marlowe's. They had hid her before the final fighting on the beach and after she'd been separated from Deb.

"But did they not want to follow Marlowe?" Sam asked. "Did not you?"

She looked at him with steady eyes.

"They thought that he was finished. They said the Scotchmen would kill everyone, they in league with evil spirits. They said they would hide in forest and that I could too. I thought I must tell Deb's William. I did not know that you had come to shore. Some Marlowe men knew of him boat, hid on the strand. They row me out in dark and let me hold on rope on side of this ship, then they row away. I not to shout until they gone. Then Captain come and let me up. That captain. Dirty man."

Sam smiled.

"Lots worse," he murmured. "We know lots worse."

Will licked his lips. He ached to ask the question. He did not wish to overween, like London Jack.

"But do you know?" he said. "Marlowe is still alive, I am glad to tell you that. But Deborah has been taken by the Scotch. They see her as some sort of safety, still. Do you know... did any of their fellows give indication... look, Mistress — we must find her. These men are very bad."

A half-smile lit up Mildred's severe face.

"I think I know, may be," she said. "There is gold for them I think to go for. But Marlowe? Is he safe? He is alive, but is he free?"

"No. Not free. I cannot dissemble with you, Mistress. He is going back to Kingston under guard. The Navy and the colonel of militia have arrested him." Brief pause. "He will be fairly tried."

The smile was gone, but Mildred made no comment. Will said: "Forgive me, but it is very urgent. Will you tell me where Deb might be? Please."

The hot air in the cabin stirred. Sam fanned himself.

"There is a fort," said Mildred. "There is a shipwreck. Along the shore from here, I do not know how far. There is gold and treasure. A great store."

Will's heart was sinking. That could only be one place. And that could not be right.

"But there is nothing," he said hopelessly. "We burned it down. There was no treasure there, there were no people. The ship is sunk beneath the waves. I thank you, Mistress, but... Oh dear."

But Mildred's eyes were steady on him.

"Is treasure. May be buried in the woods. May be the diving men go down. They said the fort was burnt and then they laugh. Scotch men have buried treasure there."

Sam said, laconically: "If there is treasure, why did your men change sides? Do not black men like treasure also?"

Her lips curved once more.

"Not much use for treasure any more," she said. "We slaves."

"Or runaways," said Sam.

"Runaways are slaves," said Mildred. "Only when we die we are not slaves. Believe me, sir, the Scotchmen will be there. And poor Debbeerah, if she has not been killed. But if you go they will kill you as well, if so they can. They bad spirit, sir. They are the devil."

Whether he was convinced or not, Will had no choice, no free will, no rationality. He knew it. He said to his co-lieutenant: "It is a hanging matter, sir. You must arrest me, I suppose, or turn blind eyes. I am going to take a boat and some few volunteers. I shall not meet Captain Swift tonight. Make my apologies."

Holt scratched his nose.

"It is difficult," he said. "I guess Swift *would* hang you, even though he is your loving uncle. But can he hang the both of us? And London Jack? Well, knowing Swift, I guess he could, an'all. But I'm prepared to risk it, that's for sure."

"London Jack?" said Will. "What's it to do with him?"

"Well, he'll sail the ship for us. And if we get slaughtered, as Mildred thinks we must, he'll be in sole command, won't he, and so responsible? Don't look so stupid, Will. Of course we need to take the ship. And the bloody people. Those Lamonts are fearsome and they'll not be alone, you mark my words. If we're to lick 'em we'll need to take a mob. Mildred, we must call him in. Big dirty captain. If he looks at you the wrong way, bite his leg!"

Will was moved, but not surprised, that Sam would risk his neck for him, but he was moved beyond belief by Gunning's reaction and that of all the rest.

"Fuck Swift," as the Londoner put it, with sublime crudity. "In any way, young William, Miss Mildred says there's treasure in it. Can you imagine Daniel arguing with that? He'd bloody hang us if we missed the chance! I'll go and call all hands. We'll have that killick up in less than half an hour. We're under way."

***

The Scots were not alone, on Biter Beach, but they had at least not had time or men enough to get the salvage under way again. Indeed the devastation wrought before the ships had set off hunting Marlowe had left them, on return, at a loss for shelter and cooked food, which became their first considerations. But it also struck them that if the Navy should return, for whatever reason, temporary shelters, well hidden from the sea, would be their best form of defence. Observers from a ship would assume, most likely, that the beach was still abandoned.

The failure of this strategy was brought about by Will's own subtlety. On the voyage eastwards, he had worked through all possibilities with the obsessiveness of desperation, and had listed no fewer than eleven ways the Scots could thwart their plan to rescue Deb. At first Sam had treated this with wry amusement, but Will had persevered. All they had on their side, he said, was a ship, and many men, and armaments. Indeed, said Sam. And what is wrong with that? This, said Will. When they see us in the offing they will merely fade away. A ship, and men, and cannons. What better way to deal with them than not be there?

The Worm, as ever, knew ways onto the beach, but the Worm, though willing, could hardly stand, let alone trudge over rock and sand and headlands. But he could talk them through best landings and most useful tracks and did, exhaustively. Before too long Will had settled where to land in yawl or cutter, how many men to take, and which would be the best point to mount the last attack. They should be in position, he decided, before the *Jacqueline* could be spotted from the land. Or failing that, when she first revealed her intention of turning in towards the beach. With this in mind he chose his people early, stocked the cutter with supplies of food and drink, and sailed ashore in darkness while the brig stood off into the open sea. To say there was no hurry was ridiculous; he feared for Deb in all his being. But the danger of going off half-cock he knew was worse. The Lamonts, given half a moment's thought, would cut her throat, or anyone's. They had not forgot Black Bob. He was to be rescued too, if it were possible. The fact they had no notion of his whereabouts brought home to Will the greatness of their task. Or hopelessness might be a fairer view.

They went ashore at night, they hoped to strike at dawn, and they had worked their way quite close up to the camp. There were six of them — Will, Sam, big Tommy Hugg, Johns Nuttall and Bamford and the useful Frenchman Imbert — and a good strong moon got them across the worst of the terrain with no injuries. It had sunk again before they got too near to the fire, but they still chose to stay some way away in case of distant guards. There was some revelling, but not a lot, and mercifully little drink in question. An oversight, Will thought, unless somehow they had failed to find any on their march, but he thanked his lucky stars. Please God his luck would hold in the question of Deb. He longed to see her, to know she lived, but he knew that if he saw her abused or brutalised he would attack in heat, and that might well prove fatal.

If the men had raped Deb, though — and it was supposed even by Will they must have done — there was no such vile activity in the hours of their wait. They took in turns to doze and François Imbert, more impatient or foolhardy than the rest, sloped off alone at some point, in despite he was forbidden to. Bentley, in the seaman's way, awoke before the Frenchman's hand actually touched his arm, and he was so excited he slipped back to his native tongue.

"Monsieur! Monsieur!" he whispered. "Je l'ai trouvée. Votr'mselle! Là bas! Your leedle doxy!"

Imbert's English, by now, was very good (if spoiled with vile words) and Will did not try his French at all. He sat upright with a gasp, waking Sam in the process. They questioned Imbert in urgent whispers, both reaching for their guns and swords.

"Là bas!" he said again. "A cable-length. Espèce de voile, awning. She is tied up. She is with a leedle black boy. She is asleep."

Why wait? The thought was with them all immediately. Within half a minute all six were bright of eye and keen, though Hugg insisted he must have an instant shit before they moved, and cited sense of smell among the sleeping enemy as a sufficient reason for the little wait. John Bamford suggested the thunderclaps that were the big man's farts were more likely to do the waking than their odour, but the others took the delay to rinse and wash their mouths out and freshen up their eyes with water from their bottles. With weapons cocked and blades eased in their sheaths and mountings, the party then all followed Imbert down the path he had picked out. The darkness was still intense inside the woods, although the sky above was showing signs of coming light, and they were almost on the shelter before it was visible.

Whispering was dangerous, but Will deployed his men in a defensive shield before he and the Frenchman went in through the entrance. The sight of Deb lying there, curled like a baby, breath almost inaudible, filled him with a sudden rush of love and sorrow. Even in the dark he could discern bruises, ragged cuts, and filthy, muddied clothing. He knew he would have to cover her mouth with his hand when waking her, and his stomach hollowed in imagined knowledge that such awakenings would be only too familiar. She was tethered by one ankle, but the line was thin and tight, designed to bite deep into her flesh if she should struggle. The other end was attached to a wooden stake driven in the ground. Mixed up with her lashing, rendering it impossible to undo except by knife, was the end of Black Bob's line, that led into his corner. The boy was but a sighing bundle, a darker patch against the dark.

The shelter was too low for either man to stand, but it was important that both prisoners were woken simultaneously. Will indicated that Imbert should take the boy, while he crouched over Deb. The Frenchman cut both restraining lines close to the stake, and they checked that there were no other fastenings. Will breathed deeply for a moment or two more, then gave the signal. He went down on one knee, put his weight on one hand, and clapped the other firmly around Deb's mouth. She woke instantly, her eyes flashed open, and her back arched in a convulsion.

" Deb," he breathed, braced against her struggling. "Deb, it's me. Hush. I am Will Bentley."

In his corner, Black Bob, tied by the neck, was struggling more violently. Will was aware of a thrashing, squirming whirlwind of furious revulsion, with muffled groans bursting out from beneath the Frenchman's hand. Then Deb's struggles took all his attention and he pushed his face to hers, willing her to recognise him.

"Deb! Deb! I am Will, I am here to rescue you! Deb, silence, please, please! You will wake the Scotchmen up!"

Suddenly, the fight was gone. She collapsed beneath him, her body loose and pliant. Tears sprang in her eyes, and as he eased his hand from off her mouth she breathed in with a juddering gasp. Her chest rose up to push against him and Will had her in his arms. Her first words were a groan, a deep, low, groan.

"Oh Will. Oh Will. God save you."

But Bob was broken free, and screaming. Imbert tried to grab his mouth, got bitten. He tried to seize his neck, but the skinny boy was twisting like a conger eel. He bounced sideways in the dark, banged into Deb and Will, rolled further into the doorway and then out of it, and still he screamed and shouted.

"Bob!" cried Deb. "Bob! It is our friends! No noise! No noise, for Jesus' sake!"

As roars burst forth in the rebels' camp Tom Hugg loomed huge to block the small boy's way. Bob went past him like a hare jumping at a hound, but Hugg stamped on the trailing line and snapped it taut. The black child's piercing scream was cut off in a dreadful croak, and his legs flew out from under him as his neck was held. By accident or fantastic realisation Hugg lifted his foot, which may have saved Bob's life, as he then rolled over and over like a kicked ball, control of his arms and legs quite gone. But if his life was saved from choking, he was lost to his rescuers, which cost him very dear. Hugg lunged for the rope's end, but the boy got clear, got to his feet, got down the path to safety or perdition. Perdition, certainly. For as he ran he came face-to-face with Chattel and Mick Carver, who had several other men behind them in the dark. Carver had a pistol and he fired it and missed, and from behind his back another gun flashed off, also to no effect. But Carver stopped his forward rush, and Hugg gave up on saving Bob, who ran off to one side, followed by Chattel and two other hunters. Deb had seen it all.

"Oh Bob," she screamed once more. "For Jesus' sake. Oh Bob."

From Carver's band there now came many shots, and Will and Sam between them hustled the maid away in safe direction. Bamford and Nuttall stood ground and fired carefully, with good result as two man fell, one black one white, believed to be Seth Pond, no loss to any nation. François Imbert, who had disappeared again, burst out not fifteen feet away from Carver's lot, and set off two small pistols at a range that had them running backwards in confusion. Hugg, his mighty arm and mighty cutlass raised, burst ahead of his band down the way that they had come, in hope that they could reach their boat in time, or push far enough into the thick to hide or separate. As the sun rose and the light grew stronger, the hope seemed more and more forlorn.

They had not seen the Scotsmen either, and that for Holt and Bentley was the worst. It was like a poison cloud hung over them, the knowledge that those three monstrous men were there. And then they heard a thin and piercing scream that could only be Black Bob, and it ended in a heart-rending, choking gurgle, and a burst of gleeful shouting.

At the same instant they heard another sound, so completely unexpected that it stopped most men in their tracks. It was the flat boom of a cannon, and as it echoed strangely round the trees and outcrops of the bay, there was another one, and then a third. Will heard the whine and buzz of an iron ball, heard the clipping and flat hisses as it carved through leaf and branch.

It was the *Jacqueline*, offshore. She had opened fire.

Chapter Thirty-Six

When his two lieutenants failed to show up for their rendezvous, Captain Daniel Swift took it with unusual equanimity. Truth was, as he made quite plain to Ashdown and Jem Taylor, he was bored with woodland life now that the "hot work was all done." What he had expected neither of them knew, for to "mop up," which had been his plan, one needed fellows to stand still for mopping, as Taylor put it. The rebels, their leader gone, their women and children off into the Cockpit lands, had abandoned their little captured outpost with indifference, Ashdown guessed. It was their normal way. They were successful outlaws, and as such held permanence in sheer contempt. The only permanence in freedom was lack of permanence itself. The whites had entered one small village, and right welcome to it they should be. If they should find the next one, that would be abandoned ditto.

At the end of the long hopeful day, Swift's "pickings" amounted to five milking cattle and pair of ageing goats, which later chewed their way through their neck ropes as bored goats will, and wandered off again quite unaware that they had been important prisoners. Swift's men, to show they had been working hard and that their commander had been right, reported many sightings of rebel men and women, and wondered aloud at their uncanny facility in the art of disappearing. Truth was, that if they had in fact seen any, they had not come close enough to identify them as rebels or the man in the moon. Their day did not bore them, though. Much as they liked fighting, they liked not fighting more, and there were the ill effects of too much pillaged rum to sleep off in the quiet glades.

The upshot was, that far from going mad with rage when Bentley and Holt did not show up, Captain Swift decided he must head back to the *Pourquoi Pas*, and then for Kingston and Port Royal, as soon as ever possible. Having failed to hang Marlowe on the spot he was taken with the fear that Mather and Co would do it without him back in town, despite the kudos ought to fall to him. For this reason, and because it would serve his people right to taste a little suffering, he had all hands — the *Pourquoi Pas* crew, Kaye's leftovers from the *Jacqueline*, the few militiamen and hangers-on — mustered in the pitchy dark and made to strike camp and prepare to take the long, unpleasant way back to Montego Bay in conditions of forced march. As ever with this iron little man, he took the front and set the pace, and had those few who dared fall by the wayside thrashed. Some few did not appear for muster when they reached the northern shore, which Swift supposed was due to nocturnal depredations by the rebels on the way. In fact the losses were men run: they swelled the ranks of rebel bands with useful English, Scots and Irish sailor-blood. Some negroes in succeeding years were noted for red hair, and temper.

Dan Swift took passage along the northern coast, and made terrific time with kindly winds. As he dropped south to double the eastern extremity, the wind hauled from west to north for him, and once round Morant it blew south-easterly. He did not even need a tow to reach the inner harbour, and the wind died as if by magic as he prepared to drop the hook inside the Palisadoes. He had received and answered a salute from the Apostles, and a smart pinnace from the Offices was there to take him off as soon as he desired. Seated in the boat — my kind permission of Captain Shearing, undoubtedly — were the elder Siddlehams, and they were overjoyed to see him. Congratulations were in order, they told him as they climbed on board, great congratulations. Not only for his triumph neither, and the capture of that murdering bloody Marlowe swine — but no, because the deeds were drawn and done, and the lawyers ready with their quills. In no time at all or even shorter — he would be the owner of their beautiful fair house and land. They were a band of brothers, veritably.

Swift, in the face of such bonhomie, such unparalleled delight, responded like a lizard to strong sun. He seized the hand of Jeremy, then Jonathan, and worked them up and down as if they were pump handles. Lieutenant Jackson, from the pinnace he had not ever left, watched sourly for a good long time before showing impatience, but made his general disaffection quite apparent. At last he suggested, mildly for him, that Captain Shearing was a very busy man, as doubtless were the members of Assembly who had gathered in the Offices to hear the Captain's tale. Swift responded sunnily to this misery, and within two minutes more was being whisked across the harbour in fine style. He asked after Marlowe — locked in jail, and safe, and comfortless — Mather, and Captain Richard Kaye, and hoped that all was well with them, by contrast. No trouble on their journey back, he hoped, no attacks, no unforeseens? But no, said the oldest

Siddleham, everything was tiptop, beautiful, no *contretemps* of any kind at all.

"Except," he said… And Lieutenant Jackson snorted, as only he could snort.

They were at the jetty now, amid a flurry of painters and tossed oars, and there was no time for elaboration. But Swift learned soon enough that his friend and colleague Captain Kaye was the shadow on the sun, and the Siddlehams were hoping he, Dan Swift, would be the cure, and that right fast. After a reception at the Assembly, after formal thanks and congratulations had been passed, they set out for the Siddlehams' plantation — his plantation very soon, they gushed — and they filled in the detail, far as they could. It was not until he asked them where Kaye was that he learned the strangest thing.

"We wished to bring him home with us," said Jeremy. "As he was betrothed to our dear sister it seemed the kindest thing, the only thing. We wished to succour him, to let him get to know our ways, indeed the house, as he will be part-owner very soon with you, and it is the place dear Marianne was born in, and died so tragically. But he would not come. He would not hear of it. In fact, he grew... well, he became abusive. He accused us of all sorts of things."

"Things?" Swift queried. "Pray, sir. What do you mean by things?"

They were on horseback, but he caught the glance the brothers exchanged. Jonathan said brutally, "Sir, we must be frank with you. He has took to drink, sir. Kaye is drinking like a nigger or a common seamen. Aye — rum. It is an awful thing."

"He has took up with bad company," added Jeremy. "On the march back he fell in with that rogue Alf Sutton and his son, who filled his mind with stuff and nonsense. Scurrility, Captain. He has become a slave to it."

Jonathan said hastily, "But drink's the worst, sir. It is not civilised. Rum. It is deplorable. We are concerned, sir, to be frank. Concerned."

That Lieutenant Jackson's snorts were thus explained struck Swift as ironical, considering the sour adjutant appeared to be dying of the same complaint. But drunkenness was anathema to him, he had seen so many officers destroyed by it, often with their ships and men. So much so that he pulled his mount to a halt, forcing the brothers to wheel back and do the same. Another glance between them, perhaps of some alarm.

"Where is he then?" asked Swift. "But I must talk to him, immediate. If he does not stay with you, where stays he? Good God, sirs, he is his lordship's son, the keeper of the wherewithal. What sort of stuff and nonsense? Is it to do with our transaction? Surely not?"

"Good God, sir, no," said Jonathan. "Oh no, sir, that could not be. The papers are drawn up. It is but the matter of a... well, sir — we have agreed, though. We shook our hands on it, all three of us. Not so?"

It was so, and Swift was furiously angry, of a sudden, to be so betrayed by Richard Kaye. And angry to be slighted by these mere islanders in the matter of his honour. That they should doubt a gentleman, a man who, unlike themselves, had not left his home and motherland to turn an easy profit. It was beyond endurance.

"Where is he, sirs?" he snapped. "I must confer with him immediately. You have my word on it, which is my bond, but I must find him out. Where is the Sutton spread? Will he be there? Or if not, where? This is of the essence, sirs, the utmost urgency."

It was as if, for a moment, the brothers did not care to say. Again the looks between them, that struck even Swift as somehow being shifty. Which enraged him even more; at Kaye's behaviour, not theirs. He thrust his hand out suddenly, at Jeremy, almost forcing him to take and shake it.

"There, sir!" he rapped. "My hand again, if you should dare to doubt me!" He wheeled his mare, presenting next to Jonathan. "An honest man does not backslide," he said. "Now where is Kaye? Where do the Suttons plant? When I have settled this, then we do business. And I must say I will not be doubted, sirs. I will not be doubted."

The young men were vehement in their denials of his interpretation; he was not doubted, nay, and never could have been. It was just that... well, their concerns for Captain Kaye; their fears as to what the Sutton men might do to him, how warp his understanding. It was their belief, also, that they may have induced him to draw money out in Kingston, on his bonds or those provided by his father. Each statement, however tentative, each interpretation, fuelled Swift's concern and anger.

Likewise their insistence that they did not know Kaye's whereabouts. He might be at the Suttons' house (which they would direct Swift to, that would be the work of moments) but he was more likely in Port Royal, in the dockside drinking dens. The Suttons took him there, they said, and plied him with raw spirit, and fed him filthy lies. They offered, even, to go down with Swift, to help him seek them out. For they were certain, somehow, that the Suttons, Alf and Seth, were not at home. And that meant, they said, that Kaye would not be, neither.

There was something in this whole affair that Swift distrusted, but he could not put a finger on the reason. He had watched Kaye, on the expedition, and in retrospect recalled he had been drinking publicly, but not, so far as Swift could see, to great excess. He recalled better that Kaye had been concerned when he had raised the buying of the plantation, and hardly shared Swift's great enthusiasm; indeed had exhorted that lawyers be engaged before a pen were sharpened or applied. So Swift, while retaining total confidence in his judgement, and the probity of the brothers Siddleham, decided to do what he did best, in his opinion; which was, to go alone and find the core of truth. Before he went, he tried just one more gambit.

"Sir," he said, to the older Siddleham. "Excuse my frankness, there is something I would like to know. Your pater was a baronet, as I believe? Or am I wrong? If you should require it, I would be more than honoured to use your title."

Jeremy Siddleham did not bat an eyelid. A smile grew on his lips, and it was supercilious. There was a moment's pause.

"Well," he said. "Captain Swift, may I congratulate you on being so well-informed? Indeed you might, sir, except for this: it is a little premature, as we are so far from London in this benighted place. I hope and imagine that the necessary order is in the mails already; who knows, it may be languishing in a ship not far offshore. Forgive me for my modesty, however. I do not feel it would be seemly, yet, to use the title. Do forgive me, if you will."

Swift bowed, and smiled, and rode off on his own. Young Siddleham was a baronet, latest in a line of noble knights. It was all the reassurance he could ever need.

At the Sutton place he found them right in one thing, but half wrong in another. The Suttons weren't at home, as was confirmed by a short and stumpy Irish woman who met him at the door, but Post Captain Kaye was. Strangely, though, he could not be spoken to or seen.

Swift bullied, and he blustered, and he raised his voice enough to raise the dead. Or the dead drunk, as Bridie later told it. When Kaye appeared he looked mortal sick, and he clung onto the door-post like grim death. Swift might have turned his heavy guns on him.

But in truth, he was too disconcerted. He would have to reload those guns, he thought. With double shot.

***

Deb, for the first time in her life, and certainly the last as she imagined it, became the Captain's Lady as they voyaged back along the coast to Kingston. She lay in Slack Dickie's bed, at first with Mildred, then alone, and then — the dream impossible come true — with Will, whom she dearly loved. It was not his idea, it filled his mind with fear and scandal until Holt and London Jack beat that out of him with verbal blows of scorn and ridicule, but once achieved it flooded him with a peace and wonder that he felt would never go away. She lay in his arms in linen (run up for her, as for Mildred, by the sailmaker) and for a long long time she did not talk but wept. William did not weep, although he was quite near it, but he lay and felt her move, and throb, and sob, and now and then he kissed her wet, bruised eyes. He was fully dressed at first, and intended to remain so, but after some few hours Deb turned to him and asked him to undress. When he demurred she did it for him, item for item, garment for garment, half-covered by a sheet. And then she stood beside the bed, unhooked the clumsy shoulder-pieces the sailmaker had sewn in, and slipped the shift down so she was naked also. She looked ashamed and frightened, not at her nakedness, but at her bruised, cut, bitten skin. She had been bitten on the breasts and stomach, and the marks were cut and blackened, with teeth-shapes in the flesh.

"I have been used," she said. "I am so sorry for it, Will. You need not look at me."

"I do not look," said Will, eyes wide open on her. "My eyes are closed. I see nothing that you should be ashamed of, Deb. I love you. Come to our bed and sleep."

Deb could not sleep, but could not make love, neither. She tried, she tried hard, she insisted, and Will — though half-ashamed of it — found his prick as eager as a pointer on a shoot. He kept it down, he lay on it, he tried to deny it had existence of its own, till Deb held it in the end and pushed it at her gleaming, curling hair, and poured his hot seed on her stomach and her thighs. And then she cried still more, and the cries turned into tearing sobs, and she lay down on her face and he half-covered her, and held her back and neck, and pressed, and stroked, and comforted.

Before she went to sleep Deb said, "What if I am pregnant, Will? Oh, what?" And she did not mean with any child of his.

They had got off the beach in their waiting cutter not long after the *Jacqueline* had opened fire. The timing — which Gunning claimed merely as fortuitous, a response to all the shots they heard on shore — was perfect in the circumstance. Mr Gunner Henderson had picked up on some musket or pistol flashes and had laid off on them with all his speedy brilliance, and the shots, while striking nothing, had led the prey to think they had been sighted. This led to confusion, if not outright panic, which Imbert added to in terms by ducking round behind the renegades and firing on them from the other side. This led to half of them racing in the wrong direction, releasing shots, and more useful flashes for Henderson to lay and range on. Tom Hugg, another man of great initiative, gave up his headlong clearing run, turned back along the path, and snatched Deb bodily from off her feet and on towards the shore. Bamford and Nuttall, their pistols empty, then rushed ahead and freed and launched the cutter, shipped an oar apiece, and jerked her stern-first outwards when the rest appeared. Hugg deposited the girl in gently, stood by to aid the two lieutenants if need be, then lifted Imbert, the last one to appear, bodily by one upper arm and swung him through the air and lightly inboard. Then he took the stem and shoved the cutter into deeper water like a raging bull, before he jumped on board, balanced on one knee.

"Hey!" he shouted, in delight. "Hey, Frenchie Amber, you're the man for me! You little Froggie bastard!" And Imbert, as if to prove it once for all, picked up a loaded musket, stood calmly on the swaying, rocking thwart, and loosed off a shot at the beach-head trees, where Thompson and Josh Ward had just appeared. And disappeared, immediate.

For the rest of the voyage back to Port Royal, a voyage all too short for Will, the idyll that sustained his spirit waxed and waned. In their times together in the bed – the windows open, the sea sounds and creakings, the shouted orders, muttered conversations on the poop deck overhead – they swooped from joy to great unhappiness. They were in love, they were together, that was reality. He was a Navy officer, she a runaway, a fugitive, a criminal in the island's eyes – that was also real. Try as they might, dream sometimes as they did, they could not see a future save for misery.

"I could be hanged," said Deb at one point. And they knew it to be true. "I killed a man for you in London once," said William. "For us. Perhaps I will again." And they knew it to be false.

Mildred, Will's friend and confidante by now as well as Deborah's, was a clear-eyed realist, although not completely without hope.

"Bridie will help," she said. "Although she still work for Sutton, I suppose. And you and your friend Sam had lodging in Port Royal, I talk to mistress there she may perteck you, Debbeerah, we give her money in the hand. And fat man Hugg done marry Nellie. Nellie all right, except she try to sell you for a whore, maybe." She smiled. "Maybe I joking, Debbeerah. You got a knife though, ain't you? Mr Bentley can give you one."

But as they slipped in past the Twelve Apostles, nothing was fixed, except that Deb and Mildred, for the moment, would stay on board. When Captain Kaye came back they would have to see. If he still believed Deb innocent, then he would help, perhaps. Or not. With Kaye, one never, ever knew.

They knew the people, though, and they knew their story could not be safe and secret long. Gunning anchored in the most open water, and forbade the bumboats to come near. For the moment, Deb and Mildred stayed "hidden" in the cabin.

Chapter Thirty-Seven

Swift had reloaded, as he saw it, and with double shot, but Kaye was too drunk to be intimidated by the rush of cold-eyed rage, though even Bridie, who had lived for long enough in the shade of violent men, was moved to feel a little fear. Not that Swift threatened physicality, for he did not move a muscle beyond those in his face. No, it was an emanation, a chill wave of hatred and contempt for this soft-faced drunkard stood in front of him. And the soft-faced drunkard only blinked, and sniffed, and belched once, and then smiled. Bridie thought at this point that the "gaudy popinjay — black in the face for sure, by now" might be taken with a seizure, might "drop dead and lie there, on the spot!"

The theme was duty, Kaye's duty to his father, friends, his Navy and his King. Duty to the race of white men and their struggle with the blacks. Duty to the promises he'd made, the commitments to his exiled countrymen and the memory of their womenfolk so cruelly butchered. Duty finally, to his own dear sisters and Mama, who languished back in England with expectations of his conduct far away and who would die with shame if he dishonoured them.

At this point, Kaye's blinking grew intense. He blinked, he pushed himself upright, and he took a series of deep breaths. Indeed, he seemed to sober up. The swaying slowed, then stopped. Swift was watching, fascinated. Kaye farted noisily then coughed and spat. Bridie muttered something, that sounded like *ochone, ochone.* She took her opportunity; slipped past Kaye and through the door. Kaye licked his lips.

"You are being gulled, sir," was all he said. "By the Siddlehams. They are bankrupt."

For an Englishman, Jamaica when the sun is high is not a place to sustain a full-blood quarrel. The air too hot, too sweet, the sky too blue. In his dark coat, tight-cravatted at the collar, Swift found himself on the verge of choking, and had to scrabble at his neck. When he was ready to speak again, Kaye was also much more in control of limbs and gestures. He waited now politely, while Swift sought to regain advantage. But his chin was still unshaven, his eyes still red, his unwigged pate still tufted with untrimmed hair.

"I beg your pardon, sir," said Swift, at last. "I thought I heard you say... That is an outrage, Captain Kaye."

His deflation, though, was so complete that even Slack Dickie knew something must have happened, that doubt, somehow, had entered this fierce man's soul, or confidence. He wondered what it was, but only vaguely, for the rum fumes were still rising in his consciousness.

"It is not an outrage, though," he said. "I believe it to be true, sir. The estate is damn near bankrupt. It is in default, in hock, in escrow to the very hilt. Or some such thing; I do not know the proper words. The Siddlehams are villains, sir. Just like their father was before them. If we had put money in, we would have kissed it all goodbye. The last, brass farthing of it. Thank God we did not sign, sir, eh? Thank God for that."

Swift stared at him, and he was very pale. But Dick's troubled mind had wandered off once more.

"To think she was betrothed to me," he said, distractedly. "To think I loved her. To think she lied."

"How lied?" said Swift. "Did she... but I do not believe you, sir. I cannot."

Kaye's eyes on him were bloodshot.

"She boasted. Sir, she boasted. I hoped she would be part of it, when we wed, we'd be lord and lady of a great estate. She told me, sir, it was a mighty prize."

"Who told you this?" asked Swift, savagely. He had got his colour back. He had crushed his doubts, knew once more that this could not be true. "Who told you? Who gave you all these lies? It is the Suttons, sir, perhaps, who are the villains! Do they wish to sell, mayhap? Is it you their hooks are baited for? They are Yorkshiremen, as I believe! That is, great rogues unhung! They have marked you for a booby, sir. They will strip you down and hang you out to dry."

"Nay, they are my friends," said Kaye. "They have gone to find the Scotchmen. And Black Bob. They have a good idea, sir, they have black bloodhounds and good spies. They have gone to bring Black Bob back home to me."

***

Marlowe was in jail and not yet hanged, Will and Sam learned as soon as they stepped on to the quay. They were met by the men they had parted with or swapped for the inland expedition, and also by Lieutenant Jackson, to whom they reported they had seen no action and learned no worthwhile intelligence down in the West. To some extent he was indifferent, he said — on behalf of his commander, Captain Shearing — because the rebel was already safely locked in chains, and the island, not the Offices, would be bearing the most part of the cost. In any way, Captain Swift seemed to think it all over, and Captain Kaye was... He smirked. Dead drunk.

They did not care to argue with this odd fish of a man, or question further, however raw and wild his innuendoes, but found out from office minions where to find the jail and what the form might be for gaining entrance there. Ashdown, who had been left outside with Tom Hugg, remarked with half a smile he could have answered both those questions from experience, and even now moved round the town with circumspection in case a keen official should recognise him and try to refresh his memories.

At the prison, given Holt and Bentley's status and bearing, getting in was actually a bagatelle. There were white men there, and nominally "in charge," but they were indifferent, and indolent. The heat outside the jail was magnified by ten inside, and the stink and filth were almost staggering. They were put in the charge of two black jailers, both dressed in baggy trousers only, with bunches of enormous keys at one side of their belts, and lead-loaded clubs drawing down the other. They did not speak, but chewed, and spat, and ran with sweat. This time Ashdown and Hugg came in with the officers. It was hoped the Irishman could communicate with Marlowe.

Whatever they were expecting — and Deb had told Will of a tall, thin, "shining" man with a nose "like Caesar's in the picture," and "blacker than the ace of spades" — what they saw was a living shock. When the door was clattered open they could see for a moment almost nothing. Light came in through one high window in a four-foot thick wall, not a window truly but a slit, and the stench of crystallised urine was so sharp it made their throats clench up. When Will discerned a person it was more a sort of bundle, angles and arms and legs, all twisted and deformed. It was encased in chains, some heavier than the chains a main yard might hang from, and the first sign of life was a metallic clink.

"Jesus Christ," said Holt, and it was not a blasphemy. "Sweet Jesus Christ Almighty."

"We've come as friends," said Hugg, strangely. "We have not come to offer harm, at all."

This time the great chains clinked and rattled to a purpose, and suddenly the pathetic bundle was transformed. Legs unfolded, an arm shot out and pushed against the floor to raise a torso, and the head moved round, a blob became a face. It was a fearsome sight, jet black indeed as Deb had said, but encrusted with dried blood and other things. One eye was closed and swollen, there were weeping cuts, and the nose was newly squashed and broken. The white men, it seemed, had done their civilising work upon the savage.

"I have news from Mildred," said Will. "And the white maid, Deb. They are safe on board my ship, and...asked after you."

"Do you want to stand?" asked Hugg, holding out a massive paw. "I am very strong."

It seemed naive to Will and Sam, to talk to this man thus. But he turned his one good eye on Hugg, and smiled, albeit painfully. He held an arm out, clanking, and the chains that hung from it must have been a hundredweight. Hugg took it near the wrist, and raised him to his feet. The face was racked with pain, but Marlowe did not let out the smallest cry. Upright, he rocked for some moments, to achieve his balance. Then he said: "I thank you. But however strong you are, you cannot break my chains. I must die King George's slave man after all. There is no help for it, from God or man. I will set down again. I thank you."

"This is not right," said Hugg. He eased the black man to the ground, and looked at William. "Sir, Mr Bentley. I swear this is not right."

Holt said: "We are getting lawyers for you, Mister. Jack Ashdown here has known Jamaica's best." He almost said, in his flippant way, "Much good they did him, ditto." But, for once, prevented it.

Although down, Marlowe was not yet out. He split his face into a grimace that he intended for a look of reassurance.

"I am suffering," he said. "Forgive me if I crave for liberty. I am glad that Mildred is alive, and you good woman, Lieutenant Will. They know I aided them, and I innocent. Tell Mildred go fight on, and if she must reach the gallows too, like me, go there with heart of blood and fire, like I will do. Freedom the right of every man, and woman, tell her, from the time of birth. It is the law of God."

Outside the jail once more, the four of them were speechless. They knew a vast injustice was happening and would soon get worse, and fatal. And they feared they could do nothing. Nothing at all.

***

Alf Sutton, and to a less extent his one surviving son, were not the men to be put down, or put upon, by mere Navy officers, however fierce and grand. Their clattering arrival in a yard behind the house had ended the argument between Swift and Kaye, but, warned by Bridie of the visitors, they had come through the house to confront them without delay. Alf Sutton held a bottle by its neck, and pushed it at Dick Kaye, who took it gratefully. He pulled the cork, and took a draught, and coughed, while Swift looked on in something like dismay. Sutton, surely an ironist despite he was a hard West Riding man, laughed.

"Eh oop," he said. "'Ast et a sour plum, owd lad? Young Dickon needs a drink now, doan't 'e? Tek one yersen, and welcome."

"Sir," Swift said icily. "I am Captain Daniel Swift, and I serve his Majesty the King. I am not here for prattling, nor for drinking rum. Captain Kaye, sir! Your duty! I beg you to constrain yourself."

Kaye shook his head, as if to clear it, and coughed some more. He addressed Alf Sutton, not Captain Swift.

"Did you find them?" he said, anxiously. "Did you see the boy? Is he all right? Did you tell my proposition?"

Seth was grinning like a monkey. This was priceless. He glanced at Swift's face, high on his horse, clenched with fury, and he almost sneered.

"Proposition?" said Swift. "What proposition, Captain?"

"Aye," said Alf. "We fahnd 'em, 'tweren't that 'ard, and they snapped up t'brass aw reet."

"Is this the Scotchmen?" Swift demanded, angrily. "Do you dare to tell me, sir, you have seen the Scotchmen? And given money? Bribes? Where are they, sir? I insist to know! Good God, sir, I am the British Navy! How did you find them?"

"Oh just a bit o' common sense, lad, bit o' money changin' 'ands, nowt special. We *ain't* the British Navy, that's an 'elp. Eh, talkin' o' money, Dickon — 'ast bought the Siddlehams out yet? 'Ave they took yer brass? Ee, they're canny folk them brothers. We tek us 'ats off, doan't us, Seth?"

"But where's the boy?" Kaye said with desperation.

"Where are the Scotchmen?" said Swift, harshly. "You will tell me, sir. It is your obligation as an Englishman."

The brown, lined, sly face creased in quiet pleasure.

"We doan't think England any more," said Alf. "This is called New World b' some folk. 'Asta not 'eerd o' it? You're in Jamaica now, m'lad."

"Anyroad," said Seth. "'Appen they'll be gone b'now. Them Scotchies. When we saw 'em they was packin' up their sticks, ent that so, Dad? They've got the nigger-boats an'all if they should fancy; owd Marlowe's. Off to Cuba'd be my wager. Hispaniola, Cayman mebbe. There ain't a shortage o' good islands, is theer now? Nobbut a cockstride away."

"But what about Black Bob," said Kaye. "If they were going, where was my... Where is the little boy?"

Alf fumbled inside his tunic. It was stained leather, and capacious. He withdrew a bundle, a kind of pouch, tied up in marling twine. He handed it to Kaye.

"Oh aye. They give me this fer thee. Summat to be going on wi', the tall one said. Wrapped up proper by a sailorman, so I couldn't get a peep, I reckon. The fat 'un done it. Englishman, not Scotch."

While Kaye clawed at it, Swift tried some more to pump for information. He tried intimidation, he tried man-to-man. The planters, son and father, viewed each gambit with contempt.

"Thee answer me a question," said Alf, at last. "'Ave them brothers took yer money yet? Is all signed and sealed?"

"What's that to you?" said Swift, furiously. "It is a private business matter."

"Oh, nowt," said Sutton. "Just interest. And did they say their fayther wor a lord? A duke or baronet, or summat? Nay, they'll not've told such awful lies, what say thee, Seth? Ah knew 'im when 'e didn't 'ave a pot to piss in, theer owd Dad. Till 'e met that rich lass. She wor a lady; would've liked to be. 'Er owd man were all fer killing Nat. Beg pardon, that's *Sir* Nat. 'Appen that's why they skipped out of England over 'ere. Cost 'em dearly though, din't it? She 'ad 'er airs and graces, but she ended up with precious little else. Am ah reet, Seth? Am ah reet?"

"Aye," said Seth, judiciously. "Int'region o' — according to the lawyers, what knows best — well, int'region o' fook all, weren't it, Dad? Fook all."

Alf stared at Swift's rigid face for a long moment, as if in sympathy. Then he said: "That's danger fer folks what doan't know our island ways, int it? Someone could've warned thee, couldn't they? They should've done. But no one would. D'ye see?"

There was a strange noise from the mouth and throat of Richard Kaye. He had the bundle in his hands, the open pouch, and there was something in it, gleaming white. His face, beneath the wind and weather tan, was almost whiter. He held it up. It was a necklace.

"Oh aye," said Alf. "They boiled up and bored his teeth fer thee. And finger-bones. Sort o' memento, you can wear it round the neck. Pretty, int it?"

"Aye," Seth added. "You can show it to yer friends. ''Ere's lickle Bob, I likes to keep 'im close, don't laugh.' Unusual, int it? Talking point."

Kaye's shoe lashed out, and caught the bottle of rum. It smashed against the wall, and raw spirit spread across the flags. The smell was penetrating.

Chapter Thirty-Eight

Dan Swift, for all his bravery and power, was not an aristocrat, although he aspired to what he saw as their values. Slack Dickie was one, born and bred, and it was a nothing to him. He refused to use his title, he found his fellow "well-borns" fastidious and effete, and he wished, the secret of his heart, he could be liked by normal men. He was, however, blind to all the reasons that could not be. He did not even realise he was a law unto himself.

Slack Dickie had not kicked the rum away by accident, but Swift, of course, knew full well that he had. It was the measure of the man, a wreck, a blasted drunk, a broken reed, and Swift, in anger, took himself away out of his sight. He left the shattered captain, he left the two sardonic Suttons, he left the dull, failed plantation (as he saw it) and rode off on his borrowed mare. He had been rogered, he had been gulled, he had been taken for the worst kind of a fool. Worse, as he saw it, there was no way at all that he could break the bargain. Whether he believed or not the Suttons' claim that Jeremy was not a baronet, he was certain that Sir Nathaniel had been a knight, and his own constraints were etched in iron, as a gentleman. He had shaken hands, he had given his word, and hand and word were bonds. If the Siddlehams held to the point, then it must stand. So Captain Swift, with dignity and courage, went to see them.

They were waiting for him, it would appear, and young as they were, comported themselves with icy hauteur. They knew which way the wind was blowing before he said a word, and had (as soon as warned of his approach) set themselves on horseback for the confrontation. His horse was big, and theirs were bigger, and both of them were tall, and straight, and — aristocratic. Swift, who could have faced an army single-handed, had little chance.

"Sirs," he said, after first normal greetings, "Sirs, I hear disturbing things. I hear that I must consult with lawyers."

They stared at him as if in blank amazement.

"Sir?" said Jeremy. "Good God alive, what can the trouble be?"

"Lawyers," said Jonathan, "on this island, sir, are considered worse than dogs. Black dogs, even. Men who consort with lawyers, sir... well, people like we... three... do not, sir. Never."

As Swift searched for another gambit, his mare farted, then pissed noisily onto the ground. It seemed to last for ever, and the smell was hot and sharp. It was a punctuation, normal yet unreal, and all three waited until the mare was finished. Then Jeremy spoke.

"If you have heard rumours, Captain Swift, then that is also island talk. I will not demean you by asking you to detail them, suffice to say there is no truth. You have our word, sir. Our word as gentlemen. We hope you—"

"Sir," said Swift. "I must ask directly. Is this plantation in escrow? I have not seen papers. Are there constraints; distraints? I do not have the language but—"

Jonathan had pulled himself up in his saddle. If it was simulation, he simulated anger well.

"How dare you, sir! By God, a man could call one out for that! A man—"

"Jonathan!" The older Siddleham was sharp. "Desist, sir! There is no need for language such as this! Good God, sir, Captain Swift here is our honoured friend! I am certain— I would lay it on our mother's grave— I... Sir? Your intentions, I am right amn't I, I confide in it. Honour sir, is a very precious thing."

"And breach of honour, sir—" Jonathan began.

"Brother! Desist! I will not have this! Captain Swift, sir..."

But round a clump of trees then Kaye appeared, and Kaye appeared, to all of them, to be drunk, as drunk as ever. Even his mule seemed to stagger as it crossed the rugged ground at speed, and his face was flushed and gleaming. He pulled up ten feet before them and, astonishingly, drew a long pistol from beside his saddle. He levelled it first at the older Siddleham, then at the younger. Both men paled but held their ground, although Jeremy's horse began a sideways stepping movement that he struggled to control.

"Ho!" said Kaye, his voice hard and incisive. "Hear me well, you villains, before I pull this trigger. Hear me well!"

Swift was amazed and let it show. He raised a half-apologetic hand at the Siddlehams, and shifted his own horse sideways as if to come alongside Kaye's mount. But Kaye also shifted sideways and made an angry gesture with his barrel.

"Sir," he said. "The field is mine, I beg of you. Siddlehams. You know my lineage, and by thunder, sirs, I now know yours. I say this loud and clear: You are scoundrels, you are liars, you are rogues. My father is of ancient family and does not part easy with his cash. You have chosen the wrong men, sirs, to tangle with, and you will now withdraw. If Captain Swift here, in probity and honour, thought he had an honest bargain with you, you must tell him that he stands mistook. He wished that we should buy something from you, which it now seems that you do not have. Both I and Captain Swift are here as agents of my father, and we have full authority from him to act as we see fit. Hereby we release you, do we not, Captain? You are not beholden to us, gentlemen. You are absolved."

Jonathan, who was the quicker-witted of the brothers, was consumed with fury. Tricks and insults, from Kaye's lips, were unexpected, and touched him on the raw.

"Absolved?" he shouted. "And you are drunk! A handshake is a handshake in our society, and it shall be observed. By God, sir, we are the gentlemen of this new place, and now you never will be, believe me! We will ruin you! Our word will make you veritable pariahs, dogs! Captain Swift! What say you to this! You are the higher officer! Make him step back from it!"

Swift had an instinct for when men were on the run. His nose lifted. His grey eyes sparkled.

"The captain is an earl or some such noble thing," he said, mildly. "I am but a common captain, for my sins. His word outweighs mine by far, sirs. You aristocrats would know the truth of that, surely?"

The brothers could perhaps have called Kaye out, but he looked as if he would shoot them without benefit of seconds if they had. In any way, in a duel, which of them would have dared face this bright-eyed sea fever? Undoubtedly he had killed men in his time, and not just chained-up slaves. Their ally Swift (or victim, call him what you will) had decamped to stand foursquare against them. It was they who must step down. They did so.

"This is egregious," said Jeremy. "Put your gun up, sir, it is offensive. It is French behaviour."

Jonathan wheeled his horse and gabbled: "We should call 'em out, Jem, the pair of 'em. We could end up bankrupt out of this."

"Just as we thought," said Dick Kaye, gaily. "Good to hear it from the horse's arse."

As they rode back to Kingston, after some long way in thoughtful silence, Swift said to him: "You surprised me, Captain. Forgive me for presumption, but I thought that you were drunk."

"Do you know the song?" said Dick, after a pause. "I once had land, but now have none… No, that is not it, hold a moment."

Suddenly he was singing, in a voice surprisingly rich.

Then I had land, which now I lack,
Was rich but now am poor.
The wine tun and the good ale tap…
Bring ruin to my door.

"I got the gypsy's warning," he said. "I do not drink brandy any more, sir, from this very moment forward. Nor rum, nor any other violent spirit." He laughed, although Swift did not know why. "I must tell London Jack," he said. "It's easy."

Swift nodded.

"That's just what Jack has said himself," he teased. "These last five years at least."

Dick sang again

.

John Hadland now some do me call,
And that name well I have.
For now I stand with my cap in my hand…
And of you favour crave.

"John Hadland lost only fields and trees and cash," he said. "I lost my poor Black Bob."

***

On the *Jacqueline*, when their errant captain returned, the mood was even more inclined towards dubiety. The mood, indeed, among Bentley and his fellows — extending down to some higher members of the common crew — was more extremely raw and raucous. The story of the rebel Marlowe chained and shackled in the filthy cell had affected them all severely and Deb and Mildred, who were already the ship's open, precious secret, spread it throughout the men like fire in a hay barn. The fact that they were secret in name only now had increased their safety from betrayal enormously. The sailors, sentimental and hungry for a woman's presence, would have fought to death for either or the pair of them. And both were beautiful, and not to be obtained.

When Kaye turned up — alone, as Swift had gone about his Navy business, and to ponder any consequences that might come from

Dickie's act — there were many people in his cabin who should by no means have been there. Will had been warned in good time of his approach, and decided that the time was ripe to convince Kaye, once for all, that Deb and Marlowe were innocent, and that the rebel was the victim of a vast injustice. Will, Sam and Gunning all knew that if Kaye chose to react as Kaye well might, they could end up in trouble of the very worst. They chose to take the risk.

He was a strange sight when he walked into his cabin, ushered in, in fact, by Hugg, who was looming as a sort of friendly threat. His dress was that of a drinker who has lost his normal bed, his face was puffed and bloated about the eyes, and those eyes were bloodshot. On top of all a smell of rum, both stale and newish, and an air of raffish jollity and confidence. All hearts sank on sight of him, and all were delighted when he began to speak. He was lucid, intelligent, and quite clearly sober, and the jolliness was turned to bitter calm. He bowed to Deb and Mildred (who were dressed now in better garments, thanks to make-do-and-mend, the sailors' special art), demanded coffee and fruit juices all round, and listened as the story was outlined. He took Deb's innocence as a given, and Mildred's too when he had heard them speak. His opinion of the Siddlehams was now so low he would have believed anything to their detriment that anyone had said.

But he had passion, too, when the part played by the Lamont brothers was brought up. His hand went into the pocket of his coat and stayed there, moving, and his nostrils flared with indrawn breath. Jack Ashdown, his normal soft mien gone, said he thought they were the greatest danger, and that they should be the ones to hang, not the poor black renegade. "But what," he asked, "but how, sir, can we bring about such justice?"

Kaye got to his feet, and moved about the deck, distractedly.

"I want to see them hanged," he said. "I want to hang them with my own two hands if possible. If we got Marlowe out, perhaps he could... We do not know where the Scotch may be, they may be, indeed, no longer even on this island. But could...mayhap your Marlowe...?"

This to Mildred, who nodded decisively.

"He would, he could. He find any one out there. He find me and Debbeerah."

"Hold hard!" said Will. "Hold hard, sir! We can't get Marlowe out, he is in Kingston prison. It is a proper jail, a fortress."

"Ladies' drawers," said Kaye. "That is all I say to you, Bentley. Ladies' drawers. Hugg! What would the men say to that, do you think? These bastards raised them on our main yardarm. These same bastards who've put Marlowe in their jail. Could you find the men to break the door down, do you think? We'll give 'em bloody ladies' furbelows!"

Hugg was a calm man, for his size, but a smile spread quickly across his face. He liked a challenge, and that of armed men and a prison gate was appealing. Jem Taylor, boatswain, was more cautious, but both agreed the men would love it, would see it as a well-earned right. It was Will and Sam who saw the flaws and problems. They saw themselves against the might of the Assembly, the militia, the law, and in the end, of England. Navy officers, they pointed out, were not paid to spring traitors out of English jails, even in an island far away.

Kaye said: "Hard cases make hard laws. I have something in my pocket that would convince you of the need. I will do anything to find these murderers."

There was a silence while all looked at him, but Kaye did not withdraw his hand. His fingers worked, however, and his eyes were haunted. No one asked. Nobody dared, or cared, to.

Ashdown said mildly: "We could not force our way inside, sirs. Perhaps we should not, as our two lieutenants say. But there is a stronger weapon for getting out of jail; or into one, indeed. The governor of the place does not live in the building, why should anyone, indeed, who could go home at night? It is a foul, filthy hole not only for the inmates. I have been in there myself, and I lacked the weapon, so I stayed. But we have it, so I assume?" He glanced round the officers. "I do not mean all of us."

Jack Gunning laughed.

"Aha!" he said, delightedly. "Hard cash; old Captain Bribe! Well said, Ashdown. Indeed they do have cash. They roll in it!"

Tom Hugg was disappointed.

"But the ladies' drawers brigade," he said. "Surely that way's better? Let's knock the doors down and break some heads! Let's show the namby bastards on this devil's cowpat what English tars can do!"

Will said: "A combination! Ashdown, how many men to pay their way inside? Too many is impossible, too few and there could be catastrophe. But if there was a riot going on outside... If the guards thought that they were under threat, distracted? By God, I'll go in myself in such a circumstance!"

Sam added: " It would give some cover to the rogues who take the bribes in, too. In the excitement anything could happen. It could be hours before Marlowe's escape was even known about!"

Kaye said: "And then we fade away like summer snow. A fratch, a roar, a brawl — and of a sudden, nothing at all. Hugg — organise the people. Gunning, you must be on board, of course. We'll bring the man straight back to here and then you keep him safe. Mather's militia itself would not dare to try to come on the ship. And if they do — well, you can shoot 'em for me, can you not? Ashdown — it is dark soon. It's best at night I guess? You go with the two lieutenants, who will have cash. Come lads, let's get a drink in here! Let's knock out the details, and then let's move! By God, I'll show those villains! Bring drink!"

Aha, thought everyone. So much for the new Captain Kaye, soberton. But to universal wonderment — he did not take a drop.

***

It fell to Ratty Baines, God spare the mark, to be the hero of the hour. Ashdown knew the jail, he knew the way that men and money worked, he knew Jamaica. But at the gates, as a riot grew up in the streets nearby, it was Baines who knew the magic words, who chose the targets, who took the cash from Bentley's hand and crossed the jailers' palms. They were big and black and armed, Rat Baines was small and greyish, entirely pathetic. Bentley and Holt were banished – Rat squawked with derision at their hopes of anonymity, these Navy gentlemen – and he went in through the gates and doors with no one else but Ashdown, who carried no weapons, and young Frenchie Amber, who did, but very secretly. And in the cell, when it was unlocked and bolted, they found Marlowe, who thought maybe that they had come to hang him. As the dull lantern broke the total darkness in his cell, he appeared quite crushed and hopeless.

"Sir," said Ashdown. "We have come to—"

But Ratty Baines was too impatient for polite and genteel conversation. He wanted to get out of here, and fast, and he could not be bothered with men who would not seize a chance when offered.

"Come on, you mangy cur!" he said. "Look lively or we'll let them hang you like a dog! Stand up, stand up, or must I kick you? You will be free, I tell you, if you want to leave or not! Be you a coward, sir, or just a fool?"

Marlowe rose, draped in his chains, and the contrast was amazing. He towered over Rat Baines in the dim light like an apparition from a tragedy, and he raised his hands as if to strike Baines down. But Rat made a pass at him with one enormous key, rattled two others, and darted for the locks. The rebel still had not had a chance to speak when half his shackles tumbled to the filthy ground that he had lain on. Ashdown, the brains behind it all, was reduced to almost incoherence.

"It is your right," he said. "The laws that hold you here are infamous. We will not see you hanged, we will not have it. You may berate us if you will, but we will free you. Pray sir, give us all your aid."

Marlowe, dazed and exhausted though he was, and vile and stinking too, responded finally, and appeared to surge with energy. Hands free, he attacked the leg-iron locks with keys, and the two unmatched human beings, in a tangle of limbs and jerking hands, quickly cleared the remaining chains and headed for the door. Outside a jailer stood, indifferent and unafraid, his money doubtless in some inner pocket. They were not challenged as they went back to the street.

In truth, as Will and Sam told it afterwards to London Jack, it was neither a noble nor a difficult operation. This Kingston jail was more a camp of brick built huts and yards then anything, and breakouts were neither uncommon nor considered of much moment. There were always other blacks to hang, and those who fled would be run down later by their fellow blacks for money, or starve, or fade from legal memory very fast. The loss of Marlowe was considered more serious than most escapes, but his time would come again, no doubt, and the senior member (black) of the guard was hanged three days later, although the poor man had not even had a bribe. The problem was, that the minor riot of the ladies' drawers had spread great excitement to the local populace, and several other criminals had been broken out as well. The Jacquelines escaped from any blame it all.

Back on the ship, out on her mooring behind the Palisadoes, Marlowe was washed, tended and dressed by Mildred (Grundy, thank God, did not even suggest that he should have a go) then left to sleep on a palliasse laid on the Breton oak, the softest bed that he had had for ages.

And the people, with the Captain's blessing and liquor by the bucketful, celebrated. Though very few, if any of them, had any real idea for what.

Chapter Thirty-Nine

Deb could not stay on Jamaica, that was well-known. Will though, was certain that their futures lay together, however it should come about. Which left them, hour after aching hour, turning their lives and possibilities around. It came down to this: she could not live without some way to feed and clothe herself, and William was in the Royal Navy. If she was found onshore she would be duly imprisoned, most probably to hang. If she were to take her chance with Mildred, with Marlowe and his people, she would be a fugitive at best, and split from Will in any case. She could not stay upon the ship; she could not go upon the land. As Deb saw it, through her frequent tears, she was lost.

America, the thirteen colonies, or another island in the Carib Sea, English or maybe Spanish, Swedish, French or Dutch? How would she get there, who would meet her and protect her? Round and round and round they talked, and always ended at the starting point. They loved each other, wanted nothing else, and could see no way that it could come about. Their life was blighted. Their love was doomed.

Dick Kaye, that strange, strange man, gave them the first hope, although it was, in fact, a forlorn one. In consultation with Captain Swift — who knew nothing of the desperate implications on board the *Jacqueline* — he had decided that the best place for him to be was out at sea, or at the very least a long way from Port Royal and Jamaica. The Siddlehams, although disinclined to try their luck since Slack Dickie had proved himself a lion not a sacrificial lamb, were in the background pulling strings, there were rumours about the English maid, there were even more about the breaking out of Marlowe. And Alf Sutton and his boy, unpopular as ever, bought themselves a little credit with tales of Kaye's outrageous drunkenness. Having agreed with Swift to put to sea (which had been his intention in any way) Kaye suggested to Will that "Miss Tomelty" should come along.

"We are going west," he said. "We are going to the *Biter* wreck, for that is where you and Holt last saw signs of the Lamonts and I must live in hope, however desperate thin that is. Marlowe is coming with me, and although the Suttons say that they are gone he might still get scent of them, I guess. Mildred is coming ditto, which will be a partner for your maid. It is a long shot, William; but the only one I have."

Will's heart — not Deb's, she was not in the cabin with him — leapt.

"How long away?" he asked. "No, that is stupid. Sir, it is fine and generous. Even any time, however short... oh, yes sir, I accept with all my heart."

It was the Suttons who had set Kaye onto the *Biter* beach as the place that might yield clues to find the Lamonts after all, for Marlowe, when questioned, had had no idea as to their whereabouts (and was not the man to pretend he did), while both Will and Sam deemed it unlikely they would have risked staying there after the raid that rescued Deb. Kaye had ridden back to the plantation ostensibly to thank them for the warnings that had saved him so much cash and trouble, and partly, too, to show off his new sobriety and dare them to make much of it. At first they denied any further knowledge – or indeed that the bay was where the Scotchmen had been "found." But Kaye's intelligence, perhaps, had grown with his sobriety. He offered money, in generous amounts, and he waxed scurrilous about the Siddlehams' secrets and their habits. He ended up with hints from the two Yorkshiremen, and nothing more. But the hints had been quite broad…

They sailed a few days later and the people, as the people often seemed to do, guessed where they were going, and ran it through the rumour mill as concrete fact. None knew that Kaye's mind was full of murder more than treasure these days, but had they done so they must have approved. Dick's change of heart and personality after the death of Bob had surprised them, but only in its changeability. To them, as perhaps to him, Marianne Siddleham, his hoped-for bride, may as well have not existed. She was forgotten.

As they neared the beach however, those who knew Dick best noted a new nervousness, a dread, about him. If the Scots were there, there would be killing done, it was inevitable. And even Slack Dickie could grasp that the Scots more often killed than suffered. Their first thing would be to run, but if cornered they would behave as rats, the rats they were. Dick became tense, and tetchy, and looked (men said) in dire need of "Lady Liquor." But he did not crack; he did not drink a thing, save juice and coffee. He practised with his small-arm, though, on the quarterdeck. He had things hung from off the shrouds and yardarms, and he shot them down. His small-arm was a long one, the horse pistol he had always favoured. Within short days he was considered deadly.

Will and Deb, like star-crossed lovers, swooped from depths to happiness and back again ten thousand times. Will, I love you; but what is love? Must I run with Mildred as a fugitive, or fly to Virginia as a farmer's servant-slave once more? I am on the wrong side, I must go, my presence is a weight around your neck, your life. But if you go, Deb, you go to — what? Some sort of death? Some sort of death in life? Is there not Stockport, if all else fails? But is not anything better than Stockport, Will? What, whoring? Servitude? At times they even laughed, so impossible had their love become. Sometimes Slack Dickie laughed, thinking of Bob and the Scotchmen. But for all three of them, the world was passing bleak.

As they rounded the point into Biter Bay, it looked obvious through glasses and through naked eye that there was no one there. No smoke, no rafts or boats, no men, no movement in the trees. Marlowe, on the quarterdeck like an invited officer, was taught to use a telescope and found it extremely fine. But neither he nor Mildred saw anything that they might recognise. Except, as the *Jacqueline* drew closer, a something on the beach, a pile of something or some things. Some things that might be human bodies.

They dropped anchor close in, and three boats were racing for the sand before Jack Gunning declared her holding fast. Dick Kaye's, by an effort from his crew that was superhuman, crunched down first, and Kaye was already in the air, sprung off the stempost. There was a smell, a rotten smell, a stink of filthy, rotting flesh, but Kaye rushed into it, and up to it, like a man who had to be their first, a man who had to know. As Will and Sam forced their feet through the thick and yielding sands behind him, a strangled cry came back, a shout of joy and horror. When they came up to him, he looked almost happy.

"It is them," he said. "Look Will, look Sam. Someone has cut their throats."

More than that, the men were butchered. Their throats were cut and crawling, their eyes already eaten. Wee Doddie's teeth were gone, his jawbone broken. Angus was disembowelled, Rabbie sans testicles. All three were blanketed by flies, that rose and fell at every interruption, pulsing like the violent, violent stench. Marlowe, who had come in Bentley's boat, called from the blackened stumps of the old stockade.

"More men dead. Bakra men, no nigger." He grinned, ebony split by a gash of white, then laughed. "I think Chattel very rich! I think he take the treasure when they get it up at last. Then thank him white masters like good slaveman, huh? Like man of Africa! I think slave drivers they go lose them whip! And them silver."

When the searching teams spread out, indeed, they found several open holes. They found depressions ringed and littered with coins, they found ingots here and there. Will said in wonder at one point: "They said they didn't want the treasure, but they've surely taken it. It was a game. A waiting game."

Sam said: "But they didn't want it like they should have done, did they? Would we have left all this stuff about? White robbers? No, we'd do a proper job! Jem, stop those bastards picking up gold coins. Jem!" He stopped, amused. "Oh bollocks to it," he said. "Slack Dickie can get it off them himself. They're welcome to it for my idea, most welcome."

There was much to do, and much to find, and the Scots and their henchmen — Fat Mickie Carver, Chris Thompson and the rest — to give good Christian burials to, as far as Mr Grundy could manage that. And Dick made it clear quite quickly that he wanted searches made, in case there was more gold buried, or in case they could come up on Chattel and his gang, and he wanted diving done, even at this late stage, in case there was more stuff to be brought up. Will scorned this, but it suited him as well. More time with Deb, more time to let their hearts and bodies speak. They had decided that they would not part. They had decided that they could not. They would separate, they would have to, but they would wait always to be rejoined. Sam was in on it, and he agreed. They would find a way.

In the meantime, they were together. And on the third night something happened. Richard Kaye had gone on shore. Even the captain of a Navy ship cannot be alone on board in any real terms, so he was rowed to the sands, and left there, and faded into the blackness, like a wraith.

And out of it, to him, came a smaller wraith, and it was Bob. He had escaped, the bones and teeth were not his, merely the Lamont's jest. He had escaped, and so observed the cruel aftermath, the sly brilliance of Chattel's night-time killing spree, brought down on men who had not the least idea that they were even hated. And he watched Chattel and his cohorts bring Marlowe's hidden boats around, and fill them with the treasure they'd dug up — and slip away.

Strangest of all was the sight that met the sailors when Dick had hailed out from the shore to be picked up. As they approached, through pale moonlight, they saw the big man and the little boy, and they were arm in arm and smiling at each other. Black Bob this time, it seemed, really had come home.

Printed in the United States
101566LV00005B/173/A

9 780972 63035